THE
LAST FULL
MEASURE

THE LAST FULL MEASURE

TRENT REEDY

ARTHUR A. LEVINE BOOKS
AN IMPRINT OF SCHOLASTIC INC.

Photos ©: 268 background: ayzek/Thinkstock; 269: Lisa F. Young/Shutterstock, Inc.;
303: Robert F. Sargent (CPhoM)/Corbis Images; 304: James Brey/iStockphoto.

Library of Congress Cataloging-in-Publication Data

Names: Reedy, Trent, author.
Title: The last full measure / Trent Reedy.
Description: First edition. | New York, NY : Arthur A. Levine Books, an imprint of
    Scholastic Inc., 2016. | ©2016 | Sequel to: Burning nation. | Summary: Danny
    Wright is considered to be a hero by many in the rebel-held area of Idaho and the
    Northwest, but he has little faith in what passes for a government there, or in the
    secretive and repressive Brotherhood — and when nuclear weapons are detonated
    in Washington, DC, and New York, the Civil War suddenly turns into World War III.
Identifiers: LCCN 2015043454 | ISBN 9780545548779 (hardcover : alk. paper)
Subjects: LCSH: Government, Resistance to—Juvenile fiction. | Civil war—Juvenile
    fiction. | Guerrillas—Juvenile fiction. | Nuclear warfare—Juvenile fiction. | War
    stories—Juvenile fiction. | Idaho—Juvenile fiction. | CYAC: Government,
    Resistance to—Fiction. | Guerrilla warfare—Fiction. | Nuclear warfare—Fiction. |
    War—Fiction. | Idaho—Fiction.
Classification: LCC PZ7.R25423 Las 2016 | DDC 813.6—dc23 LC record available at
    http://lccn.loc.gov/2015043454

10 9 8 7 6 5 4 3 2 1   16 17 18 19 20

Printed in the U.S.A.   23
First edition, May 2016

This book is dedicated to the memory
and honor of Paul Reedy (1935–2013),
a Korean War veteran and my
beloved grandfather.

"It is rather for us to be here dedicated to the great task remaining before us — that from these honored dead we take increased devotion to that cause for which they gave the last full measure of devotion — that we here highly resolve that these dead shall not have died in vain — that this nation, under God, shall have a new birth of freedom — and that government of the people, by the people, for the people, shall not perish from the earth."

President Abraham Lincoln
Gettysburg Address
November 19, 1863

"In time of war, and by a two-thirds majority vote of both houses of the Legislative Assembly, a state of martial law may be imposed, during which time the rights of the people, enumerated in the first twenty-two sections of Article I may be suspended at the discretion of the President of the Republic of Idaho. Martial law shall continue until the President or a simple majority vote of both houses of the Legislative Assembly chooses to restore the rights granted to the people in the first twenty-two sections of Article I."

Constitution of the Republic of Idaho
Article I, Section 23

⌁—• You're listening to the Cliffhanger, broadcasting pirate radio to a nation on the edge of the abyss, to a people holding on with bleeding, white-knuckled fingers to keep from falling to their deaths in a useless war. I'm on the move, coming to you over the Internet, shortwave, CB, AM, and sometimes the FM band, wherever I can find a transmitter, and the power to boost my signal and bring you the truth. It's a truth that cannot be silenced. Maybe the warmonger Governor Montaine will try to take me out for having the guts to say that his little crusade to be free isn't worth the high cost. Maybe President Griffith will try to arrest me for violating the Unity Act.

They'll never find me because I'm everywhere and nowhere. The Cliffhanger is your friend in the dark of the night, the voice we all cling to so we can feel safe in our homes while we sleep. The Cliffhanger is the unstoppable voice for peace. Go tell your friends, and keep me tuned in. If you think the warriors have shut me down, think again. I'm out there, up and down the dial. Come find me. Find the truth. I am the Cliffhanger. •—⌁

CHAPTER
ONE

"Okay, Danny, we're ready to go live in thirty seconds."

The voice made me jump. I looked through the double window on my left into the control room, where Paul the producer leaned over the mixer board. He pressed a button and smiled at me. *"Just relax, be natural, and have a good time."*

I nodded, my headphones heavy on my ears, the sound of my nervous breathing filling the soundproof booth. From the control room, JoBell offered a little wave, but then she went back to watching the dozen or so feeds that brought the news on a full-wall screen. Major Leonard, my old National Guard company commander, stood next to Paul, wearing his plain, old-fashioned olive-drab Idaho Army uniform with his arms folded. We all thought Leonard had died during the Fed invasion, but he'd spent the occupation locked in a US Army prison cell at Federal Idaho Reconstruction Authority headquarters in Coeur d'Alene. After Idaho forces had rescued him and he'd had time to recover, he'd taken over as the commander of the military security escort that had been following me and JoBell around for the last month.

Through a different window right in front of me, Buzz Ellison slid into his own chair in the main studio. He pulled his mike in front of himself and flashed a smile at me. *"Paul,"* Buzz said over the mike, *"are we ready to go?"*

"Everything's go, Buzz," Paul answered. *"Buzz will take it from here, Danny."* The bass rhythm and jangling electric guitar of the

show's intro music filled my headphones. *"Just follow his lead. Don't worry. He's an old pro at this. And in five, four, three."*

Buzz winked at me and launched into the show that my friend Schmidty had listened to for years. Before the war had killed him.

"Greetings! Greetings, fellow patriots! A new record number of you all listening in a new record number of independent countries. Sixteen million people listening to the Buzz Ellison Show, according to the most recent figures. And that's because, in these difficult times, more people than ever are turning toward those values that I, Buzz Ellison, have been talking about for years. From the very beginning, this show has been about a certain ethic, a philosophy of hard work, dedication, and independence. The idea that the individual can succeed without the help of the government, if the government will stop interfering and let him do what he needs to do.

"And that is just what is happening in Idaho, Montana, Wyoming, Texas, and Oklahoma. People are waking up, fellow patriots. This is the conservative revolution we've been waiting for! I've been saying this for months — years! For over half a century, a certain segment of the United States population has made the mistake of believing the US federal government's lies. They've been told, 'Put your trust in your government. Give your money to your government. Your government will take care of everything.' Ever since President Johnson's 'Great Society' bullshit, the US government has pledged to wipe out poverty, disease, laziness. More specifically, they said, 'Vote Democrat, or vote for traitorous big government Republicans, and your problems will be taken care of.' But people are finally, finally, after all these years saying, 'Wait a minute! Nothing's getting better. In fact, it's getting a whole hell of a lot worse! And so maybe we don't need this giant, bloated US federal government anymore.'

"This is our conservative revolution, fellow patriots. And who is spearheading that revolution?

4

"Today . . . You know, in the history of the Buzz Ellison Show, *I've had very few guests on the program. I'm serious. Maybe five or six guests. I usually don't need them. People tune in to listen to my magnificence. But today, I'm humbled — and it takes a lot to humble someone of my caliber — but I really am humbled and proud to have on the show someone who truly embodies that patriotic conservative spirit. In the studio today we have Private First Class Daniel Wright of Freedom Lake, Idaho! Private Wright, welcome."*

Buzz popped a cigar in his mouth, flipped open a Zippo, and lit up, puffing his cigar to bring it to life. Now I was on. With millions listening. In the middle of a war.

I hated doing this propaganda shit.

Buzz looked up at me as he flicked the Zippo closed and blew out smoke. *"PFC Wright, can you hear me?"*

I shook myself to get in the game. "Yes. Yes, I can hear you. Thank you. It's great to be on the show, Mr. Ellison. Longtime listener. First-time . . . um . . . guest."

"I think someone's a little nervous." He laughed. *"But call me Buzz. May I call you Daniel?"*

"Sure," I said. "Or Danny's fine." I *was* a little nervous, but that wasn't my problem.

"Thanks for being on the show today, Danny. How are you enjoying your stay here in Boise?"

He should have said Fortress Boise, since the place had transformed into basically a big Army base. But that's not what Buzz or President Montaine wanted to hear. My job was to motivate people in their fight against the United States. I tried to wedge little truths in with all my lies. "It's been pretty great. Me and my fiancée JoBell are staying in a nice hotel with steady hot water. I haven't eaten so good in a long time." Buzz frowned. "I mean, we're eating a lot better up in northern Idaho now that the Fed, er, I mean, the United States military has been kicked out." My face felt hot. I sounded like an idiot. "Just a real good chef at the hotel here, I think. Had some hash browns just this morning. The United States only wishes it could get its hands on potatoes that good."

Buzz laughed again. "*So you like the* food*?*" He had always been a pretty big guy. I would have thought that, like the rest of us, he would have slimmed down a little during the occupation. Instead he was the same old Buzz. "*Things are also getting better in other parts of the Republic of Idaho, aren't they?*"

How was I supposed to know what was going on in other parts of Idaho? Our screen and comm feeds were still out half the time. Same thing with electricity. "Oh yeah. Lots better," I said. "Way better than under US occupation."

"*I understand that President Montaine has had you on a sort of tour, that you've been traveling from country to country, helping to motivate the troops for the cause. Where have you been? What have you seen?*"

I'd been all over the new independent countries in the past month. Where should I begin? "Me and JoBell made it to the Republic of Texas. We took this series of short plane rides and secret ground transports all the way to Austin."

"*Yes! You must have arrived just after President Rod Percy and the Republic of Texas Army had come out of Houston and retaken the capitol. Amazing!*"

"Um, yeah," I said. When I got there, the old stone capitol building and a lot of the structures around it were mostly in ruins. Anti-aircraft guns and small missile batteries were set up all over the city. "Part of the Texas capitol building is underground. Some sections have collapsed, but President Percy and his team are hanging in there. It must have been a hell of a fight to take back Austin," I continued. "The soldiers looked pretty tired. Worn out."

"But you helped them keep going, didn't you," Buzz said.

"I guess." I'd wanted to puke when I gave them the rebellion sign I'd accidentally invented, raising my left fist and yelling, "Rise up!" But almost all of those Texas soldiers had answered back the same way. "Then we made it to Tulsa, Oklahoma. Half the city was under US control. Oklahoma forces were clear down in the southern suburbs in this area called Jenks."

"But the fight is going a lot better in Tulsa now," Buzz cut in. He pointed at me with his cigar. *"Oklahoma has taken most of the city back."*

"That's true," I said. About a week after JoBell and me were flown back north, I heard that most of Tulsa had been saved, if "saved" was the right word for it. From what we'd seen, homes, schools, businesses, parks, and even an old drive-in movie theater had been completely destroyed or were so shot up that nobody could really use them.

"I understand that lately you've been back up north, where our freedom fighters have really been sticking it to the United States. How has that been?"

"Almost unbelievable, Buzz," I said. "We were on a flight that was supposed to land in Cheyenne, Wyoming, last week, but coming in through the dark, instead of seeing streetlights and house lights and stuff, we saw only fires. There was nothing left of Cheyenne. The US had destroyed it. Our pilot diverted to Laramie, but it had fallen to the US too. We were so low on fuel that the pilot had to put us down on a highway. We got out of there fast before the US —" I stopped myself. This wasn't the kind of story I was supposed to be sharing. "There's just fighting everywhere."

"The fight for our freedom is on! What's been the best part of the trip so far?"

"It's hard to say, Buzz." I'd hated so much of it, encouraging all those soldiers to charge back into the fight. Throwing gas on a fire that moved good people to die in a war I wanted to be done with. I could see Buzz getting frustrated, though, so I needed to do like JoBell said and be the best actor I could be. "Montana was great. Bozeman, Butte, and Missoula were like resort towns. Idaho, Wyoming, and Canada have kind of shielded them from a lot of the ground war. Lot of cows, goats, and other animals even, grazing in people's yards."

"Yes, Montana has become a great food supplier for Idaho and Wyoming."

"But I've loved it here in Boise," I said. "One of my best friends was burned up pretty bad in the fight to end the occupation. He's getting help in a good hospital. People here have been great. People in all the new independent countries have been great."

Buzz blew out a plume of smoke on his side of the glass. *"You've mentioned your role in the battle to force the US military out of the Republic of Idaho. You broadcast the signal for a number of new countries to take action to break away from the United States. I know I was inspired by your words. How did it feel, after being in hiding and on the run from the US military for so long, to finally be on the offensive, to finally be able to take the fight to them and send them back where they came from?"*

"Good," I said. And if it hadn't felt exactly good, it was at least necessary. "I knew that we had to kick out the occupying army if we were ever going to have peace. I figured there was a better chance of that if I helped launch a precision attack, because then less people would get hurt." I slipped into my standard lines. "You know, the United States needs to realize Idaho ain't going back to just being a state again. They need to end the war and let us go."

In the control room, Major Leonard nodded. JoBell offered a thumbs-up and a shrug. Like me, she hated all of this, but we agreed

I had to do it. This tour had been the only way to get Sweeney the surgeries he'd needed. Now he was at the Boise VA hospital, nearing the end of his treatment.

Buzz smiled. *"It's been a difficult war. Before the show today, I watched the press conference with US Secretary of Defense Haden. What did he say?"* He swiped his finger down his comm screen, searching. *"Ah, here it is. He said, and I quote, 'Collateral damage is an unfortunate but acceptable statistical inevitability in modern warfare.' Normally I'd agree with him, but not when he's talking about innocent American civilians! Some US drone operator in Arizona or who knows where chased after freedom fighters who crossed from Wyoming into Nebraska. The drone fired missiles that hit a school in this tiny town of Morrill, Nebraska. Nine kids who were practicing their spring play after school are dead. Two others are in critical condition. Now you watch, Danny. They'll probably blame the kid operating the drone. I'm sure you'll agree that the United States is real good at ordering its soldiers on missions and then turning on them when the mission develops complications. And while they're neck deep in deliberations about that, how many more innocent civilians will the US military murder? I'm honestly surprised that more states don't declare independence."*

He paused and puffed his cigar. Did he want me to answer? Should I say something? I'd been a soldier whose actions had led to collateral damage. I sparked the Battle of Boise that ignited this whole war. I bit my lip to keep control of myself. Would those school kids still be alive if I hadn't started all this?

"Now, Danny . . ." Buzz's voice took on that cold, quiet, serious tone that people reserved for hospitals or for funerals. *"You and your friends and your families have been through a lot. How are you all holding up?"*

9

All I had left in my life were my friends, and this shit was rough on all of us. Sweeney had been burned so bad that we weren't sure if he was going to make it for a while. Becca had been doing all she could to help the local medics take care of him. JoBell was impatient to get home. And Cal? Shit. The Brotherhood of the White Eagle had made him one of them.

Both Major Leonard and Buzz were looking worried, so I hurried to answer. "We're . . . great, you know. We're all safe. And happy to be free. That's why . . . It's a real honor to be part of the Idaho Army, you know? Growing up, we always read about George Washington and all those guys who fought for our freedom —"

Buzz leaned forward in his chair and pointed at me with his thick cigar. *"Exactly what I've been saying here on the show! George Washington, Thomas Jefferson, Alexander Hamilton, and the other heroes of the American Revolution founded a great nation based on freedom and conservative principles, but that vision has been corrupted by liberalism in the last half century. Now we have a new George Washington in the form of President James Montaine. So you and your fellow soldiers and all of us are like the new George Washington's soldiers, wouldn't you say?"*

I didn't give a shit about any of that liberal versus conservative stuff. I never had, and I damn sure didn't now. But this interview wasn't really a discussion. "That's exactly what I'd say, Buzz."

JoBell smiled at me from the control room. She's why I was doing this. Montaine had promised that if I played ball and got everybody riled up and ready to fight the United States, he would put me on extended leave, and I could take off with JoBell and our friends if they wanted to come. We'd find someplace safe and leave the war behind.

"Danny?"

Oh shit. I'd missed his question. "I'm sorry, Buzz?"

"*Well, I can understand how this is difficult for you to talk about, but I mentioned your mother. Now, the United States murdered your mother simply because she wanted to return to her home and her son in Idaho.*"

I rubbed the scar in my aching left hand. This was the plan? To drag out the worst day of my life to put on a good show?

Buzz went on. "*Obviously, that question upset you a great deal. And I can see . . . I can tell from looking at you that this is tough. I only mention it because so many citizens of Idaho and Montana, Wyoming, Oklahoma, and Texas have endured incredibly painful losses. As someone who shares their pain, what would you like to say to them right now?*"

People were missing husbands, brothers, mothers, and friends and family of all kinds. Thousands of people were dead, and I was supposed to say something that would make it all better? "We need to end the war," I said. Then, catching Buzz's disapproving look, I went on. "I know it hurts, but we can't let our losses be for nothing. We have to make it count. We have to . . . sacrifice . . . so that we can be free. We need to beat the United States of America." I needed to jazz this up, make it sound like something I would have wanted to hear back when I was burning for revenge on the Fed. "And we can win this war! All we have to do is have courage and stay in the fight. Rise up! We will give them a war!"

I hated the words even as I said them, but Buzz smiled and clapped.

"*That's the spirit!*" Buzz said. "*I couldn't have said it any better myself. That's about all the time we have today for the interview, but thanks for being on the show, Danny. And to all our brave soldiers out there fighting for our freedom against the tyranny of the United States, I think I speak for Danny Wright, and for all of us, when I say keep up the good work. We're all counting on you, and you're doing a great job. We're going to turn it over to several important updates from the Republic of Idaho Radio News, and then we'll be right back.*"

"*You're clear, Danny,*" Paul said through my headset. "*You can come on out now.*"

Back in the control room, Paul shook my hand. "Thanks a lot, Danny. Buzz wasn't kidding. We don't have a lot of guests on the show, and you did great. Can I get you some coffee? Water?" He shrugged. "We ran out of water bottles months ago, but the tap is still pretty clean."

"I'm fine. Thanks." I joined JoBell in front of the wall-sized screen, and she pulled me into a tight hug.

"I know that was tough," she whispered. "But this is almost over. We'll go home soon."

"Buzz has another segment after the short news break, and then he wants to talk to you off the air during the longer hard break. Do you mind hanging around until then?" Paul asked.

We had no place to go around here and no ride to get there, even if Major Leonard allowed us to leave, so I nodded. "At least you can watch your news again," I said to JoBell.

"All of it bad." She picked up a comm and tapped to switch the large center feed and the sound to a different channel.

"*— tactical redeployment was a terrible idea. By the time US Army and Air Force assets cooperated to retake Fort Sill, insurgents had already seized weapons, ammunition, vehicles, and hardware. So we suffered a demoralizing defeat in Idaho to gain what amounts to a bombed-out shell of a former Army base on some useless ground. The same is true of Fort Hood and other bases in Texas. The US military has control of those places now, but they're essentially destroyed.*"

JoBell flopped down in a swivel chair. "Old news." She tapped the comm hard to switch feeds again.

"You're watching United States Television. USTV. Hope for a united America. The latest combined federal, rebel combatant, and civilian casualty estimate has topped twenty-five thousand, an increase of about eight thousand deaths since —"

Not again. At least three times a week, one side or the other gave us casualty figures. The reports were never in agreement. The US always said more rebels were dying. Idaho said the opposite. "Jo, I can't stand to hear about —"

She changed feeds. *"In an Entertainment Television exclusive, Kat Simpson, star of the teen vampire blockbuster* Nightfall, *will be disappointed to learn that her onetime on- and offscreen romance Ron Porter is the father of singer Molly Curtis's future child. Molly, who only confirmed baby bump speculation last week, says her tour will continue, and daddy-to-be Porter can watch her, quote, 'twerk that baby into the world.' Certainly much-needed happy news in the face of the civil war. The baby's name? Are you ready for this? Ron and Molly plan to name her Peace."*

"Oh, goody for them," said JoBell. She shook her head and switched the sound and main screen to another channel.

"President Griffith and the National Nuclear Security Administration are working with the FBI, the NSA, and the military to recover the two missing nuclear warheads —"

"— for a hearing regarding accusations of price gouging for generators, emergency rations, chemical toilets, and other high-demand items —"

"— the largest manhunt in United States history, in the history of the world, is ultimately hampered by a lack of trust. Air Force Colonel Arnold Woodruff and Air Force Lieutenant Colonel Dennis

Doyle, the assumed masterminds behind the theft, were in command at what we are calling Missile Silos One and Two. Both possessed the technical knowledge for removing the Minuteman IV five-hundred-kiloton warheads and for disabling certain security protocols. Both are missing. But with the United States accusing rebel leaders of harboring these men and their accomplices, and with rebel leadership accusing the United States of orchestrating these thefts for its own purposes, the task of finding the suspects becomes increasingly complicated."

"— for Disease Control in Atlanta has issued a warning about the danger of infection from direct contact with or inadequate storage of human remains. Effective immediately, the following policy has been —"

"— theft and armed robbery through the roof. You know how many homes have been flat-out abandoned by people leavin' the city? Now we gotta deal with squatters, vandalism, turf wars. And this ain't just Brooklyn. Ain't just New York. Got an old cop buddy in Dallas. His homicide division can't handle all the bodies. How's they s'posed to separate normal murders from combat deaths? Who handles that? You tell me! Lagging police response times? Get out of here —"

"— If you see something, say something. It will save lives —"

"Damn," JoBell said. The news might be getting her down, but I think at least a part of her secretly welcomed being informed, that feeling of connectedness to the world and current events she always seemed to crave. She switched the main feed again.

"Federal investigators have confirmed the identity of the human remains found in a hog confinement outside of Shawano, Wisconsin, as those of Army Specialist Randal Bishop, who had been assigned to security at Missile Silo One. Due to the condition of the remains, it was impossible to determine the cause of death, but this discovery *might lend some credence to the theory that those responsible for stealing the nuclear warheads, and the warheads themselves, have quite possibly left the rebel territories —".*

"Change it," I said. "Nothing new there. They keep blathering on about the same stuff. They're looking for the bombs. We get it."

"— Laura Griffith is strong, but she's also a mother. A grieving mother. She even gave the order to rush the Air Force Academy cadets through their pilot training, which may have contributed to her son being shot down over Idaho. It might not be inappropriate to ask if she is really mentally fit for her current position. It's a medical fact that there are certain hormonal differences, and when that is coupled with grief, fatigue, and —"

"Exactly the kind of sexist crap I'd expect from Fox News," JoBell said. "Can we get radio in here?"

"This *is* a radio station," Paul laughed. He made a few taps on the control comm and the audio switched to a radio feed. JoBell swiped and tapped some more.

"From NPR News, this is Everything That Matters. *I'm David Benson. New fires have broken out at Texas oil wells and refineries as a result of military —"*

Buzz came into the control room. "The only toxic air in here is coming from NPR! Someone switch off that liberal propaganda!" He snatched the comm out of JoBell's hands and changed the main wall screen to a debate in Congress. "Little C-Span. At least then we can see what those crooks are up to." The senator on-screen said something about an Emergency Agricultural Bill and a food shortage as Buzz lowered the volume. He puffed on his cigar. "Not bad for your first time, Danny." He patted my back. "Now for next time, we'll set you up with a list of good talking points to help you with —"

"Next time?" I asked.

15

He looked confused. "Well, yes. Didn't President Montaine tell you? He believes that ongoing appearances on my program will be the best way for you to help with the war effort, the best way for you to motivate people, and I agree."

"My friend has been in Boise for surgery, but he should be ready to go home soon," I said. "I was hoping to go with him."

"And Danny isn't going to be your sock puppet," JoBell said. "He's not going to read some propaganda script that you plop down in front of him."

Buzz laughed. "Little spitfire, this one, eh, Danny?"

JoBell folded her arms. "I'm standing right here."

"Honey, I'm not talking about providing him with a script or making him say anything he doesn't want to say. I just want to remind him of those parts of his story that so many people have found so inspiring. You gotta relax, sweetheart. You're starting to sound like Lazy Laura Griffith."

JoBell glared at him. "I'm not your honey, or your sweetheart."

Buzz's jaw stiffened. In the silence, the senator on-screen continued. "*It is our job, our responsibility to the people we represent, to make sure they have enough to eat. Their very lives depend —*"

The lights in the Senate chamber went out. The image shook, and I could just barely make out senators gripping their seats. "*Oh no —*"

The image cut to static and then to a blue screen. A second later, a dozen or so other feeds on the wall screen did the same. "Paul, what's going on?" Buzz said to his producer. "I thought Montaine's people had this fixed."

"I don't get it." Paul checked some readouts on a different screen. "We should be up. This is showing all our equipment is —"

At nearly the same time, all the blue screens switched to black with the words "Emergency Alert System" in bold white letters near the top. Three short screeches sounded, followed by a long, high-pitched tone. Seconds later, our comms began to buzz the same way.

"No," JoBell whispered. "What now?"

"This is an automated emergency recording from the United States federal government." The male voice from the screen sounded completely fake, like it was coming from an antique computer. *"A debilitating thermonuclear detonation has been detected in Washington, DC. If you are receiving this message take shelter immediately and conserve all food fuel and water. If you are outdoors find shelter immediately within a sturdy structure ditch or low-lying area. Remain sheltered and await instructions from federal authorities. All government officials designated for the line of presidential succession must immediately transmit their identification codes on Homeland Security Emergency Channel One. Repeating. This is an automated emergency recording from the United States federal government. . . ."*

Thermonuclear detonation. The missing warheads. Griffith had been trying to find them, but she was too late. Now she was gone.

This couldn't be happening.

"All those people," JoBell cried. I wrapped my arms around her shaking body. "How many live in DC?"

There were tears in the producer's eyes. "I think . . . Buzz. That we'll kind of wrap up . . . I mean, it will be all news now. God help us all."

Buzz hadn't moved the whole time. A long piece of ash dangled from the end of his cigar. He dropped it and slammed his fist into the center feed of the wall screen. "No!" The screen cracked and sparked. Three lines of deep red blood ran down over the scramble of bright static. "It wasn't supposed to be this way! We were building a true conservative nation! Not a damned . . . Not a nuclear . . . The US is

17

going to blame Idaho for this. They'll nuke us for this! Damn it!" He kicked over a swivel chair on his way into his studio.

Major Leonard came back from the corner where he'd been on his radio. "I have orders to take you back to your hotel room," he said to me and JoBell. "You'll be secure there. Obviously, the situation has changed."

I rubbed the old, aching ghost wound in my left hand. "Sir, the situation has just gone straight to hell."

⌇—• *mean the box is bigger on the inside and can travel anywhere in time and space? But that's . . . that's fantastic. Doc —"*

"This is BBC1. Now a change to the schedule as we join BBC News 24."

"We're int . . . We're interrupting normal programs to bring you terrible news from the United States, where at about half past six United Kingdom time, two nuclear devices simultaneously exploded in New York and Washington, DC. The devastating loss of human life is still being calculated but is easily in the millions, with hundreds of British citizens among those killed. British intelligence is unsure whether United States President Laura Griffith has survived. She was scheduled for a trip to California, but at present, her location is unknown, and it is unclear what form the American government will take, if it has survived at all. Prime Minister Carman's office has released a statement assuring citizens of the United Kingdom that the British military stands at the ready, and preparations are being made in the event that this is the beginning of a nuclear war.

"Taking you now to live footage of a spontaneous vigil taking place at St. Paul's Cathedral here in London, where we are told Her Majesty the Queen will be making an address later tonight.

"We have many more details to relate to you, but we are cutting now to startling footage from New York. Here you see •—⌇

⌇—• *Please stand by for an emergency announcement from the president of the United States."*

"I am horrified to have to report to you from our new, temporary national capital aboard Air Force One. A short time ago, two . . . two nuclear devices were detonated on American soil. Washington, DC, has been completely destroyed, and catastrophic damage has been inflicted on New York City, with ground zero in the heart of

lower Manhattan. So far, there have been no other detonations, though the United States military is on guard against further attacks. My senior military advisers have informed me that . . . based on the magnitude of the explosion and the radioactive fallout . . . the damage is consistent with that caused by a five-hundred-kiloton nuclear device of the kind that we have been searching for — stolen from the Minuteman IV intercontinental ballistic missiles in Montana.

"We have no reason to believe this was an attack perpetrated by foreign powers. No missiles, submarine launches, or bombers were detected before the explosions. I wish to assure the nations of the world that the United States is in full control of its nuclear arsenal. We are absolutely not launching any nuclear counterstrikes.

"We are still learning all we can about this devastating attack, and we will share more information as soon as possible. While the electromagnetic pulses released by these ground bursts were much less severe than they would have been had we suffered a nuclear air burst, my advisors estimate severe damage to electronic equipment and electrical infrastructure along the entire Eastern Seaboard. As a result, millions of people relatively far outside the blast and radiation zones may be without power. Many may not be able to receive this message. Our nation's military is moving into the affected areas as quickly as possible. Nevertheless, I appeal to all of you. If you are receiving this message, please do what you can to pass it along to those who cannot. I'm urging everyone along the Eastern Seaboard to take shelter, and to conserve all necessary resources. Remember, even if your area appears unaffected, you increase your risk of exposure to deadly radiation when you go outdoors. Have hope. Help is on the way.

"My fellow Americans, we must prepare ourselves for terrible news and for incredibly sad days ahead. The information we have is *only preliminary, but casualties are estimated to be in the millions. As both the House of Representatives and the Senate were in session, most of Congress has been lost, along with many senior government and military officials. Today we grieve a loss that is almost unfathomable, but I want to assure the nation and the world that the United States of America lives on, our government lives on, and together we will rise from the ashes of this, our darkest day. Further updates will follow.* •—⋀—

—⋀—• *I'm Al Hudson, and I promise you, we're going to stay on the air here in the CNN Civil War Situation Room in Atlanta. We've suspended our paid subscription format to bring you our programming for free. We will also be letting you know which of our competitors' networks have resumed broadcasting. Competition and profit don't matter at a time like this, and we want to help people get information no matter where they are.*

This is what we know, and, God help us, the situation is terrible. Beginning with Washington, DC. As many of you saw a few hours ago, President Griffith is still alive and apparently in some kind of control of the country, though how much control anyone might have at a time like this is uncertain. Reports suggest that ground zero is in the very heart of the capital. Despite stringent security measures designed to prevent the missing warheads from moving into DC, the origin point of the blast appears to be right along what used to be Pennsylvania Avenue. Everything — the Capitol, the White House, the Supreme Court, and nearly every residence — has been completely destroyed. Casualties are nearly 100 percent. The radiation dispersal pattern appears to be spreading as far northeast as Paterson, New Jersey, and Philadelphia and Baltimore are currently exposed to dangerously high levels of radioactive fallout.

Turning to New York. All of Manhattan as well as parts of Brooklyn and New Jersey have been leveled. Burn injuries are being reported from Staten Island to Upper Manhattan. Elevated radiation levels have been detected as far north as New Hampshire and as far west as Pittsburgh. Evacuation of these and many other irradiated cities has begun, but the task of moving millions of sick and injured people is daunting.

At the bottom of the screen you'll see a list of those New York and DC area hospitals that are still open and able to receive patients, as well as temporary emergency medical facilities that military and civilian responders are scrambling to set up. Beginning with the Washington, DC, area •—⌁

⌁—• of the Minuteman IV warheads, if that is, in fact, what we're dealing with, is that they have an enormous yield. The energy of a Minuteman IV detonation is equivalent to five hundred kilotons of TNT. To put that into perspective, the atomic bomb dropped on Hiroshima during World War II had only a fifteen-kiloton yield.

Preliminary estimates suggest that the air blast radius in the New York detonation spread from Brooklyn to New Jersey. Windows are blown out from the Park Slope area of Brooklyn all the way up to Harlem.

Adding to the emergency is the electromagnetic pulse or EMP phenomenon. Nuclear detonations produce intense electromagnetic fields that create massive electrical surges in all electrical conductors in range. Had the explosions occurred in midair, the EMP would have had a far greater range, likely disrupting the electrical grid, electronic devices, and even vehicles across most of the continent. Two surface detonations are bad enough, however, and catastrophic damage has been dealt to electrical systems of all kinds along the entire East Coast. Tens of millions of Americans will be without power for quite some time.

As if the immediate effects of the blasts weren't enough, computer models suggest that radioactive fallout •—⌃

CORAL CHU ★ ★ ★ ☆ ☆

This is why Montaine and the other rebel leaders should have been assassinated as soon as they started the first hint of rebellion. Now they've nuked us! Nuke them back!

★ ★ ★ ☆ ☆ This Post's Star Average 3.05   [Star Rate] [Comment]   2 hours ago

KHALEESI FLEMING ★ ★ ★ ☆ ☆

More fighting isn't the answer! Enough people have died! Somebody make it stop. Those poor people. We need to work together or we arent gonna make it.

★ ★ ★ ★ ☆ This Comment's Star Average 4.00   [Star Rate]   2 hours ago

KARL DUNAJSKI ★ ★ ★ ☆ ☆

Coral, I don't know how we got to be friends on FriendStar, and I don't care. The new independent countries didn't have nothing to do with these attacks! They allowed US soldiers to guard every single missile silo. It wasn't Montana soldiers who stole the warheads. That was US Air Force and Army. It's no coencidence that Griffith just happened to be on the other side of the country when the bombs went off. Hit the link for proof that these attacks were carried out by Laura Griffith and the US government just to give them reason to continue the war. www.nuketruth.com

★ ★ ☆ ☆ ☆ This Comment's Star Average 2.03   [Star Rate]   58 minutes ago

SILVIA AGUILAR ★ ★ ☆ ☆ ☆

Maybe the bombers acted alone? I read that First Lieutenant Delgado tried to stop a strange vehicle as it was leaving the grounds of Silo One. She ordered her soldiers to fire on the truck, but they couldn't stop it before it entered Montana territory.

★ ★ ★ ☆ ☆ This Comment's Star Average 3.19   [Star Rate]   50 minutes ago

KARL DUNAJSKI ★ ★ ★ ☆ ☆

Exactly! They let the vehicle drive right off the grounds with the warhead. They had M4 rifles and heavy machine guns, and they couldn't disable one truck? They let it get away! This is just screaming INSIDE JOB!

★ ★ ☆ ☆ ☆ This Comment's Star Average 2.19   [Star Rate]   49 minutes ago

CORAL CHU ★ ★ ★ ☆ ☆

Yeah, Karl, you dumb shit! They drove that truck right off the missile silo compound, right through the Montana soldiers who were stationed there to prevent anyone from leaving those compounds. So obviously the US soldiers and airmen who stole the warheads were working with the rebels since the rebels LET THEM GO! (I guess I'll use ALL CAPS since you seem to think that helps make a point. And . . . you're unfriended. Sorry, not sorry.)

★ ★ ★ ★ ☆ This Comment's Star Average 4.14   [Star Rate]   48 minutes ago

KARL DUNAJSKI ★ ★ ☆ ☆ ☆

Where do you live, Coral? You think you're all big and bad? Just try to stop us in the new independent countries! You're so big and brave with that "nuke 'em all" talk, but I bet you don't have the guts to face me in person. Better pray you never do. I'll cut you open!

☆ ☆ ☆ ☆ ☆ This Comment's Star Average 0.12   [Star Rate]   48 minutes ago

CORBIN CRUZ ★ ★ ★ ★ ☆

She unfriended you. No way she read that. I think you're a little too late, tough guy.

★ ★ ★ ★ ☆ This Comment's Star Average 4.72   [Star Rate]   46 minutes ago

KHALEESI FLEMING ★ ★ ★ ☆ ☆

Millions of people are dead. I think we're all a little too late.

★ ★ ★ ★ ☆ This Comment's Star Average 4.00   [Star Rate]   40 minutes ago

⌁—• *From NBC News West Coast headquarters in Los Angeles, I'm Adrienne Welch. On behalf of everyone here at NBC News, I'd like to begin this emergency broadcast by expressing the unbelievably heavy sadness we all feel after the loss of so many innocent lives. No doubt all of you are grieving terribly, just as we here in the studio* are grieving for people like Byron Westbrook, Dennis Gavis, and other members of the NBC News family on both sides of the camera who are almost certainly no longer with us. I am now one of only two surviving NBC News anchors, and while I'll admit that I am shaken to my soul, I promise to do my best to bring you the information you need just as soon as we have it.

"And our sorrow reflects that of people around the world as a large portion of the northeast coast has been obliterated by two nuclear weapons. We're scrolling critical information at the bottom of the screen, and you can tap any of the links in the window on the left for more information about emergency rescue, evacuation, medical, and other disaster relief facilities. We're going to try to connect now with Clint Hipolito, who is in the air south of New York City. Clint, can you hear me? Are you there?"

". . . interference . . . I'm . . . aboard a plane . . . higher altitude where hopefully our signal can get out better. There's a lot of debris, smoke, and fallout in the air. I think we're above most of that now. I've got a good uplink with my Hummingbird CX80 camera drone, and I'm going to send you the feed to that video. Oh no. Are you . . . Are you seeing this?"

"We have the video. It's a little scratchy. It seems like, we're looking at a close-up of the ruins of a burning building. I can see several collapsed floors. Is that —"

"No, Adrienne. That's a long shot of Manhattan. Not one building, but blocks and blocks of . . . destroyed homes and businesses. I'm trying to maneuver the drone closer to what looks like ground zero, or the new ground zero, I guess. It's . . . Radiation degrades silicon chips. My control is breaking down and there's a lot of signal interference. But can . . . See, there's the blast crater. I'm comparing the drone's latitude and longitude with old maps. Let me see . . . Ground zero appears to have been in Union Square. That's all gone now. The crater is maybe a thousand feet across from interior rim to interior rim. Over twice that distance from outside edge to outside edge. About, maybe, two hundred feet deep. Well below sea level, but it looks like any water seeping in is boiling off in seconds. A lot of steam and smoke rising out of there. The skyline is so altered that it's hard to find my way around. Camera control is becoming increasingly jerky. I'll see if I can pan for a long shot. . . . There, I think that's where the Freedom Tower used to be. Rubble now. The World Trade Center has been destroyed again. The memorial is gone too. Seems . . . dwarfed now by the magnitude of this catastrophe."

"Clint, I'm not seeing any rescue vehicles or personnel. Have you spotted anything of that nature?"

"I think the radiation levels are very intense in this area. It's . . . not practical to conduct rescue operations in this zone."

"But are you seeing any movement at all?"

"Unfortunately, in the area we've been monitoring, radiation levels are simply too high. But at the outer edges, we have seen a lot of panic, with people scrambling to escape rubble or to rescue family members. I'll see if I can get a shot."

"Clint, you're, er, we're losing your picture. Can you clear that up?"

"It's the electronics. They're breaking down. I'm going to try to pull the drone out, see if I can save the aircraft."

"Thank you for that horrifying first look at one of the two attack zones, Clint. We have more updates on •⌁

⌁• As we reported before the nuclear attacks, American forces have been rushing to turn over security of Iran to the new Iranian National Army. However, only hours after word of the nuclear attacks reached Iran, Tehran fell to the Iranian Islamic Revolutionary

Militia. The insurgent militia has launched coordinated, simultaneous, crippling attacks on US Air Force bases throughout Iran, and now American forces are engaged in a large-scale hasty overland movement south to the Persian Gulf, where Navy vessels are standing by to assist in security and evacuation. US military officials are calling this a rapid redeployment, as no doubt these soldiers, Marines, and airmen are now needed to help stabilize the critical situation back home. Our sources across Iran are reporting American military personnel have taken what they can carry and are rolling south to the Persian Gulf as fast as possible, destroying some sensitive equipment and leaving the rest for the Iranian National Army. We have unconfirmed reports that some of the US-trained Iranian soldiers have in fact switched sides and attacked Americans. The situation is unpredictable and changing all the time, but one thing is certain. American military forces are taking heavy casualties in what's going to be a frantic, all-night retreat. •—ᴧ

ᴧ—• WGN wants to repeat to our viewers that the Red Cross has an urgent need for blood donations and all manner of relief supplies. We are scrolling information about that at the bottom of our screen. The Red Cross is also asking for any qualified phlebotomists to please volunteer your time. In many cities, despite recent outbreaks of violence, people are lined up for several blocks to donate blood. If there is any way you can help, please, please do so. Also consider that millions of Americans have had to flee their homes and have nothing or next to nothing. Our refugee problem from the civil war has just been made many times worse. No matter where you stand on the issue of the war, we at WGN would like to remind everyone of our shared humanity and compassion. •—ᴧ

CHAPTER

TWO

Because the top half of the building next door to our hotel had long since been blasted away, I had a full view of downtown Boise through the smoky midday haze from the fires still burning in the hills to the northeast. Idaho military and well-armed commandeered civilian vehicles sped down the cracked and bombed streets, ignoring the jacked-up, randomly flashing traffic lights. Even though at least two Idaho soldiers guarded the door to our cushy luxury suite, and even though I could spot plenty of anti-aircraft gun emplacements hidden among the ruins of different buildings, I didn't feel close to safe. Holding my new Walther P99 nine mil tight, I watched the skies over the partially collapsed dome of the capitol building, waiting to see when the US would blame us for the nuke attack and send their air strikes.

"You know you're not supposed to be by the windows." JoBell was fully dressed, but she pulled the thick, poofy comforter on our king-sized bed to her chin as she sat propped up by a stack of pillows. "They warned us about snipers."

"Hank," I said to the digi-assistant on my junky old COMMPAD. "Any luck getting through to President Montaine?"

"*That's country! When I lay it all down —*" Hank started singing, but then cut to static.

"The whole Internet is jacked up," JoBell said. "A bunch of the transmission equipment and server capacity throughout the country was blown up or fried from the EMP."

28

Static and garbled gibberish sounds squawked on my comm. *"Sorry, partner . . . I keep trying to reach President Montaine like you asked, but I can't get through. In the meantime, I'd like to express my sorrow over"* — more static — *"loss of so many Americans in New York, Washington, DC, and around the country. I'd like . . . to assure you and all . . . my fans that I'm working on a song right now in their —"*

"Just keep trying to get through to Montaine," I said to Digi-Hank.

JoBell twisted her engagement ring on her finger — that promise of our shared life, back home away from the fighting and the chaos. "I haven't heard from Becca or TJ or anyone in forever. The last text from Becca has me really worried about what the Brotherhood is up to. What if there's no peace back in Freedom Lake either?"

"Then it's like we talked about. TJ's family has a cabin. If things have gone to hell in town, we'll pack up and go there."

"Live off the land?" JoBell asked skeptically. She'd never been completely convinced about the cabin idea.

"Hell yeah," I said. "There's plenty of firewood. A stream for fishing. We can hunt. We'll be safe. We can wait out the war there if we have to."

The feed to the hotel room screen had winked out for a while, but just then static popped and the picture came back. Vice President Jim Barnes was standing in front of a bunch of people, giving a speech.

"He survived the attack?" JoBell said. "He wasn't in DC?"

"Recognizing that the federal government of the United States of America no longer exists as a representative democracy," Barnes said, *"we do, on behalf of the people of Connecticut, Maine, Massachusetts, New Hampshire, Rhode Island, and Vermont, hereby make this peaceful declaration of independence."*

"That son of a bitch!" JoBell shouted as she watched the former vice president. "This is only the beginning. With the federal government gone, more and more states will be breaking loose. How long until they start fighting each other?" She switched feeds.

"— *any given day there are well over four thousand flights in the New York and Washington, DC, areas. Dozens of aircraft in the vicinity of the blasts have crashed. Some inbound flights had come in from long distances and lacked the fuel to divert to other airports. With many air traffic control systems crippled, pilots were left to make alternative landing decisions on their own. As one would expect, this has resulted in not a little chaos, a runway ground collision between two 747s —*"

Quiet sobs turned me away from the window, and I hurried to JoBell's side, wrapping my arms around her. Her whole body shook as she cried. "All those people. So many dead. And . . . and so many people will never see their loved ones again, will never even get a body for a funeral."

I ran my hand over her blond hair. "I know. I can't believe . . . I . . . It's too terrible to think about, to imagine. But maybe President Griffith will call for a cease-fire. Maybe after all this, the war will be over."

JoBell pushed her face into my chest. "Danny, I don't want to talk about the war. Don't want to think about it."

We stayed like that for hours, sad and exhausted zombies staring at the news. After a long time, a knock on the door brought room service, escorted by two soldiers with M4 rifles. When we first arrived in Boise, there had been a few different choices on the menu. Now each of us was given a plate with a couple slices of rare beef and a scoop of potatoes. The meal sat cooling in its own puddle of blood and congealed fat as we watched the aftermath of the devastation on whatever news outlets were still available.

We saw images of the blasted, burned rubble of the two nuked cities. Other footage showed places like Baltimore, Maryland, and Stamford, Connecticut, completely intact, but choked with deadly radiation. In a matter of weeks, those cities would be ghost towns. Radiation burn victims lay in agony in makeshift clinics, while scorched corpses outside lay in piles of bodies larger than any I'd seen in photos from the Holocaust. One commentator wondered out loud on the air if maybe the people who had been vaporized in the initial blasts had been the lucky ones.

Finally we went to bed, but we couldn't sleep.

"Dan . . . Daniel Wright! I have a vid call with President . . . Montaine!" Hank said late that night, just as my eyes were finally closing.

I rolled out of bed as fast as I could, grabbing my nine mil out of habit and slipping it into the waist of my jeans. "Hank, put the vid call through!" I rushed to my comm before we lost the connection or Montaine hung up on me.

"PFC Wright?" Montaine's voice.

I picked the comm up to see President Montaine in the underground headquarters the Republic of Idaho had built as its central command. In the background behind him, countless soldiers and officers worked at screens on desks and mounted on walls. Montaine usually kept himself pretty neat and professional, but it looked like he hadn't shaved in at least a day, and his ever-present tie had been loosened.

"I'm here, Mr. President," I said. "Thank you for taking my call."

He half smiled. *"Sorry it took so long to get back to you. We've been on guard for a renewed attack from the United States.*

Griffith said she's not going to launch any nuclear attacks on foreign governments, but that doesn't mean the US won't bomb the shit out of us."

I couldn't keep myself from asking the same question everyone had been repeating on the news. "How could this have happened?"

"I don't know. It's madness. I've been sending messages nonstop since the attack, trying to tell her that we had nothing to do with the nukes. We're just defending ourselves, trying to get the US to let us go and leave us alone. Pissing them off with an unholy attack like that just doesn't make any sense. Now so far, our air space is clear, and I've moved our alert level down a notch to let some of our people get some rest. How are you and your fiancée holding up? What can I do for you?"

I had to say this right, to come across as an Idaho patriot, not like some whiny, scared kid who wanted to ditch Montaine's war effort as fast as he could. "Mr. President, I want to thank you for protecting me and my friends the way you have. My buddy Eric Sweeney would probably be dead if you hadn't flown him down here to Boise for treatment. But you told us a few weeks ago that when my speaking tour was done, you'd release me from duty. We'd like to go home to Freedom Lake."

Montaine rubbed his knuckles over his stubbled chin. "Yes, Private Wright, but Buzz Ellison has more plans for you on his show, and, you know, with everything that's happened, I really feel like the safest place for you and your friend and fiancée is down here in the Idaho CentCom bunker."

I could hear JoBell sigh from across the room. "I don't know how else I can help," I said. "I've done my best to —"

"None of the presidents of the other newly independent nations have been able to get in contact with President Griffith. The US government, what's left of it, will not answer. Does that mean they're giving up — collapsing into internal fighting — or preparing to attack? We don't know. Until we have more information or unless it is safer for you elsewhere, I need to keep all my best assets close at hand."

I was an asset now? "But, sir —"

"I'm really very sorry, PFC Wright, but that's the best answer I can give you."

"I could do video calls from home. There's no reason for me to stay here in —"

"Enough!" Montaine shouted. "You're a soldier, Danny. Act like one! We all have our duties, and mine are such that I simply do not have time for these kinds of distractions. From now on, your calls will be routed to General McNabb or one of his officers."

"Mr. President, I'm sorry if —"

"Montaine, out." The screen went blank.

"Damn it!" I slapped the comm down on the table.

"I don't think breaking your comm is going to help anything," JoBell said.

I'm not gonna lie. I knew she was right and the logical one, but I wasn't in the mood for logic right then. I felt like a damned prisoner, and I didn't do so good locked up. "Piece of junk shit barely works anyway," I said. I went into the bathroom, locked the door, and sat down on the toilet lid, my heart thumping hard in my chest. When I closed my eyes, the images of the disaster played in my head. The smoke, ruins, rubble, and fire. The helpless people. The burned, bleeding bodies.

If there hadn't been a civil war, the US military could have kept tighter security over its nukes. If I hadn't fired that shot here in Boise back in August, if I hadn't run around like an idiot with my fist in the air and all that "We will give you a war" bullshit, there might not be a war right now. There might not have been nuclear strikes. It was my fault. Millions were dead. Millions.

I didn't deserve to live. Not when so many others had died, not while more would die in the future. I pulled my nine mil out of my jeans and looked at the sleek, dark metal. The gun shook in my hands. All I'd have to do is pull the slide action to chamber a round, put the gun in my mouth, flick the safety off, and pull the trigger. I probably wouldn't even feel it.

But suicide was a sin, wasn't it? Chaplain Carmichael always said if we confessed our sins and believed, Jesus would forgive us. But if suicide was a sin, I wouldn't have time to confess and repent after I pulled the trigger. Could I ask for forgiveness before I did the deed? That didn't seem right.

I pressed the side of the barrel to my forehead, felt the cool steel against my skin. How long could I go on with the nightmares? How long could I handle always feeling jittery, like any second I could be in a fight for my life?

A knock at the door. "Danny?" I jumped to my feet, ready to chamber a round and fire. A second later, I regained control, disgusted with myself. That automatic fight instinct wouldn't go away. JoBell knocked again. "You okay?"

I reached back and flushed the toilet. "Ye —" I licked my lips. "Yeah. Be right out."

"Hurry up," she said. "I need you."

I tucked the gun back in my jeans, splashed some water on my face, and looked into the mirror at this person I didn't like much anymore. But JoBell waited for me out there. She'd kept me going through all of this. She comforted me after the nightmares. She was my only hope for life outside the war. Sometimes she could even make me smile. She said she needed me, but more than anything, I needed her.

Back in our room, JoBell reached out to me until I slid under the covers beside her. She said nothing as we watched the continued coverage of the nuclear devastation. When we huddled together, I felt more warmth and peace than I did at any other time.

We slept by the light of the screen. The misery from the nuclear blasts, and the horror of all we'd been through in the war, slithered into our dreams.

I jerked awake and scrambled away from whoever was grabbing my shoulder. My fists were up, ready to fight.

"Danny! You're okay! It's me." JoBell stood back away from the bed. She was used to the rough way I woke up. "Something's happening." I reached for my gun, but she grabbed my hands. "Shhh. No. On TV. I think you better watch this."

I turned my attention to the screen, where a younger man sat at a news desk.

"*Good morning. For those of you just joining us on the East Coast, it's seven a.m. Four o'clock here in Los Angeles at the NBC News studios. I'm Carsten Packer. Some of you may have been with us through the long night as we've tried to relay the information you need at a time like this.*

"*NBC has confirmed that only twelve members of Congress are still alive — seven senators and five representatives. All of them have been transported to North American Aerospace Defense Command, or NORAD, near Colorado Springs, seventy miles south of Denver. The new capitol of the United States will be established at NORAD's headquarters in the facility formerly known as the Cheyenne Mountain nuclear bunker.*

"We're going to take you now, live, to the Air Force Academy Chapel north of Colorado Springs. The chapel is completely full this morning — lots of military officers and surviving members of the press, along with many other civilians. There are also scholars and university professors. These experts may begin to replace the members of the president's cabinet lost in yesterday's attack. I'm sure the chapel is well protected outside. Here you see, standing in front of the altar, the twelve surviving members of Congress. The seven senators are to the left of the lectern, while the five surviving members of the House of Representatives are to our right.

"Joining the remains of Congress is . . . My sources are telling me that's NORAD commander Chuck Jacobsen, previously a general, that is to say, a four-star general. He now appears to have been promoted to general of the Army, and is wearing five stars in a pentagon formation on his shoulder board. It's unclear why he —

"And there she is, President Laura Griffith, now stepping confidently to the lectern. Presidential insiders have told NBC News that she hasn't slept since the attack, but if she's suffering from fatigue, she certainly isn't showing it. And now, here's the president."

"My fellow Americans. As the dawn is obscured on the East Coast by dark clouds of smoke and deadly radioactive contamination, I will forego the customary greeting of the day, for this morning is not good. Our largest city, a world capital for industry and the arts, has been destroyed. The historic capital of our great nation lies in ruins. The monuments to our collective past are no more. Most importantly, over thirteen million of our fellow citizens, innocent men, women, and children, from all walks of life, have been killed.

"The United States government is making every possible effort to rescue and treat the wounded and sick, and to evacuate irradiated areas. FEMA, Red Cross, and military personnel are rushing to provide medicine, treat injuries, and distribute needed food and other supplies. Citizens who must be evacuated are being moved out by Air Force, Army, and Marine air assets. The United States Navy and Coast Guard are turning their vessels into floating refugee cities until victims of this tragedy can be relocated. To be sure, New York and Washington, DC, are hazardous and dangerous areas, but our military and FEMA response teams have been trained to deal with nuclear-contaminated environments. At this time, experts believe it is best if citizens in the affected zones remain in their homes, sealing up and keeping away from windows to avoid additional exposure to radiation. Federal authorities are moving as quickly as they can through neighborhoods to offer assistance. My fellow Americans, I promise you. Help is on the way.

"I want to thank so very much those who have responded to our most recent tragedy. Soldiers, sailors, airmen, Marines, Coast Guard, and civilian law enforcement and emergency crews have reacted to this devastating attack on our nation in the very best tradition of the service. The gratitude of the United States also goes out to all those who have donated food, supplies, and even their own blood to help victims. People around the world, from Saudi Arabia to Great Britain, have come to America's aid, and we are grateful. The United States of America will always remember and support our allies.

"I chose to make this address so early in the morning, before sunrise on the West Coast, because I want all Americans, and the world, to know that although we have suffered terrible losses, democracy in the United States of America lives on. Since yesterday's deadly nuclear explosions, I have worked ceaselessly to rebuild our government as quickly as possible.

"Our Constitution dictates that only a simple majority of each house of Congress shall constitute a quorum, or the minimum number of members required in order to do business. In the absence of the guidance of a Supreme Court, and for the benefit of our country, these members of Congress and I have decided this clause refers to a simple majority of surviving members of Congress. Thus able to conduct emergency business, Congress and I have passed a single emergency exception to federal laws that would prohibit active-duty military personnel from serving in high civil office. I am therefore pleased to report that the Senate has approved my appointment of General Charles Jacobsen to the office of vice president, and I know that his military experience, expertise, and training will be of tremendous value in the struggle ahead.

"Our Constitution provides procedures for filling congressional seats left vacant by death or incapacity, and details about these procedures will be coming to you from your local governments and election officials. For now, it is enough to know that our representative democracy will be fully restored well inside of the next fifty days. I know that in the shadow of such terrible destruction and loss of life, such legal and procedural details may seem trivial, but I make this speech before you all, standing with the vice president and Congress, with the hope that this honesty and transparency will foster trust in your government and faith in the future of our country.

"Many are no doubt wondering if our civil war will go on after these nuclear explosions. The answer is that the war could end today, if the leadership in rebel states would surrender and rejoin the union. At this desperate and painful time, you might wonder why the United States is continuing a war that is likewise desperate and painful. First, although the rebel leadership in Montana, Wyoming, Idaho, and elsewhere has fervently denied any knowledge or involvement in the nuclear attacks, it is inarguable that the instability caused by their rebellions contributed to the explosions. Second, even if the leaders of the rebel states were not involved in the attacks, evidence strongly suggests that at least some rebels assisted the known nuclear theft suspects. To secure America and the world from any such disasters in the future, the rebellions must end.

"Furthermore, there is no basis upon which any state might be allowed to leave the United States of America. States are not legally *allowed to secede*. President Lincoln, in his first inaugural address, stated that the 'Union of these States is perpetual,' that no provision of the Constitution allows states to secede, that 'no government . . . ever had a provision in its . . . law for its own termination.' In the nearly two centuries since, no court decision has ever disputed that position. Clearly, there are no true legal means by which states may secede from the union.

"It is, moreover, not feasible or practical for states to secede. Americans in any given state both contribute to the collective well-being and are dependent upon it just the same. Electricity generated in one state is transmitted to run a factory in another. That factory may produce farm equipment that is then transported along federally funded highways to other states where food is grown to feed people across the country. The states that have declared their independence cannot possibly offer their own citizens the same quality of life that they enjoyed in the United States, nor can the United States afford to lose the contributions of the rebel *states. The United States is bound together for myriad practical reasons.*

"Finally, morality will not permit us to allow states to secede. Secession would create a multitude of desperate or destitute nations that would soon resort to fighting over resources, and such fighting would cost even more lives than have already been lost in this tragic civil war. Our nationwide interdependence has also allowed many states to benefit tremendously from federal funding for roads, dams, universities, law enforcement resources, and much more. These projects were paid for by federal taxpayer dollars for the benefit of all. To allow states to secede from the union would be to allow them to seize these federally funded resources, in effect allowing rebels to steal the benefits of hard-earned tax dollars from Americans everywhere. Thus, the United States has an imperative to stop these rebellions.

"And stop them we will. When organized rebellion has ceased and peace and security are restored, our investigation into the criminals behind this attack will no longer be hindered, and we will be in a much better position to determine exactly how far the conspiracy spreads. In the meantime, the search is under way for those eleven individuals who are known to be responsible for these evil nuclear attacks. They have tried to destroy our government and our national resolve, but they have failed. Our people are determined, and our military is powerful and prepared. To facilitate greater command and control of the US military, almost all of our forces — both military personnel and their families — will be redeployed to our new capital here in Colorado. This morning, as commander in chief of that military, I make the following promise: The United States will make no distinction between those who carried out these attacks and those who assisted them in any way.

We have no more patience for and will deliver no mercy to our enemies.

"This morning, Congress and I stand before you in the open, offering unity to our citizens and friendship to our allies. From our new capital, we will carry out the business of soundly defeating our enemies and rebuilding the United States of America. Further announcements will follow. Thank you."

The screen cut back to the newsroom desk and a lot of people talking about Laura Griffith's speech. They named her philosophy regarding secession the Griffith Doctrine and debated for hours about what it would mean.

Its meaning was clear enough to me and JoBell. The war would continue, and we weren't going anywhere anytime soon.

I saw a picture once, a painting with these clocks melted and flopped over a tree branch and something like a concrete slab. After my mom died, I felt like that, like time had melted. For weeks, I couldn't have told anyone what day it was, what time it was. I ate sometimes, I think, when Becca or JoBell could convince me to have something. It never tasted right. I drank a lot. The pain of the world was too sharp for me back then, and the booze helped soften it all. It took moments and it took months before the blur of time finally snapped back into focus.

Life oozed by like that for JoBell and me for days and days after the nuclear attack, the screen bringing us unending images of fire, smoke, tears, blood, and death. We ate or didn't eat the food they brought up to us. We were kept company by the endless commentary from the surviving news people and their so-called experts. We watched as tens of thousands of people walked out of Baltimore along I-70, which was completely blocked by stalled-out or wrecked cars and trucks. People kept moving along, hauling whatever belongings they could manage to carry. Thousands of bodies littered the road, victims of exhaustion or radiation sickness. The scene was repeated in countless places as millions of people gave up on waiting in their basements for help to arrive and decided to take their chances on foot. Some civilian and military helicopters flew into the less irradiated evacuation zones, picking up the refugees who were worst off, but a few times, desperate people mobbed the aircraft until force had to be used to keep the birds within their weight limits. Some people survived the explosions and fallout, only to be shot on the edge of rescue.

"I'm so damned useless here!" I shouted after watching this. "Everything's going on outside, and we're locked up in this room. Can't even go home." I held up my comm for JoBell to see. "And something's wrong back there. Becca just sent this."

When are you guys coming home? Hurry. Things are getting bad.

She nodded. "I managed to get a voice call through to Becca while you were asleep a few hours ago. We didn't talk long. She was saying something about the Brotherhood right before the call cut out. I couldn't get her back."

"Maybe we could break out of here somehow."

"And be on the run from Idaho *and* the US?" JoBell asked in that annoying way she had of pointing out my stupid ideas.

I paced toward the window again. "Well, we can't just sit here!"

A hard knock pounded on the door. "Private Wright! Miss Linder!" It was Major Leonard, and he sounded pissed. Outside, the moan-shriek-moan-shriek of the air-raid siren began to echo through the city. "I'm coming in!" he bellowed. JoBell and me scrambled into our boots and street clothes as Major Leonard and two other soldiers ran into the room. "I have orders to get you to Idaho CentCom," the major shouted.

One of the soldiers grabbed JoBell's arm and I rushed at him, but JoBell shoved him off first. "What's going on?"

I squeezed the handle of my gun. "Major, what do we got?"

"Our long-distance radar beacons just lit up. Several dozen inbound aircraft. None of them answering on radio." The major met my eyes. "The United States is coming for us."

THREE

"Now hear this!" a voice boomed from speakers that must have been wired up all over the city. *"Emergency! All soldiers to action stations. All Boise residents proceed immediately to evacuation points. Emergency! All soldiers to action stations. All Boise residents proceed immediately to evacuation points."*

The two soldiers with Major Leonard were Sergeant Martonick and Specialist Valentine. Martonick drove us in an armored Humvee, with Valentine standing in the center of the vehicle manning the .50-cal, Major Leonard riding shotgun, and me and JoBell in the backseats, cradling our rifles in our laps. The spring day was beautiful. Picnic weather. The kind of day that teased kids who were still stuck in school, promising them the freedom and fun of summer.

Today would bring bombs, bullets, and blood instead.

Dozens of Idaho jets raced across the sky toward the south and southeast. Chinook and Black Hawk helicopters rose up from all over the city. The streets were crowded with speeding military vehicles and packed buses.

"I don't get it," JoBell said. "They're evacuating Boise? How is that possible? How many people —"

Major Leonard turned to look back at us. "Well, a lot of people have long since left the city."

"But there were, what?" JoBell asked. "Two hundred thousand

people living here before the war? So we're talking about moving thousands of people."

"Tens of thousands, probably," said Major Leonard. "We've been running battle drills for months. Everybody knows where to go, what bus, helicopter, or semi-trailer to board. We have reinforced shelters set up in the mountains. Right now, we have to get you two out to the flats and down into the CentCom bunker."

"The flats" was the name given to a section of the southeast corner of Boise that had been pretty much completely destroyed by earlier bombing. It made sense as the location of the Idaho base. The US might not suspect that Idaho headquarters would be under the wasteland, and if they did, they wouldn't have anything valuable left in the area to damage when they targeted it. But they might target everything else.

"We got to get to the VA hospital to get Sweeney before we go wherever you're taking us," I said.

"Negative," the major said. "My orders are to get you to safety immediately. I'm sure an evac plan is in place for the hospital. Your friend will be fine."

"Bullshit my friend will be fine!" I said. "You don't know. This little evac plan could all go to shit. I will not abandon my friend."

"We owe him our lives," JoBell said.

"The hospital is halfway across town in the wrong direction," Sergeant Martonick called back over his shoulder. He drove us up onto a sidewalk to get around some broken-down vehicles in the middle of the street, bringing the Humvee to a crawl to avoid running down civilians.

"I'm sorry," said the major.

I reached over to squeeze JoBell's hand. She locked eyes with me and I knew she understood my plan. "I'm sorry too," I said. I yanked the handle and kicked my heavy door open, sliding out of the vehicle in seconds. JoBell was right behind me.

"Damn it, Wright! Get back here!" Major Leonard had his door open.

Me and JoBell slung our rifles on our backs. I dodged through the crowd of people, sidestepping and dropping my shoulders to get around shouting men and screaming children. JoBell stayed right with me, pulling ahead a little as we cleared about half a block. I risked a look back to see Major Leonard following. He drew his sidearm and aimed at me for a moment. "Wright!"

I knew he wouldn't shoot. There were too many civilians in the area, and his mission was to protect me, not kill me.

At the end of the block, me and JoBell found a break in the chaos in front of a boarded-up shoe store. "Which way to the VA hospital?" I shouted over the screams and the air-raid siren.

"What do we do when we get there?" JoBell answered. "Eric's not in the best condition."

I held up my M4. "We can figure that out once we find him. Maybe we can take an ambulance or —"

"You won't be stealing any vehicles." Major Leonard caught up to us. "We'll take our Humvee and go get your friend. But no more bullshit. We have to work together, and we have to hurry. Those US birds will be here any minute."

"Thank you," I said, hoping the major knew I meant it.

Martonick finally caught up to us in the Humvee. Major Leonard said nothing as he climbed into the front seat. "Sergeant, get us to the VA hospital," he said when we were all back inside. "I don't care how you do it. Make it happen."

Sergeant Martonick swerved to the left, dodging through heavy traffic. Gun Hummers and civvy vehicles packed with people crowded the road. Parents hurried crying children along. A little girl dropped her doll in the street and broke away from her mother's grip to pick it up. A guy on a motorcycle dropped into a slide to scrape to a halt just a couple feet shy of hitting her. Everyone was shouting, crying, hurrying to get out before the coming attack. Over it all, the two tones of the air-raid siren moaned, like Boise herself was going back and forth between crying and shrieking in fear.

"Sergeant!" Specialist Valentine called down the turret.

The road was blocked ahead as civilians ran with everything they could carry, scrambling into the back of a UPS truck.

"We cannot wait here, Sergeant!" said Major Leonard.

"Shit!" Sergeant Martonick bumped up the curb onto another sidewalk and slowly eased ahead.

"Get out of the way!" Valentine yelled at the people who blocked our way. "Move! This is an emergency!"

"No kidding it's an emergency." JoBell held her hands over her ears. "Are they ever going to shut that air-raid siren off?"

Explosions and the sound of gunfire echoed from the distance. "It's starting," said the major.

A big white passenger van smashed into the back end of our armored Humvee, crumpling its own front end. How many people in that van were now stuck in a city about to be bombed? We drove on, block after block. Sergeant Martonick was an expert at dodging-bomb-craters-debris-and-terrified-people-type driving.

We shot past the damaged capitol building and then, a few blocks later, actually drove up and over a pile of bricks and junk that blocked Franklin Street. The scene on the other side of the rubble was completely jacked up. People hurried all around the hospital area like pissed-off ants after their hill had been kicked open. Ambulances, Humvees, buses, and other vehicles were parked in the street, on the grass, everywhere, and nobody was moving. A few helicopters flew in and out, but that was it.

"This is as close as I can get!" Martonick said. "We're screwed!"

I popped open my door. "Wait here! I'll get Sweeney and be right back!" Then, carrying my M4, I sprinted like hell for the hospital. I dodged through the small gaps between cars, rolled over a vehicle's hood when I ran out of room, and ducked under an open semi door. A quick look back let me know JoBell was a few paces behind me. She should have stayed with our ride, but we didn't have time to argue.

A loud explosion blasted close by, maybe only a few blocks away. A jet shot past overhead. Seriously hard-core machine gun fire cracked the air.

A squad of soldiers in the OD Idaho Army uniform fought to maintain order against a crowd at the front doors of the hospital. "You people have to stay back! Nobody is coming in. It's an evacuation. Get to your evac points!"

JoBell caught up with me. "What are we gonna do now?"

I looked her in the eye. "If you're coming with me, grab my shirt or whatever and stay right on my ass. Nobody gets between us. Got it?"

"Yeah, but what are you —"

"We're gonna fight our way through." She grabbed my shirt and I ran ahead. "Get the hell out of my way!" I shouted. "Private First Class Danny Wright on a mission from President Montaine!" I pushed some dude aside, elbowed another. JoBell helped behind me but kept hold of my shirt. I didn't take the time to look back. I squeezed between two women who tried to shove me. Then I reached the soldiers. Two specialists stepped in front of me, holding their rifles horizontally across their chests.

"No way. Nobody gets in!" said one of the soldiers.

"I'm PFC Wright. The president sent me here." I didn't wait for him to step aside but grabbed his weapon and pulled. As soon as he tried to pull it back, I pushed him hard and opened a gap. Me and JoBell ran inside.

The front lobby of the hospital was even more chaotic than outside. Furniture was upended. Papers littered the floor. Some guy lay bleeding from a bad stab wound in his gut. There was nobody left to take care of him. Everybody was running to leave. A guy frantically worked a screen at the desk, trying to answer the hundreds of questions coming his way at once. I didn't have time to wait in line, so I shoved up to the desk and made sure he could see my rifle. "Where is Eric Sweeney? He was being treated for burns. Had some surgeries."

The man eyed my weapon. "They've been treating the burn victims up on the second floor." He gave me directions and JoBell and I sprinted off through the mad rush. The lights flickered and then went out. More explosions shook the earth and air around us over the loud siren.

"There!" JoBell pointed down the hall.

Under the glow of the dim emergency lights, I could see a doctor or someone pushing Sweeney in a wheelchair. "Hey! Stop!" I ran up and grabbed the wheelchair handle. "We'll take him from here."

The doctor looked like he had come from Pakistan or somewhere. He spoke with a heavy accent. "Who the hell are you?"

"Private Danny Wright. I'm taking Eric Sweeney with me. Is he well enough to travel?"

"You are not taking my patient! This is madness. I am loading him on a helicopter and then we are getting out —"

"We're going to Idaho CentCom. He'll be safest there." I pushed the man out of the way and took the wheelchair from him. "Get to the bird. Get yourself to safety."

Sweeney looked up at me with a dazed expression. "Heeeey, d-dude! I got this like noise sshpinning in my head."

"What's wrong with him?" JoBell asked.

The doctor looked at us like he couldn't believe we had to ask. "He is doped up on pain medication. He's not completely recovered from his most recent round of surgery. He's in a lot of pain being moved around at all —"

"Is he well enough to travel?" I asked. "Is it safe?"

"Safer than here," said the doctor. He sighed. "You want to avoid bumping him around. His grafts are very tender. You need to keep him clean. *Gently*, gently clean his new skin with mild soap and cool to warm water." He shook his head. "You are very stupid for taking him. I cannot spare any medications for you. Wherever you are going, get him to a doctor."

JoBell thanked the man and we took off running, pushing Sweeney in the wheelchair. "Hang on, buddy. Don't worry. We'll get you out of this," I said.

"Woooo," Sweeney said through his drug fog. "Going fast now."

On the way out, things were a lot easier. We looked up. One second, a jet was in the distance, and the next, the hotel JoBell and I had been staying in burst into fire, dust, and falling rubble. Red-and-white mushroom clouds of fire rolled upward all over town.

"What if they left us?" JoBell shouted over the noise.

"Then we'll go back and take shelter in the hospital basement." I spotted our gun Hummer, the specialist crouched low in the turret waving at us. I rolled Sweeney's wheelchair as close as I could to our ride, but when we were blocked by cars, I was out of options. I slung my M4 to my back and reached down to pick him up.

"Danny, be careful," said JoBell. "His skin is so tender right now."

"Good thing he's all drugged up," I said.

"It *is* a good thing!" Sweeney shouted as I carried him to the Humvee.

Finally we loaded him into my seat, and I sat on the turret platform next to the specialist's feet. Sergeant Martonick was sweating and shaking as he shifted into drive and sped off. The roads had opened quite a bit, but there were still a lot of evacuation vehicles moving around. We passed a bus and a semi heading southeast.

A four-story brick building flashed for a second like a light had switched on inside and then blasted out in all directions. I pulled the specialist down into our Humvee as Sergeant Martonick drove through the falling debris. Bricks smacked our windshield and thumped all over our hood and roof. The Humvee bumped ahead, and I worried we'd be stuck and then buried, but the sergeant got us clear.

"Good driving, Sergeant," said Major Leonard. "Keep it up."

"I hate this shit!" said Martonick.

The road ahead opened up like the sun. One explosion after another ripped the world apart.

"They're after the command center!" the major screamed to be heard over the roar of the US bombs and the Idaho anti-aircraft guns.

"We're never going to make it there now!" JoBell shouted.

More bombs fell, and more debris flew back toward us. Major Leonard shouted something to Martonick before the sergeant whipped a tight U-turn and sped back north. The major held the radio handset to his ear, keying the mike and shouting something to someone, probably trying to call for help or instructions.

JoBell reached over and squeezed my hand. Nobody spoke for a long time, not that we would have been able to hear each other over the roar of the battle outside. Martonick gripped the wheel hard, muttering swears as he tried to keep us from getting killed.

As we neared the north edge of Boise on Highway 55, more explosions rocked the earth behind us. A jet shot by overhead and another met it — a fighter one second and a fireball the next. Heavy anti-aircraft rounds ripped up from everywhere, blasting planes and helicopters. It was impossible from this distance to tell if more US or Idaho aircraft were being shot down, but the US had to have us outnumbered, and the city was being pounded by bombs and missiles.

The road curved so that we couldn't see out our windows to the south anymore. JoBell put her face in her hands. "So many innocent people."

I looked down to where Sweeney sat, barely awake, swimming in a sea of drugs. He still wore a lot of bandages. I'd become used to that sight. But now more of his flesh was exposed, that strange, unnatural grafted skin sculpted into place. One patch of that new, raw skin came up his neck and right cheek. Even the bottom of his earlobe would be mangled for life. Sweeney had been the best-looking guy at school, the guy who always got the girl. For the rest of his life, he'd have obvious physical damage. Who would he be now?

But he was alive. He was in better shape than thousands of people in Boise, better than millions around New York and DC.

"I could hardly hear when I was on the radio back there. I asked for instructions, since we couldn't make it to the Idaho CentCom bunker," Major Leonard finally said. "We have new orders to get out of Boise and head to Freedom Lake. Then I lost radio contact."

JoBell looked up. "My dad is in that bunker." Her voice shook. "He's helping Idaho rewrite its legal system. If you lost contact . . ."

Major Leonard turned around in his seat to look back at us. "CentCom is thirty feet deep in a bunker made of steel and three feet of reinforced concrete. They lost an antenna somewhere, not CentCom."

The road in front of us exploded. Black chunks of dirt and pavement pelted the windshield. "Oh shit!" Specialist Valentine ducked down into the Humvee again. Parts of the road showered down around him. "Apache gunship right behind us!"

Our Humvee lurched to the right, skidding out of control a little on the loose shoulder. "I got it. I got it." Sergeant Martonick gritted his teeth, held the wheel tight, let off the gas, and eased us back onto the road.

"They won't miss us again!" I yelled. "Fed bird got us sighted. Our armor ain't gonna stop a hellfire missile."

"Fort McHenry, Fort McHenry, this is flashpoint. Urgent! We are northbound on Highway 55. Fed attack helo is on us. Request air support. How copy? Over." Major Leonard pressed the handset to his ear. Then he frowned at Valentine. "Specialist, get up there on your gun. Do your best to bring that bird down."

The specialist stayed crouched, his hands holding his helmet down by the chin strap, eyes squeezed shut. "Oh shit, oh shit, oh shit," he whimpered. "Can't stop a helicopter. There's no way."

"We've got some concealment under these trees ahead," Sergeant Martonick said.

"That won't last long," said JoBell.

"Damn it." I pushed Valentine back and climbed up onto the gunner platform. "I said I was getting out of this shit." I stood and grabbed the machine gun by the handle with my left hand. With my free hand, I unlocked the turret so it would rotate. Then I spun around to face our rear, ready to free gun it.

Roaring fire ripped through the high tree branches over the road, dropping leaves and some heavier sticks onto the pavement. A line of holes blasted into the road behind us, walking up on us. "Faster, Martonick!"

Plastic five-gallon cans in the steel rack on the back of our Humvee burst. Our extra fuel splashed all over the vehicle, seconds before a couple rounds shredded through it. Screams came from inside the truck. "Jo?" I shouted.

"We're okay!"

Martonick swerved back and forth to make us a harder target. Another volley opened up from the Apache, mostly missing us, but a few rounds nipped our back passenger side corner, taking our radio antenna and its mount. Red-hot tracer rounds ignited the fuel-soaked back end.

"We're burning!" I yelled. Flames licked up to the edge of the gun turret. "Get that fire extinguisher up here!" I didn't have time to deal with the fire. We cleared the tree cover and I hammered down on the butterfly trigger of the .50-cal, praying I could hit something. Damn my ammo supply. Damn cooking the barrel. I followed my tracers and sprayed bullets up at the helicopter, trying to compensate for our swerving vehicle and the movement of the Apache. Some sparks popped on the bird's weapons pods, and then tapped the engine beneath the rotors. Smoke sprayed from the side of the Apache. I lowered my machine gun and cut a hard line right down the canopy.

I hit the Apache's tail rotor, sending it into a flat spin heading right for us. I ducked as its tires whooshed close by overhead. It crashed into the pavement and rolled sideways for a moment before it ripped into a ball of fire and shredded metal.

Then we were airborne. The Humvee shot off the road into someone's sloping front yard, dodging the burning Apache wreck but taking out a mailbox. I held on tight to the edge of the turret and the gun handles as we landed. We skidded to a stop, taking out a little decorative windmill thing and about half a dozen garden gnomes on the way.

The fuel had burned off the outside of the Humvee's ass end, but we forced open the damaged trunk so we could use the fire extinguisher to put out any flames back there. Then we had a moment to rest and make sure Sweeney and everybody else hadn't been hurt. Besides the sounds of battle rumbling in the distance, the road was mostly quiet.

"Major Leonard?" I said. "You can cancel that air support."

⌇• *Republic of Idaho Radio is going to stay on the air even though the United States has bombed some of our transmitter network, just as it is bombing the entire Boise area. Our redundant transmitters are taking over for those we have lost in order to bring you the truth. As you can probably hear in the background, a fierce battle is taking place in our nation's capital right now, part of President Griffith's retaliation for the nuclear attacks.*

Neither the Republic of Idaho nor the nation of Montana had anything to do with the attacks, but once again, our innocent freedom-loving people are forced to pay the price in blood. It is far too early for any conclusive casualty counts, but it is clear that at least hundreds of innocent civilians are being murdered by the United States at this very moment.

President Montaine and the leadership of the Republic of Idaho are alive and in command, fighting back and repelling this latest United States aggression. And Republic of Idaho Radio will stay on the air through the crisis to bring you the information you need. Idaho is free! Idaho will never surrender! •⌇

⌇• *This would normally be the time for the KCTV5 Kansas City drive-time traffic report, but today I-70 is essentially closed to civilian traffic by a massive military convoy. It consists of all the trucks and armored vehicles you might expect, but buses, moving trucks, and passenger vans packed with civilians are traveling along with the military forces, everything heading west toward Colorado. We believe these civilians are the families of those serving at Fort Leonard Wood and Whiteman Air Force Base in Missouri. Some sources that we cannot reveal to you have brought us evidence that those bases are being evacuated, and we have heard that Fort Riley and McConnell Air Force Base in Kansas are also being stripped of all personnel and useful military materials. We have one unconfirmed report of the military firing on a vehicle attempting to access I-70, and we therefore urge Kansas City residents to stay off the roads. This convoy is miles long, it's well armed, and it seems to be accepting no interference. We'll continue to bring you more information as it becomes available.* •⌐ᴧ⌐

⌐ᴧ⌐• *I don't know if anyone is receiving this transmission, or if there's anyone left at any of our ABC affiliate studios to broadcast this report, but if we're stranded over here, we're going to keep filming. I'm James Novik, standing in Vilnius, Lithuania, watching a scene that is playing throughout many former Soviet states today. Several hours ago, Russian planes dropped leaflets welcoming people back to the Soviet Union, and radio and television broadcasts began communicating the same message. A short time later, Russian, or I suppose we can now say Soviet, tanks, trucks, and troop carriers, supported by their air force, deployed from occupied Ukraine. They quickly moved into Belarus, crushing the limited resistance they encountered. Now they've entered Lithuania in the same way. The Lithuanian military made some attempt to resist the invasion, but they were hopelessly outnumbered by Soviet forces.*

What you're seeing behind me is a column of well-armed Soviet soldiers marching down a major street in Vilnius, singing the Soviet national anthem, with the lyrics now updated to mention "Putin our leader." The civilian population is watching this display of military power, monitored closely by soldiers, who are handing out small red Soviet flags for the people to wave. I'm told this same footage is being shown on RT, well, on Soviet state television, where Vladimir Putin has proclaimed the people's faces to be wet with tears of joy. Somehow, as these invaders raise their crimson flag with its golden hammer and sickle, I do not think the crying people are full of joy. Putin's dreams of reestablishing the Soviet Union are apparently being realized now that NATO is no longer backed by the American military. This is James Novik, for ABC News, or . . . whoever is left to air this. •⌣

⌣• *MetLife has folded not only because its headquarters in New York has been destroyed, but because, quite simply, there is no way that any insurance company could pay out literally millions of separate insurance claims for the damage inflicted by the nuclear bombs. Look, the terrorist attacks of September 11, 2001, produced insured losses of nearly forty billion dollars, but that is going to be insignificant compared to the insured losses in life and property, not just in New York and Washington, DC, but in the hundreds of cities that have been basically destroyed by radiation.*

It may seem petty to be talking about financial issues in the wake of such a terrible loss of life, but our national capital and primary financial center are now gone. The resulting economic catastrophe will have dire consequences for us all. It's times like these that we need the federal government to step in and make decisions to try to provide some financial security and straighten a lot of this out. Unfortunately, we essentially have no federal government anymore. •⌣

⌣• *CNN's Jenna Martin brings us a disturbing report on a sad new twist in America's border crisis. Jenna?"*

"Thanks, Jerry. For decades, Americans have struggled with the problem of dealing with an influx of immigrants, both legal and undocumented. Now, however, after weeks of civil war in America and the nuclear detonations in New York and Washington, DC, the situation is reversed. Canadian Prime Minister Stewart Hadley announced today that Canada's borders are closed to refugees. He

did promise that Canadian relief supplies will be moved to refugee stations on the American side of the border. He was also quick to add that providing supplies for refugee stations in New England does not constitute the Canadian government's official recognition of the so-called independent nation of New England.

"To the south, the situation is much worse. Mexican President Emilio Nevarez has closed his country to all Americans and forti-fied the Mexican border with the US using Mexican military and law enforcement personnel. Some Americans, desperate to flee the civil war, have tried to cross the border anywhere they can, some-times attempting to climb over or even break through the wall. Many have been shot by Mexican law enforcement, firing in response to what they insisted were armed American invaders. •⎯⌁*

⌁⎯*• Shout Out founder and CEO Martin Zimmerman confirmed today that the state-of-the-art Shout Out server base in Connecticut has been destroyed by the EMP from the recent nuclear detona-tion. Worldwide users of Shout Out experienced significant lag and interruptions to service as the backup servers in California attempted to take over. That system overloaded and crashed a few hours later. Zimmerman says the company would try to rebuild, but because of the war, suitable parts are no longer being manu-factured or are reserved for military use. He also spoke about the overwhelming expense of replacing the massive server sta-tions. Shout Out facilities had been insured, but their insurance company collapsed shortly after the nuclear attack. In response to hundreds of thousands of requests for data recovery, Zimmerman offered his apologies, but forensic retrieval of important user mes-sages, photographs, or videos will not be possible. You're listening to ABC News.* •⎯⌁

⌐√—• US nuclear experts disagree on the cause of the explosion in the number three reactor at the Indian Point nuclear power plant, about forty miles north of New York City. Some experts suggest that a surge in the power lines around the city, caused by the warhead's powerful electromagnetic pulse, might have traveled to the plant and shorted out some of the fail-safe systems. Others have theorized that ground tremors might have been significant enough at the plant to cause something to go wrong.

"Whatever the cause, the immediate crisis is clear. The protective dome built around the reactor is severely cracked. This image comes to you via camera drone, and those spots you see are the result of radiation eating away at the drone's electronics. Radiation levels in the plume of smoke and other fumes are over three thousand rads. That's several times the lethal dose, far worse than the level of radiation in the fallout zones around New York and Washington, DC. If this reactor cannot be sealed, it will continue to spew an even larger cloud of radioactive fallout, contaminating the ground, air, and water, and rendering an even larger portion of North America uninhabitable. Moreover, because the Indian Point nuclear power plant is located on the bank of the Hudson River, a great deal of nuclear contamination could be carried out to the Atlantic Ocean.

"Before the nuclear attack, about seventeen million people lived within fifty miles of the plant, and despite a massive number of fatalities and a significant evacuation effort, hundreds of thousands still reside around Indian Point. Now their hopes rest on the 247th Army Engineer Battalion. The mission of the engineers is to fill the remnants of the breached dome with lead, which will absorb some of the radiation from the extraordinarily hot fire inside. Afterward, they will seal the cracked dome inside a second dome of cement, and then they will encase the entire structure in a massive steel-and-concrete sarcophagus. Since radiation degrades silicon chips, robots and drones cannot complete this work. The Army Corps of Engineers is forced to send in human beings, and many of them will be exposed to very harmful and even lethal levels of radiation. Because of this, NBC will be broadcasting videos the soldiers have filmed for their loved ones through the next several days. Here's the first of those."

"I'm First Lieutenant Winnie McBride. I want to tell my family back home that I love them, and that I'm doing this for them. We're going into the radiation zone to seal that reactor breach, and we're not coming out. To my daughter, Kristina, I need you to remember that Mommy loves you very much. As you grow up without your mother, please try to understand that someone had to go in there and do this. Try to remember that your mother did her duty. I love you, baby. Goodbye. ●⎯⋏⎯

CHAPTER
FOUR

It should have taken about four hours for us to drive from Boise to Grangeville, but our armored Humvee wasn't the fastest ride going, and a few sections of road had been bombed out. We often had to drive on the shoulder or at least go really slowly to pass over rubble. Once, we got ourselves stuck in a bomb crater so deep that we had to hitch the winch cable to a thick-ass tree so we could pull ourselves out. All that slow going had me worried about Sweeney. He kept up a good tough-guy-who-never-feels-nothing-type act, but I knew that sweat on his forehead and upper lip wasn't just 'cause it was hot. We needed to get him some pain meds.

When Highway 95 came out of the mountains a little bit, we saw the aftermath of the Battle of White Bird. The highway was interrupted by a little pond formed by a bridge that had collapsed and dammed up White Bird Creek below. We had to drive down off the ridge into the town itself.

Or what used to be a town. Way down in southern Idaho, there was Craters of the Moon national park, a place where volcanoes had shot up a bunch of lava a million years ago or something. It was an empty, dead area torn up in parts by ancient lava flows and rock stuff. That place was as lush as springtime in my mom's old flower garden compared to White Bird. It had never been much, maybe sixty houses, a hundred to a couple hundred people. Now not one house was left in livable condition. Only four or five were still standing, and those were just burned-out shells. Even the mountains themselves didn't look, well, mountainy. They used to be sort of smooth-looking and covered in dry scrub brush, not all craggy like some of the higher ranges. Now parts of them had been blasted away, leaving them jagged and cruel, like a giant's teeth that got busted out in a fight.

"Oh no." JoBell pointed out our window.

I looked at what she was pointing to and wished I hadn't. "Nobody could get in here and recover the bodies?" I asked.

"This was kind of no-man's-land during the occupation," said Major Leonard. "Idaho dug into the mountains and forced the Fed back every time they tried to enter through here. Kind of appropriate, I guess. Right around here, back in 1877, the US Army was defeated by the Nez Perce Indians at the Battle of White Bird Canyon. About seventy of them fought about a hundred US soldiers. Thirty-four soldiers were killed, and only three Indians were wounded. It was the beginning of what we now call the Nez Perce War." The major must have noticed our curious looks. He shrugged. "I worked for the National Park Service before the war. Used to do guided tours and talks and things for tourists and student groups."

The sergeant drove us through the rubble of the town, our tires crunching over chunks of torn-up pavement and the remains of people's lives. "That's awesome," he said. "We beat the US Army here just like last time."

"Well, I don't know how many parallels we should draw," said the major. "The Nez Perce did lose the war. After they surrendered, Chief Joseph supposedly said, 'From where the sun now stands, I will fight no more forever.'"

The ghost wound in my left hand flared again, and I looked down at my rifle. I wished I could stop fighting, or better yet, go back in time and never start fighting in the first place. I remember once in Sunday school, Chaplain Carmichael talked about how God existed outside of time, how God was presently with us right now and in every moment in the future and back on the cross, all at the same time. I prayed for the millionth time that God might send me back to that horrible night in Boise and not let me fire that one shot that had started all this. Sure, I'd prayed this before to save myself or my mother, but it wasn't a selfish prayer anymore. It was a prayer for millions of lost lives, for so many more losses that would come before this war ended.

That dirty, cold truth ate away at me in every quiet moment. Before the Battle of Boise — before the first Battle of Boise, I guess — I used to dream about buying out Schmidty and taking over the auto shop that him and my dad had started. I'd fix the place up, modernize it, and expand the business, maybe get into cool auto detailing. JoBell and me would get married, buy a little house, or maybe build a place in the woods where I could hunt and fish. We'd have some kids.

My nine mil was digging into my hip, and I shifted position. Now all those dreams were echoes from the old world, one I'd helped to destroy. I had no right to be sad about what I'd lost when millions had been robbed of so much more.

I placed my hand on JoBell's shoulder, closing my eyes and feeling her warmth through my fingers. She kissed my hand. I pushed my grief aside and thanked God for her.

"I just wish . . ." I whispered to JoBell, and she looked up at me. I couldn't finish my sentence. I didn't know how. She squeezed my hand to tell me she was here for me. With that, I could keep going.

I barely did shit back in high school, but I paid attention in Mr. Shiratori's American History class, and I remember there was a lot more to what Chief Joseph was supposed to have said. He had talked about a bunch of the Indian friends he'd lost, and there was a lot of language about suffering children. I think our history book had been trying to set up "I will fight no more forever" as some kind of noble declaration for peace, but I wondered if maybe it was more about his exhaustion and heartbreak. I could understand that feeling, only I'd brought all this misery on myself. On everyone.

Sergeant Martonick off-roaded up from the dead town to the crumbling highway, and we continued on in silence toward Freedom Lake. Progress was slow. I nodded off during the bumpy ride, but I snapped awake when I felt the Humvee slow down.

"Shit," Martonick said.

I made sure my rifle was ready. "What's going on?"

"Out of fuel." The sergeant sighed. "And our reserve fuel cans were shot to hell."

"I don't suppose there's a gas station around." I looked out the window at an entire ruined city. Burned-out foundations of houses. Bricks and steel girders scattered from where downtown used to be. Shell craters all over. But here and there, especially closer to the river, new little shanties had been built out of the junk. Some people were still alive in this town. "Where are we?"

"If the roads weren't so messed up, I'd say we're about two and a half hours from Freedom Lake," said the major. "This used to be the city of Lewiston. Our people held out here for a long time, even when the city was surrounded by the US military during the occupation. Finally the US Navy brought four Littoral Combat Ships up the river and destroyed this place." The Humvee rolled to a stop. "Okay, everybody but Specialist Valentine and Private Sweeney, get out. Set up a security perimeter around the vehicle."

Martonick had taken us off the road into the parking lot of an abandoned motel. The main office was in a separate building from the row of rooms, and it had been torched long ago, along with its barely readable HAPPY TRAILS MOTEL sign. The rooms themselves had busted windows and doors. Empty square holes showed where the wall air-conditioning units used to be.

JoBell held her Springfield M1A rifle at the ready. "I was going to say at least we'll have beds tonight, but I think this place has been pretty picked over."

Major Leonard tugged on some wires at the ruined radio antenna mount. "So there goes radio with any friendly units in the area. Before the war, I might have been able to contact command via satellite." He held up his comm. "Now I can't even get this thing to connect to the network. Anyone else?"

"Use mine," Sweeney yelled. He sat with his legs hanging out the door of the Humvee. "It's the best."

I laughed. Sweeney might have nearly been killed in the last battle to force the US out of Idaho. He had limited motion in his right shoulder, a nasty limp that might be permanent, and disfigured skin on the right side of his body and face that would probably earn him weird looks for the rest of his life. But whatever else happened, he was never far from his comm.

The major grabbed the comm and tapped the screen. I winced, bracing myself for another half-pornographic visit from Sweeney's digi-assistant.

"Hello, Eric. How may . . . I help you?" A calm, male voice came on instead.

JoBell gave Sweeney a curious look. "What happened to Digi-Trixie?"

He rested his head back against his seat. "Trixie was stupid. I named this one John Smith."

"Damn." The major held Sweeney's comm under his arm while he tried to tap his own. "I can't get my comm online at all. Can't access my contact list."

"Cover this section?" I said to Sergeant Martonick. He nodded, and I went to the major, holding up my hands for Sweeney's comm. "Sir?"

He tossed it to me and then turned away, surveying the area around us.

"John?" Nothing happened.

"John *Smith*," Sweeney said.

"John Smith, please get me a voice call with Becca Wells."

The comm did nothing for a long time. *"I'm . . . sorry. Network difficulties . . . for voice calls . . . again later."*

"John Smith, send a text message to Becca Wells and Cal Riccon." Usually the digi-assistant would ask me to go ahead with the message. This time, the text screen came up. I'd actually have to type. **stuck in lewiston**, I typed. **help.**

"Text message." Had the message gone through? I couldn't tell. This was a Sony SatComm Six Superdrive. A six-hundred-dollar COMMPAD. But with the Internet and satellite network jacked up, it was worthless.

"John Smith, send Cal Riccon and Becca Wells my location." I held the comm up, hoping it could connect with something.

"To assist," was all it said. Whatever that meant.

"I don't know if anyone is getting the message or not," I said to the group as I handed Sweeney's comm back to him.

"It's getting late," said Major Leonard. "We'll see what MREs we have left in the Humvee that weren't shot to pieces. At first light, we'll send a team deeper into Lewiston to search for diesel."

"Sir, maybe we should look for food and water too," said Sergeant Martonick. "If we can't find fuel, we could be here a long time, until someone starts to wonder why we haven't showed up in Freedom Lake."

"If CentCom is still there to miss us," JoBell said.

Pushing up the mangled back hatch of the Humvee felt like the heaviest military press I'd ever lifted. Finally, JoBell helped me get the thing open, and we dug out what could be salvaged of our food and bottled water. A couple days' worth, at best.

Since a fire would give away our position to US Special Ops or anyone else in the area who would want to mess us up, we decided to run straight-up tactical. But that didn't mean we couldn't use some blankets and maybe a mattress or two out of the motel, if we could find any that were in okay shape. Shortly before dark, me and JoBell started clearing the rooms. Raccoons had made a mess of the first one, judging from the scratch marks and shit all over everything. In the second, the little tactical flashlight I'd borrowed from Martorick fell on a bed with the remnants of ropes on either side of the head-board and a nasty but dry red-brown bloodstain in the middle of the mattress.

"Happened a long time ago." My voice thudded heavy in the thick, still air.

JoBell didn't answer. We moved on and found several rooms where everything had been stripped out and taken. Finally, we kicked in a door where things looked okay. A little cookstove, some pots, and a few cans of vegetables and soup were set up on a small counter next to the sink outside the bathroom. The bed was in mostly good shape. I felt the stove. Cold. "Whoever was living here isn't here now. I wonder how long —"

I was slammed in the side so hard that I hit the wall, clocking my head on the hangers on the open closet bar. I tried to swing my rifle up, but someone grabbed it. Rough hands clamped my throat.

JoBell screamed. Something crashed. I tried to yell for help, but I couldn't breathe.

"Hey." A gun muzzle was pressed next to my eye. "Hey, hey. I'll shoot your damn brains out. You feel?" He pressed the gun harder. "Huh? You done?"

Some guy with his huge gut hanging out the bottom of a wolf head T-shirt had a .38 to JoBell's temple. Her blond hair stuck out from between his sausage fingers. On one of those fingers, he wore a big silver skull ring that seemed to smile at me. In the dim light, I caught a glimpse of my guy in the mirror. A skinny little bastard with a sorry excuse for a beard and a douchey braided ponytail. I could drop him in one punch if he wasn't pointing a gun at my head. If his buddy didn't have my JoBell.

Another guy about my age took JoBell's rifle. Then he hurried to me and grabbed my M4, slinging it over his shoulder. While he took my nine mil from its holster, our eyes met, and I saw his nose, crooked from having been busted, his split lip, the bruise under his eye. He wasn't like the other two. A current of fear ran through him, and I wonder if that silver skull had played a part in his jacked-up face.

"You two okay in there?" Major Leonard called.

The skinny guy shook me. "Answer him. Tell him you're okay. Wrong word, and I'll kill you."

"We're good, sir," I shouted after a moment. "Just saw a rat."

The fat man pulled JoBell's head to the side and dragged his slimy tongue up her neck. "Mmm. This one's fresh. Showered in the last week and everything, I bet." JoBell squeezed her eyes closed as he kissed her cheek. "Welcome to the Lewiston Hilton, baby. You and me are gonna have some fun. Got the honeymoon suite reserved a few doors down."

Every muscle in my body tensed to move and destroy this asshole. Why hadn't I swept the room first? Rule number three. Always post a guard. If we'd checked the bathroom right away like we had with the other rooms, they'd never have jumped us.

"We got friends outside," I said. "If you let us go right now, we'll let you live."

The skinny guy laughed. Fat Ass grinned, showing off the tobacco all over his teeth. "That so?" He laughed and then spoke close to JoBell's ear. "I do believe he's jealous of us, darling." To me, he added, "Well, don't you worry. We're going to have fun with you too.

When the dating pool is as piss-poor as we got here, we can't be too picky. Ask the kid there."

"We're not with the United States," JoBell said. "We're Idaho Army."

"That so?" Fat Ass shrugged. "Honey, Fed or Idaho, you're all pink inside." Him and the skinny bastard laughed like this was the best joke they'd ever heard. Then, like throwing a switch, Fat Ass turned serious. "I could give a shit which army you're with. It's your damned war what ruined my landscaping business, what got my family killed. Now, come on." He pulled JoBell toward the door. Skinny Guy made me follow, and the bruised kid brought up the rear.

Outside in the parking lot, Specialist Valentine saw us first. He froze like he didn't know what to do. When the major saw him freaking out behind the machine gun, he finally turned and noticed us.

"Evening!" Fat Ass yelled. "No. No. Lower your guns. That ain't any way for guests to behave. 'Sides, check it out." He jerked his head, and I risked a look. Four men with a mix of shotguns and rifles stepped up to the edge of the motel roof. Fat Ass laughed again. "Don't look so worried. Nothing bad's gonna happen 'cept if you do something stupid to piss me off. Now see, Captain —"

"Major," said Major Leonard.

Fat Ass made a little bow but never relaxed his hold on JoBell. "Well, then I'm the damned admiral. See, *Major*, me and my boys will take that nice ride of yours. Turns out we have a spare can of diesel. We'll have that machine gun, all your rifles, and any food you got. And we'll take your uniforms — all your clothes, really."

"Who are you?" Major Leonard asked.

"I'm the guy who's going to kill you if you don't do what I say, and start doing it right now. Now get your boy out from behind that machine gun. All y'all put your guns down and step back." The major put his rifle on the ground. Martonick did the same, and the specialist climbed up onto the roof of the Humvee and got down to the ground. "That's right." Fat Ass kept his gun pointed at JoBell's head with his right hand. He let go of her hair with his left and wrapped his arm around her, his hand slowly sliding up over her shirt closer and closer to her chest.

A dull thud came from behind us. A man had fallen off the roof, and we looked up to see a sword blade slip through the throat of another. Then Cal stepped into view, pulling the blade back and spinning to slash the hands clean off another man.

Skinny Guy was watching the action on the roof. I threw my head back to crunch his face, and my hand moved to knock his gun aside. I pulled away from him as Cal slashed the last roof man's head off. Then he jumped from the roof, sliding down a pole fireman-style.

JoBell ducked and slammed her elbow into Fat Ass's tiny junk. When he groaned and backed up, she spun out of his grip and shot up with her legs, back, shoulder, and arms, bashing her fist under his chin. A piece of his tongue fell away and he yelled as blood gushed from his mouth. "Oo fuhin beh!"

Cal screamed as he sprinted toward us. He slashed his cavalry saber down and to the left to take a chunk out of Skinny Guy's face and neck. Then he took his sword in both hands and swung up and to the right, slicing through Fat Ass's stomach. Cal gripped that sicko by the throat with one big, shaking hand, eyes wide and breathing heavy. "You messed with the wrong people, asshole!" He gritted his teeth. Spittle was on his chin. "Special place in hell for you." He rammed his saber up into the guy's crotch, his bicep flexing and cut forearm shaking as he pushed the blade up into our attacker's body.

The whole thing had happened in seconds, and the younger, bruised guy who had taken our guns stood frozen. Sheriff Nathan Crow came out from behind the motel office, walking calmly with his hand out in front of him, pointing an eight-inch .44 Magnum revolver as he approached the guy.

The gun grabber held his hands up as he stepped backward. "No. Please. I ain't really with them. They made me —"

Crow shot him in the face as casually as he might swat a fly. He holstered his gun as the guy's body fell back and bounced a little when it hit the ground. Crow let out an earsplitting two-fingered whistle, and two big four-wheel-drive pickups rolled into the lot. A half-dozen Brotherhood men climbed down from them and set up a security perimeter.

"Danny, Miss Linder" — Sheriff Crow nodded to us — "we came as soon as Cal got your text message. Miss Linder, are you injured? I know you're not okay, but did he cut you or anything?"

JoBell shook her head.

Cal handed me my nine mil and M4. "How about you?"

I looked at my friend, every part of me, inside and out, shaking scared. "Shit, Cal."

He pulled a red-brown stained hanky from his pocket and wiped the blood off his sword. Then he put his arm around my shoulders. "It's cool, dude. The Brotherhood has it covered."

Crow's eyes wrinkled with his big smile as he handed the major's rifle back to him. "I'm Nathan Crow."

"Major Leonard."

Crow nodded. "Good to meet you, though I wish it had been under better circumstances."

"Likewise," said the major.

JoBell stepped close to me. I was surprised she wasn't crying. I about wanted to, and I hadn't been felt up by that sicko. I noticed a black armband with the white eagle stretched around Cal's big arm. He was an official member of the Brotherhood now. "When did this happen?" I said, nodding to the armband.

"Cal joined us a couple weeks ago. We could hardly find a band long enough for him." Crow slapped a hand on the big guy's shoulder. "We were putting a stop to some horse thieves south of Pullman, Washington, when he got this strange text message. Then your location pinged with the word *help*. I've never seen anyone drive a big four-by-four so fast. We sneaked up behind the place at just about the time those four sorry assholes took aim at you from the roof."

Sweeney had limped out to join us. "Thanks for coming, buddy."

"How you feeling?" Cal asked.

Sweeney shrugged and then winced.

A dark-haired man in a black armband stepped up to Crow. "Nathan, scouts have radioed in. They've spotted some vehicle movement deeper in the ruins. We may have more of a problem."

"Call the scouts back in. Fuel up their Humvee," said Crow. "We'll pull tight security, set up here for the night, and roll out at first light. If that's okay with you, Major?"

The major nodded. "Yes."

"No," JoBell said. Everybody watched her. Her voice broke a little as she said, "It is *not* okay. We leave tonight. Burn this place down."

Nobody answered her for a moment. Crow finally snapped to life. "You heard her, boys! Pack it up. Little gas on a couple of the beds in there." He pointed to the bodies on the ground. "Then throw those miserable carcasses in too. Torch it all."

FIVE

The thing about a fight is that the experience doesn't end after the last punch is thrown, or the last shot is fired. Whenever I was in a struggle against someone who wanted to hurt or even kill me, the world would change in the space of a few seconds. My heart rate, my breathing, and even my thoughts sped up, so it felt like everything around me was moving a bit slower. Even after the action cleared and the danger had passed, it took a long time to relax. My muscles stayed tense. Every small sound or movement felt amplified somehow.

I was about eleven years old the first time I got into a real fistfight. We were both little kids, and I could hardly remember why me and him had been fighting. I didn't even know his name. But I remembered how after it was over, and he'd run away from the playground with a bloody lip, I'd walked my bike back home, and I couldn't stop my body from shaking. I couldn't cool down, and although I wasn't hurt too bad, I found myself crying in the garage later on. There had been just too much energy and intensity to deal with.

I had that same leftover adrenaline, without the tears, later that night, as me, JoBell, and Sweeney rode in the backseat of a big four-wheel-drive pickup back to Freedom Lake. Cal drove. Nathan Crow rode shotgun. Two Brotherhood guys sat on a couch in the bed of the truck, facing backward and manning a captured US M240B machine gun. I'd had a rotten time trying to sleep since the war began, but now I'd been awake and running around for like nineteen or twenty hours. I should have been fried enough to catch a few hours on this ride, but I couldn't calm down.

It wasn't only the fight rush that kept me from relaxing, though. I could still feel that slimeball's hands on me. I could still smell the greasy stench of that piece of shit who'd threatened my JoBell. One look at JoBell showed me she was thinking the same things. She kept herself balled up around her rifle, almost like she was cold, even though Cal had the heat on against the cool spring night. JoBell had done really good in the fight against the US occupation, but that had all been removed and distant. A fight with rifles was different than fighting up close and hand to hand. And those sickos had wanted more than to just kill us. I clenched my fists tight, all pissed off again when I thought about what they nearly did.

"Cal, Mr. Crow," JoBell said after we'd been on the road for about a half hour. "Thank you for saving our lives."

Cal shrugged. "It's just what we do. Anyway, I promised you a long time ago that I wouldn't let nothing bad happen to you."

"I'm glad we got there in time," said Crow. "We, um . . . Well, the Brotherhood of the White Eagle is doing the best it can, but I'm sorry to say that we haven't always made it in time for everyone who's needed our help."

We rode in silence for a moment. "I'm sorry if I got carried away yelling at you all back at the Victory Day celebration," JoBell said. "I mean, I still think we could have found a different way to handle the situation besides hanging those people, but maybe I was a little too harsh."

"Don't think anything of it. I wish there'd been another way too," Crow said. He turned around to look at us. "I'm supposed to be a sheriff, Miss Linder. You give me a working legal system, a place I can take dangerous criminals, a way to make sure that justice will be done, and I'll be the first one on board. That's why I'm glad your father is down in Boise, helping to set up a system." Crow must have noticed the worry on JoBell's face, because his expression softened. "Hey. Hey, don't you worry. We've heard from Idaho CentCom. They're still broadcasting on RIR. It was a tough fight, but we pushed 'em back. Your daddy's okay. I'm sure of it." JoBell nodded and let out a shaky breath. Crow went on, "Problem is, what do I do until the law enforcement, the courts, and the prisons are back up and running? I don't have the facilities to lock up guys like the ones who assaulted you tonight, and even if I did, I don't think we can rightly afford to take care of monsters like that, when good, honest, hard-working Idaho people can barely feed their families. Most of all, I have to make sure these dangerous people don't run free to hurt others. So if the evidence is reasonably clear, as it was tonight outside that motel, I feel like it's our duty to take action to remove the threat. That's not how it's supposed to be. I know it. I just hope you can understand why it's that way for the time being. We're doing the best we can, but right now it's all we can do to keep people safe."

"Is it really that bad out here?" I asked.

"We've mostly been up against theft and robbery," Cal said. "It ain't like you can just stop at the Gas & Sip real quick for a beef-and-bean burrito and a PowerSlam. There's not a lot to go around, and plenty of greedy bastards out there who just don't give a shit and will hurt anyone to get what they want. We were checking on this farmhouse about two weeks ago. This guy answered the door when we knocked. He had a shotgun, but so what, right? Everybody got a gun. Be stupid not to. Except he didn't seem quite right. He was like too friendly."

"So we asked if we could come inside," Crow said. "I was noticing something a little fishy too."

"The guy just went cold," Cal said. "Tried to feed us some line about his house being too messy. Well, we had a dozen of our guys on the other side of the house. Nathan keyed the radio and yelled to storm the place. I dropped the guy at the door with one punch. Crow shot a man in the kitchen who was pulling a gun. The third guy we found upstairs, crying like a baby, begging us to let him go."

Crow ran his fingers over his mustache. "The three men had broken into the house, killed the father, and tied the mother and two teenage daughters up. They hadn't had the chance to do, you know, what they were going to do to them, before we got there."

Cal continued the story. "So I dragged that crying son of a bitch out of the house by his hair. I took him out into the woods so the girls wouldn't see. Then I slit that bastard's throat with my sword."

"Damn, Cal," JoBell said.

"Saved a bullet," Cal said.

"We've been helping people out a lot too," said Crow. "The occupation left us in a pretty bad fix. We were out of, or running low on, almost everything. As soon as the Brotherhood took over eastern Washington, we started redistributing supplies. Food, fuel, hardware, blankets, medical stuff. I mean, Idaho doctors were begging for antibiotics."

"We busted up this one — I guess you'd call it a gang," Cal said. "Tough fight. A couple of our guys got hurt, but we took them down. Found a whole barn packed full of basically everything those bastards had been stealing from people. Whatever you could possibly need, they'd taken it. For some of it, we could find the rightful owners. The rest we gave to people who didn't really have nothing." Cal smiled. "It gives you a good feeling, you know, to help people out. Especially after being stuck in the dungeon for so long during the occupation. Now we're out in the open fixing things."

I thought about Becca's message about how things were getting bad up here. JoBell seemed to think Becca'd been talking about the Brotherhood, but now I wondered if maybe she'd been worried about crime and bandits and stuff. Or maybe she'd just been having a bad day, and things were all right. We wouldn't know until we talked to her.

"How did everything fall apart so quickly?" JoBell asked. "I knew it was going to be rough — I mean, the best thing would have been to avoid all of this — but I can't believe so many people are so without decency that they'd abandon their humanity and steal and kill and rape. I thought we were better than that."

"We are better than that, Miss Linder," Crow said. "You saw the worst of the situation tonight, but when we get up to Freedom Lake, you'll see the best. We are standing on the threshold of a great new era. People *are* working together, and together we *are* making progress. In fact, I wanted to ask you both if you'd be willing to help with that progress."

That's exactly the kind of shit President Montaine had said. I knew where this was going. "We're sort of hoping to get out of the fighting and the promoting," I said. "You know, get on with our own lives."

"I know exactly what you mean," Crow agreed. "I can respect that. But what I have in mind would be all about the two of you getting on with your lives. I was talking to Principal Morgan about what we'd do for you once you came home, and we agreed that considering all you've done for Idaho and the credits you've already earned, you've earned your high school diplomas. We'd be honored if you would all participate in the Freedom Lake High School graduation ceremony in a couple weeks."

"You want us to graduate?" Sweeney's voice was tight. He was hurting. "The whole cap-and-gown thing, even though me, Becca, and Cal missed the whole second semester?"

"Even though I barely had a senior year?" I said.

"Life experiences are important," Crow said. "You've all learned a lot in the last several months. And like I said to Mr. Morgan, having you all at graduation would be a tremendous morale booster for everyone. Show people we're rebuilding our society."

"I don't know. It seems too late," I said.

"It wouldn't be fair to everybody who stayed in school," JoBell added.

"I'm surprised they've kept the school going. I thought it — *uunnhh*." Sweeney groaned in pain. "Was mostly a hospital now."

"Classes have been limited, especially since a few of the teachers abandoned their students to flee to the United States," Crow said. "But we've been keeping on. You remember Jake Rickingson? Well, he's been helping the school by teaching a new class on good citizenship."

I'd never been too into school, but Mr. Hornschlager did know a lot about chemistry even if he was boring as hell. Mrs. Stewart had read about every book ever written. Jake Rickingson had probably read less books than me. What made him know how to teach anything? And what exactly was anyone supposed to learn in Brotherhood class?

"If we're going to build a school system that really prepares people for a better future," Crow said, "we need people to believe in that system. That's. where you come in. And all you have to do is show up."

"Come on, guys," Cal said. "It'll be great. I had about the worst grades before I left high school and got my education in the real world. I can't wait to see the look on Morgan's face when I walk across that stage. Show him what all his books are worth."

"I've spoken to President Montaine about this," Crow said. "He agrees this graduation would be a real boost. A great way for

PFC Wright to serve the cause without getting wrapped up in combat."

JoBell and I exchanged a look. We both knew what Crow was getting at. "Sure," I said. "What the hell. I'll graduate high school."

The roads were banged up in a lot of places, and our convoy had to stop a few times while advance scouts made sure the way ahead was clear. Major Leonard checked in at the new Idaho Army outpost at the resort in Coeur d'Alene to pick up another armored Humvee escort and an old school bus filled with an entire platoon. Getting the troops and supplies took forever. The sun had long since come up by the time we reached Freedom Lake.

When we pulled into town, the mountain that had stood to the west my whole life was right where it was supposed to be. I could see the water tower and where we had patched it after it was shot up in the last fight against the occupation.

But in the morning light, most of our view of the town itself was blocked by a giant wall, twelve feet high, stretching out from the road for about a hundred yards to the east and west. Giant steel doors blocked off the road. The Brotherhood must have raided the scrap yards, because a bunch of old vehicles, from pickups to ancient 1990s station wagons, had been propped on their noses and shored up with dirt, cement, or welded scrap to form the wall. I thought I saw the old junked van that used to be parked behind my shop. Some kind of walkway had been constructed out of lumber, logs, and scrap metal so that armed men could patrol the top of the wall, with guard positions set up every hundred yards or so. An anti-vehicle ditch had been carved out of the ground about fifty yards away.

"Mr. Crow?" JoBell said.

Crow held up his hand to JoBell and then keyed a mike on his little radio. "Freedom Lake position one, this is talon actual. Open it up. This entire convoy is clear. Got some reinforcements for you. Over."

The two giant steel doors began to swing open. *"Roger that, talon actual. Welcome home."*

Crow smiled at JoBell. "You wanted to see the best of humanity? You were hoping that people could still work together?"

"What is all this?" JoBell asked.

"Well, you've seen the criminal elements out there," said Crow. "We didn't have enough men to patrol the whole town, especially at night. Now we just close the gates on the roads, and our town is a lot safer. Soon the wall will be complete, so there will be no way anyone can sneak in and hurt our people. We'll always know who is coming and going."

"Is that even legal?" JoBell asked.

Crow nodded. "I know. It's terrible, right? We just couldn't think of a better way to guard against the danger out there, at least for the time being. The gates are unlocked during the day, and we open them for anyone who wants to peacefully pass through. If the US military ever tries to invade again, we should be able to hold them off for quite a while with this wall up."

"What about the lake approach?" I asked.

"We've temporarily put up a barrier between town and the lake, but the goal is to build a massive wall all the way around both of them."

"That would go for miles," JoBell said.

"Fortress Freedom Lake," I added.

"That's the idea," said Crow. "We're setting up defenses like this around a bunch of different towns."

Nathan Crow had Cal drop him off on Main Street at the cop shop they were rebuilding. He told Cal to take us home.

"Nice of Crow to lend you his truck," I said.

Cal smiled and rubbed the steering wheel. "This baby's all mine."

"What?" Sweeney leaned forward and groaned. "Dude, this is like a forty-thousand-dollar vehicle."

"Yeah, well, I've earned some rewards helping the Brotherhood keep people safe from criminals and Fed synth . . . sympathize . . . from Fed traitors. And that's not all. With the danger out there, Becca moved out of your house, Sweeney."

"Did she go back to her parents?" JoBell asked.

"Not exactly. They were starting to smooth things over, but then her old man said they couldn't afford to keep feeding Lightning anymore and sold the horse to some farmer who could take care of her. I don't . . . It's complicated. I'll let her explain that if she wants to. Y'all coming home ought to cheer her up." Cal pulled into the driveway of a nice brick ranch-style house. "Let's hope there's power." He hit a button and sighed in relief when the double-car garage door opened. I could see Pale Horse inside, my badass armored Humvee ambulance with the turret and gun ports I'd installed myself.

Becca Wells stood next to the vehicle, but she didn't look like I'd ever seen her before. She wore black combat boots and dark green cargo pants, with a serious knife sheathed on her lower leg. Her big silver "Cowgirl Up" buckle and western belt was replaced by some kind of tactical belt that held a sidearm in a holster. One hand was on her hip, and the other held an M4 pointed at the ground. She stepped out of the garage and looked up and down the street as Cal pulled the truck in. The only thing still Becca about her was the purple butterfly clip shining in her hair.

"You guys okay? How's Eric?" she asked as soon as Cal shut the engine off and stepped out. Sweeney grunted, opened his door, and started slowly climbing down from the truck. Becca reached out to him. "Let me help you."

Sweeney waved her away. "I got it. Think I can get out of a truck by myself."

"You saw us pull in?" Cal asked Becca.

"Of course. I've been up since one a.m. keeping watch," she said. "Even if I wasn't on duty, with so few people driving anymore, your big, loud truck is easy to notice."

"I told you, the Brotherhood is on guard duty for us," Cal said. "We don't have to worry about stuff like that anymore. And I doubt anyone would be dumb enough to try anything at my house if they know I'm in the Brotherhood."

"Your house?" Sweeney asked.

Cal closed the door to his truck and stood up tall. "Yep. I ain't trailer trash no more. Me and Dad are both moving up in the world. He moved into the house across town that the Huffs' grandma left behind when she went to the nursing home." Cal looked down. "You know, after Randy and his family all . . . Anyway, nobody is coming to claim that house. Be a shame to let it fall apart." He smiled. "Come on inside. I'll show you around." He led us in and gave us a tour of the house, but I'd been up for well over twenty-four hours by that point and was so fried that I couldn't think straight. Finally, Cal led JoBell and me to a cool, dark basement bedroom. We crashed hard.

⌁—• in immediate proximity to the war or devastation should, when possible, avoid handling human remains. US FEMA and military teams are working hard, continuing necessary mass cremations. The risk of disease from contamination of available drinking water due to radiation or inadequate disposal of human remains is still very high, and everyone should boil water even when it comes from a certified water source.

Citizens are reminded that prolonged viewing of disaster or war footage, particularly by children, can potentially lead to serious negative mental health effects. Some studies suggest that even people not directly affected by combat or by the aftermath of the nuclear explosions can suffer acute stress symptoms. •—⌁

⌁—• Welcome back to normal broadcasting on ESPN. I'm John Soto."

"And I'm Lindsay Nang. This is MegaSports. On behalf of myself, John, and everyone here at ESPN, we want to express our sadness after the loss of so many and offer our sympathy to all who grieve."

"Major League Baseball commissioner Joseph Jackson announced today that for the first time in over one hundred years, the American baseball season has been canceled. The commissioner held a press conference from MLB's temporary headquarters in San Francisco, saying that while sports have long been one of the best ways to bring people together in friendly competition and a celebration of the human spirit, now seems like a time more appropriate to grieving. He also cited safety concerns, pointing out that large gatherings like Major League Baseball games may present tempting targets in these tragically unstable times. NFL commissioner Ronald Goodman is expected to make a similar announcement next week regarding the football season."

"The players' reaction to this? First, we'll talk to Kansas City Royals pitcher •⎯⋏

⋏⎯• *US Navy official speaking on the condition of anonymity admitted that yesterday, Chinese carriers and warships took a very aggressive posture in the East China Sea over islands also claimed by Japan. The official said that with the US Navy's increased focus on domestic waters, there is little it can do in response to an increasingly militarized China. Under modern Navy doctrine, US naval forces in the area lack sufficient resources to defend our Japanese allies if the need arose.* •⎯⋏

⋏⎯• *It is our custom here on CNN's* Talk Fire *to debate both sides of the issues with commentary from the right and the left. Tonight, with Stacey Covey on the left and Nestor Grimm on the right, as CNN switches from wall-to-wall emergency news coverage to the programming you are familiar with, I, Al Hudson, wanted to take a moment for us all to join together to express our condolences to those who have lost loved ones. Stacey?"*

"That's right, Al. Whether we're conservative or liberal, Republican or Democrat, we are all devastated by the nuclear attacks and the civil war. I think we can also agree that our country is teetering on the edge of total collapse. Now, Mr. Grimm and I have very different ways of looking at the world, so we're going to have to try to come to some kind of common ground to find real solutions for saving this country and saving lives. We need to find some unity. To that end, we all watched President Griffith's speech in Colorado last week, and I was glad to see her taking the necessary steps to restore our democracy. I was particularly impressed by her effort to preserve the party balance in place before the attack."

"Stacey, you're only impressed by that because you want the new Senate to still be controlled by Democrats. There are more Republican governors, and if governors appointed replacement senators of their own party, which is their right, then the Senate would shift to Republican control."

"Nestor, that couldn't be further from the truth. It's just President Griffith trying to preserve the will of the voters."

"The will of the voters? You can't just make that up as it suits you. You have to follow procedures. Democrats like Griffith are always bending the rules through executive orders or other means whenever it fits their —"

"She said she realized her request to the governors had no legal bearing. It's an impossible situation. But can we talk about a bigger problem? For the first time in United States history, we have a serving member of the military, an Army general, in the executive office. Doesn't this bring us closer to being a military dictatorship?"

"Stacey, this is the first good move Griffith has made in a long time. She needs to show the rebels that there is strong military leadership in the capital. Maybe now rebels will take notice of the real threat posed by serious, competent leadership in the federal government."

"So President Griffith wasn't taken seriously before?"

"I don't think she —"

"Because she's a woman or because —"

"I'm sorry. I'm going to have to stop you both there. Ladies and gentlemen, I don't know what's happened to our security here at CNN world headquarters in Atlanta, but a number of soldiers have —"

"I am General Jonathan Vogel. For the past two and a half years, I have been the commander of United States Special Operations

Command. Do not lie to yourselves about who is really in charge at NORAD. General Charles Jacobsen is the acting leader of the United States, and President Laura Griffith has become a puppet. A mouthpiece. I am the commander of SOCOM. I do not waste time or words. Believe me when I say the United States of America no longer exists.

"An order has been issued to redeploy nearly all military assets in the United States to Colorado to support the regime there. In defiance of this order, my allies, operatives, and subordinates have seized control of SOCOM headquarters at MacDill Air Force Base in Florida, Fort Jackson in South Carolina, Fort Benning and Fort Stewart in Georgia, and other smaller military installations. We have command of all military and law enforcement assets in all three of these states. We have secured the allegiance of all ships in Carrier Strike Group Two. All resistance has been neutralized.

"The former states of South Carolina, Georgia, and Florida now comprise the new nation of Atlantica. I am that nation's leader. I do not suffer any delusions of peaceful relations with the so-called United States of America. The criminal regime in their capital in Colorado will attack us, and we will destroy them. We have the best-trained soldiers in the world. We have dozens of Air Force facilities. Our Navy is powerful. Our doctrine is simple: All who oppose Atlantica will die. •⌁

United States of America
Republic of Idaho
Nation of Wyoming
Nation of Montana
Republic of Texas
Dead Zone
Atlantica
New England
Nation of Oklahoma

Atlantica? What the hell is that? This General Vogel guy looks like bad news. Go get him Griffith. I just hope its not too late.

★ ★ ★ ★ ★ This Post's Star Average 4.95   [Star Rate] [Comment]   12 minutes ago

STEVE BRAKER ★★★★★
8 countries where we used to have teh USA. It's over. This is gonna be bad.

★ ★ ★ ☆ ☆ This Comment's Star Average 3.15   [Star Rate]   3 minutes ago

⌁—• *The voice of truth, calling out in the night, to all of you afraid, with no home, clinging with all your might to what was, frightened of what will be. I am the Cliffhanger. Everywhere I go, I see the dispossessed and the forgotten, struggling against the rising tide of war and destruction.*

And in these times of uncertainty, when the Cliffhanger dares to tell the truth, who tries to silence him? The same men, the new warlords, who come to all of you saying, "Put your trust in me, and I will keep you safe." They spread the news of failure and danger and

sow distrust among you and your neighbors until you're so desperate, holding on to what little you have today, that you lose any hope you had for tomorrow.

The Cliffhanger has been on the airwaves in this place, this fortress called Atlantica. The Cliffhanger dared to speak up in New England, in Idaho, in Texas, and all over what is left of the United States. Everywhere, the Cliffhanger is hunted. Everywhere, the new leaders try to shut the Cliffhanger down.

They talk about freedom and they promise security, and they ask you to die for their flag. But here's the truth that all the people must know. This war is the same as the last war and the same as the war before that. It's another way for the few men who have much, to keep control over the many who have so little.

Don't trade your future for their empty promises! Don't sell your children for the scraps from the table of these new warlords who would be our masters. Look for hope from your neighbors. I'm not calling for a fight or advocating revolution. The Cliffhanger asks you to help one another, lower your weapons, and feed not only your own family, but the family of all mankind. •⎯⋏⎯

CHAPTER
SIX

As tired as I was, I actually managed to get some sleep for once. Nightmares only woke me up a couple times. Finally, half-dazed, I reached over and felt an empty space where my fiancée had been.

I was fully awake and rolling out of bed in seconds. "JoBell?" I grabbed my nine mil from the nightstand and hurried out into some kind of rec room. Light spilling in from the high basement windows showed a couch, screen, and video game controllers. In the corner, up against the wall, was an impressive-looking bar with three stools. There was even an old pinball machine. I held my gun at the ready. Didn't we make it to Cal's last night? Or yesterday? I checked the windows again. Or today? The thing about traveling so much and barely sleeping is that sometimes, after I crashed, I hardly knew where or when I was.

The sound of footsteps and muffled voices drifted down from upstairs, along with the most amazing, powerful aroma. I relaxed.

"Bacon?" I said. Life was always good with bacon.

I got dressed and headed up the stairs. All my friends except Sweeney were gathered in the kitchen. At the stove, Cal reached around Becca for the spatula in the skillet, but she slapped his hand away. "You don't have to cook all the time," Cal said. "You're guests in my house. I can take care of this."

"Cal, no," said Becca. "The last time you tried to make breakfast was a disaster." She smiled at him. "Seriously, go sit down."

Cal saw me. "Hey, buddy. Wow, you must have been tired. Got

you here yesterday morning. We tried to get you up for supper last night, but you were out."

I nodded and slipped my gun into the waist of my jeans, looking around the kitchen. It was a nice place. The appliances were all the older stainless steel kind, but in decent shape. JoBell and TJ sat around the table. "Have a seat," Cal said. "Hungry?"

"Where the hell did you get bacon?" I asked. This was the best food I'd seen in Freedom Lake in a very long time.

Cal leaned back against the kitchen countertop. "Like we said on the drive up here: We starved during the occupation, while people in the US had it easy. Now that the Brotherhood has taken most of Washington, well, let's just say we've evened things out a little."

"You've been staying here too?" I asked TJ.

He sat back in his chair and nodded. "Said goodbye to my folks. We got in a big fight when I wouldn't go with them, but they finally left a couple weeks ago for my cousin's farm in upstate New York. They called to say they made it safely, and I even managed to get a message from them after the nukes. They're okay. The farm isn't in the radiation zone. I could stay at home, I guess, but it's crazy lonely, and I thought I could help out here."

"But what about this house?" Sweeney limped into the kitchen.

"Hey! There he is!" Cal shouted. "The other zombie. At least you had an excuse crashing so long with the painkillers and all." He punched my shoulder. "Not like this lazy ass."

Sweeney offered a half smile that didn't force him to move much of the burned side of his face. "Cal, this place is great. How did you afford it? Even if there were a banking system —" He took a breath and leaned on the table. "Nobody would lend you money."

Becca pulled out a chair and helped Sweeney sit down. "This house belonged to Sally Hines," she said. "You know, the former owner of the Bucking Bronc Bar and Grill."

Sweeney, JoBell, and me exchanged a look. What the hell was going on here? "So you just took the house? Moved in?" I asked.

"This is a war," Cal said. "Fed traitors forfeit their property. That woman sold you out to the United States. You were tortured because of her. Now she's died for her crimes. Someone should get her house." He shrugged. "I moved all her personal stuff, clothes or whatever, out before I moved in. Donated it all to people who might need it." He held up a finger. "Kept her booze, though. You been downstairs. Seen it? That woman had a hell of a home bar."

I met JoBell's eyes and could tell she was uncomfortable too. Of the three people the Brotherhood had hung on Victory Day, Sally was the most guilty. What she'd done had almost gotten me killed, and if she was alive, I guess I'd be pissed at her for the torture she put me through. But I understood why she did what she did. She didn't deserve to die, and it felt weird being in her house.

When the food was ready, I helped Becca put it on the table for everyone. We prayed and then started eating, but everybody was quiet. JoBell poked around on her comm, its sound shut off. After a while, she held it to her chest and smiled as she let out a long breath. "He's okay." She looked at her comm again, as if checking to make sure what she'd read was real. "Dad finally got through. 'I received your message, and I'm glad you're all okay. CentCom's holding up. I'm fine. I miss you. I love you. Stay safe.'"

"That's great." Becca smiled.

"Huge relief," said TJ.

We all agreed and congratulated JoBell. She laughed a little and nearly cried. As I looked around the table, some of my war weariness melted away from the warmth of being back with all my friends. We'd been through hell, but had come out the other side together. It almost felt like old times, like a big Saturday breakfast the morning after a hard-fought football victory.

But Sweeney was in a lot of pain. I could tell by the way he grimaced occasionally as he ate. Becca had gone all commando and looked exhausted — exhausted or pissed. And we were having this meal at this table where Sally Hines might have sat, thinking about turning me and Sparrow in to the Fed so that she could collect some reward money. Even the best times still had a sharp sliver of pain these days.

"Don't you like it?" Becca pointed at my plate with her fork.

"What? No, I . . . I mean, yes. It's great." I dug into the scrambled eggs. "Just distracted, I guess. We had a rough trip up here."

JoBell finally put her comm down and pushed it away. "The network is too spotty to get much of anything, but I did finally get some articles. Boise pushed the US back, but they lost a lot of people. I'm so glad my dad was down in the bunker."

"I'm glad we got out of town," said Sweeney.

"JoBell told us about what you two have been up to over the last month, but I wasn't around to hear about your trip home. Sounds like some rough shit went down," TJ said to me. "What happened?"

I explained about the US attack on Boise, the fight with the Apache gunship, and the sickos at the motel on the edge of Lewiston. A look from JoBell told me she didn't want me talking about what those freaks had almost done to us, so I kept quiet about that.

Becca reached over and squeezed JoBell's hand. "I'm glad you're okay."

"Any other news?" TJ asked JoBell.

"Updated casualty estimates." JoBell shook her head. "We'll probably never know for sure how many died in New York and DC. It's all such a mess. The whole world is falling apart."

Cal slapped his black armband. Did he sleep in that thing? "Yeah, well, the Brotherhood is getting things back together around here. Cleaning house."

"Maybe," JoBell said. "But it's not a permanent solution."

Becca sat up straight and fixed her gaze on JoBell. I thought I saw her just barely shake her head.

Cal frowned. "What do you mean?" he said to JoBell.

"Well, obviously we need to get back to a regular military and police force." JoBell motioned at the food on the table and then at the whole room. "And we'll need to start keeping better track of resources. We can't continue with a winner-takes-all system."

Becca's chair scraped the floor as she stood up. "Jo, you still hungry? There's a little more bacon, and I could get you some toast."

"I'm good. Thanks."

"You sure?" Becca asked.

"Really, Jo? I didn't see you bitching about the Brotherhood when they got Danny out of that Fed prison cell." Cal's voice was icy. "You'd probably be dead right now if we hadn't saved your asses in Lewiston."

I was glad that JoBell didn't say anything back. She looked too shocked.

"Cal, you don't have to get mad," TJ said.

"I'm sorry." Cal took a deep breath. "It's just there ain't no state troopers no more. No courts or jails yet. We're keeping this town safe and running patrols all over Idaho and Washington, and we ain't getting paid 'cept with shit like this that, like I said, used to belong to Fed traitors."

Becca put her arms around the big guy. "Hey, it's okay. We're your friends, and we're grateful for your help."

Cal patted Becca's hand. "You all don't have to thank me for nothing. You guys and my old man are all I got. All I care about. I'm sorry for getting mad. It's just, all my life, you know, teachers would kind of half-ass try to encourage me, but I could always tell none of them thought I'd amount to shit. I used to dream 'bout getting me a newer *double-wide* trailer. One that didn't leak when it rained." He rubbed his armband, and I got the feeling that he really did wear it to bed. "Now . . . You know, Mrs. Stewart's minivan was stolen a few weeks ago. While the Brotherhood looked around town, I hopped in the truck and hauled ass up Highway 41. Found the thieves out of gas about five miles out of town."

"What did you do to them?" JoBell asked.

Cal twisted up his face. "Do to them? It was a single mom, her two kids, and her grandmother, trying to get to Canada. Everything they owned had been blasted by a US drone. I locked up Mrs. Stewart's van and drove them off-road into Canada. Then I had the Brotherhood send up a tow truck so we could get the van." He took a bite of eggs and then drank some water. "My point is, for the first time ever, Mrs. Stewart said she was proud of me, and she really meant it." He checked JoBell's comm. "Shit. I gotta get on the wall. I'm gonna be late for guard duty. You guys make yourselves at home." He looked at us carefully. "I mean that. You're all moving in with me. I have plenty of room and it's safer here. Becca and TJ can show you where everything's at."

Cal slung Schmidty's AR15 over his shoulder as casually as a businessman might grab his briefcase, and he ran out the door, heading toward his post on foot.

Becca sighed and slumped back in her chair. "Jo, you can't say that kind of stuff, at least not around him."

"Or any other member of the Brotherhood," TJ said.

"What did I say?"

"Something bad about the Brotherhood," Becca said. "Listen. This is serious. You remember Kenny Palmer, used to work for the city?"

"Black guy with the big hair?" I said. "He used to come to some of our football games. Man, that guy could yell."

"That's him," Becca said. "Well, he was mad about a lot of the things the Brotherhood has been doing. He was down on Main Street with a sign protesting about it."

"That's his right," JoBell said.

TJ leaned forward, elbows on the table. "Which is what Nathan Crow said to everybody. Very loudly."

Becca sat up straight. "But a few days later, Kenny was arrested as a United States collaborator. The Brotherhood guys searched his house and said they found all this evidence. They said he'd been giving away resistance positions to the US Army during the occupation. He was taken to a" — she made air quotes with her fingers — "'secure facility,' but nobody knows where that is or has talked about it since. Nobody's seen the guy either."

I wasn't sure I totally trusted the Brotherhood, but a lot of what Cal had said earlier made sense, and they had saved me and JoBell. "Well, it's like Cal said. There are no courts yet. No jails. And they probably wanted to prevent like a mob or something from coming to get that guy. They're probably keeping him safe."

"Like they kept those Fed POWs safe on Victory Day?" Becca asked. She met my eyes and then JoBell's. "Just — for me, okay? Do me a favor and don't say anything bad about the Brotherhood."

"Even if what you're saying about the Brotherhood is true," I said, "it's not like Cal would rat us out to them."

TJ stood up from the table, finished with his breakfast. "No, but you saw how pissed he gets. He might not go tell on us, but if he's on guard duty all upset, and those guys ask him what's wrong, he could talk to the wrong person about it, thinking he's just blowing off steam to a friend. If we piss off the wrong people, we could be in trouble."

"You really think they'd come after us?" I asked. I'd always hated my status as a living symbol for the resistance and the rebellion, but what the hell. Why not be honest? "I'm Danny Wright. I'm supposed to be the hero of Idaho. You think they'd mess with me or my friends?"

"Just because we criticized the Brotherhood a little?" JoBell added.

TJ and Becca exchanged a look. Becca shook her head. TJ held up his hands a little like he was pleading with her. "Come on, Becca. We have to."

"Have to what?" JoBell asked.

"It's better if we don't," Becca said to TJ.

"What?" I asked.

"We can't keep them in the dark. They deserve to know," TJ said.

Sweeney kept his hand pressed over his eyes, as though he had a headache. "Would one of you please tell us what the hell you're talking about?"

Becca sighed. "It's important that you don't draw suspicion from the Brotherhood because TJ and I have been doing more than criticizing them."

A cold shadow sunk inside me. What had they done? Had they hit the Brotherhood?

"Cal talked about evening out the supply distribution," TJ said. "But the Brotherhood's methods aren't exactly even."

"Or equal," said Becca.

TJ nodded. "Some people — a lot of people, actually — are getting food and other stuff just like Cal said."

"And every member of the Brotherhood gets more than enough." Becca motioned to our plates and then around the house. "But others are getting much less, or nothing at all."

"So we've been taking some of the food and extra blankets and stuff that Cal gets and sneaking it to people around town who don't have enough," said TJ.

"Some people got it bad, you guys," said Becca. "Like when we took some canned soup and vegetables to Jaclyn Martinez's house last week, they were down to two packs of ramen noodles and three cans of beans. Mrs. Martinez cried when she saw what we'd brought."

"Jackie's dad, though . . . You know the guy wasn't fat, but he always had a bit of a belly, right?" TJ shook his head. "Not anymore. That guy's a skeleton. I think he's been saving what little food they have for his family."

Becca rubbed her butterfly hair clip. "He needs to shut up. He's been complaining too much. Too publicly. If he pisses the Brotherhood off enough . . ."

"So." TJ finally broke the spooked silence. "That's why we gotta be cool. The smuggling we're doing is important."

"Cal hasn't figured it out?" JoBell asked.

"That's one of the reasons I do all the cooking," said Becca. She almost smiled. "And, yeah, except for meat on the grill, he sort of destroys any meal he tries to make."

"Maybe it's a simple accounting error," JoBell offered. "You know, with the war, it could be hard to keep track of who's getting what."

"Again, that's the line Crow uses," TJ said. "When people complain about not getting their ration cards, he says there was some mistake, but the mistakes keep happening to the same families. The same ones who have questioned the Brotherhood."

"Or who aren't white," Becca said.

Sweeney looked up at us. "Shit. I knew it."

"What do you mean?" I asked.

"Crow has always been super nice to all of you, but he's usually a dick to me," Sweeney said. "You probably don't remember this, but after we got Danny out of that Fed prison cell, I was in the radio room charging my comm, the same as a lot of people. He yelled at me and kicked me out. And he's always way less patient with me than with any of you. We've backed a bunch of racist assholes."

"We don't know that," JoBell said, but doubt and fear shadowed her voice.

Becca stood up with her empty plate. "We don't know for sure. Crow and the Brotherhood are smart, sneaky like that. But for now, we have to be very careful."

Later that day, Becca announced she was borrowing Cal's truck to drive Sweeney to High School Hospital. She wanted someone else to go along to provide cover while she drove.

"Rule number three," she said. "Always post a guard."

"In town?" I asked. "Even now?"

"Especially now."

"I'll go," I said.

I rode in the backseat with Becca driving and Sweeney riding shotgun. He stared down at the black cane leaning against one leg. "I'm like an old man. Probably be stuck with this for the rest of my life."

"Maybe not." Becca reached over and squeezed his good shoulder. "Doc Strauss says the pain will back off in time, and you might not need the cane after a while."

Sweeney smiled at her. "I'm feeling better all the time." He reached over to give Becca a little punch. "Thanks to you."

Good. Some of that old Sweeney flirty charm was coming back. Maybe he really was getting better.

I followed the two of them into High School Hospital, the place we used to call the Freedom Lake High School gym. Back on Victory Day, the entire floor had been covered with the wounded, dead, and dying. Now the place was cleaned up and a lot more under control. The regular graduation stage was set up in front of the basketball hoop at one end of the gym, but instead of the normal Freedom Lake High School cloth backdrop, two giant Brotherhood banners displayed their white eagle emblem. Between the banners was a flag with that damned bleeding fist symbol and the words WE WILL GIVE THEM A WAR.

"What happened to all the state championship pennants?" Sweeney asked.

The little flags dedicated to past sports glory had been removed from high up on the side walls. They'd been replaced by smaller Brotherhood flags.

"This is why Crow was so excited about getting us to go to graduation?" I said.

"I doubt he was excited about me going," Sweeney said.

"He must be planning to turn it all into some kind of rally," said Becca.

At a table on the half-court line, Freedom Lake's veterinarian turned emergency surgeon, Dr. Nicole, was sewing up a heavily tattooed Brotherhood man with a nasty cut on his forearm. A guy with a shaved scalp and a tattoo of an eyeball on the back of his head stepped up and handed his hurt friend a couple pills. "Here you go. For the pain."

"No," said Dr. Nicole. "We have to save the pain meds for operations and really serious injuries. Where did you even get that?"

"It's okay, ma'am," said Eyeball. "Nathan Crow says it's okay."

She folded her arms. "But we won't have enough to go around if you keep wasting medication."

Tattoos and Eyeball looked at each other and laughed a little. "Ma'am? We're Brotherhood," Tattoos said, like that explained everything and she should have already known that they were entitled to the pills.

Dr. Nicole turned her back on them, spotted us, and led us toward the doors at the far end of the gym. "Eric." She smiled. "How are you doing?"

"A little better," he said.

She gave a worried nod. "The gym is just for emergency triage now, at least until graduation, when all these patients will be crammed into classrooms. Dr. Strauss is in the old nurse's office. I'm glad you're feeling better."

We thanked her and went on our way. About twenty minutes later, Sweeney came out of the nurse's office looking both in pain and a little pissed.

"What is it?" Becca asked.

Sweeney tapped his cane on the floor. "Let's just go."

"Talk to me," Becca said.

"Doc wanted to cut my painkiller dose way down," Sweeney said. "Less than half of what I got before."

"What?" Becca said. "That's crazy."

"He says they have to save it for emergency patients that aren't stabilized yet." He met our eyes, and none of us had to say anything to see the bullshit in that. "So I told him to shove his medicine up his ass." Sweeney's knuckles were white as he gripped the top of his cane. "I'll just do without."

"Eric, are you sure?"

Sweeney started down the hall. "They're the Brotherhood," he said in the same tone Tattoos had just used in the gym.

A ton of terrible, impossible, or just plain weird stuff had gone down in the last year, but walking down the hallway of my high school with Sweeney and Becca was one of the most jacked-up experiences I'd had. For a moment I could almost believe that I was a senior in high school like I was supposed to be, that all the bad stuff had never happened.

"This seems like such an out-of-place bit of normal," I whispered. Sweeney grunted as he hobbled down the hall with his cane. Becca put her hand on his back. "Well, okay, maybe not so normal."

The door to the main office flew open, and I instinctively reached for my gun in the holster on my belt. Mr. Shiratori burst out into the hallway. Mr. Morgan was right behind him. "Michio, listen."

Mr. Shiratori didn't even look back. "Go to hell, Garrett."

"Please, not in front of the students."

Shiratori spun to face Morgan. "Fifteen *years*! Fifteen damn years I've been teaching and coaching in this school, and now I'm being shut out?"

"I'm sure the investigation will clear all —"

"Investigation!" Shiratori threw his hands up. "Tell me you're not that damned stupid. Think of the kind of ignorant jackasses who brought these so-called charges. In what kangaroo court do you think I'll possibly get a fair hearing!?"

I ran up to our old coach. "What's going on?"

Mr. Morgan held the main office door open. "Daniel, this is a discussion that would be better served in private. Why don't we go back to my office, where —"

"I'm being placed on administrative leave," Shiratori said.

Mr. Morgan wiped his brow. "Pending an investigation into allegations of cooperation with the US military during the occupation."

"That's total bullshit!" Sweeney said.

"Eric, watch your language!" Morgan looked up and down the hall.

"No, he's right. That's total bull*shit*!" I yelled as loud as I could, just to piss him off, and because it was true.

"I —" Mr. Morgan started. "There's nothing I can do. But the important thing is —"

"Who is accusing him of this?" Becca asked.

"Nathan Crow says he's not allowed to tell us that." Shiratori slid his hands down his face. "Listen, kids. I appreciate your concern, but I think it would be better for you to just stay out of this one. Something's really not right here. You need to steer clear of this. Don't try to stick up for me."

"Absolutely." Mr. Morgan twisted the end of his tie. "I think Mr. Shiratori is absolutely correct in thinking of our students first. So I hope you kids will —"

"*You* should be sticking up for me, Garrett." Shiratori turned away and headed out the front doors. "Fifteen years!"

Morgan went back to his office, and we went back to Cal's to tell JoBell and TJ what had happened.

"This is stupid. This is wrong. Criminal." JoBell grabbed my shoulders. "You have to do something to fix this."

"Me? What can I do?"

"Use your influence," JoBell said. "Nathan Crow. President Montaine. They listen to you. Call them."

"Crow's not going to do anything," Sweeney said. "Except favors for his Brotherhood guys."

"Crow's the one behind all this." Becca stood off to the side of the front picture window, holding her M4 and keeping watch on the street outside. "Shiratori's not white, so now he's accused of being a traitor."

"We don't know that for sure," I said. But my words felt hollow.

JoBell met my eyes, and I knew she felt the same way. She shrugged. "You have to try."

"Don't try to get meds for me," Sweeney said. "I don't want that asshole's help."

I took my comm out of my pocket. Funny, I used to be on it all the time, texting, checking FriendStar updates, listening to music. Everything. When we'd first lost Internet back when the occupation started, we'd all kind of gone out of our minds for a while. Now, having been off-line for so long and with such an unreliable Internet connection, I didn't miss it as much. "Hank," I said, hoping my stupid digi-assistant would actually work. "Are you there for once?"

My comm did nothing for a long time. *"I'm . . . an AmeriCAN,"* Digi-Hank finally said. *"I'm ready . . . to help."*

"Give me a voice call on speaker with Nathan Crow."

Digi-Hank skipped his usual country music ad, and after a short wait, Crow was on the line. *"What can I do for you, Danny?"*

"There was a problem at the school today," I said.

"What happened?" Crow sounded worried. *"Is everybody okay?"*

"It's Mr. Shiratori," I said. "Someone has accused him of basically being a traitor."

"Oh." He sighed. *"That. I was worried something else had happened."*

Becca circled her hand around in a hurry-up-and-get-to-the-point-type gesture.

"But he's not a traitor," I said. "So I was wondering if you could help him out. I mean, I'll vouch for him or whatever. I know for a fact that he didn't sell us out to the United States."

"I hear you, Danny," Crow said. *"Here's the thing. This is a tough time, and these situations have to be handled very delicately. I didn't believe the allegation when it came across my desk, but someone in town does, and that someone probably has friends. If nothing is done, then people get upset, thinking a dangerous traitor*

is still working against us and convinced that the law isn't going to do anything about it. Then these people try to take matters into their own hands. So he's been placed on leave, pending an investigation."

"So this is all just for show?" I said. "Coach isn't going to lose his job or go to jail or something?"

"Well, I'm going to do my duty and fully look into the matter. There have been some bad things happening around here, things I can't tell you about, that make it pretty clear a person or persons are working with the United States. So I'm going to find out the truth about Mr. Shiratori. And you have to admit, the guy didn't help himself when he was out there with a bullhorn next to Major Alsovar this last winter."

I couldn't believe I was hearing this. "For like the whole week before he did that bullhorn speech, he was hiding me, Sweeney, Cal, Becca, and Luchen from the Fed. We stayed in his basement after we launched a big attack. He fed us. Protected us. Without his help, we'd be dead!"

"Well, that's good to know," said Crow. "I'll certainly take that into account in my investigation, but we have to make sure his loyalties have been in the right place since then."

"He hasn't done anything wrong!"

"This conversation is over. Call me when you're ready to be reasonable."

I wanted to smash my comm into the floor. "He tapped out."

"I don't believe him," Becca said.

"Me neither," said Sweeney.

"I don't know, guys," said JoBell. "He said he didn't believe the accusations either. And could you imagine if there were no one here to keep some kind of order? What would happen then if people were accused of working with the US? They'd be shot right away."

"But what does it mean? 'Conduct an investigation'?" TJ paced the living room. "People in this country — I mean in the United States or North America or whatever — are always conducting investigations. What does Crow think he's going to find? What evidence?"

"Screw Nathan Crow," I said. "I'll go right over his head to President Montaine." Sure, the man had said he didn't have time to take my calls anymore, but that had been pretty much right before the US brought down a major attack on Boise. Anyway, I didn't care. I'd go through every officer in the Idaho Army if it meant I could help Coach.

I told Digi-Hank to get me a voice call with the president. The system locked up for the longest time. Finally, after a couple minutes, Digi-Hank spoke up. Kind of. "Hey . . . part-ner." Then he was silent.

"Is that it?" Sweeney said.

I shook my comm. "Hank? Can you connect that call? It's important."

Nothing.

We waited another three or four minutes.

"I don't think it's going to work," JoBell finally said.

"This is so messed up," said Becca. "Things around here are getting worse and worse."

I wanted to argue with her. We weren't hiding for our lives in the dungeon under the shop, and there was no open warfare on the streets of Freedom Lake. But I knew what she meant. Something was really wrong.

⌁• I am Captain Clarence Benedict, commander of the aircraft carrier Ronald Reagan. With the help of Captain Fletcher Star, commander of the carrier John F. Kennedy and with the help of countless other officers and enlisted personnel, I have taken command of Carrier Strike Groups Nine and Eleven, hereafter designated as Rogue Fleet. I am making this address on behalf of the sailors and Marines of Rogue Fleet, and on behalf of their families.

Three days ago, when the states of Georgia, Florida, and South Carolina declared themselves the independent nation of Atlantica, Carrier Strike Groups Nine and Eleven were given orders by the United States Navy to move to Tampa Bay, Florida, to engage Carrier Strike Group Two, and to assault hostile military and industrial targets in the area. My fellow members of Rogue Fleet and I have decided that we cannot, in good conscience, obey those orders. We will not willfully attack fellow sailors and Marines. We will not take actions to worsen the civil war or to harm our fellow Americans, no matter their political or national allegiance.

Therefore, the sailors and Marines of Rogue Fleet, allowing those so desiring to peacefully disembark, are taking our twenty-two warships and leaving the United States, bearing no ill will toward anyone, but very capable of defending ourselves from attack. Any ships entering our waters or aircraft entering our airspace without permission will be deemed hostile and may be seized or destroyed. We hope that someday the wounds caused by this terrible war will begin to heal, and that our fleet can return to the country we loved. Until then, we will take care of our own, and we will pray for peace in what was once the United States of America. •⌁

⌁• Welcome to Adam Coleman Twenty-four Seven, now on NBC. I'm standing about an hour and forty minutes north of Las Vegas,

Nevada. What you see behind me is a giant caravan of over one hundred recreational vehicles and about that many cars, trucks, and vans. It's like a city on wheels, and here with me is the leader of this group, Larry Boyd. Larry, how many people are part of this caravan and what is its purpose?"

"I'm not the leader."

"Oh, I'm sorry. Is your leader available to —"

"Ain't got no leader. This convoy is just made up of people who don't want to be in the cities when the bombs start dropping or when another nuke goes off."

"How do you decide where the convoy goes?"

"We vote. Majority wins. Folks disagree, they're free to go off on their own. Only rules we got is everybody helps out with cooking, vehicle repairs, and defending our camp. Oh, and we share fuel so everybody who wants to can stay with us."

"This convoy is armed?"

"You bet your ass we're armed. America has failed. Can't you see that? All we got's each other. So we look out for our own, the way this country should have done before the fall. •⌄⌃

⌄⌃• At zero five hundred hours Korean time, North Korean military forces entered the demilitarized zone and were immediately engaged by the South Korean Army. The armistice that has been in effect for well over half a century is no more, and casualties are mounting as intense fighting has broken out on the Korean Peninsula. The United Nations Security Council has met in emergency session, where delegates from the People's Republic of China pledged Chinese neutrality in the Korean conflict, provided all other nations adopt the same posture. The Chinese delegation warned of swift and decisive military action against any nations that might intervene. •⌄⌃

~~• *Please stand by for an important announcement here on United States Television, and the Unity Radio Network. Hope for a united America."*

"I am Vice President General Chuck Jacobsen, speaking to you tonight with President Griffith by my side. When I served as commander of NORAD, part of my responsibilities was to ensure continuity of the United States government even in the face of the most dire and unprecedented circumstances. In the wake of the terrible nuclear attacks on Washington, DC, and New York City, our nation's military and civilian governments should have been coming together to facilitate our recovery. Instead, greedy criminal opportunists have used our recent tragedy to seize power and sow division and destruction.

"President Griffith and I are here today to remind the rebel governments of Idaho, Wyoming, Montana, Texas, Oklahoma, New England, and Atlantica that of all the so-called nations in North America, the United States is by far the most well armed. We're now in complete control of over eighty Air Force wings comprised of hundreds of aircraft. We have assembled armor and multiple infantry divisions from both the Army and Marines. Our massive Navy, based in the states of Washington, Virginia, and North Carolina, is powerful and prepared. As our commander in chief's most trusted military advisor, I have recommended the implementation of far more aggressive tactics against rebel states, and the president agrees. Madam President?"

"Yes, Vice President General. I deeply value your military . . . suggestions in these troubling times. I agree that much more severe measures must be taken against the rebels, and so, I am granting you wide discretionary power over the United States military. I order you to execute your plans immediately."

"Thank you, Madam President. I promise that your faith in me is not misplaced. I promise my fellow Americans that I will take all necessary action to crush the rebellions and that I will maintain control and do my best to see us through these troubling times. •—⌁

⌁—• What does it mean if we never learn the full truth about the conspiracy behind the nuclear attacks? Can there be healing, can people begin to move on, if these mysteries remain unsolved? On the other hand, even if all those responsible are identified and apprehended, is there any kind of punishment that could possibly be appropriate to this level of destruction? Finally, what hope do we have of recovery while the civil war continues? These questions are our focus tonight here on Issues. •—⌁

⌁—• All units, all units, this is position one seven nine. We're being overrun at Snoqualmie Pass. The US is coming through. They blasted open the road barricade with cruise missiles and now armor and infantry units are rolling in. We're going to fall back to our emergency firing positions, deploying avalanches along the way. All units, be advised, the United States is coming in force. Long live the Brotherhood! •—⌁

CHAPTER

SEVEN

"Hey, wake up!"

I reached for my nine mil on my nightstand, but it was gone. I rolled out of bed and went for my rifle by the wall, but it wasn't there either. "What the hell?" I said. I'd been back in Freedom Lake for like ten days or something, and I was getting really sick of not knowing what was going on when I woke up.

"Chill, Danny," said TJ. "I have your guns right here. I didn't want to get shot trying to get you out of bed. But this Brotherhood guy came by. We gotta get down to High School Hospital. Bunch of Idaho soldiers just came in tore up pretty bad. Kemp's one of them."

Me and JoBell were dressed, armed, and upstairs with the others in the kitchen in minutes. Becca and Sweeney were right behind us. We mounted up in Cal's truck and sped over to the school.

I'd been in combat enough to be familiar with the aftermath, and as soon as I walked into the gym, I recognized the smell of blood and sweat, the groans of pain and difficult breathing. The gym was packed with cots and stretchers again. Some were even up on the graduation stage. Major Dr. Strauss was conducting surgery under a bright light in the center of the gym floor, right over the Minutemen emblem. They'd found a proper light to replace the ancient spotlight from the drama department they'd been using.

Dr. Nicole barely lifted her head when we came in. "Becca, can you get some iodine off that table over there?"

Becca nodded and ran to help.

"Anything we can do, Doc?" I asked.

"You can stay out of the way." The soldier she'd been helping groaned, and blood started seeping from his belly as she pulled the dressing off. "These guys are hurt pretty bad."

We started weaving our way around the dead and wounded, looking for people we recognized.

"Looks like a good mix of Brotherhood and Idaho Army guys." Sweeney leaned toward me on his cane and whispered, "You don't think they fought each other?"

I shook my head. I didn't know what to think.

"PFC Wright," said a gentle, quiet voice from a few cots in front of me.

"Chaplain Carmichael?" I went to the man. He held a blood-soaked field dressing to his thigh with one hand, and a little gold cross hanging from a chain with the other. "Oh sh —" I remembered to check my swearing. "Crap. I'll see if I can get someone for you."

"I'm okay. Others are worse off." He took a sharp breath in through his nose. "It's . . . good to see you again."

"What happened?" I asked.

"I don't know," said the chaplain. "There was a break in the fighting, and I thought . . ." He closed his eyes.

"Sir, are you okay?" I asked.

JoBell looked around the gym. "Let's at least get him some pain meds."

Sweeney shook his head and whispered, "I doubt they'll give him any."

"I thought I'd do what I like to call" — he opened his eyes again — "a walk with Christ with some of the men. We walk, talk about our concerns as Christian soldiers. We pray. But then the whole area seemed to explode. I don't know how I got here. My chaplain's assistant must have got me on the transport out. Specialist Baer. I haven't . . . seen her."

I'd read about chaplain's assistants in some of the brochures at the recruiter's office before I enlisted in the Guard. Chaplains weren't allowed to carry weapons, so it was up to the chaplain's assistant to protect the chaplain on the battlefield. It was possible that Specialist Baer had died doing her duty.

"I hope you find her, sir," I said. I wanted to salute or something, but I felt weird in this makeshift hospital, and I wasn't in uniform. I squeezed the man's shoulder. "Hang in there."

"By the grace of God," he said.

Across the gym, TJ waved at me. "Wright. It's Kemp. He's over here."

"Oh no." JoBell spoke first when we saw him. A white bandage was wrapped around his head and down over his left eye. His shoulder was wrapped up too.

"Hey, Sergeant Kemp," I said. "How you hanging in there?"

Kemp grimaced. "I've been better. Could be worse."

"You're going to be okay," TJ said to him. "The doctors are good here."

Kemp laughed. "I hear one is actually a veterinarian."

"Yep. Dr. Nicole," JoBell said. "But she's a damn good veterinarian."

Sweeney gave his half smile. "And not so bad looking." Then he looked at the bandage over Kemp's eye, and his smile vanished. "Oh shit. Dude, I'm sorry. Old habits. I didn't mean . . ."

"Before you ask," Kemp said, "the eye is gone. The only good thing about that is . . . the drugs."

"What happened?" I asked.

JoBell nudged me. "Danny, maybe he doesn't want to talk about —"

"It was terrible," said Sergeant Kemp. "Major Leonard led an entire company on a mission to Leavenworth, Washington. You know? That little German-themed tourist town? We established a supply base at a cabin on a river north of town for our guys and the Brotherhood to use in guerrilla tactics. We were in Leavenworth getting ready to set up some obstacles for when the US came through. Then this . . . drone. Four rotary blades and huge speakers. It comes down out of the sky right in the main tourist square and starts blasting this death metal music. So loud, we couldn't really hear anything else. Then a bunch of little rotary blade drones came zipping around corners and down over rooftops. Each one of them was carrying serious IEDs. Shrapnel bombs. Most of the drones would drop the bombs and fly away to save themselves, but some just blew up in place. Those little drones are quiet anyway, and with the music and the explosions you couldn't hear them coming at all.

"We lost about the whole company in seconds. We couldn't get to the vehicles because the drones were on them." He shook his head and then groaned in pain. "It's like our worst nightmare. IEDs that can move. A little C4, or any explosive really, packed in the middle of a bunch of nails or ball bearings. The drone can hover and hide behind trees or buildings, waiting to fly out and attack. And all the time, their operators can be somewhere totally safe, piloting the drone by its camera. Nasty."

"But you got out of there." JoBell squeezed his hand. "Thank God."

"A bunch of us made it on foot to the woods east of town. We thought we'd got away, or that the last of the drones had exploded. Then one of them dove out of the branches from overhead. Specialist Bingham shot it, and it went down in the woods. We rushed it, and I pulled the blasting cap to disarm it. But just as we were patting ourselves on the back for capturing one of their drones, another one swept around from behind this rotting tree trunk. I mostly got behind a tree before it went off." He shook his head. "We patched up and carried our wounded, found a vehicle that actually had gas, and floored it out of there. Major Leonard lost his right leg and will probably lose most of his right arm. They've already taken him and our most critically wounded to Boise. He'll never be in the field again."

"But you saved his life," said TJ.

"It was a massacre. Just like the Fed invasion that started the occupation. Except this time they're killing anything that moves. Soldiers. Civilians. They don't care." His good eye began to tear up. "I'm . . . so tired of it all."

Becca made her way over to us. "Sergeant Kemp, it's Becca Wells. Were these dressings done in the field?"

"Yeah," Kemp said. "Best we could do."

"I'm just going to take a look, make sure everything's nice and clean and that you've got good, sterile bandages." Becca leaned close to Sweeney and spoke quietly. "I'm going to need some more packing gauze, and probably more bandages too."

"You got it," he said to Becca. He looked at her for a moment, and as long as I'd known Sweeney, I'd never seen him look at a girl quite that way. Even though he was obviously still in physical pain, he looked . . . happy. Like really happy. It was different from when Sweeney was excited about making it with another girl. He had this look of satisfaction, of contentedness that I'd hardly ever seen in him. He walked off to the supply table, leaning on his cane a little less than usual.

Becca gloved up and went to work. "I know it hurts, Sergeant Kemp," she said as she cleaned the wounds on his arm. "Try to hang in there. I think we better get one of the doctors to look at you. I want to make sure you get stitched up right, and they're way better at that than I am."

Sergeant Kemp reached up and squeezed Becca's hand. "It's good to see you again, Wells. Even if it's just with one eye."

"Try to relax, Sergeant," I said. "You're safe now."

Sergeant Kemp groaned. "That Vice President General is not messing around," he said. "The US is moving across Washington one city at a time like stepping-stones. They'll destroy everything to get to us, and they're two or three steps away. I don't think any of us are safe."

"Who's that for?" I asked TJ the next day. He was stuffing a couple frozen steaks and some canned goods into a backpack.

He looked up from his work. "Making a run to Coach Shiratori's house."

"In broad daylight?"

TJ thumped a can of mixed fruit onto the counter. "I actually have some experience with this."

"Sorry," I said, remembering how he'd pretty much saved us by smuggling food and information into the dungeon during the occupation.

TJ packed the can in with the rest. "One thing I figured out is that lots of times, if you act like everything you're doing is completely normal, people will assume it is. You go sneaking around in the middle of the night and people wonder what's up."

"Can I come?" I felt weird, somehow, asking to join in the operation. I worried they might be mad, thinking I was trying to take over what they were doing. "Unless three of us would draw suspicion. I just want to talk to Coach."

"Becca's staying here to help Sweeney. He's hurting real bad."

"You were planning to go alone?" I asked. "What about rule number one?"

"I made almost every smuggling run by myself during the

occupation." He smiled, but there was a distant look in his eyes. "I can handle it. But it's cool if you come along." TJ hoisted the backpack, checked the .38 in the holster on his belt, and then chambered a round in his bolt action Remington 700. He slung the rifle on his shoulder. "Just like the good old days sneaking past the Fed. At least now I get to go armed."

It was no secret that me and TJ never got along too good in the past. Through the war, we'd gotten over that and become friends. But as I picked up my M4 and felt the familiar nervous tension that came with any mission, I realized I'd never taken the time to really think about and appreciate everything TJ had done for us. While me and my guys were hiding in the dungeon and later at the cabin, that guy had been sneaking food and messages right past Fed patrols, and without even so much as a pocketknife.

"TJ," I said. "You're one tough son of a bitch."

He laughed. "Leave my mother out of this, asshole."

"You two fighting again?" JoBell said, leaning against the doorjamb, looking good in ratty old jeans and a T-shirt, with her Springfield M1A hanging from its sling. She came into the kitchen and kissed me quick.

"We're making a run to Shiratori's," I said.

"Then I'm going too." She hurried to tell Becca and Sweeney. Outside the house, she draped her arms over both of our shoulders and led us forward. "You two need someone to keep you out of trouble."

"Are you sure you can spare it?" Mrs. Shiratori asked a few minutes later in her kitchen. "It's so much."

"There's plenty more where that came from." JoBell was trying to pump cheerfulness into her voice, like we were just delivering a few cookies at Christmas or something, like this was all fun.

"Is Coach here?" I asked.

Mrs. Shiratori kind of froze up for a second. "He's in his study," she said sadly. "Where else?"

"Can I go see him?"

She shrugged.

I exchanged looks with TJ and JoBell. "Why don't I help you put this stuff away?" JoBell said to Mrs. Shiratori. If it weren't so tragic, the offer to help put the food away might have been funny. It was a couple T-bones and about a dozen cans. Mrs. Shiratori wouldn't need much help with that.

I slipped out of the kitchen and went looking for Coach's study. I'd never really been in the man's house except for when he'd hidden us in his basement closet during the occupation, so it took me a minute to find him.

"Wow." It was the only word to describe the room. Floor-to-ceiling bookshelves were packed with books on every wall, and a big wooden desk stood in the middle of the room. Coach sat at the desk with a bottle of bourbon and a half-full tumbler in front of him. He had several days of stubble on his cheeks, and his hair looked greasy, like he hadn't showered in a while.

"Danny Wright!" He made a halfhearted effort to offer the left-fisted Brotherhood salute. "What brings you here?"

In all the time I'd known him, Coach Shiratori had always been in control, professional, from his clothes to the way he carried himself. It hurt to see him down like this. "You okay, Coach?"

"Am I okay?" He leaned his face over his glass and shook his head. "What? You here to drop off food so my family doesn't starve?"

"We brought some stuff in case —"

"I'm facing false charges of treason, and they've taken my job. Everything I've worked for, my savings, fifteen years toward my retirement pension, investments. All wasted. And my ration cards never come, so I can't even feed my *family*!" He shot up out of his chair. "Am I okay?" His hand slid along his books. They stopped at a glass case with a half-dozen military medals. "These are my grandfather's from World War II. During the war, they questioned my family's loyalty to America, forcing them all into a camp until they needed more men to fight. When the Army came asking for volunteers, my grandfather could have told them where to stick their enlistment contract. But he didn't. He told me once that he loved his country. *His* country! And he wanted to prove he was American."

"Coach, that was all a long time ago," I said.

"He shouldn't have had to *prove* anything to anyone! Just because he looked different. And now decades and decades later, I have to prove my loyalty again!" He turned back to his shelves, yanking one book and tossing it to the floor. "Look at this! *Band of Brothers*. The Winston Churchill World War II books. I read 'em all. Book on the Holocaust." Book after book fell to the floor. "All these books to study. A new World War II movie every other year. The testimony of tens of thousands of veterans and Holocaust survivors. Decades to reflect on the world's worst war and how it happened."

"Coach?"

"We haven't learned a damned thing!" Tears were in Coach's eyes as he held out another book to me. "Anne Frank's diary. Don't you see? Otto Frank saw the signs. If he could have just taken his family farther away."

What was he getting at? He staggered a little, and I helped steady him. "How much have you had to drink?"

"None. I don't drink. That bottle was a college graduation gift like twenty years ago. I just haven't slept for days. Been up keeping watch." I helped the man to his chair. "Every time I've ever read a

Holocaust story, I always wished I could go back in time to tell the victims to run. Run away and don't look back."

"That stuff was a long time ago," I said again.

"No." He looked at me, wide-eyed. "It's right now. I'm not stupid, Danny. All of this has happened before. I tried to get my family out of here a few days ago. Figured I had enough gas to make it to US territory in Seattle. About a mile out of town, we ran into a Brotherhood checkpoint. A bunch of thugs with rifles and shotguns. They" — he leaned forward, throwing his whole body into making air quotes with his fingers — " 'strongly encouraged' me to turn around and go home. For my own safety."

"Well, it is dangerous out there," I tried.

He gave no sign of hearing me. "You should have seen the condescending looks on their faces, heard the way they talked down to me like I was a damned child! Some of those guys used to be my students, used to be on my football team. And I —" He slammed his fist down on his desk, spilling some of his bourbon. "I shouldn't have to prove to my former students, or to *anybody* else, that I'm not the enemy, that I'm a citizen who is supposed to have rights."

"Well, maybe . . . maybe the investigation will clear you."

I immediately regretted what I'd said.

Coach glared at me in silence for a moment. He scratched his stubbled cheek. "You know, I worked really hard to teach you something. Tell me you're not that dumb. No, Danny. I'm too late. For my daughter. My wife. We should have got the hell out of here long ago. Now we're all just waiting for another Kristallnacht."

I'd come here to ask Coach Shiratori what to do about the Brotherhood, whether I should try to talk to Crow to work stuff out to make sure things were fair, or if they were a lost cause. If they were, what were we supposed to do? Run away? If the Brotherhood would even let us. And even if they would, where could we go? Should

I try to fight the Brotherhood? That was going to be tough with the United States on its way across Washington, ready to try to crush us.

Coach had always had answers to stuff like this, or at least he'd always been able to point me toward the right questions. But now, this man who had always been a role model to all of us growing up, who'd saved our lives during the occupation, was broken down. The war had turned a lot of things around, screwed up the way things should be in all kinds of ways, but I never thought I'd be the one coaching and encouraging Mr. Shiratori.

I moved to the side to put myself in line with his dull gaze. "I'll take care of this, Coach. Don't worry." He laughed a little. "I'm serious," I said. "I'll keep you and your family safe. I promise."

Coach only spun away from me in his chair, wiping his eyes. I stood there in awkward silence for a while before I figured the man wanted to be alone.

"I'm not gonna lie," I said to my friends as we left Shiratori's house. We passed a Brotherhood soldier who just happened to be strolling around across the street. I wondered if there was a guard there all the time. "It's getting harder and harder to see what we've gained from this war."

CHAPTER
EIGHT

My eighteenth birthday was two days later. In spite of the nervous tension around town with the United States military drawing closer and closer, Cal insisted we celebrate, and a bunch of our friends came over. Brad Robinson brought a football, and we all returned to what we used to call backyard foot*brawl*.

"Set, hit!" Jaclyn Martinez shouted a second before Brad Robinson snapped the football to her.

The other team started their five count before they could rush. "One battleship, two battleship . . ."

Cal and Brad held our offensive line while me, Becca, and Aimee Hartling took off on pass routes. Aimee and me both ran outs, sprinting ten yards ahead and then cutting to the sidelines. Becca shot straight up the middle.

"Forget it, Wright." TJ was right on my ass. "Jackie can't throw far enough to hit Becca, and Aimee can't catch. I got you."

I spun to head back inside. TJ slapped my back, covering me.

Jaclyn fired the football like an artillery shell, perfect, heading right toward Becca's outstretched hands. Then Becca slowed down, and the football hit the ground a few paces in front of her.

"Yeah!" TJ laughed. "Our ball now! Time to kick a little ass!"

I wiped the sweat from my brow. We had a good six-on-six football game going. The other team had TJ, JoBell, Crystal Bean, Timmy Macer (who was getting a little too tough to be called Timmy anymore), Caitlyn Ericson, and Mike Keelin as quarterback.

Sweeney was still hurting too much to be able to run around and everything, so he watched from a deck chair. Cassie Macer and Samantha Monohan were acting as cheerleaders for both teams, though as my team went on defense, Cassie just sat there with her arm draped around Sweeney.

"Damn, Jackie. You got a hell of an arm, girl." I jogged up next to Becca while the other team huddled up. "I thought you had that." Becca didn't answer. "You okay?"

"Fine," Becca said. "Sorry about that. Mistimed it, I guess."

"Enough bullshit," Cal said. "We'll count to five, then me and Brad are rushing. They ain't got a line. Wright, Becca, you cover deep. Jaclyn and Aimee will stay close and cover the run." Everybody agreed. "Becca?" Cal asked.

Becca snapped her attention to him as if hearing him for the first time. "Yeah. Cover the pass. Got it."

"What's the matter?" I asked her.

She frowned. "Nothing. Let's play." She dropped back a little to find her zone.

"Ready? Okay," Samantha Monohan shouted from the deck. "It's football. We love it. It's football. So suck it! Goooooooo, both teams!" Sam looked down at Cassie, who was running her fingers through Sweeney's hair. The guy would usually be way into that kind of thing, but instead he sat totally still. If I didn't know that Sweeney was suffering with no pain meds, I would have guessed he was doped up.

Mike took the snap from Tim. On my team, Cal and Brad started growling the five count. Tim, TJ, and JoBell shot off on pass routes. In backyard footbrawl, everybody, including the center, was an eligible receiver.

I should have covered TJ, but he was way the hell across the yard and JoBell ran right by me. "Becca, you got TJ!"

Mike threw to JoBell, who caught the ball and kept moving. I followed. "I don't want to hurt you," I said as I prepared to tackle my fiancée.

"Not a chance." JoBell cut back inside and shoved my shoulder hard. "You suck, babe!" She spiked the ball in the end zone at the edge of the yard. "Touchdown!"

The other team celebrated the score as they ran back to get ready to kick off. Becca jogged over to Sweeney and Cassie. "You okay?" she said to him. She must have noticed his doped-up look too.

Sweeney winced a little as he got out of his chair. Cassie patted his good arm and tried to hold on to him, but he pulled away and limped into the house. Cassie stood still, looking confused, but Becca followed him inside.

"What's going on?" I said as I reached the deck.

Cal ran up. "Sweeney okay?"

I shook my head. "Just hang on. I'll go check it out." Sweeney had been getting better, but he still hurt a lot, and lately he'd been a little out of it, kind of down. But a deeper shadow had clouded his face just now before he'd gone in. I headed inside. Low voices were coming from his room.

"Baby, they're going to be okay." Becca's quiet voice drifted out to the hall.

I was about to ask who was going to be okay when I noticed a flicker of movement in the mirror on the wall. I could see around the corner into Sweeney's room, where he sat in a chair in front of a little desk. Becca leaned down to kiss his good cheek.

"When I hear you say that, I can almost believe it," Sweeney said. He held up her hand and kissed her fingers.

What was going on here? He'd hit on her for years and never gotten anywhere. Maybe this was just the way close friends were. I'd been pretty close to Becca too, once. Very close.

She stroked his cheek with her other hand. "You'll see I'm right."

He looked up at her. "Becca . . . I know in the past, I've been a real asshole."

"Eric, no."

He held up his hand and then winced a little. "It's true, though. And I'm sorry about that. I've been a rich, spoiled, sexist . . ."

I heard his breath shake. Was he crying?

"Becca," Sweeney continued. "Since I was burned. Just . . . thank you. I never would have made it through any of this without your help."

They were quiet then for a long time. I took a couple steps away from my view of the mirror and leaned back against the wall. Did Sweeney and Becca have a thing? Sweeney, the guy who went through more girls than Starbucks made lattes? He had warned me not to hurt Becca, and he was getting with her now? He'd just been sitting out on the deck all snuggled up with Cassie Macer.

I started back to join the others, stopping in the kitchen to get a glass of water. Was I mad about this? That would be insane. I wasn't mad. I was engaged. Becca could date whoever she wanted. She'd congratulated me and JoBell on our engagement. It was just that I worried about her dating Sweeney. Right. That was it. Sweeney *had* treated women like recyclable products. I didn't want him hurting Becca. There was nothing else to it. Really. Nothing.

"Are you going to be okay with this?" Becca asked from behind me.

I jumped and spun so fast that I spilled a little water. She stood with her hands on her hips. She'd been out of the football game for maybe five minutes, and she'd already reholstered her nine mil and slipped her knife into the sheath on her lower leg. Yet she still wore her butterfly clip in her red-brown hair. The war had hardened her, but she was still Becca.

"What?" I took a sip of water. "What do you mean?"

"You're not half as good a spy as you think you are, and I'm way more alert now, not as easy to sneak up on." She folded her arms. "You know exactly what I mean."

Did she know what I thought I knew, what I thought I'd seen? "I was just checking on Sweeney."

"Damn it, Danny. You're the bravest person I know in a firefight, but when it comes to love and relationships, you're such a coward."

"So you and Sweeney?"

"Yeah. You got a problem with that?"

Why couldn't we have stayed outside playing football? Backyard footbrawl was so much easier than all this. "Of course not. Date whoever you want. Or you don't even have to date, you know. You could just mess around. Have some fun." She said nothing but stared at me. "Um. Because you know Sweeney. He's with one girl one minute and the next —"

"Yeah, I *do* know Sweeney," she said sharply. "Do you?"

"I've known him all my life. We've been in fights together, both of us on the football team since junior high."

"That was all before," Becca said. "You've hardly talked to him since he was burned."

"How could I? He's always at the hospital or —"

"And I've been with him at the hospital, right after his accident and now. I brought him food and water, and I made sure his wounds didn't get infected. I held his hand when he hurt so bad that he wanted to die." Her eyes were sharp and pinned on me. "I made sure he was never alone. And we talked. He's changed. *I've* changed." She looked down for the first time. "I love him." Her attention snapped back up to me. "And I'll knock your ass out if you try to treat either of us like we just have silly little crushes. This is different. It's more than that.

And I know we're in the middle of a war, and so all of this might sound frivolous, but these feelings are real. They matter. Maybe they matter more now, *because* we're in a war. And anyway, we don't get to choose how we feel."

It was my turn to stare at my boots. "No, we don't," I said quietly. I kind of understood right then why she was attacking me, why she was so upset. And I knew why Sweeney and her hadn't said anything about their thing. She'd been expecting me to accuse her of all that she'd just defended herself against. And hadn't I started with those arguments? Anyway, it was none of my business. If I was honest, I guess, weirdly, a part of me felt bad that she'd moved on so quickly from caring about me.

"You and JoBell are engaged." For the first time since I came back to Freedom Lake, Becca sounded like her old self. The sweetness was back in her voice. "It killed me inside, but I congratulated you. I've supported you. I hope that you can support me and Eric with —"

"I'm happy for you," I said. "Happy for you both."

She almost smiled. "Really?"

"Hell yeah," I said. "You guys are my best friends. My family. I want you to be happy. I was just surprised, is all. Can you be patient with me while I adjust to all this?"

She laughed a little as she stepped up and held up her hand, first for a high five, then for a fist bump.

"Come here." I pulled her in for a hug and felt her squeeze me tight.

"Thank you, Danny," she said.

"Thank Sweeney."

She stepped away from me, raising an eyebrow. "Maybe I will." She frowned. "But later. He said he wants to be alone for now."

"He in pain?"

"Yes," she said. "But it's more than that. Come on." She put her arm around me and led me toward the back deck. "Might as well tell everyone at once."

Everyone went silent when we got out to the backyard. It looked like they'd given up on the football game and had just been tossing the ball around or talking. Becca closed the sliding door and leaned back against the glass. "Eric's dad called, said he and Mrs. Sweeney are on their way home. They made it out of Florida, but the roads are bad, and there's a lot of fighting in different places. Bandits and stuff. Eric tried to get a better idea of where they were, but then the call dropped."

"Are his parents all right?" JoBell asked.

Becca shrugged.

"But even before that call, I could tell something's really wrong with him," said Cassie. "It's like he doesn't even know me anymore. I'm worried about him."

Becca shot me a look like, *That's why we didn't want to tell anyone.* I nodded and put my arm around JoBell, who was sitting on top of the picnic table.

Sam dropped down into Sweeney's chair, no more cheer in her. "I hope his parents are okay. But also, I don't think he likes watching football. He was pretty down, mumbling about never being able to play again."

Nobody said anything for a moment. Finally Cal squeezed Samantha's shoulder. "We'll cheer him up!" He pointed at me. "*And* it's Danny's eighteenth birthday! We'll wish him a happy birthday the way we Freedom Lake Minutemen do best." He held out his free arm like he was making a big announcement. "My friends, we shall have —" He looked around to make sure he had everyone's attention. "A raging kegger!"

Cheers went up from the whole group.

"I have bratwurst and burgers for the grill," Cal continued. "A bunch of bags of chips. Hell, I've even liberated some cookies and shit! We need to party! We've earned it."

I caught a look from Jaclyn Martinez and knew exactly what she was thinking. We were getting ready to pig out the same way we had before the war, while the best her family could hope for was canned soup, fruits, and vegetables sneaked in by her friends.

It was my birthday, but it was not happy.

Cal must have been planning this for some time, because that night at the party, Samantha surprised us all with a full-on birthday cake, my name written in frosting and everything. Becca started to ask where she found all the ingredients, but it was clear that being Cal's girlfriend had its benefits. Cal put burgers on the grill, then pulled me up in front of everyone.

"Now for your birthday present!" he said.

I tried to tell him I didn't want anything, but he wasn't listening. Instead, he pushed Brad Robinson and TJ apart like a curtain, revealing an entire keg of beer.

The big guy put his arm around me. "Happy birthday, buddy!"

How much would something like that cost? How had Cal gotten it?

When the food was ready, we sat around on the deck and told stories about old football games, fights, trucks, and parties. Stuff that didn't matter anymore. With the beer and the food, it should have been a perfect evening, but I couldn't help noticing Jaclyn gulping down her meal like she hadn't eaten in weeks. She wasn't alone. Everybody but Samantha and those of us who lived with Cal ate like they hadn't had anything this good, or even much food at all, in a very long time.

After we ate, the party went on like a lot of other parties. A big group out back on the deck by the keg. Some guys playing video games. Music from someone's comm. Hank McGrew came on once with some song about freedom. I couldn't handle that stuff anymore and switched to really old rock.

"Man, I hope the Brotherhood will let me join soon," Dylan Burns said to me, munching some chips. "They get all the best stuff. About the only snacks we've had at my house have been some canned peaches my mom had from last year." I took a sip of beer. Dylan continued, "They're really careful about who they let in. It's a super-secret process how they decide who they'll accept. But the Brotherhood loves you. They'll let you in no problem. When are you going to join?"

"Yeah," I said. "I was actually hoping to kind of take it easy."

Dylan grabbed more chips from a bowl on the table. "What? Are you kidding me? The Brotherhood is the coolest. Once you're in, you're set."

I was happy when the doorbell rang and I could get away from that guy. But then I answered the door and found Nathan Crow — former sheriff Nathan Crow — smiling on the step outside.

I shoved my cup of beer behind my back and smiled like an idiot, trying to act like everything was normal. "Mr. Crow," I said. "Great to see you. I didn't know you were coming."

Crow laughed and then smoothed his mustache. "Relax, Danny! And call me Nathan. I'm not sure what the legal drinking age is in the Republic of Idaho, but in my book, if you're old enough to serve your country in the military, you're old enough to have a beer. And trust me, nobody is going to bust the legendary PFC Wright." He nodded to the house. "May I come in?"

I spoke quietly. "We got a lot of friends here. A bunch of them are younger than me. Not serving in the military."

He nodded again. "Nobody's getting busted tonight, long as nobody tries to drink and drive."

I stood aside from the door. Cassie Macer looked up with horror as Crow walked in. I figured I better do something before my friends started running away. "Hey, everybody can chill. Nathan Crow's just, um, here —" Why was he here? "Um, for the party. We're not getting busted."

Even with my reassurance, the party completely froze. Cal came in from the deck with Samantha on his arm. His face lit up when he saw Crow. "Hey, you made it! Great! Anybody else?"

"Are you kidding?" Crow said. "I wouldn't miss Danny's big eighteenth birthday. I shuffled the guard rotation so a bunch of our Brothers can make it. With this birthday party today, and graduation in a week, things are good." He patted my shoulder. "You and your friends are still planning to attend the graduation ceremony, aren't you?"

Graduation. I'd almost forgotten about it. My friends had missed most of the school year. I'd been gone longer than them. And now with Mr. Shiratori under some joke of an investigation, the whole idea felt stupid. But Crow seemed really excited about it, and it would be best not to piss him off. I didn't know what he was so fired up about. I'd been to graduations before. They were always held in the hot gym, with all these boring speeches. Old people cried. Was he just excited because he had all his Brotherhood flags up? "Of course. Wouldn't miss it," I said.

"Great!" Crow shouted. He put his arm around my shoulder and led me into an empty corner. "I'm going to make sure everybody in town is there. I think this is going to be a great way to bring some more unity to this town for the struggle ahead. And best of all, Danny, I've been talking to some of the leadership of the Brotherhood of the White Eagle, and they all agree with me. You're exactly the kind of man we're looking for."

"What?"

Crow laughed. "Don't be so modest, Danny! We want you to become one of us. I'll be speaking at graduation, and I've set aside some of the time before we hand out diplomas for your armband ceremony." He looked off across the room like he was gazing at the future. "Just think, you'll be able to walk across that graduation stage with your own Brotherhood armband. Later, after you do your initiation mission to prove your loyalty to us, which should be no problem for an experienced soldier like you, you'll be a full member of the Brotherhood of the White Eagle."

"I, um . . . geez."

"Aw, don't worry about it," Crow said. "You don't have to thank me. It's the least I could do for you after all you've done to give the Brotherhood the big chance we've been waiting for. The whole ceremony will be on local TV and on a radio network we're getting set up. I think a lot of people will be more motivated to support the Brotherhood's mission if they see you joining us. So what do you say?" He offered a handshake.

Joining the Brotherhood of the White Eagle was the last thing I wanted in the whole world. It seemed like the worst thing I could do if I wanted to get out of the fighting. But TJ and Becca had warned me to play it cool with these guys. I shook his hand. "Sounds great."

Crow kept hold of my hand. He looked me in the eye, and his smile faded. "It's about loyalty, Danny. Some people don't understand all the good the Brotherhood is accomplishing. They can't see our great future. They doubt our mission and sneak around trying to undermine what we're doing. But I know you understand. Your father understood." What the hell was Crow saying? What exactly had my father understood? Did I really want to know? His hand-shake was so firm, my hand was starting to ache. Finally he let me go. "Think about it."

"Can't wait," I said.

"Well, don't waste your time hanging around an old fart like me." Crow refreshed his smile. "Go have fun with your friends. This is your night. It wasn't easy finding a whole keg of beer, but you've done so much for the Brotherhood of the White Eagle that we just had to come through for you in a big way like this. Go! Party!"

Crow had organized this whole thing. Why? To show me the advantages of joining the Brotherhood? Did I even have a choice? I took a sip of my beer, but it had gone warm.

What followed was the weirdest party any kid ever had. We had freshmen in high school and guys in their forties or older. The parents of some of our friends showed up. Most of the drinks were provided by the only guys in Freedom Lake who were remotely like the cops. Sweeney limped up to me on the deck and commented, "What the hell is going on here? I've never had much respect for the twenty-one-year-old drinking age, but these old dudes welcoming us to the keg? That's all kinds of jacked up."

After several hours and I don't know how many beers, it got to be too much, so I found an old two-liter plastic Mountain Dew jug, washed it out, and filled it with beer. Then I bummed a couple cheap cigars and a lighter from a member of the Brotherhood and went off to be alone for a while.

Sally's . . . Cal's house was only a few blocks from JoBell's, so I lit up one of the cigars and thought I'd walk by her old house. The streetlight at the corner wasn't working, so it was real dark in front of JoBell's place. Of course the lights were off inside. JoBell was back at the party, and her father was still in Boise. Mr. Rourke's house next door was dark too. Nobody had heard from him since Major Alsovar and his US soldiers arrested the guy for driving without permission during the occupation. I chugged some more beer.

Down at the end of the block, a section of sidewalk had been pushed up years ago by a big tree root growing underneath it. When we were kids, we all used to jump our bikes over it. But a US Army Schwarzkopf tank or some other tracked vehicle had crushed it back down, probably on the night the Fed occupation began.

As I neared Main Street, two Brotherhood guys raised their shotguns at me. "Stop! Who are you? What are you doing out so late?" one of them shouted.

I held my fist up at an angle over my head, my cigar still smoldering. "'m Danny Wright. Pissh off." I took another drink and kept on walking. One of the guys said something about it being an honor, but I wasn't listening.

I tripped at Main Street and damn near dropped my beer. Looking down to make sure I had my footing, I noticed the yellow painted curb that had nearly dumped me. Me, Cal, and Sweeney had sat here one summer for the Fourth of July parade. The band had been marching by, and JoBell had played her flute, wearing these tiny little shorts. I smiled at the memory.

Then a noise down the street caught my attention. Some Brotherhood guys were coming to relieve the guard shift in front of the old cop shop where Crow had set up the Brotherhood headquarters. A lot more Fed soldiers had been outside that base the day I'd set off a roll of barbed wire stuffed with C4. I never saw the bodies, but back in Major Alsovar's torture cell, he'd made sure I'd seen the dog tags from one of his friends I'd killed.

I walked down the empty streets of my hometown. I remembered driving here in the Beast with JoBell at my side. I remembered me and my friends running for our lives from the Fed.

I'd lived my whole life in Freedom Lake, and I knew every street, house, and bump in the road. Every part of this town carried with it a memory of growing up here. But now those memories had turned to shit. Everything had been ruined.

My beer was getting a little warm by the time I made it to the front porch of the house where me and Mom used to live. It was never much of a place, but we used to do good keeping it nice. This spring, Mom's flower beds were a wreck. The gutters needed to be cleaned out. The white paint was starting to chip pretty bad. I sat on the wooden handrail at the side of the porch, hoping the old thing would hold me.

My cigar had gone out, and I flicked it to the porch. It had been something like nine months since life had been normal for Mom and me. Now she was gone, and times when it was real quiet like this, I could still hear her screaming in pain as she bled out in my truck from that Fed bullet. The sound blended with the memory of Specialist Sparrow's screams, echoing around me when Major Alsovar caught us in the basement of the Bucking Bronc.

I closed my eyes and shook my head to escape the noise.

But behind my closed eyes I couldn't forget crawling past Bagley and First Sergeant Herbokowitz back in the shop. My hand had brushed Herbokowitz's intestines, the thick, blood-soaked pink-white hose.

This is Private First Class Luchen. Out. That explosion.

My lungs couldn't pull enough air. I put my hand to my chest to try to help. Short, sharp gasps. Then my nine mil was out, and I squeezed the pistol grip hard until my arm shook. My free hand moved over the cool, even metal of the slide, and my chest opened to let in a gulp of cool air.

I yanked back the slide and let it go, chambering a round. It was such a satisfying sound, that smooth metal scrape and click. So easy.

It'd be over.

A noise behind me. I stood fast and swung my gun arm in its direction. The gun went off.

"Shit, Danny! It's me! Don't shoot!" TJ was on the ground.

My heart pounded and my breath came heavy as I pointed the shaky gun for a moment. A dog's bark echoed from a few blocks away. "Damn it. Sorry." I holstered the gun. "Acshident. Y'okay?"

TJ stood up. "I'm fine." Jaclyn Martinez came around the corner of the house next door. TJ led her up onto my porch. "Almost shit my pants, but I'm fine."

"You scared the shit out of me. Serioushly. I'm sorry. I thought it was somebody tryin' to jump me."

"What the hell are you doing here?" TJ said. "What happened to rule number one?"

"When JoBell couldn't find you, everybody freaked out," Jaclyn said. "People are looking for you. JoBell and Cal went out to the football field. Becca and Sweeney are checking out the shop. Some of the Brotherhood are driving around."

"I didn't plan to go like all around," I said. "I'm shorry. I'ma total jackwad."

TJ picked up my plastic bottle from where it sat on the porch rail. He sniffed it and took a drink. Then he pulled a little radio from his pocket. "I better call in and let them know you're okay."

"Fine," I said. "But no." I reached out and pushed his radio down. "Don't call 'em . . . you know. Letsh jes walk back. I don't want a big thing."

"Should we get going, then?" TJ asked.

I took my beer jug back from him and chugged the rest of it down. It was so warm that for a second, I thought I might puke it up. "Ushta be able to walk 'round and not have to worry. Not have to carry a damned gun."

"Or have a giant wall around the whole town," Jaclyn said.

"I jes' hadda get away from my birthday party," I said. I couldn't tell them about how I'd thought about getting away from everything. "Shit, TJ, they celebratin' me? Affer everything I done? Affer I've killed so many people? And the whole war. Millions dead. A party ain't right. I been dreaming of getting out of the war and trying to get back to normal life, but . . ."

"It'll never be like it was before," Jaclyn said. "For anybody."

"Tonight Crow said he's gonna make me one of 'em. Damn armband an' everything."

"What did you say?" TJ asked.

"The hell you think I said?" I rubbed the back of my hand against my eye. "I don' wanna be one of 'em, but what d'ya think Crow's gonna do I say no? Like you an' Becca said. Don't pish 'em off, right? I acted like it was so cool."

TJ let out a relieved breath.

"TJ, whatta hell was it all for?" I asked. I leaned against the wall of my house. "I tried to tell myself maybe the Brotherhood was okay. That they was doing the best they could? I wanted to believe all that good shit Cal and Crow was saying. And maybe they done a few good thingsh. But you and Becca were right. They ain't no good. What they done to Shiratori. You didn't see him the other day, TJ. Wouldn'ta recognized him." I tried to meet Jaclyn's eyes, but it was too dark. I was too drunk. "What they're doing to Jaclyn's family." I looked down at the worn floorboards. "And it's my fault! I helped those assholes."

Jaclyn put her hand on my shoulder. "It's not your fault."

"It's all my fault," I said. "And I can't fix it. What we gonna do? Fight the Brotherhood? They jes kill anybody disgrees with 'em. They got guys everywhere. Got everybody boxed in here. Ain't like fighting the Fed, 'cause half the town is on their side."

"Plus the US is on its way," Jaclyn said.

"Right? We can't fight 'em both. So. Tired. Of. Fighting." I smacked the wall behind me with each word. I looked up at TJ. "Your folks had that cabin. Could we go there? All of us? You, me, Shweeney, Becca, JoBell —"

"And Cal?" TJ asked.

"Cal ain't gonna agree to come with us," I said. "He's *so* wrapped up with those assholes."

"Go ahead," Jaclyn said to TJ.

"What?" I asked.

"Let's let him sober up first, at least," TJ said.

"No, come on. We have to tell him."

I was clumsy as I pushed myself off the wall. "Tell me what!?"

TJ looked up and down the street, making sure we were alone. He draped his arm around the back of my neck and pulled me in almost like a football huddle. "I wanted to tell you about this for a long time, but I couldn't because I wasn't sure where you stood, and we can't risk the wrong people finding out about this."

"A lot of people have been thinking like you, wanting to leave," Jaclyn said. "You're right. Plenty of people here in town, even good people, are solidly with the Brotherhood. But some of us, a growing number we can trust, are tired of putting up with those guys. But we aren't going to fight them, because that would just mean more deaths of good people here in Freedom Lake."

"We're leaving town, Danny," TJ said.

"Who? When?"

"About a hundred of us," he said. "Soon."

Jaclyn rubbed my back a little. "Let's get you home so you can sleep this off. We'll talk more about it in the morning."

"I'll take you to the Macers' house tomorrow," TJ said. "We

already planned a meeting there. But you can't tell anyone about this. Nobody."

"JoBell?" I asked.

"Yes." TJ watched the street. "Of course tell JoBell, but don't tell anyone else. We have to keep this quiet, or we could end up in deep shit."

CHAPTER
NINE

Once, in English class, we were assigned to do argument speeches. I forget what mine was about, but Sweeney did his about lowering the drinking age to eighteen. "Besides drinking and driving, which is illegal anyway, there are really no problems with eighteen-year-olds drinking alcohol," he said.

I remembered that argument the next morning as I stood in the shower. "Sweeney. I'm eighteen. I drank alcohol," I whispered with my throbbing head pressed to the cool tile. "*This* is a problem." I threw up once in the shower, and again in the toilet once I'd finished and dried off.

It turned out Becca and Sweeney were already in on this thing TJ had started to tell me about, so just JoBell, TJ, and me headed out to the Macers' that morning. I still felt like shit. By the time we knocked on their front door, I had to heave into the shrubberies beside the front steps.

Cassie opened the door without her usual smile. I couldn't tell if she was down because she'd figured out that Sweeney wasn't into her anymore, or if she was ready for the serious stuff that TJ had brought us here for. Or maybe she was just hungover too.

"Come in," she said.

Tim and Mr. and Mrs. Macer were in the living room. An old woman sat on the couch. Skylar Grenke and his dad stood in the corner. Everyone held some sort of rifle or shotgun. Most carried a sidearm too.

"Welcome," Mrs. Macer said. "Have a seat. Can I get you anything?"

"Wa —" I shuffled my dry tongue around enough to talk. "Water. Please."

Mr. Macer chuckled. "Rough night, buddy?"

"Yes," said the older woman. "I hear you were partying with Nathan Crow last night. Close to the Brotherhood of the White Eagle, are you?"

"Not really," I said.

"Word is the Brotherhood is going to make you one of them," said the woman. "That you've accepted Crow's offer to let you join the Brotherhood on graduation day."

I had no idea how this woman knew about that, but then again, word traveled fast in a small town. "Crow pretty much insisted that I join them," I said quietly. "What was I supposed to say?"

"He's figured them out. He's with us," TJ said. "We can trust him."

Cassie's dad spoke up. "Danny, JoBell, this is my mother-in-law, Tabitha Pierce. She's kind of been in charge of all this from the very beginning."

Mrs. Pierce stood up with one hand on her hip and the other on the handle of the pistol in the holster on her belt. Her jeans and blue button-down shirt fit loose on her thin frame, and her frizzy, dark gray hair was pulled back in a bun. "I didn't trust this Brotherhood of the White Eagle as soon as they made themselves public," she started, "and honestly, I'm a little surprised that you ever did."

I ought to have knocked TJ on his ass for hauling me out of bed for a lecture. "The Brotherhood saved my life a few times," I said, "so, you know, I gave them a chance. I didn't know things would go down this way."

"You didn't know?" she asked. "My father was in the Army. He helped liberate the Nazi death camp at Dachau. One time he had to guard some German POWs, prisoners who probably worked at those camps or at least knew about them. He said they didn't seem evil. Friendly as some of our neighbors back home. Then he told me, 'The evil's always at the door. It's not in far-away mysterious monsters. It's always around us, even in us, and we must always guard against it.'" A faraway look had come into the old woman's eyes. Then she snapped back to the present. "The Brotherhood is dangerous, and we are not going to wait around until they finish that wall and control everything we do. It's time to take action. What I need to know is, are you with us or not? Can we trust you or not? Because you're either completely committed to our cause, or you can get out of here right now."

Mrs. Macer came back with some ice water, and I gulped down half of it right away. Then I sat up in my chair. "Fine," I said. "I'm not Crow's friend, I didn't even want that damned party, and I damn sure don't want to join them. I've seen enough to know that the Brotherhood is bad news."

Mrs. Pierce allowed a hint of a smile. "Then welcome to the resistance."

"Oh no." I glared at TJ. "I've been in the resistance before. I told everyone, *including* TJ, that I'm done fighting wars." My head kept throbbing, and I closed my eyes for a moment. "You can't beat the Brotherhood. The Feds were just soldiers from far away who happened to be assigned here. The Brotherhood knows every inch of this town just as good as we do, and they won't give it up without a hell of a fight."

"We're not going to fight them," said Skylar's dad.

"Then what kind of resistance are you?" JoBell asked.

"We're leaving Freedom Lake," said Mrs. Pierce. "A hundred of us are getting ready to leave town. They're all people we absolutely know we can trust, people who the Brotherhood doesn't take kindly to, or who can't stand the injustices under their control."

"How do you know the Brotherhood will let you leave?" I asked, remembering what Mr. Shiratori had said about trying to go to Seattle.

"That's part of the problem," Mr. Grenke said. "I tried to get my family out of town last week. The Brotherhood . . . I guess you'd say guards, stopped us before we left town. They didn't say we weren't allowed to leave, but they kept warning us about all these terrible things that would happen to us if we went."

"Everybody needs to stay here and work together," Skylar said. "That's what they kept saying."

"Read between the lines," said Mr. Macer. "They won't let people leave. They need people to help them fight if the US makes it back here again. And I think they have some idea of starting some kind of youth brainwashing program at the school. They're looking at the long game."

"So we're working on a plan to sneak or fight our way out," said Mrs. Pierce.

"I still say we fight our way free," said Mr. Grenke. "Take out the guards on the north end of town and roll through the gap in the wall."

"That's suicide," I said.

"Maybe not if we had Pale Horse with us," TJ said.

They wanted my truck? I gripped the chair harder for a moment. "Even then," I said. "They'd come after us."

"You have a better plan?" Tim asked.

I massaged my temples with my fingertips. "Right now, all I got's a headache. But even if we could get out of town without getting everyone killed, we'd need a place to go. I seriously doubt there's room for a hundred people at your cabin, TJ."

Mrs. Pierce spoke up. "When I came home from Vietnam, I wanted to get away from things, be at peace with the world and with nature. I wanted to help people. So I took a job as a nurse at the Alice Marshall School, deep in the River of No Return wilderness area. The place was built in the nineteen thirties and turned into a kind of girls' reform school in the mid-sixties."

"A girls' reform school?" I asked. The old Sweeney would have been super excited. "We're just going to bust in there and invade their school? Like the Feds took over our high school?"

Mrs. Pierce shook her head. "I was talking on FriendStar with an old teacher friend of mine. Because of the war, they closed down the school and sent the girls home. The place is sitting empty." She smiled. "It's a large property. Several buildings. Classrooms. Bunk cabins. Should be in fine shape. Safe. Far out of the way from anyone."

"Are we sure it's safe?" JoBell asked. "Have you heard this pirate radio guy, the Cliffhanger? He's like always on the run, broadcasting the real news and calling for peace. He says the Brotherhood is expanding its territory, offering what they call 'protection' to more and more cities."

"This school isn't really near any towns," said Mrs. Pierce.

"Assuming you could get out of Freedom Lake, how would you get to the school?" I said.

"To move a hundred people, along with all their clothes and food and other supplies, we plan to take two buses, a good-sized RV, and a pickup hauling a horse trailer."

"And my souped-up Humvee ambulance," I said.

"I moved all those machine guns and the ammo we captured out of the dungeon under the shop," TJ said. I gave him a sharp look, and he hurried on, all defensive. "The Brotherhood knows about that place. I worried they'd go down there to check it out and 'claim' the stuff for themselves. Relax. Everything's well hidden in the basement of your old house."

"What? You just go breaking in?"

"Danny," JoBell warned me.

TJ folded his arms. "The point is, with you and Pale Horse and the stuff from the basement, we have the guns. We have the ammo. We can protect ourselves for the ten-hour drive or whatever it is that we'll need to reach the school."

JoBell and I looked at each other. "Have you been out on those roads since the war started?" she asked them. They shook their heads. "It's like a different world."

"I'm sorry, but with every gun turret on Pale Horse fully loaded, it still might not be enough," I said.

"We've been working hard to get ready," said Mrs. Pierce. "Our goal is to stay in hiding at the school for the rest of the war."

"Which could mean years," said JoBell.

Mrs. Pierce nodded. "The school is designed to be pretty self-sufficient in the first place. Wood-burning stoves for heat. Electrical generators that will be handy, since the power must be shut off. There's a good heavy-duty kitchen, a well-stocked toolshed, and even recreational stuff like canoes, horseshoe sets, and sports equipment. And we'll be bringing plenty of supplies with us. Mr. Cretis is on our side." I was surprised to hear they had my old shop teacher involved in this. Mrs. Pierce continued, "He's arranged to take welding equipment and about every other tool we might need both from the school's shop and from his house. We've collected blankets and cold-weather clothing for winter. We have canned food and powdered milk. We have seeds, gardening tools, and some experienced farmers and gardeners so we can try to grow our own food. There's more work to do before we're ready, but I'm proud of how hard our people have worked, and of what we've accomplished so far."

Mrs. Macer spoke up. "Our big concern is fuel — gas for the vehicles making the trip. We've saved up some, but not enough. We need to find where the Brotherhood is storing its supply."

"It will be guarded," I said.

"We're still working out some parts of the plan," said Mrs. Pierce.

"Let's just not rush this," I said. "We have to take the time to do this right, or a lot of people are going to get hurt."

"You're right," said Mrs. Pierce. "But we don't have unlimited time. The United States military is moving across Washington, getting closer and closer. It'll be a bloodbath when they arrive. And when the Brotherhood finishes building that damned wall, nobody's getting out of here."

"Why do you have to be this way? What is your problem?" Becca shouted after TJ, JoBell, and me made it back to Cal's living room and talked about the plan to leave town.

I was sitting on the couch, and I pressed my hands to the side of my aching head. "Please don't yell."

"Oh." Becca stood in the middle of the room. She stage-whispered, "I'm so sorry. What's your damned problem?"

"The problem is that this is never going to work," I said. "A hundred people aren't going to be able to sneak out of here without being noticed, and the Brotherhood isn't going to let us go. We'll probably all wind up being branded as traitors, and who knows what they'd do to us if they caught us. And even if we could escape, we don't have diesel."

"The Brotherhood has plenty," Becca said. "Cal always has enough for that big truck of his. We'll have him get us some."

"I don't think he's going to fuel up a whole convoy of vehicles for a group of people sneaking away from his precious Brotherhood," I said.

"You're just pissed because for once it isn't the Danny Wright show," Becca said to me. "You can't stand the fact that while you were prancing around with Montaine and Buzz Asshole Ellison, the rest of us were back here making plans without you."

"Hey," Sweeney said. "Come on. Let's all chill a second."

This was about as mean a thing as I'd ever heard from Becca. Worse, she was at least partly right. I felt left out. I took a sip of ice water. "I didn't see you bitching about us being gone when it meant getting your new boyfriend to a good hospital."

I knew it was the wrong thing to say as soon as I'd said it. Becca's glare went cold. Sweeney kind of grimaced. JoBell's mouth dropped open. TJ looked like he wished he could be anywhere else but there.

Everyone started up at the same time.

Becca: "You really want to get into relationships right now?"

Sweeney: "Kind of a low blow there, buddy."

JoBell: "You two are together?"

I put my water down and stood up. "That's not what I meant. Just that maybe you could have included us in the plan from the beginning."

Everyone spoke at once again.

TJ: "We wanted to."

Becca: "Kind of hard when you weren't even here!"

Sweeney: "I wanted to tell you as soon as I heard about it when we came back here, but then you and Jo were defending the Brotherhood, and I didn't know —"

Me: "You should have trusted us!"

JoBell: "Back up! You two are a thing? Becca, why didn't you *tell* me?"

"Listen to me!" Becca yanked the knife from the sheath on her lower leg and held it up in front of her. She wasn't threatening us. It was more like she was showing it off. "You weren't here dealing with things, okay? You were off on the publicity tour. It was TJ and me, with Cal sinking deeper into the Brotherhood every day. A lot of people around town were getting frustrated with what was happening and wanted to leave. I didn't know when you all would be back. But I'd seen way too many people die. I'd seen Eric almost killed. Too much shit had happened for me to wait around to see what you guys would want to do." She pointed the knife at the front window. "You act like the war is over. Like we won and everything is fine. But it's not. We're worse off than before, and we're running out of time. So yeah, it pisses me off when you're all 'this will never work,' but aren't even trying to help us figure out how to get the hell out of here!"

Silence fell over the room, and she put her knife away.

"So," JoBell finally said. "You and Eric?"

Becca blew out a frustrated huff until she saw the smile on JoBell's face. Then she busted out laughing, and JoBell ran and threw her arms around Becca. "Come on, warrior girl. You know we're on your side." She kept her arm over Becca's shoulders as she turned to face us. "It's great you two are together."

Sweeney put his hand on his chest, a look of confusion on his face. "Kitten," he said to JoBell, "you know she's dating *me*, right?"

"Shut up, Eric," JoBell said. "Before I change my mind about you being a good guy."

We all laughed. "Now that we have all that straightened out. And we're all sharing —" TJ stopped for a moment when a smiling Becca wrapped her arm around his shoulders. "Um, everything, I guess. What are we going to tell Cal?"

"How about you tell me something awesome?" Cal said from back in the kitchen. He was taking off his boots near the door to the garage.

"Oh shit," Sweeney breathed.

Cal came into the living room, stretching his arms with his hands up behind his head, his giant biceps popping. We all exchanged a look. He picked up on the heavy weirdness in the room and dropped his arms to his sides. "You guys okay?"

"Cal, honey, we need to talk," Becca said.

"Oh shit," he said. "Those words ain't never good. Maybe I need to sit down for this." He flopped down on the couch, sitting like he always did, the way that took up at least two normal people's spaces.

She was really going to go for this now? Did she think we could talk Cal out of the Brotherhood? Or maybe she only wanted to know the location of their fuel depot. Whatever she had in mind, Cal was already on the defensive, and we hadn't even begun. "Cal—" I started.

"You know we love you," Becca said. "You're my brother. We'd all be dead without you. You've saved us a bunch of times."

"You saved my life when I was shot," JoBell said.

"I'd do it again," Cal said loudly. "Ain't nobody gonna hurt my friends."

"You helped get Danny out of that Fed prison cell," Becca said. "And any one of us would throw in our lives for you."

That was smart. Remind him of his loyalty to us, of our loyalty to each other. That would make it easier when we had to ask him to question his loyalty to the Brotherhood.

"Something's up." Cal frowned. "Just say what you gotta say."

"We know you like the Brotherhood," I said.

Cal tensed up in his seat, spreading his fingers and then tightening them into fists. "Oh no."

"Just listen a second," Becca said. "Cal, I know you think they're great, but there are some real problems going on around town. Some problems with the Brotherhood that —"

149

"Of course there are problems," Cal said. "Even Nathan Crow admits there are problems. The Brotherhood is the only group trying to fix things."

"Cal, they are starving out the people they don't like," I said. "Jaclyn Martinez's family can barely get enough to eat."

"That's because her dad works laying carpet, and nobody is buying —"

"Mr. Shiratori has been accused of —" TJ started.

"Other people accused him of being a traitor! The Brotherhood didn't have nothing to do with that! And Crow is trying to get him cleared." The beginning of that dangerous animal look was creeping into Cal's eyes.

Sweeney leaned forward in his chair, placing his chin on top of his cane. "I didn't quit my pain medication just to be tough. They're out of meds for everybody but the Brotherhood. And don't you think it's convenient that only people who aren't white are being accused of selling us out to the US? That people like me can't even get a job building the wall? That their ration cards never arrive on time?"

"Come on, Sweeney," Cal said. "Don't go making this a race thing. This ain't like one of your old Asian jokes."

JoBell sat down beside Cal. "They won't even let people leave town."

"Because it's *dangerous* out there!" He flew off his seat, moving to the middle of the room like a bull in the rodeo ring. "Damn it! You were out there! Those bastards in Lewiston would have killed you, Jo! You weren't bitching about the Brotherhood then!"

JoBell held up her hand. "Hey," she said calmly. "Relax. We're all on your side here."

"Like hell you are!" Cal's hand was on the hilt of the sword on his belt.

"You going to cut us, Cal?" TJ asked.

"I should! You're damned right I should!" He breathed heavy, marched across the room toward the door to the kitchen, and turned around to face us. "I . . ."

"Listen to us for a second. Hear us out," Becca said.

"I let you live in my house. Eat my food." He pointed at me. "Give you a kick-ass birthday party, and then you ambush me when I get home? I didn't see you bitching about the Brotherhood when you were drinking their beer."

JoBell tried again. "If you'll calm down for a little bit, we can explain this so —"

"Yeah, Miss Valedictorian? Explain it so the big dummy can understand it?" He shook his head. "This ain't about the Brotherhood. Not really. It's about how you guys can't handle me having some success." He whirled on Sweeney. "You always gotta be the guy with all the cool stuff, the best house and car and snowmobiles and shit! And Danny, you can't deal with me being the guy people look to for help in the fight. Well, you should have thought of that before you decided to turn into some kind of anti-war hippie. You all liked me best when I was simpleminded trailer-trash Cal. Well, I ain't the guy I was before."

"Cal, it's not about that. There's more we have to tell you," I said. "It's important."

Becca grabbed my wrist and shook her head. "We can't."

"We have to," I said. We couldn't just pack up and leave Cal. Not after everything that had happened.

Cal went through the kitchen and started putting his boots back on. "You all are lucky I'm a good guy, not a shitty friend like you. Because I should kick you all out of my house. Dump your shit on the curb." He stood up. "But see, I'm a good guy. A good friend. I'm a member of the Brotherhood of the White Eagle. We help people. I said this was your house, and I meant it. But I ain't hanging around here listening to this anymore."

A cold fear shot through me. Where was he going? Who would he talk to? We could be in serious trouble. "Cal!" I yelled. "Cal, I know you're mad at us, but do us a favor and don't tell the Brotherhood about what we've said."

"Oh, so that's how it is," Cal said. "Brave enough to talk about them behind their backs, but you know you don't have jack for proof. And maybe you're feeling a little guilty bitching about the Brotherhood while you live off their food, while Crow has offered to let you join? Don't worry. I won't tell the guys. I'd be too embarrassed." He slammed the door on his way out.

"Now you see why we were afraid to tell you about the evac plan?" Becca asked me.

I felt sick, and it had nothing to do with my hangover. I met Becca's hard eyes. "I know it's a risk, but we can't ditch Cal. We can't leave him behind."

"You heard him, though, Danny," JoBell said. "He's a fanatic. We'd be putting everybody at risk if we told him about the plan."

"We don't even have a plan." I rubbed the heels of my hands in my eyes. "And now our group is falling apart. Everything's a mess."

⌇—• special report. Live from the NBC newsroom in Los Angeles, here's Adrienne Welch."

"Good evening. My colleagues in the news media are calling today Separation Sunday, for although the timeline of a number of historic and perhaps tragic events is unclear, we do know that there are now thirteen countries where once there were eight, where once there was one, in the territory that used to be the United States of America. Resentment has been on the rise for weeks, as US forces pound cities in rebel states in an effort to force them back into the union. In response to those attacks and to aggression from Atlantica, the states of Louisiana, Mississippi, and Alabama have formed the Southern Alliance of America, moving quickly to seize control of the Florida Panhandle south of Alabama. New York, Pennsylvania, New Jersey, the eastern part of Maryland, and Delaware have broken away as the Keystone Empire. Illinois, Indiana, Ohio, and southern Michigan have formed the nation of Liberum, the Latin word for 'free.' North and South Dakota have joined together as one nation known as Dakota. And finally, some kind of political military coup has turned California and western Oregon into a country that is being called Cascadia. We here at NBC will continue to bring you information as we have it, assuming the leaders of Cascadia will allow us to continue to report fairly and freely.

"So this is what the map of Pan America looks like as of this broadcast. Keep in mind that borders are arbitrary and fluid, and that rebels . . . Excuse me. I am being told by my producer that the leadership of Cascadia has asked me to refer to the former rebels as 'residents of newly independent countries.' So keep in mind that . . . residents of newly independent countries might not stop at some invisible state line drawn long ago on a map. They might control areas outside of their official territory and vice versa. The *map on your screen is meant to show the current situation according to the most reliable and up-to-date information we have.*

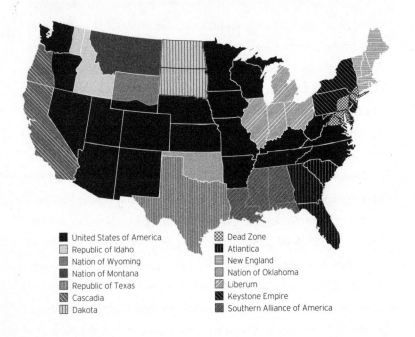

■ United States of America	▨ Dead Zone
▢ Republic of Idaho	▨ Atlantica
▦ Nation of Wyoming	▨ New England
▦ Nation of Montana	▨ Nation of Oklahoma
▥ Republic of Texas	▨ Liberum
▨ Cascadia	▨ Keystone Empire
▥ Dakota	▨ Southern Alliance of America

"As you can see, the territory that is not in dispute, that unquestionably belongs to the United States, is increasingly surrounded by newly independent countries. These hotly contested borders create a situation ripe for war. •⌁

⌁—• If anyone can hear me on this channel — guys, does this CB even have power? If anyone is listening, this is Sergeant Rine of the Idaho Army. My fire team is alone, without any other commo, and separated from the rest of our forces. We may be the only survivors. Ellensburg, Washington, is gone. US drones came down out of the mountains to paint the target, then bombers flew in and all hell broke loose. After the bombing, infantry and armored units rolled in to pick off survivors. To any Idaho Army or Brotherhood positions,

154

you've got to get out of the cities or get some serious anti-aircraft batteries up. The US had no mercy. They hit military positions, businesses, streets, bridges, houses — even the school, I think. My team is heading back toward Idaho, but it's over two hundred miles and our Humvee is done for. If anyone is getting this message, please spread the word. The US is coming for us. Sergeant Rine, out. •—⌇

⌇—• Citing a violation of the Chinese directive against foreign military intervention in the war between North and South Korea, Chinese warships attacked Japanese vessels in the East China Sea and the Sea of Japan. Japan, claiming to act in self-defense against the threat posed by an increasingly desperate North Korea, only recently joined South Korea's effort to topple the Kim Jong Un regime. Even with rapid Japanese armament in the wake of the Diet's abolition of Article IX of the Japanese Constitution, the strength, capacity, and manpower of the Chinese Navy greatly exceeds that of the combined forces of South Korea and Japan. •—⌇

⌇—• of many former Americans who have decided to flee the war by reentering what is left of their homes in irradiated northeastern cities. Some have even moved into New York and Washington, DC, where radiation is still at a lethal level. While the damage to the health of these resettlers would vary depending on where they go, experts say it's only a matter of time before radiation sickness and •—⌇

⌇—• Wildfires extinguished last week were reignited by United States missiles, once again threatening thousands of homes in San Diego county and adjacent areas. The challenge this time? Looters,

who wait for residents to evacuate, then enter neighborhoods and take whatever they can. One resident who would identify herself only as Eliza said, quote, "I'm not leaving until the fire gets my home. If I evacuate, the looters will get it anyway, probably burn down what they don't take." End quote. •—ᐟᐠ

ᐟᐠ—• a heightened level of security around the European Union and NATO countries. Drills are being conducted in cities in Poland, Germany, France, the UK, and all over Europe in an effort to prepare the population for a possible Soviet attack. In response to concerns over the missile defense system in the absence of significant US support, German Chancellor Jutta Martell issued assurances today that the EU missile defense system is online, ready, and technologically superior to any offensive system the Soviets may have. •—ᐟᐠ

CHAPTER

TEN

For the next few days, all of our group except for Cal were busy preparing for Operation Exodus. I'm not gonna lie. I was impressed with how well Mrs. Pierce had gotten everyone working.

Space on the buses would be tight, so she'd issued a packing list, just like we used to have in the Army. Every member of our group was to pack three warm-weather and four cold-weather outfits. Eight pairs of socks and underwear. One pair of light-duty shoes and one pair of boots. I spent some time going around showing people how to GI roll their clothes so they could fit tighter into less bags and suitcases. One thing Mrs. Pierce hammered into us over and over: Everyone was to bring all the hats, gloves, snowmobile suits, long underwear, and other cold-weather gear they could find. "Winter at the Alice Marshall School," Mrs. Pierce said, "does not screw around."

The group had also saved up more food than I would have thought possible, given there was so little to go around. Cans of beans, pears, peaches, olives, and about everything else had been hoarded over time. They were kept in boxes and duffel bags hidden in attics, crawl spaces, bathroom plumbing hatches, and sometimes even between wall studs behind the drywall. A few of our people had preserved what beef they could by drying it out in the oven for hours and hours to make jerky. On Victory Day, someone had grabbed four whole cases of Fed MREs. Food would be tight, but if we could hunt and fish up in the mountains, if the gardeners of our group could pull off growing some potatoes and things, we'd do all right.

I met our bus driver, Norm, in the bus barn at the school that Monday. He'd picked out our two biggest, newest buses. They had bins down below for luggage, and they even had heavy-duty solar assist systems installed on the roof. But as the two of us went over maps, checking all the possible routes to the Alice Marshall School, we couldn't get around the fuel trouble.

When Mr. Morgan found us out there, I thought we were busted, but he dropped the code phrase, "Pioneer backwatch."

"Really, Mr. Morgan?" I said. "You're part of this too?"

"Like I told you all those times you were in trouble in my office, this is *my* school. I call the shots here." The principal shrugged. "At least I did until Nathan Crow took over. It was hard enough providing a decent education for students during the US occupation. Now the Brotherhood is making it about impossible. My family and I are getting out. Tabitha Pierce told me about the fuel problem. I think there's the better part of fifty gallons in the basement boiler room of the school. It's been standing by in case we need to start up the emergency generator. We can use that to help fuel the buses."

I smiled. My old principal. I'd always thought he was kind of a jackwad, but in the final fight against the Fed, he'd taken a bullet to the leg and kept on fighting. Now he was coming through again.

Norm frowned. "Fifty gallons'll get us farther, but it still won't be enough."

"We'll keep looking," I said.

These kinds of meetings happened in secret all over town, each a little more concerned, more desperate as the days wore on, especially after even more territory broke away from the United States. We worried that would make the US only more angry, more ruthless, when they finally came for Idaho.

A cold, awkward quiet had settled between Cal and the rest of our group. The big guy went to work doing whatever the Brotherhood had him doing. Then he'd come home, drink by himself at his basement bar, and go off into his room.

"Care if I join you?" I asked him that Tuesday, pulling out the stool at the bar next to him. With all the stress we were under, I figured I could use a drink. Cal only shrugged and poured himself another Scotch. I leaned over the bar to the counter down below and grabbed a tumbler, then poured myself a splash. I took a sip of the Scotch and pursed my lips to blow out the burn.

"You know, it's funny." I held the glass up in front of my face, looking at the bar lights through the glass and the tan liquid. "Drinking used to be such a big deal. Like it was so cool if anyone could score even a twelve-pack of beer. And then there was the excitement of finding a safe place to party, the thrill of not getting caught. But now —"

"That something else you don't like about the Brotherhood?" Cal asked. "You want to go back to a twenty-one-and-up drinking age?"

"No. I only meant that it takes some of the fun out of it." I sipped more Scotch and shook my head against its strength. "I don't know what I'm trying to say." I knew that I hadn't come down here to talk to Cal about booze. I'd wanted to patch things up, to make things cool between us again. "I guess I miss those old parties."

Cal grunted and took a long drink to finish off what was left in his glass. Then he stood up, snatched the bottle from the bar, and went upstairs, leaving me there by myself.

Knowing you're having a nightmare while you're in the middle of a nightmare doesn't make it any less terrifying. In my dream, it looked like the entire US military, thousands of tanks, Strykers, Humvees, helicopters, and jets, was rumbling toward us from the west. Weirdly, dismounted infantry ran alongside the rest on foot, all of them moving at the same speed, in one line, like a front of storm clouds in summer. The Brotherhood scrambled to the walls around town, some of them driving west in pickups and old cars to meet the fight. But they were slaughtered in seconds, not by the main military force, but by hundreds of little drones that zipped in and exploded, shredding everything and everyone around them with shrapnel.

Then the drones came after us. Me and my friends ran to get away, but Sweeney and Becca couldn't keep up. Cal stayed behind with them to fight. A drone exploded, and I watched their bodies get torn to pulp. JoBell and I held hands as we ran. We were close to the gap in the north part of the wall. I had this idea that if we could get out of town, we'd be safe. We were almost there when a quadcopter drone lowered itself down in front of us. I could see the stick of C4 wrapped in nails and ball bearings, the silver blasting cap sticking out of the explosive charge . . .

I jerked awake, clutching my sweaty chest over my thundering heart.

"You're okay, Danny." JoBell was on the far side of the bed. She must have moved there for her own safety when I started thrashing around.

"Son of a bitch," I whispered.

"You're all right," she said soothingly.

"I'm better than all right." I threw off my blankets, put on a T-shirt, and grabbed my nine mil. "Jo, I figured it out. The whole damned thing."

"Danny, wake up," JoBell said a little louder.

I leaned over the bed and kissed her full and hot on the mouth. "I love you so much." I kissed her again, and she ran her fingers through my hair. As much as I would have loved to stay there and play, I broke the kiss. "But I have to go tell the others. Yes!" I punched the bed. "I figured it out! For once the Feds are going to help us."

Upstairs, Becca was standing in the middle of the living room, fully dressed with her M4 slung from her shoulder. "Another nightmare?" she said quietly without breaking her gaze out the front window. The sky was lightening up in the east. It was just before dawn.

"Yeah, but a good nightmare, I think. Have you been standing there your whole shift?"

She finally looked at me. "I'd fall asleep if I sat down. What do you mean, a good nightmare?"

"Listen, I'm sorry I've been kind of a dick about this whole thing. I guess I was frustrated because there didn't seem to be any way to pull off the escape." She nodded. "But I think I've figured out how to make it all work. We gotta go talk to Sergeant Kemp."

"You okay?" JoBell asked me.

"What?" I said. Me, JoBell, and Becca were standing outside the Bucking Bronc. The Budweiser, Pabst Blue Ribbon, and Rolling Rock fluorescent lights in the windows were all dark. I hadn't been back here since the day Major Alsovar and his soldiers caught me and Specialist Sparrow in the basement. This place was the beginning of my torture at the hands of the Feds. After the bar's owner, Sally Hines, was hung for treason, the Idaho Army had turned the place into a barracks. But I'm not gonna lie. I did not want to be here.

"You're shaking," JoBell whispered.

"I'm fine." If everything worked out, I'd be leaving this place far behind. "It's no big deal." I forced myself to enter the barracks, the girls close behind.

The specialist guarding the front door saw who we were and lowered his rifle right away. When we asked for Sergeant Kemp, he directed us to the back room.

"Hey, Sergeant," I said when we found him on his cot. "How's the eye?"

He turned over and showed us the black eye patch over his left eye. "How is it? Am I getting closer to rocking the pirate look?" There was still white gauze and packing under the patch, but his smile was a good sign. Worry washed over his expression a moment later. "But the pirate look isn't enough to get me out of duty. Word is the Idaho Army is moving us all up to the line soon. We're taking a stand at Spokane. I wouldn't be surprised if they call you up too."

I looked around the room. The Brotherhood had taken the pool table and pinball machine a long time ago, so the room was filled with cots, soldiers, and their gear. I didn't know a lot of the guys. "Is there someplace we can talk in private?"

"Privacy? In the Army? Wright, you *have* been on cushy duty too long." He laughed a little as he stood up. "Actually, Crocker's down in the basement working on some things. I could kick him out."

"Or maybe there's some other place?" Becca asked.

"The hell with that," I said. "It's fine. We could probably use Crocker's help."

Moments later, we were down in the dark basement. Crocker must have been working out since I'd seen him last, because he looked rock solid in his OD Idaho Army uniform, now with sergeant rank insignia. He looked up from his workbench. "Oh, hey guys. What's up?"

"Crocker," Becca said. "Good to see you. What have you been up to?"

Crocker sighed. "I joined the Guard to pay for college so I could learn computers. I enlisted into commo 'cause I figured that was as close as I could get to my major. Now college and the computer industry are shot, but I've been all over fixing Brotherhood and Idaho Army computers and radios. I keep putting in a request for some more commo guys up here, but they only say they're working on it."

"What are you complaining about, Sergeant Crocker?" Kemp gave him a little punch to the arm. "You got a promotion out of it. You're making the big bucks now."

They both laughed sadly. Idaho was way behind on payments to their soldiers. We'd been getting Certificates of Payment to be redeemed for an equivalent value in silver at a future date.

Crocker straightened his glasses. "Even if we were actually being paid, I probably won't live long enough to spend any of it, and what's left to spend it on? The Brotherhood controls everything, at least in northern Idaho. I'm better off trading my radio and computer repair skills for the stuff I need."

JoBell looked at me, and I nodded. "How much of a chance do you think we have against the US in Spokane?" I asked.

Kemp and Crocker exchanged a look. "I was there recently working on commo," said Crocker. "They're putting in a ton of anti-aircraft guns, and some of our fighter jets and attack helicopters are stationed at Fairchild Air Force Base, but . . ."

"What?" I asked.

"You weren't out in Washington for the US counterattack," Kemp said. "General Jacobsen wasn't screwing around when he promised to crush the rebel forces. The United States does not care who they have to kill to stop us. They're brutal."

"We might be able to hold them off, but . . ." Crocker trailed off.

Weirdly, that was what I wanted to hear. "Listen," I said. "We've been through a lot together. So I know I can trust you with this." I told him about what the Brotherhood had been doing, why we couldn't trust them, and what we wanted to do about it. "We'd be safe at the Alice Marshall School. It'd be our best chance to wait out the war, our best chance to survive. And it's my only chance of not getting drafted into the Brotherhood." I crouched down next to the boiler where Sparrow and I had hidden before we were captured. Dark bloodstains still splattered the cement floor. "If you guys stay with the war, the best that will happen is you'll see a lot of your fellow soldiers die, and we'll win the war, and these racist psychopaths will control everything. And the worst . . ." I stood up and knocked on the hollow old boiler. "Come with us. I'd hate to lose either one of you, and we could use your help setting up a new community."

"What do you say, guys?" Becca said. "Idaho will survive the attack or not. Two more people won't make that much of a difference, will it?"

Sergeant Kemp carefully slid his hand down over his eye patch. "When I enlisted, I never thought I'd be agreeing to something like this, but then . . ." He motioned all around us. "Everything." He nodded. "Okay. I'm in."

"Sounds like fun." Crocker reached out and grasped my hand in one of those half-high-five-half-handshake moves. "I suppose you're going to need someone to rig your radios."

"Actually, there's something we need from you guys way more than radios," I said. "Sergeant Kemp, you said you'd captured a US drone. Do you still have it?"

"The drone?" Crocker went to a pile of boxes in the corner, dug around through some junk, and pulled the thing out. He put it down on his workbench. "What about it?"

I leaned toward them. "It's like this. There's no way we can get a hundred people out of this town without the Brotherhood noticing. The trick is to be long gone before they come after us."

"Okay," Kemp said. "So how do we do it?"

"The United States is coming. They're sweeping across Washington. The Brotherhood and Idaho Army are already moving tons of men, weapons, and supplies to the Spokane area. Everyone around here is on edge about the fight. When it heats up in Spokane, we'll launch our own attack here. A diversion on the south side of town. The remaining Brotherhood here in town will think it's the US, and most of them will go down there. Then we use that US drone to take out the Brotherhood guards still patrolling the north side gap in the wall. That will be our best chance of getting out of town without being spotted. With any luck, the Brotherhood will figure the whole thing was a US attack. If and when they do pin it on us, they won't be able to find us."

Becca smiled at me, fire in her eyes. "We use US weapons. They'll blame the US."

"At least long enough for us to get the hell out of here."

"It could work," she said. "If we can figure out the fuel problem."

I nodded. "It's the best way I can think of."

Crocker spun on his stool and held his hands out toward his workbench. "Well, you're in luck, 'cause I almost have the programming on this vicious little bastard figured out. I'm pretty sure I'll be able to use my comm to fly it."

"The fuel issue will be tougher," Sergeant Kemp said.

Crocker turned back to face us. "The Brotherhood has a captured US fuel truck parked at a secure camp in the middle of the woods where they have their warehouses. It's well guarded and super secret. They took me out there to work on some of their equipment once, and they made me wear a blindfold for the whole trip. If anything goes wrong at the camp, they have a heck of a transmitter to call their buddies for help."

"Could you disable the transmitter?" Kemp asked.

"Absolutely I could, but it would be easier to take out the antenna. The trick is getting onto that base. They have pretty good security."

"It's like every time we overcome a problem, another one pops up in its place," I said.

JoBell rubbed my shoulder. "Sergeant Crocker can get the drone working. We can get our convoy out of town. Maybe that's enough in the short term. We can worry about the fuel later."

"I agree wholeheartedly," Crocker said.

I didn't. But I nodded anyway. "All of this is classified, got it?"

Kemp made a half-assed salute. "Yes, *Private*."

CLARK BAKER ★ ★ ★ ★ ☆

I took over my business from my old man when I was only 27. I've expanded beyond house construction to industrial projects and state highway contracts. Now I'm 54 and even if people were building right now we'd probably still be going out of business. The Army and Marines came in with guns and took a bunch of my equipment. They said they needed it for the war effort. I was worried about my employees so I told them not to resist. Those soldiers looked serious. Some of my workers are relocating to Colorado. But I'm not so young anymore. I have a family and a life here in Little Rock.

★ ★ ★ ★ ★ This Post's Star Average 4.95   [Star Rate] [Comment]   20 minutes ago

CODY BROCK ★ ★ ★ ☆ ☆

I'm sorry to hear that, Mr. Baker. You won't remember me. We only met once when you visited a house construction site. I worked on one of your crews after high school and for a couple summers when I was home from college. I'm a lawyer now, and I'm trying to represent clients who have suffered similar losses. But the courts are backed up for probably years. The whole legal system is in chaos, with some district courts now in supposedly independent countries. I honestly don't know why I bother going to work anymore.

★ ★ ★ ★ ★ This Comment's Star Average 5.00   [Star Rate]   16 minutes ago

KRISTIN SUMMERS ★ ★ ★ ☆ ☆

Grandpa, we're having the same trouble up in West Virginia. 1st we had enough of a problem with people trying to get out of the radiation zone around DC. Then this military group came through. They took whatever they could use. They had their own fuel trucks, but they took what was left of the gas. They even stole a lot of the county road equipment. Anyone reading this if you have anything valuable, hide it. And you better have a gun to protect it.

★ ★ ★ ★ ☆ This Comment's Star Average 4.00   [Star Rate]   13 minutes ago

╰╴• *In Idaho's ongoing effort to sever the United States' key transportation route between its port facilities in western Washington and the rest of its remaining territory, the First Idaho Special Forces Group launched a devastating attack in Baker City, Oregon, yesterday. Several military supply depots were destroyed, and impassable craters were blasted in Interstate 84 south of the city, rendering the road useless. While US forces suffered hundreds of losses, Idaho casualties were minimal. Onward to victory. AM 1040 Republic of Idaho Radio, RIR.* •╰╴

╰╴• *For some time now, the only cooperation between the United States and the newly independent countries has been in the ongoing effort to locate the remaining eleven nuclear theft suspects and their coconspirators who are still at large. Although many believe Idaho President Montaine or Montana President Brenner is responsible for the attacks, all evidence gathered so far seems to indicate that the nuclear theft and detonations were carried out by an unidentified element. Unfortunately, progress in the investigation effectively came to a halt on Separation Sunday. With thirteen countries in the Pan American territory and peace in short supply, it will be virtually impossible to locate and apprehend the eleven known surviving suspects in what should be the most important investigation in history.* •––⌇–

––⌇–• taking you live to Tel Aviv in Israel, where BBC correspondent Thomas Baker has a firsthand look at the situation."

"I'm reporting from the roof of my hotel in downtown Tel Aviv, and you can see behind me the glowing specter of Israeli anti-aircraft batteries trying to repel the air attack. A large-scale, carefully coordinated barrage began about one hour ago as the new, more aggressive and radicalized Iranian government, emboldened by the withdrawal of United States forces from their country, declared war on Israel. Israeli intelligence believes the Iranian military is joined by Iraqi forces operating independently from the Iraqi central government, and by a large contingent from the rising terrorist network known as Global Jihad. There are more questions than answers at this time, but one thing is certain. Israel faces an existential threat and one of the largest wars in its history. •––⌇–

––⌇–• I'm joined today in the NBC studio by California Governor Gary Black."

"That's okay, Ms. Welch, I know that calling me the interim president of Cascadia is both a mouthful and a lot to get used to. Thanks for having me on, and for this opportunity to address the people of Cascadia."

"Well, we weren't given much choice. Let me just get right to it. Mr. Black, although the civil war has been a challenge militarily and economically for the entire United States, so far, California has been lucky in that it has been less affected than other states. Now that you and your allies have turned this into a rebel state, haven't you brought the war down on us?"

"Great question, Ms. Welch. It's simple. While the leadership of Cascadia abhors the tactics of General Jonathan Vogel's military dictatorship in Atlantica, he was at least correct when he said the United States no longer exists. That's just the sad reality of the situation. An active military officer is serving as vice president, and how much influence he has over the president is unknown. What is also unknown, at least by the majority of the Cascadian public, is that the United States's recent movement of troops, Defense Department civilians, their families, weapons, vehicles, and equipment from all US bases to the area around NORAD in Colorado was a larger military movement than was necessary for even World War II. But this was not just a reallocation of military assets. This was also an effort to hoard civilian supplies. Food and water was confiscated. Industrial equipment was requisitioned. They're trying to build a new capital in Colorado with enough power to control us all by force, and that is something that the people of Cascadia will never be part of. It is something we must all resist.

"Before the war, California was the fifteenth-largest economy in the whole world — not in the United States, but the world. The leaders on the Interim Legislative Council and I didn't want to see our hard work and economy taken from us. So we worked with the California National Guard and other loyalist military forces here and in Oregon to break free from this sham of a government that calls itself the United States of America."

"But now more than ever, shouldn't we be supporting our country, trying to help it through this difficult time?"

"Maybe it's just time for the United States to dissolve. We had a good run. Sadly, it ended in unbelievable tragedy. I wish it hadn't. But maybe this idea of one giant nation spanning most of the continent is an outdated concept from another century. We can stop pretending that people in Idaho have to live the same way as people in Los Angeles. Over half of American marriages end in divorce, a statistic, a reality that we've become rather comfortable with in recent decades. The breakup of the United States is simply another kind of divorce, and it's up to President Griffith — and more likely Vice President General Charles Jacobsen — to decide if this will be an amicable divorce. Hopefully, the other countries in the Pan American territory can accept this so that we can end this war. •⌁

⌁• You're watching United States Television. USTV. Hope for a united America. Coming to you from our new state-of-the-art studio in beautiful Colorado Springs, our nation's capital, I'm Peter Bronson. For at least some time looking forward, USTV will be broadcasting over the airwaves and Internet twenty-four hours a day, seven days a week, to bring you the information you need, to help you as you struggle through the devastation caused by this rebellion and terrible war. Joining us today, is Cindy Kreenan, one of the leaders of the growing Pan American Peace initiative. Cindy, thanks for being on with us today. Now, your organization is demanding a full, immediate, unconditional cease-fire. With the exception of General Vogel's brutal Atlantica and Dakota, almost all the rebel territories are calling for an end to the war. The United States is offering gener-ous terms for the leadership and citizens in rebel territories who might wish to surrender. What makes your organization different? What is Pan American Peace all about?"

"Thanks for having me on, Peter. Our message is very simple. The war must end. Now. It's become difficult to see what we've gained by this war, but it's very clear what we've lost. Millions of our people have died. Unless something is done quickly, millions,

millions *more will die, not just from the fighting, but from malnutrition, disease, and exposure to the elements. We have an all-time record number of homeless and refugee citizens. We're not producing enough food. We're not manufacturing medicine and other essential goods. Our systems for distributing all the goods we do have are collapsing. Our electrical grid is growing increasingly unreliable. Killing more people isn't solving anything. And the United States government is just as guilty as the rebels in this. Its tactics have become more and more brutal, with noncombatant casualties skyrocketing. And I'm sorry if criticizing the US government is in violation of the Unity Act, but this must be said."*

"You make some good points, Cindy. And I'd like to point out to our critics who claim USTV is only a propaganda piece for the United States government that USTV allows and encourages free speech in pursuit of peace and the truth. Now, Cindy, you mention trouble distributing food and medicine. Did you know that United States military personnel have risked their lives by entering disputed territories so that they could deliver thousands of pounds of shelf-stable food, tens of thousands of gallons of water, and •⎯⋏

⋏⎯• *Zoe Guerrero would like her family in Indianapolis to know that the fighting was too bad, she couldn't find you, and she has gone with the Newtons to Greensburg. If you make it there, leave the family code word on a note at the old post office, so Zoe will know how to find you.*

And that's the last of the connection messages the Cliffhanger has for you this evening. As we near the end of this broadcast, the Cliffhanger must be moving on. The voice in the dark, the voice of truth, is coming to you tonight from a hijacked transmitter on

Liberum's growing radio propaganda network. We've got this antenna blasting out hope and the true message of unity, full power. If we cranked it up any more we'd burn out the system. Stay close to your loved ones tonight, my friends. The dawn brings a new chance to make things right. Have hope. Be at peace. I am the Cliffhanger. ●—◠—

ELEVEN

The whole time I'd been working with the people involved in Operation Exodus, Mrs. Pierce and JoBell had been on my case, urging me to do something I really didn't want to do. The night after we talked to Kemp and Crocker about the drone plan, I finally worked up the stomach to do it. I was going to lie to my buddy Cal and use him in our plan to escape.

"Hey, man," I said, joining him on the deck that night. He was laying back on one of his reclining outdoor chairs, watching the stars or something. "Care if I join you?"

Cal didn't even look at me. "Free country."

I sat in the other chair and reclined, trying to act casual, like I didn't feel like throwing up, knowing what I had to do. The stars were bright that night. "The sky has always been pretty awesome above this little town. But I think less lights are on all over. Looks even better now." Cal didn't say anything. "Listen, Cal. I'm sorry. You were right. Jumping your case about the Brotherhood was a dick move." I waited for him to respond, but he just lay there. At least he didn't walk away like he had the last few days. I had to hurry up with this, though, so I didn't lose him. JoBell had drilled me over and over with what to say and how to say it, but I couldn't remember any of that now.

"Cal, that stuff you said about us thinking you were dumb or something."

Cal sighed. "Great. Here it comes."

"No, just listen a second. Cal, you know I wasn't no whiz kid in school. I basically only passed my classes so that I could stay eligible for football. If the girls hadn't let us copy their homework so often, we'd have flunked out. Both of us. Together." It felt good to be telling the truth. "That's how it was always supposed to be. I'd take over the shop from Schmidty. You'd get yourself a construction business going or maybe get a solid gig working for the county. We were supposed to raise our kids here in Freedom Lake. You know, our boys would end up on the same football team and everything."

"That can still happen." Cal's voice wasn't very convincing.

Now for the bullshit. "The other day, I wasn't so much mad at the Brotherhood as I was just tired of the war. I thought that once we'd ended the occupation, I could leave the fight behind and try to get to that future I used to imagine."

Cal finally looked at me. "Yeah, but dude, did you really expect the US to roll over and quit? You gotta be realistic. We can still have the life you talked about, but we gotta win the war first. That's what the Brotherhood is about."

"You weren't in that Fed torture cell, Cal. No sleep. Electric shocks. Waterboarding. Sitting there in my own piss and shit. I wanted to die. Anything to end it. So when Crow said they'd be making me a member of the Brotherhood on graduation day . . . I don't know. I started thinking that joining the Brotherhood would drag me back into the fight, where I would be running good odds of ending up in a torture cell again. I panicked, I guess." Never mind the fact that I'd wanted to get out of the war before the Fed had even captured me.

"I'm sorry you went through all that," Cal said.

"Well, thanks for coming to get me."

"Wouldn't have left you there, man. Woulda died myself before I let that happen." It was working like JoBell said it would. Playing on his sense of loyalty. Cal sat up in his chair and turned to face me.

"But doesn't what they done to you make you want to kill the US bastards?"

"Maybe." I wasn't sure if that was a lie or not. "But more than anything, I can't go through that kind of hell again. I can't be involved with anything like that. So I was mad at the Brotherhood for trying to pull me back into it all."

"We look out for our own. You wouldn't be captured again. No way."

I remembered part of what JoBell had told me to say. "Thing is, I've been thinking about that. The US is coming for us, whether I want to be in the war or not, whether I'm in the Brotherhood or not. Every single one of us is going to have to fight for our very survival."

A little of that murderous glint showed in Cal's eyes. "We'll be ready for them. We're making our stand at Spokane. We'll kick their asses."

"Right," I said. "So I'm all in with the Brotherhood. I'll give it my best."

Cal's smile was huge. This was exactly what he'd been hoping to hear. "You won't regret it, man. And I was thinking, you know, we find all kinds of tools and stuff on our patrols. We could get your shop all set up again so you'd be in business after the war. It could be as good as new."

If I could ever get the bloodstains washed out of the cement. "I'm glad we're putting this behind us, man," I said.

"Me too." Then Cal slumped a little. "But what about JoBell? Sweeney? They really don't seem to like the Brotherhood."

"They'll come around," I said. "Anyway, it's like I said. The war is coming back. We're all going to have to come together to win it." He seemed to have bought it, because he smiled and nodded. "I'm actually kind of embarrassed to admit this, but when I joined the

176

Army Guard, I went to basic training and the drill sergeants just yelled at me and told me what to do. With the Brotherhood, I'm worried I'll make an ass of myself."

"Naw. Don't worry about it," Cal said. "The guys are cool. Plus, I'll help you out."

Now or never. "You think I could ride along with you sometime in the next few days? Like I could help you with simple Brotherhood duties, even, just to see how things go before they make me a member at graduation?"

"What?" Cal looked skeptical.

"Go ahead and make fun of me," I said. "I'm nervous, okay? If you don't want to help me, fine. Sorry for asking."

"No, I wasn't making fun of you. I was just surprised you were nervous. After all you've dealt with, I thought this would be cake for you. But yeah. No problem." He laughed. "You can take over my position on the wall when I gotta go take a dump!"

I forced a laugh back, feeling terrible for using Cal like this. "Sure. Anything to get the hang of life in the Brotherhood."

"Don't worry it about, buddy," Cal said. "I'll try to get you in on some cool stuff too. This is going to be great. You'll see."

Several hours later, I had the guard shift at the house, so I sat in the dark living room, watching the street out the window. In another ten minutes, I'd have to do a patrol of the house. It was usually a lonely duty, but that night JoBell stayed up with me.

"I know it was tough, lying to Cal, but you had to do it," JoBell said. "We have to find where they're keeping the fuel."

"I know. I know. But the thing is, I meant those things I said to Cal. I don't have any real brothers. Him and Sweeney are it."

JoBell squeezed my hand. "And TJ?"

"Eh. He's a friend."

"That's an improvement," she said.

"It made me feel dead inside, tricking him like that."

JoBell's soft fingers found my cheek in the dark, and she leaned in to kiss me. "Maybe we can still convince him to come with us." We kissed again.

I held her close to me. "I couldn't get through any of this without you," I whispered. "I got nothing without you."

The lights flipped on, and we spun around to find Cal standing in the doorway to the kitchen.

"I thought you were on guard duty tonight," JoBell said.

Cal smiled. "Sorry to interrupt you lovebirds, but Danny, if you were serious about starting to get a feel for Brotherhood life, I could use your help."

JoBell sneaked me a knowing look, and a few minutes later, I was riding shotgun in Cal's truck.

"The place we're going is Brotherhood only," Cal said. "No outsiders are supposed to know where it is, but since graduation is this weekend and you'll be one of us, I figured, what the hell?"

"Well, thanks for bringing me along," I said.

"Yeah, no problem. Crow himself tapped me for this supply run. Why he wants the stuff on this list in the middle of the night, I have no idea, but orders is orders. And it's good to have you here, because rule number one, you know?"

"Crow sent you on this mission alone?" I asked.

Cal shrugged. "Said he wanted it kept a secret, but I can trust you, right?"

"Right." I sank down in my seat a little. Cal stopped the truck to talk to the guards on the north side of town. A moment later, we were driving off into the early morning dark.

* * *

About an hour later, I was still fighting to remember everything I could about the route we were on. Cal was driving us up a narrow gravel road, and he finally started to slow down as he rounded a curve and a gate came into view. The chain-link fence was at least twelve feet tall with a coil of concertina wire around the top. Floodlights popped on as we rolled to a stop, and in seconds, the truck was surrounded by four men with rifles drawn on us.

"Cal?" I asked.

"This is normal," Cal said. "Every vehicle gets stopped like this." He rolled his window down and held a paper out to the man pointing a shotgun at his face. "Nathan Crow sent me to pick up supplies."

The man examined the paper, and then blasted a flashlight in my face. "Who's this?"

"That's Danny Wright." Cal sounded like he couldn't believe the guy didn't know. "His induction ceremony is this weekend. I needed someone to cover me while I made the run."

The man clicked off the light and lowered his weapon. "It's an honor to meet you, Mr. Wright," he said. He offered the salute the Brotherhood had stolen from the day my mom died. "My name's Alex. I got a brand-new baby boy that me and my wife just named Danny after you."

I returned the salute and made myself smile. "The honor's all mine."

"Crow called us about this load," Alex said. "It's all ready for you on a pallet by the office trailer."

The floodlights switched off and the gate rolled to the side. Cal saluted and drove ahead. The place was simple enough. To the right of a big open field were three giant aluminum machine sheds, probably where the Brotherhood kept all the stuff they'd stolen or salvaged. About a hundred yards to the left of the sheds was a trailer house with a tall radio antenna out front, just like Sergeant Crocker had said. I spotted a US Army HEMTT, a Heavy Expanded Mobility Tactical Truck, thirty yards beyond the sheds. "That the Brotherhood's fuel truck?"

"That's what keeps us running!" Cal parked the truck by the trailer. A chunky man came out onto the little wooden steps and saluted. We returned the salute. Cal dropped his truck's tailgate. "Help me with this?"

The pallet held a big coil of rope, some canned food and boxed pasta, and a couple duffel bags. It was light enough for us to carry the whole thing to the bed of Cal's truck. We covered it with a tarp and used bungee cords to secure it all.

"You can sleep if you want to," Cal said, issuing the Brotherhood salute as we left the compound.

I couldn't, though. I had to stay awake to make sure I understood the route to the compound. Cal had just shown me how to get my people out of town and away from the Brotherhood.

Back in Freedom Lake, Cal parked in a garage the Brotherhood had built after they set up their headquarters in the old cop shop on Main Street. It was a proper dock, where we pulled up next to a high concrete platform. Stacks of pallets and a bunch of fifty-gallon drums cluttered the whole place. "Great." Cal yawned as he shut off his engine. "Where the hell are the guys? We can't just leave this stuff in here." He flopped back in his seat and looked over at me. "Come on."

"Maybe I should just stay here," I said. "The less Brotherhood guys see me, the better."

"Don't worry about the guys. Everybody's excited you're joining us. It's cool."

I followed him out of the garage, squeezing my rifle and hoping Cal was right about the Brotherhood being cool with me being there.

After a quick check of the yard inside the HESCO barrier wall got us nowhere, Cal turned back. "There must be someone inside."

"This the stuff to fix the burned kid?" a man said, back in the garage.

Cal stopped around the corner, out of sight. He looked at me, confused. "Burned kid?" he whispered.

"No," came another voice. "It's for that Chinese teacher. Ex-teacher, I mean."

Cal frowned and held his hands palm up in front of him like, *What the hell?*

"You're both wrong." Crow's voice came from inside the garage. "This is for someone else. And I'll knock you both out if I hear you talking about this stuff just anywhere. That's inner circle only. Brotherhood captains and higher. Where's Riccon?"

Cal started ahead, but I held him back for a moment. "Don't go in yet," I whispered. "Don't let them think we were listening right out here."

"It's no big deal," Cal whispered back. "Who knows what they were talking about? Probably nothing."

He didn't sound convinced. "Okay, let's go," I said. "Be cool."

Cal nodded and led the way into the garage. "Hey, Nathan. We were looking for someone to check this load in."

Nathan Crow stared down at us from the platform. Jake Rickingson and another man I didn't know were with him. Crow smiled. "Danny Wright. Didn't expect to see you here."

"Cal's kind of showing me the ropes before my induction this weekend," I said. "Besides, someone's got to keep him from falling asleep at the wheel."

He laughed. "Well, thanks for the help. You all set for graduation?"

I'd felt bad lying to Cal earlier, but I had no problem playing this asshole. "You bet. I even found a tie, and I think I can fit into my old suit jacket."

"Fantastic." He motioned for the two men with him to get the load from the truck. "Well, thanks for making the supply run. Sorry about the late notice."

"No problem," Cal said flatly.

I snapped to attention and offered Crow my best Brotherhood salute, squeezing my left fist so tight over my head that my arm shook. Cal did the same, and Crow returned the salute.

Minutes later, we were safely outside the compound, driving back to Cal's.

"What do you think that meant, 'fix the burned kid'?" I asked.

Cal shrugged, refusing to look at me. "I don't know. Maybe there's medicine in the duffel bags for some patient? Maybe even for Sweeney."

The guys hadn't sounded all nice and helpful. "And the 'Chinese teacher'?" There was only one Asian teacher in Freedom Lake, and he wasn't Chinese.

"Dunno, man." Cal gripped his steering wheel hard. "Could be anything. Something on that pallet that some teacher needs? You gotta remember that the Brotherhood are helping out a lot of people all over northern Idaho."

Something was wrong, and Cal knew it. Still, I didn't want to push him too hard, or he'd push back. "You don't think they were talking about Sweeney and Shiratori, do you?"

"What?" Cal said. "No. I mean, maybe. I don't know. It could be stuff they need in Spokane. Like I said, big territory."

We'd reached his house, but he stopped in the driveway. "You're not pulling in?"

"You go ahead," Cal said. "I'm going to go for a little drive."

"Alone? It's after three in the morning."

He slapped his armband. "I'll be fine. Seriously, go get some sleep."

"Rule number —"

"Enough with the rules!" Cal shouted. "This ain't the occupation! The Brotherhood has things under control. I'm one of them. I'll be fine."

"Okay, man." I climbed down out of his truck. "Be care —"

He leaned across to shut my door and was backing out of the driveway a second later. Something bad was about to go down.

CHAPTER
TWELVE

"I hope Cal's okay," I said the next morning, as me, JoBell, and Sweeney walked toward High School Hospital, where Sweeney had an appointment with Doc Strauss. Cal hadn't come home last night, and I'd told the others about what had gone down.

" 'Course he's okay," Sweeney grunted as he limped along, leaning on his cane. "It's the 'burned kid' you should be more worried about."

JoBell put her hand on Sweeney's good shoulder. "We're always worried about you. That's why we make you keep going to these doctor's appointments even when you think you don't need to." Sweeney had been fighting through the pain, forcing himself to move around a lot more. He didn't have a huge choice in the matter, with the Brotherhood hogging all the meds, but now I think he was putting up with the pain in part to get back to his old confident self, and in part to privately say "go to hell" to the Brotherhood.

I heard a vehicle coming down the street behind us. I wouldn't have noticed that before the war, but these days, the streets were mostly empty, and the only people driving in town were the Brotherhood. I grabbed the handgrip on my slung M4.

Cal pulled up in his pickup, and we all relaxed. His window was down. "Hey," he said. He looked like hell, greasy hair and dark circles under his eyes. He wouldn't look at us. "Hey, could you guys get in? I need your help with something, and I can get y'all wherever you're going."

Sweeney lifted his cane like he was saluting or toasting. "Thanks, but we're good. It's a nice morning, and I need to get used to getting places on my own anyway."

"Please," Cal said quietly. "Please. I need your help."

JoBell went to his truck first. "What's wrong?"

"Come on," he said. "Can you hurry?"

We climbed into the truck. I rode shotgun with Sweeney behind me and JoBell behind Cal. Cal's hands shook as he shifted into drive and headed down the road.

"Have you been up all night?" I asked. "Did you get any sleep?"

"I couldn't stop thinking about what those guys said last night," Cal said to me. He seemed to notice the others, and added, "Did you . . . ?"

"I told them," I said.

"Well, it's probably nothing, but I got to thinking that maybe they *were* talking about Mr. Shiratori. Maybe they were worried about people trying to hurt Coach because of the Fed traitor stuff. So I parked in the alley behind Coach's house and did patrols around his place a few times through the night, just to be sure he was safe. Everything seemed fine."

"Then what do you need us for?" Sweeney asked.

"I want you to come talk to him with me," Cal said. "Help me convince him to watch out for —"

"Oh no," JoBell said. "No."

Cal hammered the gas and we flew down the street. A second later, I saw what they'd spotted.

Two bodies hung from a tree in the Martinezes' front yard.

"No, no, *no!*" Cal screamed. The truck hit the curb and we bounced up into the yard, shooting right by the tree. Cal hit the brakes, slammed the truck in reverse, and backed the truck's bed under the bodies. "Help me!" He opened his door to jump out.

"Cal, stop the truck!" Sweeney yelled.

Cal stomped on the brake, shifted to park, and was out. I hurried right behind him. He dropped his truck's tailgate and was up in seconds. With an arm around each body, he pushed up with his legs, trying to get the pressure off their necks. "Help me, damn it!" he shouted.

But I could see we were too late. Whole clumps of Mrs. Martinez's hair had been yanked out, creating bald patches on her scalp. The rope cut into her swollen, red-purple, stretched-out neck. Like Mr. Martinez, her eyes bulged. Her lips were blue. Both of them had notes pinned to their chests, hateful words scrawled in red crayon.

FED TRAITERS!

I put my arms around Mrs. Martinez's cold, stiff body. "Cal! Your sword! Cut 'em down!"

"Damn it!" He jumped up on the wall of his truck bed and drew his blade.

"Where's Jaclyn!?" JoBell shouted.

Sweeney caught up to us. "Danny?"

I looked at him and shook my head. "Pull security! Jo, find Jackie!"

"I'll check the house!" She ran toward the Martinezes' front door.

"Wait. Rule number one!" Sweeney followed her.

"Right," I said. "Go!"

Mrs. Martinez dropped into my arms, her dead weight surprising me. I laid her down clumsily in the truck bed.

"Get the rope off her neck!" Cal yelled.

I grabbed Jaclyn's dad. "Cut him down first!"

Cal sliced the rope in one big slash. I thought I was ready, but Mr. Martinez was heavy, and I fell, landing on Mrs. Martinez with her husband on top of me. The truck shook as Cal jumped down to the bed. "Come on! Help me."

I freed myself from the corpses as Cal fought to loosen the tight noose around Jackie's dad's neck. I rolled to my knees next to my friend and put my hand on his big shoulder. "Cal."

"Help me, damn it!" He shook me off so hard, I almost fell down.

"What's going — oh no." Mr. Shiratori stood behind the tailgate.

Cal groaned something between a human scream and an animal roar. I couldn't tell if his fingers were bleeding from clawing at the rope or if it was Mr. Martinez's blood.

"Cal, we're too late," I said.

Mr. Shiratori joined us in the back of the truck. He put his hands on Cal's shoulders. "Cal. Cal?" He let go of Cal and stood up straight. "Riccon!"

Cal finally gave up, his body shaking as he hung his head. "Yes, Coach."

I put my arms around him and leaned down, trying to get him to see me. "Buddy, you did all you could. You did everything — we were just too late."

"Those bastards," Mr. Shiratori said.

It was quiet then, except for Cal's sniffles. Then I looked up to see Jaclyn shaking, staring wide-eyed at the horror in Cal's truck.

JoBell and Sweeney came back out of the Martinez house. "Danny, we can't find —" JoBell started. "Oh, Jackie." She ran toward her friend.

But Jaclyn was too fast. She threw herself onto the back of the pickup, clawing and kicking her legs like mad to get closer to her parents. "Mama!" she gasped. "Papa!"

I reached for her, but took an accidental elbow to the face. Like Cal had done, she tried pulling at the ropes. "They're not breathing!" She pressed her mouth to her mother's cold lips and blew. She tried again. "Please!" she grunted as she pushed on her mother's chest. "No! No! No!" Her screams faded into whispers as she ran out of breath.

Mr. Shiratori pulled her back. "Jaclyn."

Cal sat against the wall of his truck bed, hugging his knees to his chest like a little kid, crying. JoBell joined us on the truck, putting her arms around Jaclyn, who screamed until she was out of breath, gasped for air, and screamed again. Jaclyn's parents had been murdered, hung by a red ski rope with blue flecks — the very rope that me and Cal had hauled to town last night. I met Cal's horrified eyes. He knew who was behind this.

Minutes later, Jake Rickingson pulled up in a new-looking Jeep Wrangler four-by-four. He hurried out of his vehicle with his hand on his belt-holstered .45. "What's going on here?"

"Jaclyn's parents were murdered!" Sweeney shouted.

Rickingson frowned at him. "Damn it. This is why all of us have to be on guard. We have people who would sell us out to the US, and others who want to play vigilante and take the law into their own hands."

"You're the ones —" Sweeney started.

"Shut up, Eric!" JoBell yelled at him.

"Come on. You're not buying —"

"No, Sweeney," I said. "Really, shut up."

Mr. Rickingson climbed up on the truck and looked down at the bodies, shaking his head. "Everybody's emotional at a time like this. I can understand that. Thanks for helping here, PFC Wright." He patted my shoulder. Then he frowned and acted like he was surprised to find the crayon-scrawled note. He held it up to show it to all of us. "This accusation is very serious. I'm going to need to search the house for evidence of cooperation with the United States." Jaclyn had dropped limp in JoBell's arms, tears and snot running down her face. "Riccon, you done good here, getting them down and all. I'll take over the investigation. Why don't you walk on home and rest?"

Cal rose to his feet, standing on the bed of his truck, his shoulders heaving like a rodeo bull. He grasped the hilt of his sword and pulled it out a few inches, but I took his hand and pushed it down.

"Easy, buddy," I whispered. I moved in front of him so he'd have to see me. "Hey. Hey, look at me." His panicked eyes finally locked on to me. "It's done. We gotta help Jackie now."

Jake Rickingson hadn't noticed Cal getting all pissed. He climbed down from the truck. "Riccon, after I search the house, I'll need to borrow your truck to take them back to headquarters and look for clues about who did this."

"No!" Jaclyn screamed. "You're not taking them, you bastard!" She launched herself after Rickingson, who had reached the Martinezes' front door, but me and Coach grabbed her. "Let me go! Let me go! They killed my parents!"

Rickingson put on a sad face. "She's out of her mind with grief. It's understandable."

"We'll take care of her," JoBell said.

"Yeah." I forced myself to be cool. "Thanks for helping, Mr. Rickingson."

"She shouldn't be alone," Mr. Shiratori said.

"You live right down the street?" Rickingson asked him. "I'd like to talk to you about what happened here."

Mr. Shiratori frowned. "What are you talking —"

"Coach," I said loudly. "Why don't we all go to Cal's house? Your family could come too." No way was I going to leave Coach and his family alone and unprotected. I had to let the Brotherhood know that they'd have to go through me to get to Mr. Shiratori. Jake Rickingson watched us from the front door of Jaclyn's house. Time for more of that acting I'd been doing lately. "Mr. Rickingson, you should get some backup. If the killers are still nearby, they may come after you."

"That's a good idea." Rickingson grinned. "You're a good man, Wright. It'll be good to have you as one of us."

I smiled as I gave the Brotherhood salute, and Rickingson returned it. I'm not gonna lie. It took everything in me not to rip his damned arms off.

When Rickingson had gone inside, I let out a breath of relief, then grabbed Cal by his shirt and whispered, "Get your shit together, buddy. We need your help. Get Jaclyn back to your house. Carry her if you have to."

"Don't you get it?" Cal started. "The rope they used. It's the stuff we brought. . . . Oh shit, Danny. This is all my —"

"Cal, honey, I know this is tough." JoBell had left Jaclyn sitting on the pickup's tailgate, Sweeney's arms wrapped around her. "But he's right. Jaclyn barely knows what's happening right now. We need to get her safely to your house."

Cal nodded. He started trying to claw off his Brotherhood armband, but I stopped him, watching the house. Rickingson might be looking out the window. "Cal, no. Whatever happens, you have to act like you're still a proud member of the Brotherhood of the White Eagle. Didn't you say you'd do anything to help your friends?"

He kind of gasped his words. "I will. I always will."

"Then act like you're still cool with the Brotherhood, and get everyone back to your house, to your basement, right away. I'm going to Coach's house first. Then we'll meet you there." Mr. Shiratori looked like he was about to argue, but I cut him off. "Trust me. Everybody, trust me."

The war had given me plenty to hate about myself, and after Jaclyn's parents were murdered, I recognized something else that made me a shitty guy. I was sad, pissed off that Mr. and Mrs. Martinez had been killed, but after we left their bodies back there with Jake Rickingson, I came alive, like someone had thrown a switch. It was hard to explain. Maybe I'd become addicted to the adrenaline. Maybe it was that prepping for risky combat ops, or being in the firefight itself, kept me busy, so I didn't have time to sit around thinking about all the terrible things I'd done.

At Coach's house, he stormed into his dining room and dumped a bunch of papers from a cardboard box onto the floor. Then he pulled these old-looking cups out of a glass china cabinet and stuffed them in the box. "Why doesn't anyone study history?" he whispered. "Why doesn't anyone listen? It's all happening again." He dropped the box on the dining room table and looked up, wide-eyed. "Kelsey? Kelsey!?"

His wife came running down the stairs. "Michio, what's the matter?"

"Where's Emma?"

"She *was* taking a nap. What's going on?" She finally saw me. "What's he doing here?"

"Pack up all our suitcases. We need all the clothes, blankets, and food we can take with us."

"Tell me what happened," she said.

"Coach," I tried.

"Just do it! Now! We're leaving now!" Coach was shaking. "They killed Carlos and Rosa! Lynched them."

Mrs. Shiratori gasped and put her hands over her mouth. "Oh no."

"I saved a full tank of gas in the minivan," Coach said. "We're leaving."

"Listen to me!" I shouted. "You go on your own, the Brotherhood will stop you, and with no witnesses around, outside of town . . ." I let the thought trail off. He understood. "We have a plan. A bunch of us are leaving town together."

He shook his head. "No. No. They told me about that. You people think you'll have better luck getting out of town in buses and everything than I will in my one little van? You're asking for a firefight you can't win."

"I really think I can sneak us out of here." I told Mr. and Mrs. Shiratori my plan. Now that Cal was on our side, we had an even better shot at getting our hands on enough fuel. "If it does come down to a fight, me and my guys can hold off the Brotherhood long enough for the civilians to escape." I could hear someone walking around upstairs and lowered my voice so his daughter wouldn't hear. "Coach, I was with Cal last night, and we heard Rickingson talking about plans for attacking your family. If you try to go alone, you'll all be killed. Come with us. That way, you'll at least have a chance."

Mrs. Shiratori put her hands on Coach's shoulders and spoke very quietly to him. Finally, he nodded. "Okay. Okay. But when do we leave?"

"Oh, we're not waiting around anymore," I said. "I'm putting out the go call tonight."

When the Shiratoris had packed clothes and blankets in one suitcase and grabbed all the food in their house, we went back to Cal's. JoBell met me at the door. She'd been standing guard with her dad's rifle. "We've been trying to calm Jaclyn and Cal since we got back," she said as we led the Shiratori family down to the basement. Becca showed little Emma Shiratori the pinball machine while Coach and Mrs. Shiratori whispered together.

I kissed my fiancée. "He still blames himself?"

JoBell bit her lip for a moment. "The rope used to hang them was the same —"

"I know. Red with blue flecks." I rubbed my aching left hand. "I had no idea they'd go after the Martinezes. No idea they'd go this far."

"It's a good thing Jackie was at Caitlyn's last night," said JoBell.

Becca joined us. "Sweeney is with Jaclyn. TJ's with Cal. We figured they shouldn't be alone. So far, we've kept Cal from telling Jackie too much about what happened."

"It's not like he knew what they were going to use that stuff for," I said. "If we had any clue that the Martinezes were being targeted . . ."

"Right, Danny," Becca said in her old, soft voice. "But nobody's thinking straight at a time like this."

"Well, this is it. There's no doubt anymore," I said. "The Brotherhood is killing people, whoever pisses them off or isn't white. Shiratori and Sweeney are next on their list. We can't wait around. We're launching the op tonight."

"You sure you don't want to wait until the US attacks Spokane?" JoBell asked. "We could use that distraction."

"In three days, the Brotherhood is going to make me one of them, and then who knows what they'll have me doing? I don't want to get stuck in a position where Crow's sending me on some crazy Brotherhood mission and I can't help with Operation Exodus. And Cal's really shaken up. You know he won't be able to keep his anger bottled for long. If the Brotherhood notices, they'll watch him more carefully, and then he won't be able to help us get that fuel. We're out of time. We have to make our move before we lose our chance."

Becca nodded, and I clasped my hand on her shoulder. "You, Sweeney, and TJ will tell Mrs. Pierce to give the go call. I'll get the fuel thing figured out with Cal."

Moments later, me and JoBell sent TJ with Becca and Sweeney and joined Cal in his bedroom. The room was at least four times the size of his bedroom in the trailer where he grew up, but he'd set it up a lot like his old place, with an old, tattered poster of Thor from the third Avengers movie. Thor had been his role model when he started lifting weights. "Gonna be big as Thor. Big as Thor," he'd say before a bench press. A plastic model of an F-35 jet was on his dresser, next to some trophies that each of us got for flag football in like the fourth grade. Another wall was covered with his huge collection of Freedom Lake Minutemen football and volleyball posters.

Cal sat on the edge of the bed in the middle of it all, sniffling with his eyes all red. When he saw me, he broke into sobs again. "Oh shit, you guys. Oh shit. It's my fault."

JoBell sat next to him and wrapped him in a big hug. "Cal, honey, you couldn't have known what they were going to do with the rope."

"JoBell's right. And if you hadn't gone to get that stuff, someone else would have," I said. "But I gotta talk to you, man. I need you to get your shit together and listen." I didn't want to be hard on him when he was hurting like this, but we were out of time. "You want to help Jackie now, and me, and a whole bunch of other people? A bunch of us have a plan for dealing with the Brotherhood." I picked up the armband he'd thrown on the floor and shook it in front of him. "Are you in?"

"Anything." He choked. "I'll do anything."

"Good," I said. "Put this damned armband back on. We're

leaving town to go someplace safe. Until we get there, you keep this on and pretend like you're a good little Brotherhood trooper."

Cal frowned. "That's it?"

"No. The Brotherhood hit us hard today. Tonight we're gonna hit 'em back."

THIRTEEN

Cal gripped the steering wheel furiously as he drove us up the long and winding road through the dark woods. "I know this is supposed to be a quick, easy mission, Danny," he said. "And a lot of guys have been pulled from warehouse guard duty to prep for the fight in Spokane. But I ain't complaining if these assholes decide they want a fight."

"This isn't a battle, Cal. You'll drive in there like you're still cool with the Brotherhood, just like you did last night, just like we got past that patrol when we left town. You'll explain that they need the fuel truck in Spokane, and your friends came along to drive your pickup back. That's all."

"Don't misunderstand me," Sergeant Crocker said from the seat behind me. "I wholeheartedly hope we can avoid a fight, but if it comes to that, at least we have our little insurance policy in the back of the truck."

Crocker was talking about JoBell and Becca, who were hiding under a tarp. JoBell carried Specialist Danning's Barrett 82A1 .50-caliber rifle. We'd found a hell of a scope for that beast of a gun, and with it, JoBell could shred any target before he even saw her. Becca had an M240B machine gun with plenty of 7.62 rounds.

"But we're not gonna . . . I mean, like you said, this is kind of a sneak in, sneak out situation, right?" Skylar Grenke's dad sat hunched over his shotgun, his chin resting on the end of the barrel like an idiot.

I jerked a thumb back toward him. "Mr. Grenke, you want to be sure you practice muzzle discipline."

"Oh. Right." He sat up. "Sorry."

What was he saying sorry to me for? It would be his own head blown off if the gun accidentally fired. We hadn't wanted to bring Grenke along. Skylar was kind of a jackwad, and it was looking to be a like-son-like-father-type situation here. But Tabitha Pierce had made us bring him. "You and your friends need to start getting used to the fact that you're not in this alone anymore," she'd said to me.

The weird thing wasn't that we were working with people outside our group. It was that adults were listening to me. I was used to getting bossed around by adults. In the Army, the older guys had all clearly outranked me.

Working with Operation Exodus was different. Not only did the older people hear me out on my ideas about different parts of the mission, but some of them took orders from me or treated me like I had authority, even though compared to them, I was just a kid. The war had turned everything upside down.

I squeezed the barrel of JoBell's father's Springfield M1A Scout Squad rifle. Mr. Grenke here was going to obey my orders, or he'd end up getting us killed.

"Here we go," Cal said as we approached the compound. Like a bizarre flashback to last night, the lights came on and the truck was surrounded by gunmen again.

"Cal?" Crocker asked worriedly.

"What do we do? What do we do?" Mr. Grenke sounded like he was about to freak out.

"We don't panic," I said. "We act like everything's cool. Here we go. You got this, Cal."

"Right," Cal said. "Everybody calm the hell down."

"Come on, buddy," I said. "Sell it."

Cal nodded and got out of the pickup with his hands up. "Hey. I need your help. We gotta hurry."

The men eased up on their rifles. "Cal?" a big, bearded man said. "Nobody is scheduled for a supply run tonight. Who's in the truck with you?"

"Nathan Crow sent me here to get the fuel truck. We gotta gas up a bunch of vehicles in Spokane for the battle. He couldn't spare none of our brothers, so I brought some civilian friends to drive my pickup back. I gotta move fast. That fight's gonna go hot any minute now."

"We're going to have to call that in," said the guy with the beard. "Our comms haven't been working. Damned US Army jamming us up. We got a radio, though." He motioned to someone at the gatehouse, and the chain-link barrier in front of us rolled to the side. "Stop in at the office to get the key to unlock the fuel truck's steering wheel."

"I got bolt cutters!" Cal shouted as he climbed back into the truck. "I'll find a new chain for it later. We need to move." He shut the door, threw the truck in drive, and sped up the gravel lane. "The radio antenna is about a hundred yards from the fuel truck," he said to Crocker.

"Roger that," Crocker said. "After you cut the chain on the steering wheel, I'll take the bolt cutters. It's only a matter of cutting one cable."

"I'll go with you," I said.

"I can handle it," said Crocker.

"Rule number one," I said. "Nobody goes alone."

The pickup slid to a halt beside the big, dark green M978 HEMTT fuel truck. There had to be thousands of gallons of diesel in that trailer. Cal left his pickup motor running, and we all hurried out. All of us but Mr. Grenke.

"And, um . . . What do you want me to do?" Mr. Grenke asked.

"Right," I said. "Can you sit here and guard the pickup?"

The man gave this big nod. "Yep. Absolutely. Should I aim the gun or . . ."

He was still talking when I left. Cal was up in the fuel truck cab in seconds. "Here!" He threw down the bolt cutters and, seconds later, a heavy chain and padlock.

I caught the bolt cutters and sprinted after Crocker, who hadn't waited for me. "It would help . . . if we had more light," Crocker said when we reached the heavy-duty antenna. It was so tall that it had to be held up by a bunch of support wires. Behind us, the fuel truck started up, and we heard its air brakes pop-wheeze. Crocker found a thick cable at the base of the antenna tower. "This one right" — sparks burst from a wire and Crocker jumped back — "here. That should do it. Their radio is useless now. They won't be able to transmit or re —"

"Come on!" I yanked him by the arm and ran back toward Cal's truck. We couldn't waste time talking. The Brotherhood could figure out what we were up to any second, and Operation Exodus was set to launch, with or without us, in an hour and a half. It had already taken us forever to get up here. We'd have to really gun it on the way back. "What are you doing?!" I yelled at Mr. Grenke, who was out of the truck walking around, holding his rifle up all weird. "Get in the truck!" When we reached the pickup, I patted the wall of the truck bed. "We're all good," I said to the girls. "Hang in there." I jumped in the driver's seat.

Seconds later, I was following Cal in the fuel truck as we drove down the lane toward the front gate. My heart thudded heavily, and an electric current ran through every sense I had. All along the bumpy road, I checked my mirrors — side, rear, side — over and over, watching to see if they'd figured us out.

Cal's HEMTT stopped at the closed gate. "What the hell? Why aren't they letting him through?" I said.

"Oh no." Mr. Grenke rocked back and forth in his seat. "This is bad. This is so bad."

"We could be in trouble," Crocker said.

"From the 'no shit' department." I drove the pickup off the road and pulled up to the driver's side of Cal's cab. The four Brotherhood guys were back out with their rifles ready again.

Cal leaned out his window and smacked his hand on the outside of the metal door. "Open the gate! Crow needs this fuel!"

"Just hold on a second," Big Beard said. "The guys in the office called down here on the field phone and said they're having trouble with the radio. They can't call to check on any of this. So why don't you and your friends get out of your vehicles and set for a spell over here in the guard shack?"

There were four of them. While Big Beard was talking, the other three drew beads on Cal, me, and Crocker. If they got us into the guard shack, we were screwed. Eventually one of them would figure to go check the antenna. They'd discover the sabotage, and then it'd be all over.

"Come on, Brother," Cal said. "We really need to get to Spokane. Our people got the biggest fight of the war coming up, and you're worried about a busted radio?"

"I'm not kidding," Big Beard said. "Shut off your motors and get the hell out of your vehicles." ·

There was no way out of this. We'd have to play their game for now. I put the truck in park and killed the engine.

"Hey, you guys think this machine gun makes me look fat?" Becca's voice came from behind the cab. The guys looked up for a second before the M240B roared into them. Big Beard's skull split just below his eye. Another guy folded in half at the crotch as the red-hot streak of a tracer round sliced his groin. At least three rounds shredded the third man's chest. The guy on the far right held his hands over his gut an instant before his shoulder and throat turned to pink mist.

I was out of the pickup by then. I leaned over the hood and aimed at the two guys in the gatehouse. One made it out the door of the shack, but I dropped him with two rounds to the chest. The other I blasted right through the window. He left a red smear as his body slid down the back wall.

An even louder shot came from behind me, and I ducked for a second before I saw JoBell firing clear up the hill toward the trailer in the distance. "This night vision scope is perfect," she said calmly. She shot again in the same direction. I had no idea who she was aiming at way out there in the dark. "Damn. Stop moving, bastard." She fired another round, then slowly swept the area through the rifle's scope. She shot twice more, and that time we heard someone scream. She fired again to finish him. Then she brought the rifle back, I guess to check the office trailer up the road. "Okay, that's everybody in range! Let's roll out!"

That's when I noticed a row of three pickup trucks a few yards back from the gatehouse. "Jo, rifle!" I held out my hands, and she tossed the heavy weapon down to me.

"Here." She threw me a second magazine.

I ran to the first pickup, crouching to aim the .50-cal rifle straight at the grille. I fired twice for good measure, the rounds tearing huge holes through the radiator and into the engine block. While Cal opened the gate, I reloaded and moved to each truck down the line. If anyone was still alive in this compound, they wouldn't be following us in those trucks until they got new engines.

JoBell met me back in front of Cal's pickup. "You be careful." She kissed me warm and deep. "I hate missing the op."

"You're not missing it. You're protecting Cal and the fuel." It didn't make sense to draw more attention to ourselves by driving the HEMTT into Freedom Lake. Instead, Cal, Jo, and Mr. Grenke would take it south, away from town, and wait for our convoy. "When you get to the rendezvous point, keep that vehicle out of sight and stay on guard." I glanced over my shoulder. "Oh, and try to look after Mr. Grenke. He's kind of helpless with all this. We'll join you soon."

We kissed again. "I love you," JoBell said.

"I love you more," I said.

"Mr. Grenke," I said. "You're going with Cal and JoBell. Guard that gas." Mr. Grenke was shaking, but he made his way toward the fuel truck. "You'll be fine," I said to him.

He stopped and wiped the sweat from his brow as he passed me. "What the hell happened to you kids? Becca mowed those guys down like it was just an average day. You shot the guys in the gatehouse. JoBell Linder, you were taking out guys like some kind of sniper. What have you all become?"

"Come on!" Becca shouted out the window from behind the wheel of Cal's pickup. I was grateful for her impatience. I didn't like thinking about the answer to his question. After squeezing JoBell's hand, I ran to the passenger seat of Cal's truck. JoBell took the big .50-cal rifle and followed Mr. Grenke into the fuel truck with Cal.

"Don't worry, Wright. She'll be okay," Crocker said from the seat behind me as we rolled out of the Brotherhood compound toward the dangerous mission ahead.

Back in Freedom Lake, everything moved very quickly. Tabitha Pierce, Brad Robinson's dad, Aimee Hartling's first stepdad, and Dr. Nicole were waiting for us at Cal's, as expected. Sweeney and TJ had mounted all the guns on Pale Horse. With .50-cal machine guns on both sides and a .50-cal in the rotating turret on top of the ambulance module, Pale Horse would lead the way in getting a hundred people out of town and away from the Brotherhood.

"Here you go, Eric." Becca handed over her machine gun so Sweeney could mount it in the back door. "Test fired it for you already."

"I'm glad you're okay." Sweeney took the weapon. "I was worried about you."

"Don't worry about me," Becca said. "Worry about the Brotherhood. They better stay out of our way tonight."

"How did it go?" Mrs. Pierce asked.

"We ran into a little hiccup," I said. "We took care of it."

"Anyone hurt?" Dr. Nicole said.

I shook my head. Mrs. Pierce looked at me for a moment and then nodded. "Let's hope that's the last hiccup for a while. Sergeant Crocker?"

Crocker just about snapped to attention. "Yes, ma'am?"

"You better send the signal."

Crocker went to the ASIP III radio we'd installed in Pale Horse. The other two secure radios that Crocker had encrypted to our network were on board the two school buses. The only radio contact we'd have with Becca's dad's pickup and Mr. Hooper's RV would be through little Motorolas. There wasn't much range on those, so we'd need to stay together. Crocker held down the transmit button on the ASIP handset and on a Motorola. "All calling stations. All calling stations. This is Pale Horse. Phase one complete. I say again. Phase one complete. All stations, sit rep. Over."

"*Bus one is ready. Standing by,*" Mr Morgan radioed.

"*Bus two. Standing by,*" said Mr. Macer.

"*Camper is okay,*" said Mr. Hooper in his RV.

"Horse race is ready." Mr. Wells had his pickup and horse trailer ready to drive down this crappy dirt road on the east side of town, where he would pick up Becca, Kemp, and TJ, who would be riding bicycles. They were going to plant the diversion on the south side of town, then sneak away quietly, without the sound of an engine to draw attention down on them. Before the diversion could launch, Becca and TJ had to get down there to join Kemp.

Crocker radioed. "Phase two is go in . . ." He looked at Becca, who held up both hands, fingers spread. "Ten minutes. How copy? Over."

After a moment, Mr. Morgan's voice came back. *"Um, ten four. Bus one understands."*

Crocker smiled. "Got a bunch of truckers on the other radio." The others chimed in the same way.

"They might not be familiar with Army radio lingo, but they've been planning for this op a long time. They'll do their jobs." Mrs. Pierce turned to Becca. "I wish I could talk you out of this."

"That's what I was saying," Sweeney said.

"Not a chance." Becca held up her M4. She wore six full mags in different pockets of a fishing vest. "I've been waiting for this for a long time too. Don't worry. Sergeant Kemp has a ton of C4 charges set up. If the Brotherhood comes after us, they'll be torn up by a bunch of homemade shrapnel bombs."

"But we could send grown men to launch this diversion," Mrs. Pierce said.

"Old guys with less than half the combat experience I have, less than a quarter of my speed?" Becca said. "I'm doing this."

"I'll look after her, guys," TJ said.

"Bullshit. I'll look after you," Becca said. "Let's go. We're late."

Sweeney grabbed her and pulled her close so fast that Becca's rifle slipped down to the crook of her elbow. It was about as smooth and sure as I'd seen him move since he'd been burned, and he kissed Becca warm and deep.

Crocker looked up from where he'd been dinking around near the Humvee. "Hey, guys, the drone is all set up on the roof, ready to deploy. When it's time — oh." He froze as he saw Becca and Sweeney still kissing. Me and TJ looked at each other. At the floor. The ceiling. Dr. Nicole laughed softly. Mrs. Pierce coughed.

Finally, the two of them parted. Becca looked at Sweeney wide-eyed and openmouthed.

"I love you," Sweeney said. "I mean that. It's never been like this before. I love you."

"Okay," Becca gasped. She ran her fingers back through her hair and licked her lips. Then her expression hardened. "Right. Let's go set our people free."

Becca and TJ pedaled away on bikes. TJ had a Motorola. He'd signal before his team — code named United States — launched their distraction attack.

Mrs. Pierce checked her watch. "The distraction team is getting ready." She spoke quietly, as if checking things off a mental list. "Mr. Wells is in position to pick them up when it's over. The infirmary is set up in the RV. Everyone's at the school's bus barn, loaded up and ready."

"I hope nobody saw them heading over there and started wondering what was going on," Mr. Robinson said.

"Dwight, that is exactly what we don't need to hear. They'll radio if there's trouble, and then we'll be over there in a few minutes." She pointed at Pale Horse. "Look at this thing! Armored and with four machine guns? And we're up against a bunch of thugs in pickups and beater cars. Now, let's go. Stations, everyone."

Tabitha Pierce did not mess around. I'm not gonna lie. She was scarier than a bunch of my drill sergeants back at basic training.

We all climbed into Pale Horse. Mr. Robinson had the .50-cal on the back driver's side. Dr. Nicole was on the .50 opposite him. She shook her head as she sat down and took hold of the gun's handgrips. "I'm a veterinarian who spends most of her time fixing up people, and now I'm on machine gun duty."

"It's a jacked-up world," Sweeney said.

Darren Hartling had volunteered to take the .50-cal turret. Sweeney would cover our six on the M240. I climbed into the driver's seat, with Sergeant Crocker riding shotgun so he could work the radio and the drone when the time came. Mrs. Pierce took her place on the bench next to the door hatch between the ambulance module and the cab.

Then we waited. The heavy, hot air dripped with tension.

A beep and short static pop went off on our Motorola network. I reached for the start button, figuring it was TJ letting us know they were about to begin the diversion. Instead, Chaplain Carmichael's voice came on. *"How about a word of prayer? Lord, Heavenly Father, we ask you to please look out for each and every one of us tonight. We pray for your protection, your guidance in our ultimate pursuit of peace . . ."*

"What does he think he's doing?" I said. "That's not a secure radio. If any Brotherhood guys have their radios on that channel, they'll —"

"He's comforting scared people." Mrs. Pierce's sharp voice cut in behind me. "We have folks with us who are older than me, we have babies who aren't even a year old, and we have dozens of terrified people in between. Let the chaplain help them. Meantime, bow your head and pray so you don't annoy God and botch this whole thing."

She had a point there. I closed my eyes and bowed my head, leaning over the steering wheel.

"In the name of the Father, and of the Son, and of the Holy Spirit. Amen."

"Amen," I said quietly with the others, adding silently to myself, *Lord, please forgive us for what we are about to do.*

"This is the United States." TJ's voice came on the net with his code phrase. *"The attack on Freedom Lake begins. Now."*

An explosion sounded from across town, just like we planned — a loud-as-hell C4 charge inside a can of kerosene, sending up a mushroom cloud of fire. Gunshots rang out, and I turned around in my seat to try to see Sweeney, but it was too dark back there. I was sure he was worried about Becca too, the way I worried about JoBell.

I pressed the power button on Pale Horse. The yellow "wait" light came on while the vehicle readied itself to start. Shouts and more gunshots sounded from far away. "Come on. Come on," I whispered. The light went off. I punched the start button and Pale Horse roared to life. Crocker hit the door opener to let us out of the garage, and we were off. Since I wore my night vision glasses, I left my headlights off as we flew down the empty street.

I rounded the corner and continued on for a few more blocks. Soon enough, coming up on my left was the church me and Becca had gone to since we were kids, the place where I always thought JoBell and me would get married. "It would have been so great," I said quietly. Now we were leaving town. Maybe forever.

"What are you doing, Wright!?" Mrs. Pierce yelled. "Speed up!"

I slapped my own face. No time to be thinking of stuff like that. "Mission first," I whispered to myself as I stepped on the gas.

The buses had to drive about four blocks east and another five north, until we reached the edge of town near the gap in the wall. If everything went according to plan, we would link up with them at the turn. Another explosion rocked the distance. And another. Tons of gunfire.

"There they are," I said as the corner came into view. We hooked a right to pull in front of the two buses, with the RV between them.

Crocker turned on his comm. "Hartling," he shouted toward the back. "Flip that switch in the center of the top of the drone, and then get away from its propellers."

A few seconds later, we heard a quiet buzz above us, and Crocker tapped and swiped at his comm. The glow from the screen made his face look even more pale as he bit his lip. "Didn't have a chance to test this. The controls are harder than I thought, but the drone is away."

"You gotta time it perfect," I said. "Keep them guessing. Don't give them time to react."

"I know," he said.

"We're like three blocks away. You want to hurry and —"

"Shut up, Private! It's not easy. I'm trying to get it back down toward the . . . They've spotted it. Two guards left. One has a radio."

Shots rang out from up ahead.

"They hit the drone!" Crocker said. "One of the rotors is messed up."

"Sergeant," I said, "if they see us coming, they'll call us in, and then our cover is blown."

"I know!"

"Just fly it down there and —"

"Wright, let him do his job!" Mrs. Pierce yelled. "You can do it, Sergeant."

"A pickup has pulled up behind bus two. Are we expecting company?" someone said on the radio. *"They got a rifle pointed at us out the passenger window, motioning us to pull over."*

"Oh shit!" I pulled to the side and hit the brakes. "Ready on the guns. Nobody in that pickup survives! Crocker, do your thing." I grabbed the handset for the ASIP. "All stations, this is Pale Horse. Pull past us. Whatever happens, you do not stop. You roll on to the meeting point. Pale Horse out."

"And I looked!" Sweeney shouted the verses we'd learned years ago in Sunday school, the verses my truck was named for. "And behold a pale horse!"

We bumped up the curb into someone's yard as the first bus and the RV passed.

"And his name that sat on him was death," I said. The second bus zipped by.

"Gun ain't going!" Mr. Hartling yelled.

"Or maybe not," I said.

About six shots went off as the pickup passed us. Mr. Hartling screamed. I hit the gas and came up behind the pickup.

Mr. Hartling yelled. "Aw, damn it!" he groaned. "I'm hit!"

"Doc, you stay on your gun," I yelled back. Besides the turret, we had no forward guns, and Hartling was hurt. We'd never go fast enough in this heavy thing to pass that pickup and get them with the side guns.

"I'm a nurse!" Mrs. Pierce yelled. "I'll take care of Hartling. Eric, get him down out of that turret."

"Hurry, Sweeney!" I keyed the radio mike. "Bus two. Slow down. Now!" The bus's brake lights flared red, then the Brotherhood's lights lit up. "Ready on the gun, Doc!" I passed the pickup on its left and Dr. Nicole let loose with at least twenty rounds. Their whole cab was torn apart, and the pickup rolled off the road and hit a tree.

"I need bandages," Mrs. Pierce said calmly. "Eric, give me your shirt. They got him right in the shoulder and I can't find an exit wound."

"I brought extra bandages," Sweeney said.

I wished I could see what was going on back there. Wished I could help. I could hear Mr. Hartling, breathing heavily through clenched teeth. The convoy was ahead of us. The lead bus would roll into plain view of the northern wall in just about two blocks.

A panicked voice came over the Motorola. *"We got a wounded baby here! Portia Keelin! Doc Randall, we need you!"*

"Stop the vehicles," Dr. Nicole shouted. "Let me out. I gotta go help."

"We have to keep moving," I yelled. "We have to get out of town before the Brotherhood stops us, or this whole thing falls apart."

A big explosion rocked the air ahead of us. "Got 'em!" Crocker shut off and stowed his comm. "The guards and the drone were just shredded by shrapnel. Just when I was getting the hang of flying that thing too." He radioed on the ASIP to tell the convoy the gap was clear.

I radioed back with Crocker's Motorola. "Which bus for the wounded kid?"

"Second."

We were off-roading as we rolled out of Freedom Lake, bumping over the uneven ground. Hartling cried out in pain from being knocked around. Without Dr. Nicole, we would be down two gunners. And stopping this close to the wall was a bad idea.

"Please! She's bleeding all over! We need Doc Randall!"

"Stop the convoy!" Dr. Nicole yelled.

Mrs. Pierce leaned into the cab and grabbed both the Motorola and ASIP radios. "This is Pierce. Hit the gas. We have to get out of here before we're spotted. Nobody stops! It's too dangerous."

A bunch of frantic radio traffic came back, screaming for help.

"Mrs. Pierce?" I asked.

"Drive, Danny! When we get over that hill up there, *only* bus two and us will stop," Mrs. Pierce said. "Nicole, get to the back door. Get ready to run up there as soon as we stop. No time to move anyone to the RV. You'll have to use the med kits on the bus and work on the move." After a two-minute eternity, we cleared the hill that would hide us from view of the town. Pierce radioed, "Bus two, stop now. Everybody else, keep moving!"

When we stopped, the back door opened and then shut, and I watched Dr. Nicole sprint ahead. When she was up in the bus, we took off again.

"Mr. Hartling," said Mrs. Pierce. "The bad news is, that shoulder is going to hurt like hell, and to be honest, you'll probably be dealing with chronic shoulder pain for the rest of your life. The good news is, I've stopped the bleeding, and you, sir, are going to live."

"What happened on the gun?" I called to the back.

"Just a mistake," Sweeney said. "I checked it. The safety was still on. I'll cover the turret."

The safety. Unbelievable. We'd gone over and over the guns a dozen times while we prepped for this mission. Now Mr. Hartling and a baby were shot, and we were down two gunners, all because the guy couldn't remember to flick a switch.

"We can't have any more screwups like that," I said. "We're lucky that it wasn't worse back there. None of that shit should have —"

"Enough, Wright," Mrs. Pierce said. "Things happen in war that none of our training prepares us for. We adapt and move on. You're not helping anyone by throwing a fit."

"It's my left shoulder," Mr. Hartling said. "I can run the passenger side fifty-cal back here."

When we reached North Priest River Drive, the convoy turned south. Hopefully, anyone who saw us leaving town would keep heading north searching for us. I passed the buses so Pale Horse could lead the way in case there was trouble. We weren't due to stop for at least another hour, when we'd meet up with Cal, JoBell, and Mr. Grenke in our fuel truck.

"*I, um . . . don't know how to use this radio right.*" Dr. Nicole's voice came over the Motorola. "*Calling Pale Horse. Portia Keelin is dead. I did everything I could. Too much blood loss. I'm so sorry.*"

My hands slid down either side of the steering wheel a little. The whole point of all this was to get people to safety. How safe were we? How safe were we gonna be? I didn't trust myself to say anything with all that pissed-off rage boiling up inside me, with the sadness and regret crushing me down.

Crocker finally radioed back. "Bus two, this is Pale Horse." He licked his lips. "Roger that. We're sorry for the loss." He let go of the transmit button. "What do we do? Stop to bury the child? Take the body with us and bury her at the Alice Marshall School when we finally get there?"

"That could take days," I said. "That body won't be . . ."

"Give me that radio." Mrs. Pierce reached out her hand to Crocker, who passed her the handset. She keyed the mike. "This is Tabitha Pierce." Her voice was a little rough, but she spoke with confidence, reminding me a little of First Sergeant Herbokowitz. "We've suffered a terrible, heartbreaking loss. All our thoughts and prayers are with Portia's family, especially with you, Cora Keelin. I know nothing I can say now will help dull the pain of this tragedy, but when we planned to leave Freedom Lake, we committed our lives to one another and to our shared, brighter future. Now we are traveling on the first part of that dangerous journey, our journey to escape war and oppression. It's up to all of us now to come together, to draw strength from one another, so that little Portia's death will not be in vain, and so we can protect all of our people still with us." She paused for a moment. "We're radio silence except for emergencies and official business from here on out. We will not stop until we've reached the rendezvous point with our fuel truck. Pale Horse, out."

I hit the steering wheel as we drove on through the dark. "Another one dead, and we could have stopped it. She's not going to be the last. What good is breaking free from the Brotherhood if we're all dead?"

"We're not all dead," Sweeney said from the back.

Mr. Robinson spoke in a deep, kind voice. "And if we'd stayed in Freedom Lake, the Brotherhood would have eventually got to Jaclyn Martinez, the Shiratori family, and even Eric Sweeney here. They'd run all our lives."

"Right." I kind of laughed. "So you're saying it's a bargain price. One dies so we can save five?"

"I wouldn't put it exactly that way, but —"

"I'm sick of having to make these kinds of exchanges. I'm tired of choosing who gets to live and who dies." I slowed down and swerved into the other lane to avoid a big hole in the road. "I wish I would have died at Boise."

There was a little silence, then Mrs. Pierce spoke. "I was twenty-three years old when I went to Vietnam as a nurse. I had barely been out of Idaho. The only time I'd left the US was for a couple fishing trips in Canada. During my nursing training, I imagined what it would be like over there. I knew it was a war, so I tried to mentally prepare myself for treating bullet wounds. Cuts. But I never could have imagined the things I saw in Vietnam.

"I was stationed at the 312th Evacuation Hospital in Chu Lai, right in the thick of things, so of course we treated American soldiers, but we also had a Vietnamese ward. This one boy came in burned up so bad, I couldn't tell if he was one of ours or one of theirs. He was so young, so small, but somehow that boy had the strength to hang on for over a week. When he died, I didn't think I could handle much more. My friend Sharon Lane, a fellow nurse who came in country with me, helped me stay strong and focus on our duty of helping whoever came through our unit. A couple weeks later, she was killed by a rocket attack."

Mrs. Pierce was quiet for a moment. "That was over fifty years ago. I still wonder why I got to live and go home, but she died. Sometimes I can still hear that burned boy's cries, or the cries of hundreds of others just like him. Sometimes my dreams are shaken by the roar of the rocket that killed Sharon."

She put her hand on my shoulder, and I jumped a little. "We don't get to go back, boys. Not completely. But in time, we can figure out how to . . . put some of those old memories away. We can develop ways of avoiding thoughts or situations that pull us back to the nightmares of our past. I know it doesn't seem like it now, but you hang in there. It is possible. We're going to get through this."

We drove on, reeking of blood, sweat, and death, into the morning.

FOURTEEN

Sergeant Crocker monitored Brotherhood radio bands for as long as we were in range. At first there was a lot of chatter and confusion about a US attack. They tried calling for reinforcements from Brotherhood units that had been deployed to prepare for the Battle of Spokane, but there were none to spare. Then they radioed, looking for Cal. Then for me. Then they found that pickup we'd shot up, and someone who'd seen our convoy must have ratted us out, because they put out a call looking for two school buses and a large RV. There was a lot of stuff about "US collaborators" and "shoot on sight." After a while, we were deep into mountainous terrain, and we began to lose the signal.

I silently thanked God that the Brotherhood didn't figure out something was up until we were south of Coeur d'Alene. We bumped our way east along torn up I-90, then headed south along the east side of Lake Coeur d'Alene on Highway 97. That road was sometimes right up by the lake, and a few times, we had to slow way the hell down at places where half of the road or more had collapsed into the water. It reminded me of the Abandoned Highway of Love back in Freedom Lake.

Farther south, the land bridge over the Harrison Slough was bombed out, so we had to take a huge detour all the way around Thompson Lake, including some time on some pretty shaky trail-type roads. Finally we got back on Highway 97 and headed south onto Highway 3. As we neared the town of St. Maries, we started trying to reach Cal on the radio. When he finally answered, he sounded down, worn out, sad, but he said they were okay.

The fuel truck pulled out from behind an aluminum maintenance shed where Cal had been hiding east of town, and as we'd planned, we followed the signs to the local golf course. The course looked like it hadn't been kept up since the war started, and the whole thing was beyond rough. We drove our convoy right onto the back fairway, where we'd be hidden away, surrounded by trees. As a precaution, we parked our vehicles like walls around a space about the size of a base-ball infield.

Even before all the engines had been shut off, people were scrambling out of the vehicles. They jumped from the rear emergency exit on the buses and ran down the steps up front. Men and women hurried to the trees to relieve themselves. Some came off the buses crying. Others looked pissed. Everyone was all-out fried and exhausted.

A warning buzzed at the back of my mind. We didn't know who was out here or how the locals would react to a big convoy rolling through their area, and tons of our people were stepping out into the woods, breaking rules one and two. But in that crowd of frightened families, there was only one person I wanted to see. I'd worried about JoBell all night, even fantasizing about her shouting my name and running into my arms as soon as she saw me.

Instead, I saw her first. She was leaning against the cab on the fuel truck, her rifle propped up next to her, hugging herself as if she was cold as she stared off into space. When I finally reached her through the crowd of people, she kind of fell into my arms with a groan.

I kissed the top of her head as she rested on my chest. "You need some sleep. We all do." She started shaking with sobs. "Hey. Hey. JoBell. We're okay. We're going to make it. We're together."

Cal joined us. "We had kind of a rough time getting here, Danny."

By instinct, my hand slid off JoBell's back, headed for my rifle. "Are you guys okay? The fuel?"

Cal shook his head. "It ain't that."

"Grenke?"

"He's fine." JoBell stood up straight and wiped her eyes. "He's useless, but fine. We passed this house fire on the way. The building was a total loss, but Cal slowed down to see if we could help. Out front like six assholes with guns were dragging this family through the yard, all laughing. Drinking. The mother's shirt was ripped off. She was screaming. Cal and I were getting ready to take them out, but Mr. Grenke threw a fit, saying how our orders were to get the fuel truck to St. Maries without stopping."

Cal kicked a weed. "We tried to convince him that we had to do something, that the three of us could take the assholes out quick, firing from up on the road. He wouldn't go for it. He freaked out."

"Cal and I weren't sure the two of us could take out all six of them. We worried they'd overtake us. Take our truck." JoBell started crying again. "And so many people are depending on the fuel."

"You did what you had to do," I said.

"I'm so tired of making these kinds of decisions," JoBell cried. It was the same thing I'd said on the drive here.

"You made the right choice." I hated the words as I said them, but they were true. "Better to save this whole convoy, even if it meant, you know." Why couldn't I believe people when they said these kinds of things to me?

"It's like I'm a scale that has to keep so many lives in balance," JoBell said. "They shot the father as we drove by."

Sergeant Kemp found us. "This is a security nightmare. Everybody going all over, and we don't even have a head count. Anyone could get picked off. We'd never know until it was too late."

"It looks like the old lady's way ahead of you." Cal pointed to the middle of the crowd, where Mrs. Pierce was pulling aside different people and giving them instructions. Others she was motioning to sit down or take a knee around her. She was setting up a meeting.

"Sergeant Kemp," she called out as the crowd gathered and started to quiet down. "You're the ranking soldier. Would you please organize an armed party to form up a security perimeter? Keep it tight, close to the buses, so you all can hear."

Kemp moved toward the center of the camp, looking more like a pirate than a wounded man thanks to the black leather eye patch Dr. Nicole had found for him. Me, Cal, Sweeney, Becca, JoBell, and TJ were first in line for guard duty, but when Crocker volunteered, Kemp told him, "Sorry, Sergeant. You know what you gotta do. Monitor that radio. Try to stay awake, buddy." Finally, enough guys volunteered or were voluntold by Kemp to stand guard, and we had a solid perimeter.

"Well done, everyone," Mrs. Pierce said. "I know it's been a long night, a tough night, but we've stuck together and made it this far. All indications suggest the Brotherhood doesn't know where we are. Now we —"

"But that could change any time." Mr. Keelin had his arms around his daughter, Cora, who held a blanket-wrapped bundle that must have been the body of her daughter. "We need to fuel up and move on. We won't be safe until we get to the school."

Mrs. Pierce looked at him sadly. "We all need to rest. If there's trouble, we won't handle it very well if we're exhausted. Sleep the best you can through the day. We'll roll out at sunset."

"But won't we draw more attention to ourselves driving around at night?" said Mr. Grenke. "Everybody will be able to see our headlights."

"I think we got enough night vision glasses," I called out. "We could drive with the lights off. Go full blackout. We'd probably have to slow down a lot, though."

Kemp nodded his agreement.

"I'm with Keelin," Mr. Grenke said. "Let's leave now. We have to keep moving."

"We're much more likely to be spotted in broad daylight," Mr. Shiratori said. "Yeah, people might see our headlights moving through the dark at night, but a lot more people will be asleep then, and we have a better chance of getting by unnoticed." He was sitting next to his family and Jaclyn Martinez. Jackie must have cried herself to exhaustion. She looked like she was almost in a coma now, and she let Mrs. Shiratori hold her.

"We gotta stick to the plan," said Brad Robinson's mom.

"The plan?" Mr. Keelin pointed to his dead granddaughter. "Is this part of the plan?"

"We should also take this time to mourn our loss and lay the child to rest," said Chaplain Carmichael. "I'd be honored to conduct a funeral service if —"

"I'm not leaving her!" Cora Keelin held her dead daughter tighter. The baby's feet had come out of the blanket and dangled beneath her.

"Well, we can't take her on the bus," said Tucker Blake's grandmother.

"Easy for you to say!" Mrs. Keelin fired back. "When your grandson was killed, you had the comfort of knowing his body was in a proper grave. Now you want us to just dump baby Portia out here?"

"We can dig a good grave," said Cal's old boss, Lee Brooks.

"No!" said Mr. Keelin. "We are taking her to the school, and we are taking her now! We've got a map on the bus. I say we just go. Who's with me?"

"I'll go. We could be like an advance party," said Mr. Grenke.

"We are absolutely not splitting up!" Mrs. Pierce yelled. "That is not an option! We'll take the girl's body with us and bury her at the school, but first we will wait here until dark."

"So you're just going to decide everything now, Tabitha?" Mr. Grenke said. The guy looked like he was ready to fight, his arms all back and his hands in fists. Skylar put his hand on his dad's elbow, but Mr. Grenke wouldn't stop. "This is exactly the kind of shit we all risked our lives trying to get away from. You're worse than Nathan Crow!"

We hadn't even been on our own together for a day and already we were falling apart. I was the one who had made sure we left so suddenly after Jaclyn's parents were hung. I had to do something. "Shut up, Mr. Grenke!" I said.

"No! You don't get to talk to him like that," said Mrs. Keelin. "This isn't all going to be run by a kid."

"I know!" I had to shout to be heard. "It's going to be run by Tabitha Pierce! I've got the firepower to back her up, and I've got a lot of people with me, people who've been fighting and living on the run like this a hell of a lot longer than any of you. So, cut that 'kid' shit. I'm eighteen, and I know what I'm doing."

"It won't be a dictatorship," Mrs. Pierce said.

"Respectfully, Tabitha," said Mr. Shiratori, "that's what a lot of dictators say. I agree with your strategy, and I'm with you. But I can't blame these people for being scared. They're being threatened with machine gun persuasion." He pointed at Pale Horse.

"Coach, it ain't like that. I only —"

"They're being told to obey the biggest guns," Shiratori continued. "A situation that we have *all* risked our lives to escape. How do we know that it won't always be like this?"

"We will elect a council," Mrs. Pierce said. "We will have a democracy. I promise."

This was all kinds of jacked up. We were basically on a military operation, out here in a war zone, trying to keep a bunch of civilians safe, and there was barely any chain of command. Maybe it would be better if we got to the Alice Marshall School faster. Or maybe the key was to make sure we had one solid commander in charge. Right then, my bet was on Mrs. Pierce.

"If we stay together," Mrs. Pierce said, "we have a chance, a good chance, of making sure that little Portia is the last among us to die from this war. Becca Wells once told me the three rules she and other Idaho soldiers lived by during the occupation. Rule number one: Nobody goes alone. That means you can't go running off in the woods without someone with you, even to go to the bathroom. More than that, it means we're all in this together. Rule two: Nobody goes unarmed. Always have your weapon with you. We don't have enough guns to go around, so we're making sure our best shooters are packing. If you don't have a gun, always be with someone who does, and always carry some kind of a weapon. A knife. A stick. Whatever you can find. It's too dangerous out here with no protection. Rule number three: Always post a guard. If two people are working on something, a third person should be standing by with a gun, watching for trouble. Do those rules make sense?" People nodded. "Toby Keelin? Ryan Grenke? Everyone? Are you still with us?"

Mrs. Pierce had everyone's attention now, so she continued. "I promise you that I'm not just bossing people around because I enjoy being in charge. If we split up, eventually we'd be out of radio range. If either group broke down or was attacked, the other would have no way of knowing. If we lost a big portion of our group, we'd lose physical resources as well as people we'll need to help us at Alice Marshall. The school's location might be compromised. We stay together, okay? For now, we live by the three rules."

Gradually everyone agreed. People settled in wherever they could to try to sleep, and some food went around, cold hot dogs and other stuff that we had packed in coolers that wouldn't last long. Cora Keelin was convinced to put her dead little girl into one of the empty coolers for the ride to the Alice Marshall School. It looked like we'd made it through our first big crisis, but I still caught a pissed-off look from Mr. Grenke.

Since nobody went alone, all guards worked in pairs. Kemp picked the teams himself, which was how me and Sweeney ended up on guard duty together, hanging out on top of Pale Horse. From there I could get a pretty good look over the buses to watch the perimeter of our camp. I didn't have to stay standing the whole time, but I stood a lot anyway to stay awake. Sweeney leaned with his back against the roof hatch on the .50-cal turret. If any big trouble showed up, we were supposed to charge in with Pale Horse.

Sweeney slapped his own face and sucked in a deep breath. "I hope Kemp finds someone to relieve us soon."

I looked over to a group of people asleep by the first bus. I vaguely realized Sweeney was still talking. "What?"

"I've never been so tired in my life."

"This ain't nothing," I said.

"Right. The torture. I forgot."

I wished I could.

"The roads were really jacked up," Sweeney said. "I guess I was kind of out of it on the way from Boise to Freedom Lake, so I didn't notice it so much. This was the first time I got to see things with a clear head. It's pretty bad."

I didn't know what to say to that. I sat down on the front of the ambulance module and let my legs dangle down over the hood.

Sweeney went on, "I haven't heard anything from my mom or dad in a week. If the roads are even half as bad in other parts of the country as they are here, it could take them forever to make it home. And if there's no gas . . . I know they left Florida, but I don't know if they made it out of the southeast before it became Atlantica. They're probably trying to get through a hotter war zone than we're in."

When I heard a sniffle and saw him wipe his eyes, I did the kindest thing a guy can do for another dude in that situation. I pretended I didn't notice. "They'll be okay," I said instead. "Your parents are two of the smartest people I know. They'll find someplace safe."

We were relieved of duty a few hours later. I don't even know who took over for me. I was so tired, I was seeing things that weren't there. It was a perfectly beautiful spring day, and I found a spot in the shade by the buses next to JoBell. I cleared my weapon before lying down to sleep with my fiancée, my friends, and all our guns.

I jerked awake sometime later after hearing Cora Keelin's screams again. I was on my hands and knees reaching for my weapon before I realized how calm the camp was. There had been no screaming. Nobody rushing around. I hung my head. Another bad dream. That's how life was now. When I needed to stay awake and do important stuff, I could hardly keep my eyes open. But whenever I had time to sleep, too many thoughts shot through my head. And always the damned nightmares. I crashed again, praying for oblivion.

After sleeping on and off for a few hours, I finally gave up and staggered in the midday sun toward the center of camp, where someone had put out some cases of bottled water. How old did this stuff have to be? Since the occupation, not much bottled water had been shipped into Idaho. I twisted off the cap and downed the water in seconds.

Brad Robinson joined me. "Hey, Wright." He motioned around the camp. "This is pretty crazy, huh? I mean, we're all homeless now. Kind of outlaws with the Brotherhood after us."

"The Brotherhood isn't the law," I said. "And if what Mrs. Pierce says about this school is true, we won't be homeless for long."

"My family's been hanging out with Crystal's family. She always had a pain-in-the-ass curfew of eleven. But now . . ."

I smiled. "You get to be with her all the time."

Brad looked around to make sure nobody else was close enough to hear. He spoke quietly. "Yeah, but it's no hot date. Her little brother and sister are scared shitless, you know? Micah tries to act tough, but I can tell he's freaked. So I've been trying to cheer the two of them up, telling Micah football stories, asking Mara about the book she brought along." Brad took a deep breath. "I don't know if I'm doing any good. How can I help them when I'm probably more scared than they are?"

I put my hand on his shoulder. "Brad Robinson, you are one of the most badass guys I know. If we could have finished our football season, we'd have been state champions. You were that good of a center."

"Yeah, but Wright, that was just a game. Kid stuff."

"You remember that crowd of reporters and pissed-off people after that game at Bonners Ferry?"

"After the news said you'd been a shooter at the Battle of Boise? Yeah. That was a jacked-up night, man."

"We had to go into a Point After Touchdown formation to bull-doze through that crowd to get to the bus. You were all, 'Nobody gets between us.' All business. No fear."

"Are you kidding? When that crazy redheaded bastard with the gun showed up, I about shit my pants. I was freaking."

"No, but see, that's my point. You were scared inside. Fine. We all were. We are right now. But you didn't let the fear cripple you. Not then. Not in the fight to kick the Fed out of Freedom Lake. Not now. It's a jacked-up world, and shit's probably gonna get bad again. When the time comes, I know we can count on you."

Brad laughed a little. "Damn, Wright, you sound like you're forty or something. What happened to you?"

My eyes stung, and I turned away from him. "The war, man. The war happened to me."

∿—• I don't know if you can hear me with the anti-aircraft machine guns firing all over the city, but I'm standing on the Post Street bridge here in downtown Spokane. Oh! There's another explosion. I'm not sure . . . Kellen, can we get a shot of that? . . . I don't know. I'm going to keep reporting for as long as I can. Jets are everywhere. By the time you hear them, they're past, but they're all shooting at each other or dropping bombs. Another one! That explosion was close. The water is surging downriver! It's like a tidal wave. A tsunami! They must have blown up the dam upstream.

Oh my gosh! Kellen, are you okay!? You're still rolling? There, folks, you see a bomb or missile has hit the Monroe Street bridge. It's collapsing! Two pickups crossing it are plummeting all the way down to the river. We're — I'm coming, Kellen! We're going to keep filming, but we're going to try to find someplace safer, though that may be . . . difficult at a time . . . like this. Spokane is an all-out battlefield.

Kellen! Viewers, that blast you just heard . . . I don't even know if this camera is still working. That blast you just heard was the Post Street bridge exploding. We were off the bridge just in time. My cameraman is hurt. A shard of concrete has sliced his leg and something's hit his head.

It's possible US military forces are trying to destroy all our bridges, to cut the town in half. Take cover, everyone. As the sun sets on our city, we wait to see what will remain at dawn. Liz Asher, KHQ News, Spokane. •—∿

∿—• Welcome back to the WGN Network, Liberum's Very Own, broadcasting from our newsroom in our new nation's capital here in Chicago. I'm Robert Bell.

Liberum military forces are in the middle of a tough fight. United States Marines dispatched from Kentucky have fought their way across the Ohio River and seized Cincinnati and surrounding areas. However, Liberum forces have successfully prevented the US military from advancing any further into Ohio's coal production country, which provides Ohio with almost 70 percent of its electricity.

The Liberum military recently destroyed Government Bridge between Rock Island Arsenal and Davenport, Iowa, along with all other area Mississippi River bridges, in order to prevent invasion by the United States. Rock Island Arsenal on the Mississippi River is the largest government-owned weapons manufacturing facility in Pan America. Anti-aircraft batteries from Naval Station Great Lakes in North Chicago have helped our soldiers maintain control of the island. United States forces in Davenport, Iowa, which planned an amphibious assault across the river, were quickly thrown into disarray when heavy artillery pieces manufactured on the island were used in extensive shelling of the city of Davenport. •⌁

ALABAMA UNIVERSITY CENTER FOR WOMEN ★ ★ ★ ★ ☆

Another casualty of this war: The death of our reproductive rights! The legislature of the Southern Alliance of America has outlawed all abortion procedures. Women in Louisiana, Mississippi, and Alabama no longer have control of their own bodies. We at the AUCW are disgusted by this action, and horrified by the fact that a government so dedicated to killing people in this war can still be so manipulated by the so-called pro-life movement.

★ ★ ☆ ☆ ☆ This Post's Star Average 2.43   [Star Rate] [Comment]   23 minutes ago

REBECCA PATTON ★ ★ ★ ★ ☆

This is sick! Our leaders say this is a war for freedom while they take ours away! And of course, they offer no exemption for victims of rape or incest at a time when sexual assault and even human trafficking is up by probably 500%. I can't believe this is happening.

★ ★ ★ ☆ ☆ This Comment's Star Average 3.25   [Star Rate]   21 minutes ago

SHANNON ROMERO ★ ★ ★ ☆ ☆

Believe it! Your so-called freedom to murder innocent unborn babies is over! Now babies will have the freedom to live! Praise the Lord! Thank God for the SAA government.

★ ★ ☆ ☆ ☆ This Comment's Star Average 2.09   [Star Rate]   11 minutes ago

RON NEAL ★ ★ ★ ☆ ☆

I'm generally opposed to abortion, especially as a means of birth control, and especially later in the pregnancy, but I think Ms. Patton makes some good points. I'd also add that while the war has taken its toll on our medical community, it's possible that there may be more pregnant women whose lives are endangered by their pregnancies. Under the new law, a woman must continue with her pregnancy even if it kills her and her unborn baby. Obviously, our society allows killing: of soldiers in war, of convicts on death row, of dangerous armed criminals on the street. Is it unreasonable to allow the killing of an unborn baby to save the life of the mother? What's missing in the discussion of this law is patience, understanding, and compromise.

★ ★ ★ ★ ☆ This Comment's Star Average 4.00   [Star Rate]   7 minutes ago

REBECCA PATTON ★ ★ ★ ★ ☆

Ron, patience, understanding, and compromise have been in too short supply since the Battle of Boise.

★ ★ ★ ★ ☆ This Comment's Star Average 4.25   [Star Rate]   5 minutes ago

⌁—• *The United States initiated a savage sneak attack on the Keystone Empire early this morning. US ground forces murdered desperate refugees hiding in the irradiated wastelands of New York, New Jersey, and southeast Pennsylvania before attacking buildings, houses, soldiers, and civilians. The assault was widespread and largely indiscriminate, killing thousands before Keystone defenses were able to force the US military back to the coast, where they soon retreated to ships that had been standing by for evacua-*

tion. Keystone Empire President Caroline Craig condemned the attack as an "unnecessary tragedy," repeating her assurance that the Keystone Empire will not engage in an offensive war. Quote, "We are at war with no other nation, but we will defend ourselves if necessary," end quote. Erin Heddleson, Empire News. ●—◊

◊—● After a brave struggle, United States forces have liberated a substantial part of western Texas, only to discover several large mass graves, each filled with an estimated three hundred bodies. Army commanders are investigating to determine who is responsible for these horrendous mass murders, but the diverse nature of the victims makes the determination of a motive very difficult. United States Army Major Carol Lassen."

"I do not believe this kind of killing would have happened before the war, and this is simply another example of why rebel leadership needs to come to their senses and surrender. A lot of the victims were children. It breaks my heart. But it does not diminish my resolve to find those responsible or to continue to liberate Texas from rebels and insurgents."

"USTV. Hope for a united America. ●—◊

◊—● Unfortunately The Last Full Measure blog has been forced to make major changes. Since there are so many different fronts in this war, since there are no longer merely United States military and Idaho combatants, and since the level of civilian casualties has skyrocketed as the result of all this senseless fighting, The Last Full Measure is now tracking all combatant deaths together in one column as well as all civilian casualties in the other. It's important to understand that keeping the death totals up to date is nearly impossible, so the actual number of deaths is much higher. Please *send me a private message to report a confirmed death as a direct result of this war. However, IN ORDER TO REDUCE DUPLICATION, PLEASE SEARCH THE LIST BEFORE SUBMITTING THE NAME OF A CASUALTY!*

CIVILIANS: TOTAL 13,684,952	COMBATANTS: TOTAL 524,869
Raina Washington	PVT Vincent Quinn
Dallas Peterson	LCpL Lance Gregory
Casey Morton	Cpl Dan Walsh
Willa Walker	PV2 Gunner Jefferson
Isaac Marshall	SPC Joanne Burns
Zoey Fowler	Jerrold Albright
Diego Delgado	Pvt Albert Pittman
Arturo Cooper	PVT Carl Guerrero
Leigh Medina	SA Ron Holt
Natalie Nash	Pvt Jason Wright
Kareem Tucker	Reed Beal
Jonah Harvey	Pvt Jess Harmon
Gabe Grant	Florencio Lemieux
Melinda Woo	PO2 Alton Lambert
Gemma Montero	Louie Pippin
Ariel Samuels	PVT Jane Bryan
Sang Altman	Frederick Wakefield
Dean Hunter	SA Garrison Meyer
Lucas Tyler	PVT Shane Woods
Dylan Jenkins	Pvt Don Williamson
Kaleb Brooks	PV2 Rachael Fox
Genevieve Watts	Claude Mendez
Ariana Figueroa	Pvt Gordon Howard
Inez Bell	Gen Trevor Becker
Jaime Herrera	SPC Declan Collier
Philip Higgins	CPO Tasha McCoy
Luke Saunders	Pvt James Hale
Brad West	PFC Doyle Swanson

Winston Pratt	SA Benjy Lewis
Erika Carroll	Pvt Oliver Rowe
Chelsea Fox	SFC Alamo Austin
Ruby Brewer	PVT Peggy Tarver
Lillian Barton	Pvt Hugh Erickson
Charles Sullivan	SA Andre Franklin
Arthur Gibson	PFC Jeff Robbins
Hector Romero	Pvt Willis Matthews
Meaghan Freeman	PVT Laurie Bates
Kate Porter	SFC Michael Webster
Monica Shaw	Pvt Emma Torres
Becky Klein	SFC Dexter Bowman
Anita Reyes	PFC Bernard Garrett
Enrique Lopez	PVT Robert Newton
Jose Carson	SFC Ron Evans
Stuart Blair	LCpl Jaime Williams
Pedro Podesta	PFC Lucy Fernandez
Arjun Sinha	LCpl James Reid
Kayla Peterson	BGen Amy Lynch
Kimberly Joseph	PO1 Carleton Arnold
Georgia Padilla	SCPO Sabrina Hopkins
Mike Thompson	SN Matt Smith
Sook Joon	Cpl Steve Kelly
Richard Gregory	Pvt Heidi Olson
Manuel Mathis	Gabe Ridgeway
Adrienne Mullins	Ethan Reaves
Sadie Harris	SSG Craig Perkins
Rosalie Wolfe	Jon Wiseman
Sara Vaughn	Ahmed Hadad
Clara Wheeler	Cpl Stephanie Richardson
Victoria Butler	Pvt Martin Grace
Ellie Hunter	PO2 Sharon Thornton
Glen Perkins	PVT Anna Robertson
Roberto Lopez	SA Johnny Farmer

Brett Peterson	Melody Pratt
Adrian Jimenez	Hope Evans
Franklin Henderson	Paul Richard
Ling Zhang	PVT Ellen Boyd
Maggie Lewis	SSgt Roxanne Oliver
Evelyn Holland	Nathaniel Murray
Scarlett Walker	Debbie Wilkerson
Gabriella Hernandez	CPO Andrew Huff
Sherry Burke	Heather Blair
Natasha Collier	MajGen Sheila Kinney
Timmy Simmons	PO1 Wilson Keller
Jian Wong	SR Penny Clarke
Marco Santos	PO1 Jerome Drake
Hiroto Takahashi	CPO Will Anderson
Wesley King	SN Luka Hanson
Sophia Holloway	GySgt Marty Boone
Camilla Gutierrez	Rodolfo Martinez
Elana Flores	Howard McBride
Whitney Schuster	CPO Jeff Walker
Shawna Kelley	SA Shizuko Yoshita
Louise George	PO1 Asher Ortega
Daniel McKinney	PVT Sarah Connor
Sean O'Brien	PFC Renée Lamb
Pablo Ramos	PO2 Lana Walton
Ken Hogan	SA Joyce Jacobs
Jose Gomez	Maj Niki Weber
Mia Mendez	Capt Dana Stanley
Chaaya Ganesh	Jaclyn Gregory
Mae Owens	Dot Jensen
Meredith Vargas	SPC Jeffrey DeSilva
Maryanne Scott	SGT Scott Lawson
Catherine Gross	Maj Angie Alvarez
Cristy Rodriguez	Kara Davis
Erin Barnes	Simon Volmar

Claudia McCoy	Kelsey Riley
Carla Lopez	SSG Hayden Russell
Gina Ramirez	Berry Castellano
Hudson Winters	Andreas Lombardi
Evan Fletcher	MG Ben Weber
Preston Neal	PVT Brendan Leonard
Alexis Ortiz	Molly Frazier
Nick Creary-Sher	Lindsay Jones
Alice Estrada	PVT Gavin Spencer
Nora Daniels	SFC Leslie Norman
Sofia Garcia	Marcia Rhodes
Elsa Chapman	Carey Graham
Mei Yamanashi	SFC Edward Perez
Nadia Reeves	PVT Charlie Allen
Stella Park	Pvt Elijah Robbins
Roxy Yates	Rebecca Crawford
Cedric Jones	Sheila Walters
Sid Kearney	Pvt Ken Ellis
Eduardo Zamora	SSG Darrel Bush
Dorian Garland	LCpl John Dawson
Nathaniel Heaton	Pvt Brian Cortez
Richie Fulmer	Russ Patton
Seung Cho	SSgt Edgar Ramsey
Siena Morris	SSG April Walsh
Maria Castillo	Dean Morgan
Melody Griffin	Lisa Parks
Helen Wong	Jasper Clark
Gloria Rodgers	PV2 Allan Phillips
Sabrina Curry	Isabel Morris
Cassandra Harper	Sadie Wagner
Sage Hobbs	SFC Xavier Leonard
Isabel Robertson	PVT Vivian Owens
Camille Chavez	Lydia McDonald
Lynne Stone	Leif Dennis

Eddy Polanco	PFC Don Saunders
Milo Bingham	PVT Andrew Long
Jack Engle	PFC Sylvia Marsh
Tyrell Christopher	Nicole Hill
Molly Summers	Tate Notkin
Tessa Hofman	Alyssa Townsend
Jennifer Barrett	PVT David Hunt
Chris van Houten	SPC Joe Glover
Renata Alvarado	Teresa Moran
Tricia Reed	ADM Tripp Swanson
Olive Hudson	Jack Pierce
Cleo Gardiner	PV2 Paul Santiago
Ashley Richardson	PO1 Vanessa Payne
Kendra Ball	SFC Jeff McBride
Denis Novak	Emile Stevens
Leo Seeley	PVT Neil Griffin
Kathleen Harmon	PV2 Joel Russell
Lauren Elliott	SPC Benjamin Pierce
Julie Martin	PO1 Adrian Anderson
Angelina Thomas	Stuart Vitale
Ciara Halvey	SPC Lucy Scott
Lilian Hendricks	Stefan Rodrigo
Arielle Durant	Len Mattos
Colleen Mayfield	BG Todd Rodgers
Molly Jamison	SSgt Clarence Pratt
Chloe McGee	PV2 Salvador Harris
Thana Lane	Sgt Kelly Goodwin
Nicole Matteson	PFC Dwayne Hines
Darryl Walsh	SrA Gabriel Valdez
Hugh Murray	PO3 Andrea Sanders
Jeff French	Arun Song
Omar Lucas	Abe Dunaway
Jasper Sperry	Sgt Carrie Hubbard
Nikita Rajani	Pvt Sara Smith

Pippa Morley	CAPT Josh Horton
Kirsten Terrio	Rick Morrison
Beatrice Elliot	Sgt Eric Gomez
Sue Oliver	Maj Gen Sherman Leonard
Padma Ganchi	Harry Santos
Faith Stewart	Col Josh Morton
Maurice Ford	Lt Col Neal Barber
Beth Phillips	LCpl Rachel Brown
Jenny Morris	PFC Nicole Wise
Nina Leonard	Fred Lambert
Tina Perry	SSG Mitchell Gonzalez
Diana Lawrence	Winston Thomas
Amy Wright	SFC Adam Wade
Olive Zaubler	A1C Bill Morrison
Miranda Perez	SPC Cameron Moore
Suzanne Terry	Cpl Shaun Jenkins
Shane Ward	Pvt Lance Sharp
Jazmin Weaver	2ndLt Miles Bradley
Dennis Cheng	SN Elisa Smith
Horace Haynes	LG Alejandro Herrera
Luther Scott	Pvt Victor Brooks
Tai Coyle	LCpl Jaime Tucker
Catarina Meade	PVT Morgan Jackson
Marylin Correa	Brig Gen Frank Allen
Devin Corley	PVT Claire Joseph
Marshall Francis	SSG Bill Weaver
Derek Love	MAJ Drew Murray
Maria Summers	Pvt Eddie Ling
Lila Corbett	PFC Jonathan Shaw
Deborah Greene	PO1 Lauren Paul
Booker McCarthy	Pvt Terrance Clayton
Henry Maxwell	Cpl Ivan Sandoval
Joey Diaz	Pvt Dave Fields
Ray Logan	PVT Justin Floyd

George Henry	Everett Carson
Adam McLaughlin	PFC Curtis Osborne
Gary Newton	Cpl Lynn Carlson
Danny Houston	Todd Duncan
Travis Thornton	Darren Adkins
Quincy Gray	PVT Donald Weber
Shannon Fitzgerald	Tyler May
Sean Duncan	SR Cody Benson
Jesus Ruiz	GEN Roosevelt Colbert
Miguel Ortega	SN Gordon Harvey
William Nguyen	Caleb Massey
Clem White	Ruben Farmer
Patrick Mann	MSgt Marcos Mendez
Garrett Williamson	Christopher Fitzsimmons
Adara Betts	Colin Mack
Elane Lemke	Lt Col Amos Holmes
Sharita Groves	Pvt Thomas Fisher
Conrad Nelson	MG Ross Miles
Hector Cobb	SPC Gerald Hudson
Guy Medina	PVT Jess Abbott
Gerard Saunders	Gen Bert Welch
Marcus Cohen	Cpl Noah Osborne
Francisco Valdez	Col Neal O'Leary
Stanton Hill	Maj Irving Burns
Jonathan Mendez	Col Billy Hammond
Zane Hunt	Brig Gen Douglas Reed
Luis Ramos	Sgt Roman Mason
Scott Castillo	SR Teddy Schneider
Derrick Chambers	SA Edwin O'Brien
Esther Mendoza	PO3 Cliff Greer
Becky Straub	SA Ned Wildstein
Michele Ortiz	SR Ryan Armstrong
Sheldon Henderson	Rory Sheehan
Jerry Sims	Zach Treadaway

Noah Holt	Isaiah Root
Darnell Patton	Hua Min
Ben Woods	Elroy Toledo
Miriam Skolnick	SGT Spencer Maldonado
Lindsay Stephens	Capt Peter Carlson
Heather Mitchell	Russel Laughlin
Mary Pilker	Jefferson Schubert
Paul Fisher	SN Maurice Crawford
Alan Lawson	SFC Ally Schmidt
Thomas Moran	Tracy Ingram
Austin Williams	SA Pablo Henry
Jermaine Bridges	PO3 Mark Day
Walter Patterson	Lou Castle
Lora Tate	Emily Keller
Allison Rice	Capt Ambrose Kirk
Jeannette Wagner	Gen Harland Sexton
Carlos Dixon	Megan Alexander
Delaney Moore	Madison McBride
Peter Moss	PO3 Larry Beck
Ron Gordon	SN Joel Chambers
Donald Vaughn	Bethany Newman
Andy Spencer	Grace Kennedy
Jackson Griffith	CPL Zachary Nelson
Steven Black	ADM Jay Myers
Marc Wells	PO1 Justin Cook
Sophie Barnes	SN Sam Simon
Candace Zimmerman	Louise Hopkins
Maisie Watson	Stan Spicer
Samantha Nichols	Sterling Boggs
Paloma Rios	Stephen Moffitt
Julia Young	Tod Dawkins
Lila Kuttenkuler	1SG Gary Fleming
Jaime Schneider	BG Alonzo Burke
Josh Townsend	PO2 Randy Schwartz

Ernesto Peña	Bob Pauley
Corrine McCaskill	Michaela Singleton
Rose Sullivan	SA Adam Bell
Colin Percy	PO1 Jack Bryant
Saul Walton	Trenton Wingate
Julian Olson	Deon Rosado
Allan French	Katherine Ramsey
Charlie Thomas	SN Bryan Harrington
Victor Vega	PO2 Dominic Collins
Chris Ferguson	Audrey Davidson
Anne Edwards	Jamaal Spears
Mona Lyons	SN Randy Adams
Alicia Ballard	SA Ryan Silva
Oscar Wilkerson	PO1 Mohammed Abukwaik
Dwight Arnold	CPO Clint Hughes
Milton Strickland	PO1 Frank Moreno
Lamar Berry	Dion Bourne
Craig Harris	Sheryl Foster
Darren Cook	Heath Quintana
Barbara Clayton	Sebastian McCutcheon
Hyo Kim	Oren Copley
Danielle Brown	CPO Geoffrey Grant
Tracy Knight	MSgt Hank Goodman
Rita Armstrong	PO3 Olivia Hamilton
Jeremy Vasquez	PO1 Phil Tate
Lee Park	CPO Milton Petrocelli
Dominic Cruz	PO1 Tim Jenkins
Nicholas Murphy	Freddy Cantu
John Wheeler	PVT Larry Clayton
Steve Richardson	CPO Lucas Noble
Julia Payne	PO1 Claude Park
Sheryl Ryan	Minnie Coffey
Ella Webb	Lyndon Colburn
Robin Morris	PO1 Craig Sutton

Suzanne Lloyd	RDML Aaron Gardner
Dara Fisher	LT Ron Chambers
Joanna Torres	Harry Aguilar
Austin Larson	CDR Luther Brooks
Jeff Carpenter	Brad Rodriguez
Toby Romero	LT Javier Hernandez
Ernest Buchanan	Pvt Lionel Turner
Jordan Lewis	A1C Damon Willard
Hope Thornton	TSgt Thomas Powers
Monique Sawyer	Christopher Smith
Ann Goodwin	Geraldo Vang
Amalia Tolliver	Barton Bittner
Hazel Miller	Carson Polk
Donna Carson	LT Damion Carnahan
Timothy Morrison	Alec Fincher
Shaun Waters	Sydney Pelletier
Evan Fletcher	CAPT Ignacio Garza
Preston Neal	Amn Glenn Baldwin
Armando Morales	AB Conrad Riley
Lucas Sullivan	A1C Chester Pierce
Taylor Campbell	PVT Anthony Charles
Max Soto	SrA Chris Davidson
Tony Pittman	AB Rex Herrera
Stewart Bailey	Amn Jay Saunders
Dominic Herrera	SSgt Daryl Manning
Carmen Stanley	Reynaldo August
Gwen Marsh	Weston Espinoza
Renee Bennett	SMSgt Charlie Sanders
Kim Watkins	Neville Murrell
Benny Spencer	Jason Stiles
Joe Burgess	Amn Percy Chavez
Jeromy Erwin	SN Ralph Lopez
Alec Kinder	Brig Gen Joaquin Romano
Darius Ochoa	SFC Reid Goldberg

Miles Cowley	PVT Adam Dennis
Logan Bollinger	Pvt Ernie Martin
Matt Buford	PO1 Dave Mann
Daisy Parks	PVT Nick Vetter
Samantha Nuñez	TSgt Dalton Velez
Naomi Lane	SSG Lucas Fan
Rachael Porter	VADM Teodoro Angulo
Bridget Armstrong	Saul Reiter
Ollie Cote	Malik Gaither
Giovanni Felton	SSG Neal Zimmerman
Deshawn Guevara	PO1 Louis Wyatt
Lola Santiago	SFC Clifton Warner
Martha Christensen	SGM Raphael Levy
Jerrod Heard	GySgt Porter Bonneville
Warner Spaulding	SSG Jerald Delagarza
Donovan Burton	PV2 Nellie Summers
Diego Isom	Pvt Leo Haynes
Sonny Dugan	SSG Edgar Daniel
Lucio Humphries	Col Shayne Bolin
Eleanor Burton	Mitch Hudgins
Mackenzie Johnston	Tyree Sibley
Lori Santiago	SGT Courtney Lowe
Amelia Grant	PO1 Frederick Shelton
Lucy Wade	CPO Reggie Mills
Madi Crawford	Enoch Solomon
Damian Ayala	Wilfred Reagan
Jasper Roland	Aaron Bergeron
Parker Hannon	Darcy Helton
Julius Hines	PFC Kathleen Davis
Arnold Morris	PVT Jackson Green
Paul Cummings	SPC Colleen Gonzales
David Chambers	Melina Vazquez
Nick Garner	Zaida Epperson
Scroll down for more . . .	*Scroll down for more . . .*

CHAPTER
FIFTEEN

That afternoon, me and Sweeney were back on guard duty, sitting around on Pale Horse. JoBell joined us, and I'm not gonna lie. This was a miserable, tense situation, but all I could think of in that moment was how good she looked in old jeans and a button-down flannel shirt, her blond hair pulled back in a ponytail. The rifle she carried only made her look hotter, though I wish she didn't need it.

"Come to save us from our boredom?" Sweeney asked her.

"Be glad you guys are on guard duty. Otherwise you'd be stuck chasing after little kids to make sure they don't wander off, or you'd be over there listening to Mr. Grenke and his pals bitch about how we should be on the road by now."

"Yeah, it's all jacked up," I said.

"Hey!" A voice came from the perimeter just down the line. "Don't move! Freeze, asshole!"

I dropped down off the ambulance pod to stand on the hood, yanking my charging handle to chamber a round. "What the hell is it now?" In two steps, I was on the ground.

One of our guards had walked out about twenty yards from the perimeter, his shotgun raised stock to shoulder, aimed at an older man and a little kid who were stepping out of the tree line with their hands up.

"Who's the guard?" I asked.

"Craig Rankin," JoBell said. "Skylar Grenke's stepdad." She must have noticed the confusion on my face because she continued,

"Yeah, he's like ten years younger than Skylar's mom. He used to drive that old Buick with —"

"The Buick Regal with the stupid green neon underglow lights and the loud as hell cherry bomb glasspack muffler." The mechanic in me often knew people by their cars instead of by name. The way Rankin was holding that gun, he might shoot those people at any moment. "Jo, cover my guard position. I'm going to go fix this."

"What about rule number one?" she asked.

"I gotta make sure Rankin's not alone." I was already running. I pulled the Motorola from my pocket and keyed the mike. "Pirate, this is Pale Horse."

Kemp came on the radio. *"Go ahead. Over."*

"Get to the west perimeter. ASAP. Over."

"Roger. Out."

"Hey, Craig. Ease it down," I said as I ran up on the scene. The man and kid still had their hands up and looked scared, but Rankin's finger was on the trigger, and he was shaking all over. "You don't have to aim the gun right at them. They're unarmed."

"We don't know who else they got with them." Craig eyed the tree line but kept his shotgun pointed at the man and the boy. "Could be an ambush."

Right, I thought, *because the really smart enemies tip everybody off by sending in two unarmed people before they launch their attack.* But I didn't say anything.

"We don't want any trouble," the man said. "I'm Eliot. This is my grandson Tyson. He was off playing in the woods when he saw you all, saw your fuel truck."

"Yeah, well, he should learn to mind his own business," Rankin said.

"Rankin, lower the gun," I said, a little more firmly.

"I'm supposed to be standing guard."

"Lower the weapon," Sergeant Kemp said, all business, coming up behind us. "Now." Craig finally stopped aiming right at the newcomers. "Is anyone else with you?" Kemp held his rifle at the low ready, scanning the woods.

"We're alone," said the man.

"We don't want any trouble either," Kemp said. "We'll be moving on soon."

"Please," the man said. "Could we bother you for a little fuel? You got diesel, right?"

"Maybe," Kemp said.

"We could trade some food or something else for it. If we could just fill up the tank on our fire truck. Right now we have about enough diesel to drive the truck to a fire. After that, it's stuck. Bunch of us are actually working to build a hand-crank water pump system with a hose that we could mount on a horse-drawn wagon. But that thing would take forever to get to a fire. By then . . . Please." The man looked serious. "Please, it's not for me. You'd be saving lives."

"No way," Rankin said. "This is ours. We need it. Get your own."

How very Brotherhood of him, wanting to keep it all for ourselves. On the other hand, people all over Idaho needed fuel. There were fire trucks and ambulances in every town that wouldn't run, useless bone-dry generators that were needed to power everything from houses to medical equipment. Kemp turned so he could fix his good eye on me.

The man took a step forward. "Please. Like I said, we can trade. We have some food. Potatoes. Canned beets."

"Nobody likes beets," Rankin said.

"Just calm down," Kemp said to him. "Right now, we have more fuel than food."

"You know how much diesel sells for?" Rankin said. "A hell of a lot more than some old beets."

"The gas is worth jack shit if we starve to death," I said.

"Come with us," Sergeant Kemp said to the man. "Let's talk to our leadership." Me and Kemp led the man and his grandson into our camp.

"We're not handing over our fuel, man. No way!" Rankin followed us.

"Craig, you didn't lift a finger to get us that fuel, so shut the hell up," I said.

"Listen, kid. I don't have to put up with your —"

"Get back to your post! Right now!" Sergeant Kemp yelled. Rankin started to point at me, but Kemp cut him off. "Wright was relieved. Someone is covering his guard position. Go back to yours."

Rankin gave in and went back to the perimeter. Me and Kemp took the man and the kid to Mrs. Pierce.

Instantly, another giant argument flared up.

"We're doing this to save ourselves, not to be heroes for everyone else," Mr. Grenke said.

"It's not that much fuel," said Crystal Bean's mom. "We can spare it."

Our old shop teacher, Mr. Cretis, shook his head. "We don't know that. If there's another bridge out along our route, we may have to backtrack hundreds of miles. We may have to drive around searching for another place if we can't get where we're going."

Chaplain Carmichael pulled a cross necklace out from under his uniform. " 'I was hungry, and you gave me no food. I was thirsty, and you gave me no drink. I was a stranger and you did not welcome me.' "

"This ain't a Bible lesson," said Mr. Grenke.

"Everything is a Bible lesson," answered the chaplain.

"Okay," Grenke said. "How's this, then? They can go to hell!"

"You see why I divorced him?" said Skylar Grenke's mom to no one in particular. Skylar's dad pretended not to hear.

Samantha Monohan's dad spoke up. "We're talking about filling up one fire truck. There've been a ton of fires with all the bombing and fighting. How'd you like your home and community burning up with no fire truck to help? We'll still have more than enough fuel, and this one act could save dozens, maybe hundreds of lives."

JoBell stepped up and put her arm around me. She held up a hand as Kemp was about to say something. "Don't worry. Sergeant Crocker relieved me. I couldn't miss this." Then she spoke louder so that everyone could hear her over the growing roar of the argument. "On the drive down here with the fuel, which we stole from the Brotherhood, who had stolen it and were hoarding it, we passed by people who needed our help. They're dead now. Or worse."

"We couldn't help them," said Mr. Grenke.

"You wouldn't even let us *try*!" JoBell stomped her foot on the last word. "On our way back from Boise, Eric, Danny, and I got stuck in Lewiston because our Idaho Army Humvee was out of gas." She let out a small, sad laugh. "We were caught by these sick bastards who would have raped and murdered us. But Cal and the Brotherhood came and saved us. The *Brotherhood*! Are you seriously saying that we will be no better than the group we're trying to get away from? I understand that we have to protect ourselves, that we have to look out for our own, but I refuse to accept that we can't do that and still help people when we can."

Caitlyn Ericson's mom actually raised her hand. "Okay, JoBell. Fine. This little boy found us here. How long until the whole town knows we're here?" She pointed at the old man.

"It's just me and Tyson," said the man. "Nobody else knows you all are out here. I'd tell as few people as I could, as few as possible so that I could still bring the truck to fuel up."

"This guy is nice," said Mrs. Ericson. "He comes asking for fuel, offering a trade. Who's to say the next guy won't bring a bunch of his friends and kill us to take everything we have?"

"You all make good points," Mrs. Pierce said. "So this is how it's going to be. Everybody load up and get ready to move. If our location is compromised, we can't stay." She turned to the man and his grandson. "Meanwhile, if you want that fire truck fueled up, you need to hurry and get it here. We'll fuel that truck, and then we'll roll out."

A half-dozen people started to object, but Sergeant Kemp shouted over them, "You heard her! Pack it up. We need to be ready to move."

"Let's go!" I yelled. My buddies all fell in with me, and then other families went along with them, until we had enough people to force a decision.

The stranger was quick. He had the fire truck up to our camp within a half hour. By that time, we were mostly ready to go. We'd be driving through a few hours of daylight, but it would be dark soon enough.

We would be shuffling duties a little for this stretch of the journey. I would be driving Pale Horse. Kemp would ride shotgun and cover the radio. Sergeant Crocker and Tabitha Pierce would ride in the ambulance module right behind the door to the cab. Becca would take over for Brad Robinson's dad on the driver's side .50. Cal would be on the turret. Sweeney still had the 240 covering our six, and TJ would man the passenger side machine gun. JoBell would ride with us too, moving around and relieving people as needed.

Tucker Blake's uncle, Derrick, had some experience trucking, so he would take over driving the M978 fuel truck. Even with his wounded shoulder, Mr. Hartling insisted on riding shotgun with him. When Mr. Robinson offered to be the third man pulling security with them, Mr. Grenke agreed immediately.

"Oh no," Kemp said, looking over the top of the radio he'd been adjusting in Pale Horse. I sat up in the driver's seat. A team of four horses pulled a modern tractor across the golf course toward us, one man sitting on the front to drive the horses and another in the cab steering. "More people heard about the fuel," Kemp said.

It wasn't the guys on the tractor I was worried about. Walking on either side of the tractor and horses were six men armed with a mix of shotguns and rifles. Another crowd of people were back behind them, some armed, some not. A lot of them carried fuel cans.

TJ called down from the turret, "You guys seeing this?"

"Yeah," Sergeant Kemp answered. He turned around to look back into the ambulance module. "Jo, go get Pierce. We need her up here yesterday."

Becca came up to the hatch and looked out the front. "We can't give them all fuel."

"They might not ask so nicely," I said.

As the tractor got closer, one of the riflemen waved at us. "We don't want any trouble," he called out. "We need fuel for this tractor, and just a little extra. Then we can plow our fields and take care of our crops. Take care of our people."

Mrs. Pierce made it back to us surprisingly quickly. She took one look at the mob approaching and turned to shout at Cal. "Cut that fire truck off! Wrap it up! We're rolling now!"

The group had come around the trees, so everyone in the buses could see them too. *"This is just what I was talking about,"* Mr. Grenke said over the Motorola network. *"Now they're going to take all we got."*

Kemp keyed his Motorola. It must have been dead, because he tossed it aside and took mine. He keyed the mike. "Damn it, Grenke! Stay the hell off the net."

Cal ran up into the back of Pale Horse, taking TJ's place on the turret. "I don't care what they're packing. A few seconds with this fifty, and I'll mow them all down."

"No, you won't," Mrs. Pierce said. "These aren't bad people. They're just desperate." She looked around the ambulance pod. "Eric, close her up. Stations, everybody. Sergeant Kemp, radio the go call. We're moving out."

Kemp called on both the tactical and unsecured radio. "All units, this is Pale Horse. We're going now. Keep the vehicle interval tight. Tap bumpers if you have to, but nobody gets between us. Whatever happens, keep moving. Do not stop! I say again, do not stop. Pale Horse. Out."

As soon as they saw our convoy moving, circling around so all our vehicles could follow Pale Horse in a tight line, the riflemen spread out, raising their guns. "We just want to talk," one of them called out. "Come on, you gotta help us."

I drove ahead, pulling around the side of the tractor. "I'm just going to drive slow, let them get out of the way. Cal, stay low in that turret!" But when we reached the two riflemen in front of us, they didn't get out of the way. They started yelling, telling us to stop so we could talk. They slapped the hood, getting more and more pissed. One of them ran back a few steps and aimed his rifle right at me.

Cal screamed from overhead, "If you shoot, I will kill you all! This fifty-cal will mow you down, and then I will shred your precious tractor. Back off!"

I sped up a little, hoping to get us the hell out of there before the whole situation went to shit like in Boise. Soon we were driving through a crowd of hundreds of people. Almost the entire lane from the golf course back to the highway was filled with folks after our fuel. They slapped the side of Pale Horse. Rocks hit us. Cal shouted at them, threatening to fire.

"Riccon, get down inside here!" Mrs. Pierce said. "You're not using that machine gun on them. We'll be clear soon enough."

"They've busted one of the windows on the door of bus one. They're trying to get in," someone radioed.

"It's like a damned zombie attack," Cal said.

A girl with jet-black hair and a black eye, maybe eighteen or nineteen, jumped up on the hood of Pale Horse. Others tried to follow her or maybe to pull her off, but she kicked them away. I swerved and she rolled off.

A gunshot went off. Another one.

"Hit the gas, Danny. Don't worry about who's in the way. More people are going to get hurt if we stay here," Mrs. Pierce ordered.

"But I can't just hit them," I said.

"Drive, Wright!" Mrs. Pierce shouted.

"Get out of the damned way!" I shouted at the mob. Then I hit the gas and we charged ahead. The front cattle-guard-steel-bumper-type thing hit one man with a sickening clunk. Then another. Finally they ran. More shots rang out. At last we cleared the crowd.

"Pull to the side," Kemp said. He keyed the mike on the ASIP. "All Exodus elements. All Exodus elements, roll on past us. We'll cover your six."

First the fuel truck, then one bus, Mr. Hooper's RV, Becca's dad's pickup and horse trailer, and the last bus drove past.

I hit the gas to follow our convoy. Now that we were clear of the mob, I'd have to pass all our vehicles so we could take the lead again.

Kemp turned and looked at Mrs. Pierce. "Orders, ma'am?"

I felt her hand on my shoulder. "Drive on, Wright."

CHAPTER
SIXTEEN

The next four days were rough. On that first day, we headed south on torn-up Highway 3, making good time, until we came up to a giant wall made of dirt, junked cars, parts of houses, and other crap. A sign said: BOVILL! WE TAKE CARE OF OUR OWN! TRESPASERS WILL BE SHOT!

The whole road was closed and dozens of people stood on top of the wall, aiming guns at us. We might have won in a fight, but not until after too many people were dead. So it was almost three hours back north to hook around onto Highway 6, which was a far rougher drive that went up and up and up for like twenty miles. Mr. Hooper's RV overheated three times on our way to the peak. It was a pain in the ass to try to keep that old thing running, but it had a lot of our tools and most of our medical equipment. Then on the way down, I seriously worried about the brakes on the buses.

All through the night, we corrected for wrong turns and navigated around blasted-out roads, sometimes backtracking for miles to take a different route. At dawn, we pulled off to make camp on a side road off Highway 12 just north of Kamiah.

The next night, we skirted around the town on an impossible series of back roads. Mr. Grenke and his friends kept getting more and more pissed every time we took a wrong turn or couldn't figure out where we were. Highway 12 took us to 14, and then to another series of crazy back roads where we almost got stuck about half a dozen times before we finally made it onto Highway 95 south of Grangeville.

Once again, a drive that should have taken a few hours took us all night, and we began to worry about our food supply. We'd prepared the best we could, but in the end, we'd still been forced to leave Freedom Lake before we were ready. Now we all prayed for good hunting and fishing up around the school. Worse yet, more and more of our group was starting to split between the Grenkes, the Keelins, the Ericsons, and people on their side, and the Monohans, the Beans, the Robinsons, the Blakes, and people on Tabitha Pierce's side.

At daybreak, we made a hidden camp on a little road off Highway 55, clear up on a pass. We were above five thousand feet, and although it was nearly June and the sun was out, we were all pretty cold. The next night we would drive through the city of McCall. After that, we'd head deep into the wilderness toward the tiny village of Hindman and then on to the Alice Marshall School. Gunfire and a few explosions echoed in the distance. We were closer than ever to our goal, but it sounded like we'd be passing through one hell of a battle to get there.

A bunch of us on Mrs. Pierce's side gathered around the front of Pale Horse. Me and JoBell huddled close together with my trusty old Army poncho liner over our shoulders. Becca and Sweeney had the same idea with a wool blanket from the horse trailer. Her mom and dad both stood close to her. Her parents had blamed me for getting their daughter into the war. Becca hadn't spoken to them much since then, and her dad selling Becca's horse hadn't helped matters. I'd stayed out of the situation, figuring Mr. and Mrs. Wells might still be mad at me and I'd only make everything worse. But with both my parents dead, I knew how important family was, and I was happy to see Becca and her folks had made up.

An extra-loud blast sounded from far down the road ahead of us.

"What the hell is going on down there?" Mr. Macer said.

"It sounds like the fighting on Victory Day," Becca said.

Sweeney snorted. "Victory Day." Becca kissed his cheek.

Brad Robinson spoke up. "How are we going to get through all that? Wright's rig is unstoppable, but our other vehicles aren't anything much."

"I'm worried about us driving down there," said Mr. Morgan's wife, Teresa. "We have some guns, sure, but we also have a lot of bus seats filled with scared little kids and some elderly people. We aren't soldiers."

"Maybe it's not as bad as it sounds," TJ said. "Maybe we could drive through quick and avoid whatever is going on."

"Is there another route to the school?" asked Chaplain Carmichael.

Mrs. Pierce shook her head. "There are two routes to Hindman, one straight east out of McCall, and the other far south of McCall on Highway 55. Either way, we have to go through the city. And once we get to Hindman, we still have a hell of a drive back into the mountains to Alice Marshall."

"We need to send someone on ahead to see what the trouble is," said Samantha Monohan's stepmom.

"Maybe," said Mrs. Pierce. "But I'm not going to make my decision until I hear from everyone." She sighed a little as she looked over at the other cluster of people in our camp.

She called a meeting, and minutes later, when everyone had gathered around, she told us the situation. "At the rate we've been going, we're about a day from the Alice Marshall School. But we've all heard a lot of gunfire up ahead. Unfortunately, we'll have to go through whatever is up there. Some people want to send a recon party ahead to find out what's going on, and I think it might be a good idea. We have this well-armed and armored Humvee ambulance. We just need a team to volunteer to man the thing."

I felt sick as soon as she brought up the idea. I didn't want to go on any advanced recon party, but nobody was driving Pale Horse except me and my close friends. More importantly, splitting up seemed like the wrong idea. If we drove down there and got in trouble, who would be left to bail us out? Mr. Hooper in his broke-dick RV? And who would protect the group while we were gone?

"I'll go," Cal said. His eyes flicked to Jaclyn, who sat with a blanket wrapped around her shoulders, staring off into space like she had been through the whole journey. "I'll help any way I can."

Sweeney and TJ stood up at the same time. Sweeney leaned on his cane. "If that big bastard is going, I guess I'm in," he said. The three guys looked to me.

"Hell no," Mr. Grenke said before I could speak. "What about rule number one? Nobody goes alone, remember?"

"Three of us just volunteered. We wouldn't be alone, dumbass," Cal said. A chorus of people jumped on Cal for saying that. "Well, it's true!" Cal said. "And we'll be in Pale Horse. We'll be fine."

"If we've learned anything from fighting the Fed, it's that armored Humvees aren't invincible," said Mike Keelin's dad. "What if you get killed?"

"Or what if you just break down?" said Dylan Burns's dad's girlfriend. We had one complicated mess of families on this mission. "Tire trouble or engine trouble, or what if you just get stuck on a torn-up road?"

"Well, we'll have radio contact," TJ said.

"But then we'd have to send someone else on ahead to rescue you," Mr. Grenke said. "And if you're dead and we never hear from you? Or if the Brotherhood or some other psycho manages to take you out and steal the vehicle, then we've lost our most valuable weapon." He wiped his hand over his sweaty bald head and smoothed down what little hair he had in back. "No. You can lecture me, threaten me. You can go on and on about how Mrs. Pierce is in charge until we get to the school and set up a council or whatever, but I call bullshit. I demand the right to vote now. I will do everything in my power to prevent you sacrificing our main weapons and leaving us alone up here without them."

"Damn it, Ryan," said Mr. Robinson. "You're just determined to ruin this whole venture, aren't you?"

"No, Dwight," said Mr. Grenke. "I'm trying to save it."

Robinson pointed at Mrs. Pierce. "That woman is responsible for putting this whole thing together. Without her, we'd all still be back there in Freedom Lake, some of us damn near starving. They'd probably have strung up Mr. Shiratori's whole family by now and come back for Jaclyn —"

"Whoa!" Mr. Morgan's daughter, Tessa, shouted.

Grenke took a step toward Robinson. "I'm getting real sick and tired of being accused of —"

"He's right," I said. In the past, I never would have dreamed of jumping into a big thing with adults. Most of the time, they bored the shit out of me and didn't really take me seriously anyway. But that was before the war. "Grenke's right. There's no fuel, so nobody's on the road. Until we can recharge our night vision glasses, we have to run with headlights, so if we drive Pale Horse anywhere near that city we'll be spotted. Say there are dangerous people down there. Say we gotta throw down. That means that our recon party would drive in, fight our way back out, and meet up with the rest of you. Then we'd all drive back to town, where the psychos would be waiting for us with a bunch more of their backcountry friends for round two."

JoBell raised her eyebrows like she was impressed.

"See?" Mr. Grenke said. "I hadn't even thought of that. But the boy's right."

Cal took a couple steps toward Grenke. "Hey, ease off the 'boy' shit, or I'll break your damned arms. Show you who the man is."

"If you think I'm scared —" Mr. Grenke started.

"Come on, you guys," Skylar spoke up. Others joined him in trying to get everyone to calm down.

"And as long as this isn't a democracy," I said, fixing my eyes on Mrs. Pierce, "Pale Horse is mine. I built her up from a wreck, installed all the gun ports. Me and my friends salvaged the guns and ammunition. Maybe things will be different up at the school, but while we're on this mission, I'm telling you, sending in a recon is a jacked-up move. Whatever's up ahead, we're going to roll through it fast, taking them by surprise if we gotta. Fighting if we gotta."

Mrs. Pierce's ice-cold glare cut right through me and did not break away. My eyes dropped first. When she finally spoke, her words were calm but precise, like she was reading each word she said. "Well, then. That's settled. Rest up, everyone. Fuel up our vehicles. We will roll out at sunset and plunge into whatever battlefield awaits us in the dark."

We came down out of the mountains, running fast on Highway 55. The closer we got to town, the more jacked-up stuff we saw. Burned or scrapped cars littered the road. We had to swerve around more than a few wrecks, some with bodies.

Once again, Kemp was riding shotgun in Pale Horse while I drove, leading the group. He keyed into both our radio networks. "Everybody stay tight and keep moving. Speed is the key here."

The city's electricity was out, and only a tiny sliver of moon hung above Payette Lake. It was tough to see just with our headlights, but it looked like most windows were boarded up, and makeshift walls and fences had been built around some properties. Unlike Freedom Lake, where everybody was all walled in together, the people here seemed to have divided the city into different sections.

"This used to be a resort town," Mrs. Pierce said through the hatch behind the cab. "What happened?"

"I can see over some of the walls up here," Cal said from the turret. "Some Brotherhood guys are gathered around a fire a few blocks off."

"The Brotherhood is all the way down here?" JoBell asked.

"I saw their armbands, but you're right. This is the first I've heard of it. Maybe they've just moved into the area, looking for new territory," Cal said. "Maybe the people here are fighting back."

"Everybody look alive," Sweeney said. "We got trouble. I see those bastards, I'm gunning them down."

"Not unless we take fire first," Mrs. Pierce said. "We're not starting anything."

"I think someone else just started something," I said.

We'd hooked a right to stay on Highway 55 and had just cleared the McCall Hotel. Two cars rolled out to block the street in front of us. Men with guns had pushed them into position. They aimed at us now.

Pierce and Kemp checked the map. Kemp radioed. "Trouble! Hook a left onto Lake Street!"

"It's blocked!" someone radioed back.

"They've blocked the road behind us too."

"Stop right there!" a man shouted outside. He wore the Brotherhood armband. "You're in the Brotherhood section of the city. We're going to need some of that fuel."

Had Crow and the others up north told these guys to be on the lookout for us? Did they know we had their stolen fuel truck?

"We're just passing through," Cal called back calmly. "We don't want no trouble."

"Well, you found trouble," the man said. "We ain't letting you take all that fuel and them supplies into Vandal territory."

"Into what?" Crocker asked.

"The Vandals are the McCall High School mascot," JoBell said. "I remember they went to the state volleyball tournament one year."

Cal must have ducked down into the ambulance pod back there, because I could could hear him better. "They got some shooters up on some of the roofs of the buildings nearby."

"We can't stay here," Kemp said. "They'll set up on us and take us all out."

It was like that day back in Spokane, the first day I ever killed someone. Me and Staff Sergeant Kirklin had been gun to gun, and if I had waited much longer, he would have shot me. So I shot him first, to stay alive and to protect my friends and my mother. At least that's what I'd thought at the time. Now I wasn't so sure.

"We gotta make our move now," I said.

Kemp radioed to the convoy. "Everybody who isn't armed needs to duck down out of sight of the windows. We're going hot. When you hear gunfire, shoot anyone out there who has a gun."

"How much room we got behind us, Cal?" I asked.

"'Bout eight feet. Why?"

"I'm gonna back us up, so when you pop back up out of that hatch, their snipers won't have a fix on you."

"Then you light them the hell up, Cal," Kemp said. "JoBell, have belts of ammo standing by for everyone to reload. You gotta keep them shooting."

"Let's just hurry and do this!" Becca shouted.

Kemp radioed. "All units, you are to hook a left and go under the archway at the hotel, into the hotel parking lot. Do not stop. Keep moving. You have the maps. Look for a way to hook up with Railroad Avenue on the other side." He let off the mike. "Now, Wright."

"Please help us, God," I said.

"Amen, my brother!" Cal said.

I threw Pale Horse in reverse and hit the gas. Then Cal was up. The loud *cah-cah-cah-cah-cah* of the .50-cal cut loose. "Suck it, you Brotherhood bastards!" Cal screamed. Rounds cut the men in front of us in half and shredded through the roadblock cars. Our side guns fired, and the front of the hotel on our left erupted with big blast holes. Shooters fell from the roof. I switched gears and drove forward hard, crashing into the two little cars and shoving them out of our way.

The first bus and Mr. Hooper's RV went under the arch. Then the fuel truck. Becca's dad's truck and trailer went under next. Finally the last bus went through.

"Don't back up, Danny! It'll take forever. Just go forward and we'll catch up!" Cal shouted.

"Do it," Kemp said.

I kept pushing through the little roadblock. "They should have used something besides a Honda Civic and a Dodge Stratus," I said under my breath.

Bullets cracked against the outside of Pale Horse, sounding like hard hammer smacks on metal. "Cal!?"

"I'm good!" Cal said. A second later his .50-cal spoke for him, firing three five-second bursts. I hit the gas and we shot by a couple more shops before swinging a hard left onto Railroad Avenue.

"I'm gonna light these bastards up for trying to follow," Sweeney called.

"Don't shoot unless you got a target!" I said.

"Pale Horse, where are you? We found a way through the back of the place. We're back on the right road." It was Mr. Morgan on bus one.

Kemp answered, "We're right behind you. We see you. Keep going. We'll catch up."

"Come on, Wright!" Mrs. Pierce yelled.

The convoy was around the corner from Railroad Avenue. We'd be there in three seconds.

"They cut us off! Somebody help! This is bus two! They cut us off! Steph, turn! No! Just turn! Here!" It was Mr. Grenke.

Kemp keyed his mike. "Bus two! Bus two, what road are you on? Where are you?"

"Floor it! Oh shit! They're shooting. We're taking fire! Just shoot 'em back! Who cares about the ammo!? Shoot 'em!"

"He won't stop keying the mike," Kemp said. "He'll never hear us."

Pale Horse rounded the corner. I couldn't see any of the convoy, but I spotted the roadblock. "He must have turned here."

"We gotta get up there!" Mrs. Pierce shouted. "The whole convoy has almost no cover!"

"I don't know where we are! Why won't anyone answer? Oh. Okay, if anyone is getting this, we're clear over by the lake. Um . . . Lake Street! It's just called Lake Street. We turned right onto Lake Street."

Kemp tried the tactical radio. "We got a hot mike! Tell Grenke to let go of the transmit button!" Finally, Grenke got off the Motorola network.

"This is bus one, in the lead. We're way up Davis Avenue now. Do you want us to stop and wait?" Mr. Morgan radioed.

"Negative!" Kemp called back. "Keep moving! Stay on the planned route and get the hell out of town. We're going back for the other bus."

Crocker had been dinking with the map. He held his hand out to Kemp. "Give me your radio." He keyed up. "Bus two, stay on Lake

Street. You're going to reach a spot where the road curves to the right onto Hemlock Street. Stay on that. We'll meet you on Hemlock."

"Okay. Ten four. We're turning onto Hem — It's blocked! They got us blocked! Oh shit!" The sound of gunshots came over the radio and from the near distance. *"They're everywhere! Stephanie! Our driver's hit! Someone else is hit back there!"*

I didn't need to be told. I turned left onto Hemlock and headed down to them with the pedal to the floor. "Come on, baby," I whispered, patting the steering wheel.

"Brotherhood sons-a-bitches everywhere!" Cal said. He opened fire.

We were coming up on the barrier fast — another couple cars they'd rolled onto the road. The bus was on the other side of them, facing us. I tapped the brakes to slow down a little and bumped us up the curb into someone's front yard, circling the barrier and skidding out as I cranked the wheel to bring us back around on our bus's side of the roadblock. Two, three, then four guys screamed as I ran them over. Pale Horse actually bumped around as their bodies went under our wheels. Now we were out on the street, front bumper to front bumper with bus two, with our ass end toward the roadblock. Instead of wasting time trying to turn around and ram through like last time, I threw the truck in reverse and backed up toward the cars. We hit hard, but not hard enough. I didn't have a good running start like last time. I gave her more gas, and our tires squealed on the pavement. "Come on, you bastards!"

We were taking rounds again. Getting pelted. Three or four shots hit our windshield, and I jumped so hard that I pissed myself a little. But I broke through the roadblock, backing up to open enough space for the bus to follow.

"Oh yeah! I'm the lead gunner now!" Sweeney shouted. "This is for starving my friends!" His M240 opened up with ten solid seconds of machine gun fire. Ten seconds was a lot of rounds coming from that badass gun. "This is for Jackie's parents! Come eat lead, assholes!"

I cranked the steering wheel to the side to put our back end up on the curb in someone's yard. Then I threw Pale Horse in drive and sped ahead of bus two.

"Bus two, this is Pale Horse!" Kemp radioed. "Stay tight on our six. We should be kissing bumpers all the way out! How copy? Over."

"*Pale Horse. This is bus two.*" Mr. Grenke's voice held less panic and more horror now. There was more shaking behind his words. "*We copy. Hey, ah, we gotta get Doc Randall. We got some hurt people.*"

We could hear screams in the background over the radio.

"*I'm ready,*" Dr. Nicole radioed. "*The convoy is stopped on Lick Creek Road. I have my kit ready. I'll need Becca Wells to assist me, please. Can I get details of the wounds? Over.*"

As I listened to Mr. Grenke tell Dr. Nicole about all their wounds and injuries, we drove past street after street, until finally we turned right onto Lick Creek Road, which would take us clear the hell out in the mountains to Hindman. From there we'd finally go deeper into the wilderness to the Alice Marshall School.

╱╲—• *This is the official radio network of the Brotherhood of the White Eagle. Rise up to victory. My Brothers, we are pleased to bring you live to Freedom Lake, Idaho, for a special address by Brotherhood General Nathan Forrest Crow."*

"Citizens of Freedom Lake and of the Republic of Idaho, members of the Brotherhood of the White Eagle, honored members of this year's senior class. Greetings. Graduation is normally a time of celebration, of looking back on a job well done, and of recognizing and embracing change.

"But today our celebration is diminished by pain, loss, and bitter betrayal. The photographs amid these many flowers at the foot of the stage represent each of the students who would have been proud to receive their diplomas today. Each of them has fallen in our struggle to be free.

"No doubt many of you are greatly shaken by the attack on Freedom Lake by United States Special Forces infantry. I'm sorry to report that our enemy was given valuable assistance by traitors among us. Principal Garrett Morgan betrayed his entire community by assisting the United States. Mr. Michio Shiratori, a beloved teacher and coach for many years, was willing to sacrifice all our lives to the US for his own comfort. Others in this community have betrayed us as well.

"I share your feelings of hurt, fear, confusion, and disbelief. I find myself questioning my own recent judgment. Before this terrible attack, some evidence did suggest Mr. Shiratori was collaborating with the enemy. If I had arrested him then and questioned his friends, maybe the traitors would not still be at large. Maybe some of the young people pictured here would be alive today. But I am a man of the law! I believe in the sacred truth that all men are innocent until proven guilty. I did not have that absolute proof until

we searched the home of the US collaborators Carlos and Rosa Martinez, where we discovered communications among them, Shiratori, and the US. Where we found hundreds of thousands of dollars in cash, blood money paid by our enemy, which helped bring about the deaths of so many of our people. Where we found boxes and boxes of extra food, more than their families could possibly eat, while the rest of us starved. So today I make this solemn vow before God Almighty! Those who would sacrifice our lives and our children's lives to our enemy — traitors like Mr. Morgan and Mr. Shiratori — will be hunted down and delivered upon the righteous altar of justice!

"We lost many in the cowardly attack, but I am proud to say that our defenses held! The Brotherhood of the White Eagle met the enemy and forced him from our home!

"I do not deny that our struggle against the United States has been long, or without cost. I have suffered as you have suffered, asking no more of any man than that which I myself am willing to give.

"Another man who fought along with us, who understood the tremendous sacrifice asked of all of us for victory, was Private First Class Daniel Wright. When the United States government came after Wright, we were shown by his example that we no longer had to be slaves in our own land! He showed us that we could break free to live our lives, not the way Fed parasites told us we must live, but as we ourselves would choose to live them!

"And so . . . I'm sorry. I can hardly find the strength to say the words, can hardly believe that it is true. It is my sad duty to report to you that Private First Class Daniel Christopher Wright, along with his fiancée, JoBell Linder, and several of his closest friends, were killed in action early Friday morning as they fought to defend their home. Private Wright, who was excited for the opportunity to join the Brotherhood of the White Eagle on this, his graduation day, has at last made the ultimate sacrifice. Daniel Wright is dead.

"As we suffer the shock and grief that follows such a tragic death, let us find comfort in the knowledge that Daniel Wright's dream lives on! The Brotherhood of the White Eagle is strong, and united with the community we serve, we form an unstoppable force for peace and freedom. Do you share Daniel Wright's passion!? Do you!? Knowing it was Wright's fervent desire to become a member of the Brotherhood, will you join together and, with the Brotherhood, declare with one voice that we will not surrender!? We will not give up the fight until every US soldier is driven from our land, until every US collaborator among us is brought to justice! Do you hear the voice of destiny calling you to our great future!? Do you!? Honor the memory of Daniel Wright and follow as the Brotherhood of the White Eagle leads you to glory! •—⋀⋁

⋀⋁—• USTV now brings you live to a press conference with the presidential press secretary, Vivian Huck, in the new media room of the United States Capitol, deep inside Mount United States, formerly Cheyenne Mountain."

"Good afternoon, ladies and gentlemen of the press. Welcome. On behalf of President Griffith and myself, I hope you have enjoyed your stay in the capitol. Before we get started with the questions, I want to remind you all to please avoid asking questions about US troop movements or other defensive plans. I will not release classified information or provide answers that might endanger American troops or assist rebels and prolong the war. With that in mind, you have all been invited here today in hopes of improving government communication and getting reliable information to all the American people. First question. Yes?"

"Robert Bell, WGN News. What is the administration's reaction to news of the death of Daniel Wright?"

"President Griffith feels that every death in this war is a tragedy, and that is why she's working so hard to end the war and bring the United States back together."

"But given the controversial nature of Wright's involvement in —"

"Wright's death, like all the deaths in this war, is tragic. Now, I'm sure we have more important things to talk about. Next question."

"Thank you. Hart Wibley, Atlantica News Network. Ms. Huck, since the appointment of her new vice president, General Chuck Jacobsen, President Griffith has made very few public appearances or addresses. Isn't it true that the United States is, in fact, under the military dictatorship of General Jacobsen, that it is no longer anything like a democracy?"

"I know that General Vogel has suggested as much, and I won't get into the irony of such an accusation coming from the self-proclaimed leader of Atlantica, but let me assure you and everyone else that President Griffith is our commander in chief and that she is absolutely in control."

"Then why haven't we seen —"

"Hart, President Griffith hasn't made many public appearances because she's really very busy directing this war. She's also organizing the reappointment of the Senate and reelection of the House of Representatives in accordance with the procedures set forth in our Constitution. Next question. Go ahead."

"Rebecca Cho, NBC News. Ms. Huck, what can you tell us about the investigation into the nuclear attacks? Has any progress been made tracking down the remaining eleven suspects believed to be responsible for the theft of the warheads? And since most experts agree the eleven would have needed accomplices even to remove the warheads from the silo compounds, what can you tell us about the search for those accomplices?"

"While finding those responsible for the nuclear attacks and bringing them to justice is important, the war has made the investigation into this matter very difficult. President Griffith and senior United States military leadership have shifted their priorities to preventing any further nuclear catastrophes. The number three reactor at the Indian Point nuclear power plant has been sealed, and no further radioactive contamination is flowing from that breach. The rest of the United States' nuclear arsenal is secure, and other nuclear power plants are being safeguarded or shut down."

"Erin Heddleson, Empire News. So the United States has abandoned its effort to apprehend those responsible for the nuclear attacks?"

"Please don't twist my words, Erin. The investigation continues, though it is presently severely hampered by the war and insurgent activities. However, the most important thing is preventing future nuclear attacks or disasters."

"Tyson Clement, Minnesota Public Radio. How can you be sure that ICBMs or nuclear weapons aboard bombers or submarines will not fall into the wrong hands or be used by the newer, perhaps less stable governments in a nuclear attack?"

"This is actually one of the bright points in this terrible war. The leadership of Montana and Wyoming have honored their agreements from the sad day they made the mistake of declaring independence. They have allowed the United States to station platoon-sized elements at each of our ICBM silos, and they have allowed us to rotate and supply those troops. Furthermore, as soon as the first two nuclear warheads went missing, the United States government immediately secured all nuclear weapons in bombers *and submarines. In short, the United States maintains full control of its entire nuclear arsenal."*

"Keira Montley, Dakota News Channel. When you talk about control of the nuclear arsenal, do you mean that the United States is determined to use its nuclear weapons?"

"I cannot comment on that. ●—⋏

⋏—● apologize for interruptions to NBC programming, as our studios and transmitters here in Los Angeles have suffered some intermittent power losses. The footage we are showing you now was shot about ten minutes ago above Los Angeles. There you see a number of United States attack helicopters firing rounds and rockets at Cascadia military targets in the city. We're going to slow this footage down for you to make it easier to see the remarkable events unfolding in the skies. There you see at least fifty F-22 fighters from the 163rd fighter wing of the Arizona Air National Guard. In seconds, they destroyed all United States attack helicopters as well as inbound US aircraft bringing in Special Operations soldiers, presumably to conduct guerrilla operations in Cascadian cities. The jets moved quickly to unleash a deadly attack on United States forces around southern Cascadia before refueling in flight to return to Arizona, where Governor Jean Bates and her allies around the state and in Las Vegas have declared Arizona an independent nation. Arizona has annexed the Las Vegas area and has declared war on the United States. ●—⋏

TARIQ JACKSON ★ ★ ☆ ☆ ☆

Idaho and all of Pan America has lost a true hero. RIP Private Wright.

★ ★ ★ ☆ ☆ This Post's Star Average 2.95   [Star Rate] [Comment]   25 minutes ago

TELL ME AGAIN ABOUT HOW THE MURDERER DANIEL WRIGHT IS A HERO

〜• *Republic of Idaho Radio. AM 1040 RIR. Onward to victory. Minnesota, Wisconsin, and the upper peninsula of the former state of Michigan have declared independence from the United States and entered the war as Minnecongan. Minnesota and Wisconsin National Guard and militia forces, in addition to defecting United States military personnel, moved quickly to launch devastating surprise attacks on the United States military in their territory and on the Great Lakes. Finally, the former states of Tennessee, Kentucky, West Virginia, the western part of Maryland, Virginia, and North Carolina have established a new country called Appalachia. With this development, the United States not only loses several former military installations, but also coastal access to the Atlantic. Thirteen states are all that remain of the US: Alaska, Arkansas, Colorado, Hawaii, Iowa, Kansas, Missouri, Nebraska, New Mexico, and Utah, and significant portions of the states of Nevada, Oregon and Washington. The US is in a fierce battle to maintain its hold on eastern Oregon and the state of Washington, to ensure its access to the sea. As of this broadcast, sixteen independent nations now comprise the area of what was once the United States of America. President Montaine issued a brief statement welcoming new allies to the war against the United States. He urged all newly independent countries to stop fighting among themselves and focus on securing a lasting, stable independence.*

Among the tens of thousands of Idaho citizens drafted into military service, several thousand have registered as conscientious objectors who will serve the nation, but will not be placed directly

in combat roles. Where will most of these conscientious objec-
tors serve? The forest service. Idaho's top military official, General
McNabb, recently announced that with summer on the way, Idaho
faces a new danger in the form of possible wildfires. Preparations
are being made to take as much preemptive action as •⌁

⌁• *From the information we can gather here at ANN in Atlanta,*
here is the most up-to-date map of the Pan American territory.
Please note that some of these borders are in flux, while fighting
continues among nations, often breaking out between rival citi-
zen militia groups battling for territory and valuable resources.
Certainly under the leadership of General Vogel, the old Florida
Panhandle will soon be Atlantican territory again.

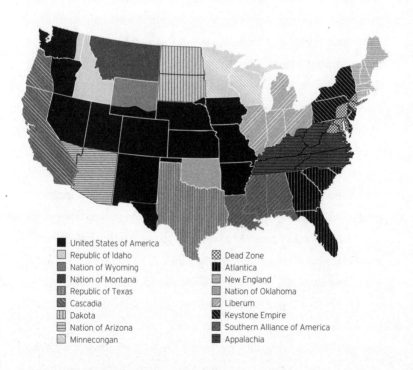

United States of America
Republic of Idaho
Nation of Wyoming   Dead Zone
Nation of Montana   Atlantica
Republic of Texas   New England
Cascadia   Nation of Oklahoma
Dakota   Liberum
Nation of Arizona   Keystone Empire
Minnecongan   Southern Alliance of America
                        Appalachia

⌁—• *For generations, American farmers have grown corn that was used for animal feed, automotive fuel, and sweeteners in everything from cookies to soda. None of it was useful as human food. Many farmers throughout all the new nations across the Pan American territory still have not broken free from this pattern of growing only corn and soybeans. As a result, we are heading for a food crisis the likes of which this continent has never experienced.* •—⌁

⌁—• *Fellow patriots, welcome back to the* Buzz Ellison Show. *The number to call if you'd like to be on the program today is 1-800-555-INDY. That's 1-800-555-4639. It's . . . Forgive me, Buzzheads. In the many years I've been bringing you the truth on this program, there have been times when the events of the day have been so painful that it has been a challenge to offer my brilliant commentary. I know that I make this seem easy, but it was difficult to step up to the microphone to talk, for example, about the election of Barack Obama, or about the recent nuclear attacks. Even then, though, calling upon my superior skill and intellect, I was able to pull through.*

Today . . . You know they say, when someone has lived a great, full life, it is not necessary to mourn his death. Daniel Wright's life, while great, wasn't full. He was so young. And yet, what he lacked in years, he made up for in courage, strength, and integrity. He inspired millions of people to stand up to the oppression of the US federal government, and in many ways, he was one of the most important catalysts of this war, our conservative revolution.

Daniel Wright was a close personal friend of mine. When I heard the news of his death, I couldn't help but remember the several meals I shared with Danny and his fiancée, JoBell. How we laughed . . . JoBell was the kind of girl who brightens up any room.

Danny absolutely adored her, and I could see why. Not only was she beautiful, but she was also full of the most thoughtful conservative insights. She and I got along like we'd been friends for years, like family, really. I . . . Excuse me, it's . . .

It's times like these that we all have to remember how PFC Daniel Wright inspired us. Raise your fist in salute with me, and rise up!

Because I can see hope coming to all of us! The Buzz Ellison Show *has always been about optimism and hope through solid, time-tested, conservative principles. And I know we are going to win this war, and build the prosperous conservative society we've been dreaming of for years. The United States can no longer triumph. How will Lazy Laura Griffith bring the new countries back into the United States? With her feminine charm? Ha! General Jacobsen has more femininity than her. No, people will never forget what the US has done to them, how many the United States has killed. None of the newly independent countries are ever going back. The United States may have taken Daniel Wright from us, but they will never kill the spirit of independence that he has sparked in all our hearts. Peace and freedom are right around the corner if we just keep up the fight!* •⎯⋀⎯

SEVENTEEN

The fight through McCall left us with three dead and many wounded. At first, I tried to keep away from everyone who was talking about how it had all gone down, but then I figured I should hear the victims' stories. I owed them that much, at least.

Casey Hayes was twenty-four and a plumber. His girlfriend split shortly before the war, leaving him with a one-year-old daughter named Josie and no explanation. They say Casey held his daughter down out of harm's way with one hand, and fired back at the Brotherhood with the rifle he held in the other. He was shot in the neck. Angeline Atkins, who graduated with Casey, promised him she'd take care of Josie as he bled out.

Steph Ollins was a tough-as-nails bus driver — never the one you wanted for a school field trip because she was so mean. But she drove safe. And brave. She'd held on until well after Dr. Nicole had treated the gunshots in her shoulder and chest. She kept talking about how she was going "to make damned sure everybody made it to the school." She said it over and over again, until finally she didn't say anything else.

Harold Gates had served in the infantry in both the Korean and Vietnam Wars. He loved his granddaughter Crystal Bean, and Crystal's siblings, the twins Mara and Micah. The man was in his nineties, but he still picked up a rifle and fought back against the enemy. They say rounds hit the bus all around him, and a few zipped right past him, but he stood his ground. He told his family that he was grateful to have fought in three wars and he was happy to know they'd be safe. "I'll be with Jesus, waiting for you, years from now when your time comes," he'd said as he died shortly after the battle from complications following a heart attack.

I watched Becca and Doc Nicole taking care of our wounded in the feeble light from a couple flashlights. Our high school English teacher, Mrs. Stewart, had fired at the Brotherhood with a twelve-gauge Remington 870 shotgun. They say she was silent and vicious, getting off six or seven shots before being taken down by a bullet in her belly. Dr. Nicole said she'd survive, but I worried. We'd thought Specialist Danning would survive when we'd done that surgery on his abdominal wound back when we were stuck in the dungeon. Mrs. Stewart was in a hell of a lot of pain, but still in good spirits.

One of the wounded who was not in good spirits was Jaclyn Martinez, who had picked up Casey Hayes's rifle and fired round after round, screaming like mad, maybe hitting the enemy, maybe not. Her arms were cut up pretty bad from the glass in the broken bus windows.

"Hey." Mr. Grenke pulled me aside between Pale Horse and bus one. Bandages covered his left shoulder and left side, next to his ribs. Both bullets had gone clean through. Even though the guy was kind of a jackwad, he'd gotten that bus out of town after Steph Ollins had been shot, people applying makeshift bandages to his wounds while he drove. "I'm sorry," he said.

"For what?"

"I've been throwing gas on the fire in our meetings. I know you've been kind of pissed at me." I started to answer with some sort of denial, but he held his hand up. "No, it's okay. I get it. And I'm sorry. And . . . When we were cut off from the group, and then stopped out there in front of that last roadblock bullets were flying at us from all directions. I looked at Skylar. At my wife and at Skylar's mom. At everybody." The guy's eyes were tearing up, and he turned away from me to hide it. I knew the feeling. "I thought I'd got them all killed. I shouldn't have argued with Mrs. Pierce about the recon. I should have figured out how to get the bus back on the right road without getting us pinned down." He shook his head, and his voice was full of tears. "I got people killed."

"No, the Brotherhood killed them. You helped save everybody else."

He looked up at me. "No. *You* saved us. You guys in Pale Horse came in like something out of an action movie and got us out of there. That's what I'm trying to say. My family is alive because of you, and I won't forget that."

I wished he hadn't said that. For all I knew, Grenke was right, and me and him had both screwed up by going against the recon before McCall. But we couldn't have known that then. We'd made the right call at the time. Hadn't we? I didn't know, but I did know I didn't want the man's gratitude. It was stupid, but I almost preferred Mr. Grenke when he was pissed and arguing with me.

I'd promised JoBell that I was getting out of the war, but so far I'd done a terrible job living up to that promise. The truth was, I'd gotten used to fighting. If someone wanted to mess with me or with the people I loved, I was ready to throw down. Give me anything but gratitude. After all the wrong I'd done, all the pain and death I'd caused, I didn't deserve thanks.

But that wasn't the kind of thing Mr. Grenke wanted, or needed, to hear. Instead I offered him a standard line, the kind of shit I'd been barfing out all over the morale-boosting tour Montaine put me on, the kind of slogan Mr. Shiratori had warned me about. "We're all in this together, Mr. Grenke. No big deal." I gave him a little punch to his uninjured shoulder.

★ ★ ★

The morning sky had just begun to brighten when we reached Hindman. The place was a ghost town. I mean, it must have been a ghost town before the war too. A sign at the edge of the village boasted a population of forty-four, with just a handful of scattered houses and sheds, a post office, a little grocery-bait-mail-combo-type store, a small diner, and a log-cabin-style bar. Most of the buildings were boarded up, and there were no other vehicles in sight.

"Veer right here," Mrs. Pierce directed. "We're close now." We rolled on in silence for a few miles. "Slow down," she finally said. "The turnoff is around here somewhere. There."

"There's nothing here," I said as I stopped Pale Horse and the convoy.

"Come on," Mrs. Pierce said. "I'll show you."

Kemp radioed over the Motorola. "Standard security perimeter like we discussed at the camp outside of McCall. Everybody else, stay in your vehicles. Be sharp. We don't know if we're alone or not." He clipped his radio to the pocket on the front of his uniform. "Wright, Riccon. Go with Pierce. The rest of us will keep a lookout."

Mrs. Pierce, Cal, and me climbed out of Pale Horse. She led us a little ways off the road.

"Here it is, by this white wooden post sticking out of this cement block," Mrs. Pierce said at last. We could barely see a dirt road there, blocked by a tall pile of scrub brush. "Someone pulled these branches over the entrance to hide the place."

Whoever hid the road must have done it a long time ago. The pine needles on a bunch of the branches had long since rusted to orange. Cal slung his rifle and walked up to the pile. He patted the trunk of a tree that lay on its side. It had to be a solid eight inches thick.

"I'll go back and get some help," I said.

Cal widened his stance and grabbed a couple nubs on the trunk. "Pussy." He heaved and the brush pile shook. "Come on, you son of a bitch," he grunted as he pulled.

"You're never gonna get it," I said.

"Bull —" He yanked the tree hard and it started sliding. He dug in his feet and worked like an ox to haul the tree out of the way. "— shit."

"Damn, Cal." I grabbed a much smaller tree, more of a shrub, and hauled it away.

After about ten minutes, we had it cleared. We moved the convoy onto the dirt road, which rose sharply up into the wilderness. It took another ten minutes to conceal the road again, and then we drove on. Tree branches scraped the sides of our vehicles. Cal had to duck down out of the turret inside Pale Horse to avoid being hit.

We passed a brown sign that read DESIGNATED WILDERNESS AREA. NO MOTORIZED VEHICLES BEYOND THIS POINT. After that, there wasn't a road anymore, but two tire ruts filled with pine needles.

"Is this even passable for trucks?" I asked.

Mrs. Pierce only laughed. "Just keep driving. We're getting closer."

The road was steep going up the mountain. Pale Horse's engine strained. Sometimes the road would level off and turn a little, but it kept going up and up. I worried that the big buses and the heavy fuel truck wouldn't make it. We bumped over some small washouts in the road, and I radioed to everyone else to keep driving no matter what happened. If someone chickened out and let off the gas, they might get stuck or start rolling backward.

Finally we rounded a corner to see a closed and locked cattle gate. If I stopped the convoy to get out and open it, the vehicles behind me might not get going again on the slope. I gave her more gas, drove past the NO TRESPASSING and AMS signs, and busted right through the gate, pulling into a small, loosely graveled parking lot surrounded by giant fir trees. I parked at the far edge of the clearing. The first bus was right behind me, and Kemp got out to direct it to park next to us.

Kemp tapped on Norm's bus door and he opened it. "We're gonna have to pack 'em in tight. There's not a lot of room."

The other bus rolled in, then Derrick Blake in the fuel truck, Hooper's RV, and finally the pickup hauling the horse trailer, with the bikes and a bunch of luggage.

The sun had finally begun to come up, and golden streaks of light made their way sideways through the trees to light up what everybody hoped would be our new home. It was a sort of flattish shelf sticking out from the mountainside. Gravel paths led back through a thick stand of trees, I guess toward the school. There on the mountain in the cool morning, the sunlight on this last day of May promised that it might be possible for the war to be over for us.

But we weren't stupid enough to take any more chances. We immediately created a security perimeter around the parking lot. A couple people set out five-gallon-bucket toilets behind nearby trees as a hundred hungry and exhausted people piled out of the vehicles.

"What do we do now?" Mr. Morgan asked. His voice echoed across the quiet parking lot, the only sound besides the whisper of a gentle breeze in the trees.

Mrs. Pierce was about to say something, but Kemp squeezed her hand and stepped ahead of her. "It's been a long trip, and not without a terrible cost. I know everybody wants to find the nearest rack and get some sleep, or maybe see if there's a kitchen —"

"There is," Mrs. Pierce said.

"— and get something to eat." Kemp unslung his rifle. "But we have to make sure nobody else is here. We'll take a small group to do a proper clearing of the buildings. As soon as we know the place is secure" — he smiled — "we'll make ourselves at home."

"Is all this security really necessary?" Mr. Cretis's wife asked. I couldn't remember her name, but it was clear that a lot of people agreed with her. "The last road up here was hidden. The pine needles on the road were fresh enough. The place is abandoned, and we're tired of waiting around."

"Please be patient," Mrs. Pierce said. "Someone else might have had the same idea about hiding up here. We have to make sure."

"It won't be much longer," said Mr. Grenke. "For now, we'll all get something to eat. Some of us will pull guard duty while everyone else rests. We made it. Let's just be happy about that."

I nodded him my thanks.

"I'll take Wright, Sergeant Crocker, and, um, Private Wells." Kemp smiled. "You all have some experience at clearing buildings."

"I'm coming too." Mrs. Pierce held her AR15 with the butt stock on her hip and the barrel pointed up.

"Mrs. Pierce." Sergeant Kemp fought to keep the laughter out of his voice. "We're going to run through these buildings really fast. I'm not sure —"

"I was in a war before you were born, boy. I'm not even eighty, and you won't be able to find the buildings without me. Anyway, nothing you can do to stop me." She started for the edge of the parking lot. "Come on, we'll begin with the guest dorm building."

"Stay sharp. Don't let your guard down," Kemp said to Mr. Grenke. "Monitor the radios. We'll call if there's any problem." Then me, him, and Becca took off after Crocker and Mrs. Pierce.

Mrs. Pierce led us down the trail through the woods until we arrived at a clearing with a giant old wood-sided, two-story rectangular building that had been painted a kind of tannish yellow. Next to that was a much smaller cabin with the same paint job and white trim.

Pierce stepped up to the door of the cabin and jiggled the handle. "Locked."

"That looks like some thick wood," Crocker said. "It's going to be tough to break down."

"Shooting the lock will draw too much attention if there's anyone else up here," said Becca.

Glass broke behind us, and we all spun to see Mrs. Pierce smashing a low window with the stock of her rifle. "Come on then, hotshots. Do your thing."

I laughed. The whole point of sweeping a building was to take any hostiles by surprise. If there had been anyone in the cabin, they'd have heard us by now. Still, Kemp led us into the cabin through the window. There wasn't much there. An open room with a couch, a couple chairs, shelves full of paper books, and a desk. The only other room was a simple bedroom with one small bed, a nightstand, an empty closet, and a dresser with a mirror behind it.

Mrs. Pierce was in the cabin for about thirty seconds. She reached into the tiny closet and felt around until we heard a jingling sound. She pulled out a giant steel ring with like a hundred keys, then held it up and shook it. "You guys did a bang-up job of searching the place."

"We were mostly checking for people . . ." Kemp started to say, but Mrs. Pierce had already left the cabin. "You know, people hiding here who might want to kill us?"

Becca was laughing. I found it hard to hold back too.

"Oh, come on," Kemp said.

By the time we caught up to Mrs. Pierce, she was up on the big covered wooden porch of the guest dorm building, the door already unlocked and open. She waved us inside. "Have fun. And can you check the main-floor library first? It's to the right. I want to sit down and take it easy while you all run through the rest of the place." She laughed, and we joined her. We still had to be careful and clear the building, but we were starting to believe we'd finally come home.

We stormed the guest dorm building, room by room, stacking ourselves up by each door and rushing in with our rifles at the ready. The main floor had its own small kitchen, a dining room, a bathroom, and a kind of lobby. It also had a big library with a nice, solid wood table, an open fireplace, a big old globe in a stand, a zillion more paper books, and two rolling ladders. JoBell would love it. The second floor had a large latrine and sixteen small but comfortable dorm rooms.

When we were satisfied the building was clear, Mrs. Pierce led us down a trail to the staff cabins, six buildings in all, each with a single bunk and a desk. The faculty latrine cabin was just behind them. We swept the cabins and then followed the path to the English, math, science, and social studies cabins. They were like any old classroom back at Freedom Lake High, only clear up here in the mountains. The rec lodge held hiking, fishing, sports, and canoeing equipment and even a little shed at the back with some tools. Maybe we could get to a point up here where we could relax and use some of that stuff.

Another trail led us to a group of nine student cabins. This was a jackpot for lodgings, with three sets of double bunks in each one. Families could be safe and comfortable here.

A little closer to the lake, we swept through the bathhouse. Row of toilets. Row of sinks. Row of showers. It was just like the latrine at basic training except with no urinals, and the showers had divider walls and curtains. Next we cleared the dining lodge, with its big room filled with long tables and bench seats. In the heavy-duty kitchen, we found a giant walk-in freezer and refrigerator.

"Don't open that," Becca said. But I'd already pulled the handle. The sour, salty stench burned my nose and eyes, and I gagged before I shut the door. Becca patted my back. "Tried to warn you."

"They must have taken off in a hurry and left all their meat behind," said Mrs. Pierce. "Let's hope they did the same with the pantry." She used her master key to unlock a big wooden door at the back of the kitchen. She swung it open, and just enough light fell into the little room to let us know what we'd found. Mrs. Pierce laughed as she looked from the room to us. "Jackpot."

"Wow," said Crocker.

The pantry ran about twelve feet deep and eight feet wide. The walls were lined floor to ceiling with shelves, and another rack of shelves ran right down the middle. All of it, all of it, was crammed with cans and boxes and crates of food. There were like gallon cans of green beans, baked beans, pears, peaches, and mixed fruit. There was beef jerky and jars of berries and big round tins of government surplus cheese.

"A fifty-gallon drum of" — Becca leaned down to read the lid — "peanut butter? Seriously?"

"Six cases of cans of Spam," Crocker said. "Why would they leave all this here?"

"Lots of times in winter, delivery trucks can't make it up the road," Mrs. Pierce said. "Alice Marshall made the rule that there should always be enough food on hand to keep everybody fed for at least a month."

"But why didn't the teachers and school administration take all this with them when they left?"

Mrs. Pierce shrugged. "They closed down the school early in

the Idaho Crisis. Maybe they were hoping that the situation would get better so they could open the place back up. It hardly matters now. We were worried about food. Now we can relax, at least a little bit."

A few minutes later, we were back at the parking lot.

"Any trouble?" asked Mr. Morgan.

"There's no trouble," Mrs. Pierce called out. "For all of us, the war is over. We're safe now. Welcome home."

⌁—• *Israeli Prime Minister Gideon Livnat spoke today in Tel Aviv regarding the ongoing war between Israel and the combined forces of Iran, Iraq, Egypt, Syria, and Global Jihad. The prime minister said, quote, "Israel will use all necessary measures to ensure its right to exist. If necessary, we will employ nuclear weapons to stop the enemies that threaten to destroy us." End quote. This is the first time that Israel has openly admitted to possessing nuclear weapons, and some experts worry that such an admission is evidence of Israel's increasing desperation in their first major war without significant US military support.* •—⌁

⌁—• *Breaker, um, anyone on this channel. Anyone listening. I'm Matt Hennes, a long-haul trucker out of Danville, Kentucky. I'm . . . I always worked hard. Never wanted nothing too much for myself. Took care of my family. Made sure my baby girl had food on the table and a good, safe home. But now . . . Jesus in Heaven. I got nothing. My daughter's three years old, and she's just too skinny. Me and her momma eat just once every two or three days, give all we got to our baby girl. But it ain't enough. I'm no freeloader. No welfare case. But please. I'm desperate. I don't need nothing for me, but does anyone on this channel have any food to spare? Please. I'll do anything. I'll give ya anything. I don't have much, but you can have it. Please. My baby needs something to eat.* •—⌁

⌁—• *for a united America. The United States Congress made its final decision today on the apportionment of US representatives. With so much of the United States in a condition of rebellion, many states are not allowed representation in Congress, but for those that do remain in the union, today's Restoration of Congress Act allows each one the same number of representatives it had before the war. Accordingly, Congress now consists of twenty-six* senators and fifty-nine representatives, in contrast to the one hundred senators and four hundred and thirty-five representatives before the war. States such as Washington, Oregon, and Nevada, which are partially occupied by rebel forces, will be allowed representation as they were before the war. Congresswoman Deena Degotti of Colorado, the new Speaker of the House, hailed the legislation as, quote, "the best way for the United States to move forward, and a system that will allow for the rapid reintegration of former rebel states when the US wins the war." End quote.

In other news, the leadership of the newest so-called independent countries, Arizona, Minnecongan, and Appalachia, were forced to face the terrible consequences of their treasonous decisions after devastating attacks last •—⌄—

⌄—• Hey there, road warriors tuning in on CB or shortwave radio. If you've got fuel and you're looking for action, come on up to the Red Bull, just off I-80 at exit 121 and up South Centerville Road. Our arena is hot tonight! We caught ourselves one hell of a tough Yew-nited States Marine gunnery sergeant, and this evening at ten, he'll be fighting to the death against our two-time champion, former FBI agent Greg "the Snake" Smithson. It's speed against power, and if the Snake survives one more fight, he's earned his freedom. So come and check out the action! We've got cold home brew, hot card tables, and some clean and eager ladies waiting to entertain you too! •—⌄—

⌄—• With the war expanding across the continent, controversial figure PFC Daniel Wright of the Idaho Army National Guard had been fading from the public spotlight, but as the news of his death spreads, so too does his legacy. Even in newly independent countries where Wright was less well-known, these posters are appearing in more and more places.

WE WILL
GIVE YOU
A WAR

When we come back, Dakota News will bring you shocking cam drone footage of the aftermath of a bloody battle near Rapid City.

◦—• *official radio station of Appalachia. We'd like to apologize to our listeners for periodic gaps in our programming. United States and Atlantican forces have been engaged in a deliberate attempt to prevent your government from bringing you, the people of Appalachia, the information you need. However, despite our ene- mies' best efforts to silence our voice and crush our freedom, Appalachia prevails. The United States Marines who invaded Memphis last week were forced back across the Mississippi River today in a hasty retreat that cost them hundreds of lives. Meanwhile, in our North Carolina territory, the advance of Atlantican forces was halted, and Atlantica now struggles to maintain control of Charlotte, Fayetteville, and Wilmington. Colonel Brandon Steele, commander of the First Appalachian Infantry Division, estimates that his forces have killed nearly twelve hundred Atlantican soldiers and will likely surround and liberate Charlotte in a matter of weeks. •—◦*

◦—• *A rare pair of E4 tornadoes cut a swath of destruction in southeast Nebraska last night. The tornadoes moved in a north- east direction, destroying precious farmland that was growing much-needed food. The twisters leveled most of the houses in the small town of Beatrice, Nebraska, and left over half of the town's population of roughly twelve thousand homeless. With many FEMA resources exhausted by the war or captured by newly indepen- dent countries, the survivors of this disaster must come together to help one another. •—◦*

◦—• *The Cliffhanger has traveled all over this collapsing society, broadcasting the truth wherever he goes. He lifts the mask on those who would proclaim themselves your next heroes, to point out the corruption and dangerous self-interest beneath. I'm broadcasting out of a van, always on the run from opportunists like Montaine,*

General Jacobsen, or General Vogel. They want to silence my voice so they can continue to deceive and control a people desperate for hope.

But people must realize that hope is already within them. The people of Pottsville, Pennsylvania, have discovered this truth. This city, just outside the edge of the DC fallout zone, had a population of only fifteen thousand before the war, and now fifty thousand live there in peace.

Refugees from everywhere have come to Pottsville with nothing but desperation and the clothes on their backs. The regular news media, the puppets of the new dictators, would stir fear in your hearts, telling you that all the refugee camps are dangerous traps full of crime and disease. But in Pottsville there are no camps, for the people there have welcomed the newcomers with open arms and open doors. People offer rooms in their own homes. Every office, classroom, church basement, and business stockroom is now an apartment, and more housing is being constructed as fast as the people can work. Apartment vacancies are filled. Derelict houses are restored and reoccupied. What food they have is shared, and every square inch of available ground in the area is dedicated to growing more.

The people of Pottsville, Pennsylvania, have proved that the lies of the new warlords aren't the only answer! That the power of the gun isn't the only truth! The warlords would ask you to rise up and help them kill, but the Cliffhanger calls upon all of you everywhere to rise up and help each other heal! •—⌁

EIGHTEEN

The Alice Marshall School's new cemetery rested in a little valley, ringed by boulders and little cliffs rising six to eight feet on three sides. Four rough crosses made from pine limbs marked the graves of Portia Keelin, Casey Hayes, Stephanie Ollins, and Harold Gates.

"We must find strength in one another," said the chaplain as he continued the funeral service. "We must remind one another of what our Lord Jesus promises us in the Holy Gospel according to Saint Matthew, chapter twenty-eight, verse twenty, 'Behold, I am with you always, even unto the end of the age.' Won't you join with me now, and with those around you, in a word of prayer?"

I bowed my head with most everyone else. In church, before the war, prayer came easily to me. I could focus on what Chaplain Carmichael was saying. It wasn't as easy now. Too many bad memories rippled through my thoughts. I squeezed my eyes closed and forced myself to concentrate.

". . . We ask you to please bring us together, Lord, as brothers and sisters in Christ. As a family. In the name of our Lord and Savior Jesus Christ. Amen."

The sound of sobs and sniffles followed us as the funeral service began to break up. The cool mountain air sent a shiver through me, even with the sun shining, my sweatshirt on, and JoBell's arm around me.

Sergeant Kemp found us as the crowd departed. "Good news and bad news."

"I don't know if I can take any more bad news," JoBell said.

Kemp laughed a little. "Well, compared to everything else, this news isn't that bad. The guys are having trouble getting the generator started, so we can't get power anywhere, but especially where we need it — in the fridges in the kitchen. So, because some people have steaks and pork chops in the coolers, we're going to cook all that up on the grills tonight and eat like kings. Pierce figures it will raise morale to have a sort of 'welcome to our new home' feast."

"And we have to eat it now before it'll go to waste," said JoBell.

"I know engines," I said. "I can help them with the generator."

"Nope," Kemp said. "I need you two to get to the front of the line and eat first and then hit the rack early and try to sleep."

My shoulders slumped. I knew the bad news. "When do we go on?"

JoBell must have figured it out too. "What? Oh, come on, Tom."

Kemp held his hands up in surrender. "What do you want from me? I have to put together a guard roster. The overnight is when the guards are most important, and you people have the most experience. You'll be on from nineteen hundred to zero one. Then again at zero seven to thirteen hundred. I doubt we'll have time to dig in established fighting positions by your shift, so it will be a roving patrol kind of thing."

JoBell held up her Springfield M1A. "I'll never be able to put this thing down."

"Sure you will," I said. "While you're asleep. Anyway, rule number three. We have to make sure what's out there doesn't make its way in here."

"Will you two be able to keep a lookout if I pair you together, or will you be too" — he smiled and raised his eyebrows — "distracted?"

I flipped him off. JoBell wrapped her arms around me and rubbed her leg up and down mine. "I don't know, Sergeant Kemp. You see how hot my boy is. I don't know if I'll be able to control myself."

"Good. Then I'll put you two out in the front parking lot, covering the trail we came up on."

"She's kidding," I called after Kemp as he walked away.

JoBell nibbled the bottom of my ear. "I am not," she whispered.

"Then maybe we should skip the steaks and get right to bed," I said. "That guard shift will come early."

"Forget that," JoBell said, letting me go and walking down the trail toward the chow hall. "I'm hungry."

I laughed and followed her. Cal caught up to me. He was holding hands with Samantha Monohan, but he whispered something to her and she nodded. "Hey, Jo! Wait up!" She ran ahead to catch up with JoBell.

"You get the night shift too?" Cal asked.

I nodded. "It's cool. I'd probably be up all night with bad dreams anyway."

We walked along in silence for a while. Ever since we were kids, Cal was the fun-loving, wild, and crazy one in our group. Sweeney'd be all, "I don't know, Cal. Maybe the ravine is too wide," and Cal would laugh, rev up his dirt bike, and gun the engine to make the jump.

That was before the war. Now . . . I'm not gonna lie. Ever since Cal found out the truth about the Brotherhood, he was like the midway at the county fair with all the power shut off. He used to walk like a tank, but now his arms and shoulders were slumped, and he dragged his feet a little.

"How you doing?" I asked.

"You believe in God?" he asked, his eyes fixed on the ground. "Like the chaplain was saying, I mean?"

"Sure," I said.

"My old man never gave a shit if I went to church or went to jail," Cal said. "He was never around, always on the road. But I . . . I always believed in the Big Man Upstairs, you know?"

"I guess."

"You know how Carmichael was talking about Jesus forgiving and stuff?" He got real quiet. "You think that's true? Like even after all I done, joining the Brotherhood and everything, picking up the rope they hung —"

I grabbed him under his arms and shoved him back against the trunk of a big tree. I wouldn't have been able to do it if Cal had resisted, but his back hit hard. "Hey!" I was right up in his face. "There ain't no way either of us could have known what Crow was gonna do with that rope he sent you to pick up. Jesus forgives you for it, and I forgive you. But you don't talk about any of your Brotherhood stuff around here. One thing I learned in the Army is that the fastest way to make sure the whole unit knows about something is to tell only one or two trusted friends. In a group this small, if you mention hot gossip to one person, everybody is going to know it in a few days. People might not be so understanding."

Cal opened his mouth like he was about to say something, but only a weak sigh escaped his lips. "But . . . Jaclyn. How do I tell her?"

"You don't," I said. "She can't handle that right now. It doesn't matter anyway, because, you big bastard, it isn't your fault. If some guy shoots up a store, is it the gun company's fault?"

Cal frowned. "What? No. That's stupid gun control crap."

"If a guy sells a perfectly good car to another dude, who then gets in a crash and dies, is it the salesman's fault?"

"Okay, I get what you're saying," Cal said. "But if I hadn't —"

"Cal, they would have done it anyway. With or without you."

He finally nodded and stood up straight.

"I wish I could go back in time. Do things different," he said.

The ghost wound in my left hand flared with pain as I thought of the Battle of Boise, the death of my mother, and a hundred other things that had happened in this war. Why was it so easy for me to forgive Cal and accept God's forgiveness for him, when I couldn't let go of all the wrong I'd done? "I hear that, man."

We walked down the long trail toward the chow hall. Most everyone else was way ahead of us now.

"You were right," Cal finally said.

I kicked a rock down the trail. "About what?"

"When we were hiding in Shiratori's basement, and I was covered in blood from cutting the hell out of those Fed assholes."

"Maybe we ought to let the past be the past," I said.

"What I mean is that, you tried to warn me about getting too far into it. Into the war or into fighting. And you were right. I loved the fight too much. The thrill. That adrenaline rush. And yeah, sometimes, lots of times, the fight was for something good, like saving you and JoBell outside of Lewiston. But the power to take out the bad guys and do something good is still power. I think I got hooked on that." He drew his sword and pointed it ahead of him.

"Would you watch it with that thing?" I said.

"I got like addicted to riding in like cowboys and shit and being like" — he stabbed the air — " 'You're done, asshole! I'm Cal Riccon, and I'm going to tell you how things are going to be.' " He shook his head. "It's like a drug, man. And I think my old man was addicted to it too. That's why I knew I couldn't talk to him before we left. It's the thrill of the fight. The power. I gotta give it up."

Chow was kind of messed up. There weren't close to enough seats or plates, so people sat outside on the rocks or on logs. A lot of people ate caveman style, just holding their whole piece of steak or chop in their hands and biting into it. Mr. Morgan's wife had her flute and his daughter brought her violin, and they played a couple songs while we ate. When I first heard about it, I thought bringing the instruments was a stupid waste of space for the trip, but then I realized how long it had been since I'd heard music, how much I missed it. With our playlists from our comms all in the cloud and the Internet all jacked up, our songs were basically gone.

After chow, we hit the rack. The school had sixteen rooms in the big guest dorm, nine student cabins, and six faculty cabins, but space was still scarce, so people had to pack it in. Kemp wanted the people scheduled for guard rotation in the big guest dorm building, so me and JoBell wound up sharing a room with two twin-sized beds with Sweeney and Cal. Sweeney had tried to get Becca to crash with him, but she wanted to spend some time with her family, who was bunked in faculty cabin four.

In the past, we all would have bitched about having only two racks for the four of us, but all of us had been through hell and dealt with worse. Sweeney and Cal insisted JoBell sleep in one of the beds, an offer she accepted right away. She fell across the bed and pulled a ragged quilt over her head, using her sweatshirt for a pillow. Us three guys argued for a couple minutes about who would get a bed and who would get the floor. I didn't want Cal or Sweeney to be screwed over just because I was dating JoBell.

"Shut up!" JoBell finally yelled, holding up the quilt. "Danny, get in here. Sweeney, Cal, you're both fully dressed. Share the other bunk. It's not like you're getting married or anything."

"Um, right," Cal said. "Plus, it won't be weird because you can sleep under the blanket and I'll be on top so —"

"Oh, good thinking, Cal," JoBell said. "That way neither of you will get pregnant. Now go to sleep, or don't, but shut the hell up."

I laughed at that and then lay there on my back with JoBell pressed in next to me, her head on my chest. I breathed deeply, forcing air in and slowly and steadily letting it back out, trying to calm myself, trying to wipe all the bad thoughts from my mind.

Kemp woke us all up at about six. Someone had brought chow over from the dining hall, and coffee, heated over the fire, would be available down in the library all night for the guards. But when we got down there, we could hardly get to the food and coffee. The library was so stuffed with people that part of the crowd had spilled into the big, empty entryway right next to it.

Becca came up behind us and kissed Sweeney on the cheek. "Maybe they could hand us our food?"

TJ found us too. "Right? And maybe they could hurry? We're on duty in less than an hour."

"Screw this," I said, starting to push my way into the crowd. "Excuse me. Excuse us. We just need to get in here to get . . . Excuse us. Can you just —" As I plowed my way through the mass of bodies, my friends followed close behind.

When we finally made it into the library, we found Mrs. Pierce and her family up by the fireplace. Other family clumps were crammed in throughout the room. The Robinsons were behind the Macers. The Grenkes were back in the corner by the table, Skylar perched up on one of the rolling ladders. The Monohans, Blakes, Beans, Ericsons. For a moment, I was kind of pissed that I had been left out of whatever this was all about. But then JoBell squeezed my hand, and I smiled. For me and my friends, the hard part was over. We'd helped them make it here. They could figure out the rest.

"Now, see, that just doesn't seem right to me, ma'am," said Mr. Robinson.

"Oh, come on, Dwight," said Samantha Monohan's stepmom. "You were a national champion fisherman. You've been on TV for catching fish."

Mr. Robinson held up his hands. "I haven't fished a serious tournament for years. Anyway, fishing is what I do for fun, to get away from work. I'd feel guilty out there by the water with everyone else working. I want to earn my keep."

Mrs. Pierce smiled. "Mr. Robinson, we need fresh food. You can fish, and teach others to fish. We also need you to figure out how to make one of those old-fashioned icehouses. We'll harvest ice from the lake this winter to use through the summer."

"I saw some old photos of an icehouse at a bar once," said Lee Brooks. "It's a big pit with some shelves and an insulated roof. You pack the ice with sawdust. I can help."

"That don't hardly seem fair," said Dylan Burns's stepdad. "What if other people want to fish?"

"You want to fish, Mr. Ratcliff?" Mrs. Pierce asked.

The man looked down. "Well, no. It's nothing I've ever enjoyed for myself, but, well, someone might like it."

Tucker Blake's dad spoke up. "Years ago I had this idea that I was going to be a chef. But you know how it goes. One thing leads to another, and I never found the time for culinary school. But if we're picking jobs, I'd really like to work in the kitchen."

"Please let him!" said Mrs. Carmichael. "We need a lot more help. We need people to help prep, cook, and wash dishes. And we'll need people to fill in for the kitchen staff sometimes so the same workers aren't in there all day every day. We need a rotation."

Mr. Blake smiled. "My wife and I would love to help."

An old man standing next to them held up his hand. "I used to be a butcher. You bring in that fish, I can prep it. Or if a hunting party bagged us a deer or moose."

"Now hunting I can do," said Mr. Ratcliff. "Never got into fishing, but I was always a good hunter. Got me a good-sized deer most years."

More people started jumping in to volunteer to hunt. Me and my friends finally made our way to our food, meals on metal plates wrapped in paper. A little pork chop and a scoop of mixed vegetables from a can. It wasn't much, but I passed the plates to my friends and we all scarfed it down.

"The other problem is that there's a little gas left to run the ranges and ovens, but once that's gone, we're in trouble," said Mrs. Carmichael.

"Can they be converted to wood stoves somehow?" Mrs. Pierce asked.

Our old shop teacher, Mr. Cretis, raised his hand. "We brought that welding gear and other tools for a reason. With all that and the tools in the shed at the back of the rec lodge, we have a pretty good shop. I could probably figure out a way to rig those stoves and ovens to burn wood. Might not be pretty, but I bet I could get 'em to work."

"I want to know what I'm getting for those steaks and chops," Caitlyn Ericson's dad said. "I had to trade my Harley for them. How am I being compensated now that everybody's had something to eat?"

"Are you being serious?" Becca said.

"Well, I don't see you complaining while you're eating," Mr. Ericson said.

My second-grade teacher, Mrs. Van Buren, put her hands on her hips. "If this is going to work, we're going to have to share."

"What are you going to share, Rachel?" Mr. Ericson asked. "Teaching?"

"Yeah!" said Mrs. Van Buren. "We're going to want our kids to get an education."

"And what about when my kids are too old for grade school?" Mr. Ericson said. "What then?"

A lot of people chimed in, arguing.

I didn't come all this way to live in some communist compound.

What are we supposed to buy things with? Our money is useless.

We can trade! Trading works fine.

Then who gets the food in the kitchen?

What's a fair trade for child care? Or for education for your kids?

What about the people too old to work?

I am not turning over my family's food!

"Everybody shut the hell up!" I climbed up onto the big wooden table. "I didn't bring any food, Mr. Ratcliff."

"Well, Danny, you should have been thinking ahead."

"Oh, I was," I said. "I was thinking about the Brotherhood guys and other thugs we ran into along the trip. So I brought bullets. Me and my guys and Mr. Grenke here risked our asses to steal diesel from the Brotherhood so we'd have enough fuel to get here. So when we get the diesel generators working again, maybe you don't get any electricity. Hope you brought candles."

"Now hold on a second," Mr. Ericson said.

"We are going to have to work together," I said. "Like Mrs. Van Buren said, we must share to make it through this."

"Just giving away what's ours? That's socialist-style," said Craig Rankin. "That's just un-American."

JoBell climbed up and stood on the table beside me. "America is dead," she said.

"Fine," Mr. Keelin said. "But I've lived my whole life by conservative principles. Danny, you've been on the *Buzz Ellison Show*. You know how he stands for everybody working hard and then getting the rewards that come from that hard work. You're sounding like some liberal Democrat."

"Democrats are dead," JoBell said. "By the millions. So are Republicans. There are no parties anymore."

I felt weird up here above everybody else, so I led JoBell down to stand in the middle of the group. "Damn it. Don't you get it yet? All that political bitching, the stupid arguments? They're what got us into all this!" I shook my head. "Buzz Ellison . . . You know who used to love listening to Buzz Ellison? My business partner, Dave Schmidt. Now Schmidty's dead! Ellison used to bitch about President Rodriguez all the time. Rodriguez is dead. Millions are dead, because everybody was busy trying to find someone else to blame instead of fixing the damned problems in the first place." I put my empty plate down on the table. "Now me and my friends gotta go on guard duty to protect everybody through the night. We ain't doing it to get paid, to see what people will trade for our time, but because it has to be done. I was a mechanic once." I held up my M4. "Now I guess my main skill is fighting. I'll do whatever you think I'd be good at. However I can help."

"No offense, Danny," Mr. Grenke said, "but the war was also caused by people trying to one-up other people, shouting them down like this."

I was about to fire back when Mr. Shiratori cut me off. "Ryan brings up a good point, Danny. So did Craig. I'm not saying he should get direct compensation for his food, but say what you want about our old capitalist system, it provided reasonable order for our society, with the expectation of reward for hard work. If you take away the direct reward, do you also take away the incentive to work?"

"I had an uncle," said Lee Brooks. "When he was young, he joined this artist colony commune. It was a whole bunch of hippies sharing everything. My uncle was a carpenter. He joined up for the free love, I think, but also because he wanted to spend his days making wood sculptures and stuff like that. The problem came when he kept getting tapped to fix up their ancient house. He and the farmers who spent their days plowing fields in the hot sun didn't think it was fair that some of the others used all their time for painting or writing. The commune lasted for less than a year."

"The alternative to these systems of sharing is to force everyone to work, often under the threat of force, like in the old Soviet Union," said Mr. Shiratori.

"We're nothing like them," said Darren Hartling.

"Of course not," Mr. Shiratori said. "We're going to have to spend some serious time discussing how we're going to make this little society of ours work."

"And we'll need to be patient," Mrs. Pierce said, her eyes fixed on me.

I knew what she meant, so I nodded at her. Then me and my friends squeezed through the crowd, heading for a long night of patrols.

When we got outside the building, we found Jaclyn Martinez standing on the pathway, a tactical shotgun leaning back against her shoulder.

"Jackie, what are you doing? Are you okay?" I felt like an idiot as soon as I said it, and the look on Jaclyn's face told me she thought the same thing.

"I'm pulling guard duty with all of you," Jaclyn said. "I want to help protect everyone."

I noticed Cal tightly gripping the wooden railing on the steps to the porch. He stared at Jaclyn openmouthed.

"Thanks, Jackie," Sweeney said. "But we got this."

"Why don't you get some rest?" Becca said.

"Everybody's been telling me to rest, as if that's my problem," Jackie said. "Not that my parents were murdered, but that I'm tired."

"It's not that," said JoBell. "Just that you've been through a lot, and you should take some time to try to recover."

"Spare me your psychobabble bullshit," Jaclyn said. "They're dead. There's no recovering from that."

Becca hopped down the steps and tried to put her hand on Jaclyn's shoulder. "But we'll be up all night, and you probably didn't sleep much on the trip." Jaclyn pulled away as Becca continued, "I know nothing can make up for what happened, but you have to take care of yourself. Why don't you try to get some more sleep?"

"No!" Jaclyn said. "Don't you get it!? I can't sleep! I don't want to sleep! Whenever I close my eyes, I see the ropes around their necks. Too much jacked-up shit has happened for me to sleep!"

The murder of Jaclyn's parents had been a nightmare for me. It had to be a thousand times worse for her. My mother's death had been different, but even now, it still cut me deep. I knew something of what Jaclyn was facing. I saw the looks on my friends' faces, and I hated like hell that they too understood what Jaclyn was going through.

"All right," I said. "Welcome to the team."

which might at first seem trivial, but is, in fact, becoming a serious problem. Before the civil war, there were nearly eighty million pet dogs and ninety million pet cats in America. Now many owners aren't able or around to take care of their pets. The result? Dangerous packs of feral animals. The dogs have become a particular danger, with hundreds of reports of children being viciously attacked when

DAVID AUDLY ★ ★ ★ ★ ☆

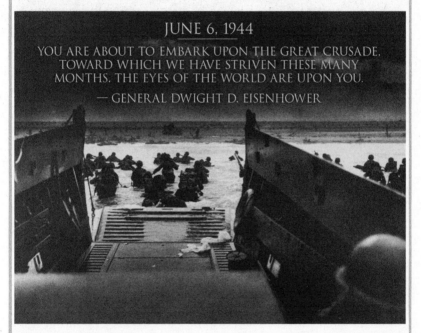

JUNE 6, 1944

YOU ARE ABOUT TO EMBARK UPON THE GREAT CRUSADE, TOWARD WHICH WE HAVE STRIVEN THESE MANY MONTHS. THE EYES OF THE WORLD ARE UPON YOU.

— GENERAL DWIGHT D. EISENHOWER

The eyes of the world are upon us all now, but we're not eliminating tyranny or bringing about security.

★ ★ ★ ★ ☆ This Post's Star Average 4.02   [Star Rate] [Comment]   11 minutes ago

JESS GERKIN ★ ★ ★ ★ ☆

They call the Americans who fought in WWII or supported the war effort the Greatest Generation. They will call us the Worst Generation.

★ ★ ★ ★ ☆ This Comment's Star Average 4.55   [Star Rate]   9 minutes ago

LYNN LATTA ★ ★ ★ ☆ ☆

The Last Generation.

★ ★ ★ ★ ☆ This Comment's Star Average 4.00   [Star Rate]   8 minutes ago

⌐—• *This is BBC Television from London. Normal programming has been suspended, and we now join Michael Lancaster in the news studio."*

"I'm instructed to advise you that the entire United Kingdom has been elevated to Alert Condition Three. All nonessential travel and communications are suspended. Be prepared to proceed to your local designated emergency shelter, but do not conduct movement to that location at this time. Moments ago, NATO's automated missile defense system came online, warning of short-range missiles fired from Soviet-held Ukraine and Lithuania. Most of these missiles have been shot down, and it must be stressed that so far, these missiles are armed with conventional warheads. However, the world is on full alert against a possible nuclear attack. Soviet troops and armored units have entered Poland, Romania, Hungary, and Slovakia. Soviet bombers and fighter planes are attacking NATO

positions in those countries, with some Soviet air assets headed toward Berlin. British and French aircraft are moving to intercept and join the fight. British Royal Marines have deployed to Germany to supplement the German defense and help secure Poland. The Soviet leadership is justifying this blatant aggression, saying, quote, 'The Soviet people have a right to defend themselves against attacks from an unstable NATO.' End quote.

"I'm also authorized to reveal to you at this time that the Soviet Union has signed a mutual defense pact with the People's Republic of China as well as with Iran, Syria, and Iraq. They have dubbed this alliance the Free Federation of Nations. In response, all NATO member countries as well as Japan and South Korea have signed on to an alliance. Prime Minister Dennis Carman has confirmed that as of five a.m. United Kingdom time, World War III has begun. •—⋏

⋏—• Soldiers of the First Oklahoma Infantry Division, in addition to well-armed area civilians, fought a bloody battle in the city of Clinton against United States infantry and armor, finally pushing US forces back into Woodward and the Oklahoma Panhandle. President Fergus's office estimates over two thousand Oklahoman casualties. •—⋏

⋏—• Frank Wood was a young man barely out of high school when he participated in the Allied invasion of Nazi-occupied France. Now in his nineties, Frank has depended on a wheelchair to get around for the last several years. But that has never stopped him from showing his pride in the flag he helped defend all those years ago. As a result, Frank Wood has not missed one Fourth of July parade in Bristol, Rhode Island, in over fifty years."

"I come home from the war in '45, married Beverly in '47, and we moved here in the spring of '50 when I got a job fixing boats. I marched with the other veterans behind our flag in every Fourth of July parade since then. 'Course, in . . . 1953, I was worried I'd miss it, but my daughter decided to be born July 2. She and her family were in New York when . . . Every year, we'd lose some of the old-timer veterans like me, but I never thought it would come to this."

"This year, since Rhode Island is now a part of the independent nation of New England, there is no Fourth of July Independence Day celebration in Bristol. Worse, many Bristol residents have fled the city for fear of radioactive fallout from New York. Mr. Wood is making this year's Fourth of July observation alone."

"Some people say the radiation will kill me, but when you're my age . . . You know, plenty of times in the war, at Normandy, in the Ardennes, I passed by the bodies of good men who didn't make it, thinking it was a miracle I lived through that day. Another miracle the day after that. And I said to myself, at the end of the war, 'Well, Frankie, you done it. The war didn't take you. You gotta live good now. You owe it to those men who didn't make it.' Well, now here's World War III, and I have outlived my country, outlived my family. I'm not going to survive this war. I look out there to where my friends and fellow veterans used to march. All gone now. 'I'm right behind you, boys. Old Frankie Wood's used up his last miracle.' •⌇

⌇• The combination of this record-high temperature of 110 degrees and sporadic power outages is creating a dangerous situation in Chicago land. In Naperville today, residents endured the loss of electricity for several hours, and despite the efforts of Liberum soldiers to distribute water and run generators for air-conditioned public "cold centers," twenty-six deaths were reported, including six in a Naperville retirement community.

Several hundred more are reported dead in battles along the

Mississippi at Rock Island and at Muscatine and Burlington, Iowa. WGN's reporters take you to the heart of the action with •—ᴧ̃

ᴧ̃—• For those of you just joining us here on NBC News, a recap on the stunning events in Korea. The rumors are true. Official confirmation came in a few hours ago. North Korea has fallen. The Korean Peninsula is unified. There is no more North Korea or South Korea, only Korea, controlled by the democratically elected government in Seoul. The Korean War, which officially began in 1950, has finally come to an end. We have reports that most of the remaining ranks of the former North Korean military have defected, and a united Korean military now stands by near the border with China, preparing for the possibility of a Chinese invasion.

"We go now to footage of the joyful reunions of many Korean families. Grandparents who were just children when their country was divided decades ago are seen here weeping with joy and introducing their extended families to their long-separated relatives.

"Elsewhere, over fifty thousand prisoners were liberated from the notorious Pukchang Political Prison Camp and other political prisons and reeducation camps across the former North Korea. You can see here the obvious effects of starvation and the scars and bruises of torture on the prisoners. United Korean troops are providing comfort and medical care.

"But we want to take you to this footage recorded just a few minutes ago. Here you see the former supreme leader of North Korea, Kim Jong Un, in handcuffs in the Great Hall of the Korean Supreme Court in Seoul. The elite members of the South Korean 707th Special Mission Battalion, who were responsible for the daring surprise capture of the North Korean dictator, are standing guard along those white columns. At the top of the stairs, standing under the statue of the goddess of justice, is

Korean Prime Minister Jung Park. Here's the prime minister now. I'm getting the translation."

"Kim Jong Un, your reign of terror is over. No longer will you torture the Korean people. You will stand trial on tens of thousands of charges of crimes against humanity and many other violations of Korean law. Do you have anything to say before I remand you to the custody of your guards?"

"I am Kim Jong Un, the rightful leader of the Democratic People's Republic of Korea! I will lead our people in the march to victory and prosperity!"

"No, sir, you will not. You will be led by your jailers in a march back to your cell. •⌁

⌁• continuing our live broadcast of the American Freedom concert at the full to capacity World Arena in Colorado Springs. Here's country music star Hank McGrew."

"How y'all doing tonight? You enjoying this free concert? Are you ready to rock for America? I can't hear you! You're going to have to be louder than that if we're gonna bring our country back together! Give it up for the USA!"

"USA! USA! USA!"

"All right! That's better, y'all. Now . . . now I wanna get real serious, 'cause this one's dedicated to the troops. It's called 'America, Help Us.'"

When I was young, my pappy drove a truck with a big gun rack,
A raised-up four-by-four with shiny six-inch chrome
    smokestacks.
He'd drive us down to Skippy's Bar, drink beer, and get
    tanked up,
Then we'd go hunting possum with some help from my
    favorite pup.

Now Old Glory no longer flies at the silent baseball field,
and the church doors are all shuttered, so our spirits can't be
     healed.
The eagle's dying painfully, bleeding out on our ruined farms,
And the cowboys have stopped riding. Instead they take
     up arms.

Americaaaaaaaaa!
Listen to this country song.
Americaaaaaaaaa!
'cause this war is just plain wrong.
Sometimes getting back together don't seem like it's in the
     cards,
But we can work it out, my brother, if we only work real hard.
Americaaaaaaaaa! •⌁

⌁• *Stand by for an important live announcement on ANN. Citizens of Atlantica, here is a special message from our leader, General Jonathan Vogel."*

"Moments ago, submarines under my command launched a devastating attack on Seattle and Joint Base Lewis-McChord just south of the city, firing two hundred Tomahawk missiles from the north end of Puget Sound. United States countermissile measures had no time to engage. These missiles destroyed all Seattle bridges, airports, harbor facilities, and US anti-aircraft gun batteries. Near total damage was inflicted on Joint Base Lewis-McChord. The carrier Obama and the destroyer Boehner have been sunk. Casualties from this attack, both military and civilian, will likely exceed one million.

"This is a message to United States Vice President General Chuck Jacobsen. You have threatened our cities with nuclear *attack, but I have just destroyed your last seaport, using only conventional weapons. The difference between you and me is that I am strong, and as a result, the people of Atlantica are strong, and we are prepared to use our weapons to effect the total destruction of our enemies. Civilian casualties are not our concern. If you do not stand down your attacks on Atlantica, your military will be crushed and more of your people will be killed. Atlantica is victory.* •—⋏

⋏—• The Chinese Navy had divided the Korean and Japanese navies in the Sea of Japan until the extraordinary appearance of the former American Rogue Fleet. Two full state-of-the-art carrier groups complete with submarine escorts have entered the war on behalf of the Allies. In the first minutes of Rogue Fleet's air and submarine attack, a dozen Chinese destroyers and battleships were crippled or destroyed. Against official United States protest, Rogue Fleet has been granted full state recognition and safe harbor by both Japan and Korea. •—⋏

⋏—• My fellow Americans, I know the news sometimes seems to bring only heartache and despair. Certainly the death of nearly one million US citizens in Seattle has filled us all with the deepest grief and a quiet, unyielding anger. In such times, one of the first casualties can be our hope for the future. But, as your president, I'm here to assure you that the United States will prevail. Our best days are yet to come.

Even as I'm speaking now, United States officials are hard at work increasing food production as well as fuel and energy distribution. Citizens of the United States, know that you are not forgotten. A new, even more aggressive offensive is being planned, and victory is within our grasp. Until that great day, we must continue to sacrifice, and to find comfort in our unity. Thank you. •—ᴧ

ᴧ—• In a stunning surprise attack, United States forces have advanced much deeper into Texas. Early this morning, Marine infantry and armor followed close behind a heavy aerial bombardment moving in from the northwest. Within hours, they occupied what remained of the cities of Amarillo, Plainview, and Lubbock. Casualties on both sides, including civilians, are estimated to be over twenty thousand. Texas President Rod Percy, commenting on the events from his bunker in the capital of Austin, said •—ᴧ

ᴧ—• must thank the Republic of Idaho for special permission to make this report from Boise. Hopefully this is a sign of increased cooperation between the Republic of Idaho and Cascadia. I'm standing here at the intersection of North Capitol Boulevard and Bannock Street, in front of the partially collapsed dome of the Idaho capitol building, where one year ago today, August 27, National Guard troops opened fire on demonstrators, leaving twelve dead and nine wounded. This so-called Battle of Boise set into motion events leading to the present civil war and the deaths of tens of millions worldwide. It is a sad irony that the Guardsman alleged to have fired the first shot, PFC Daniel Wright of Freedom Lake, Idaho, has not survived to this grim anniversary. This war has cost everyone dearly, and yet, even after facing such terrible adversity, the Republic of Idaho and all the newly independent countries in the Pan American area fight on toward peace and freedom. Rebecca Cho, NBC News. •—ᴧ

NINETEEN

We figured it wasn't practical for every single person to weigh in on everything our little village did, so we elected a thirteen-person council, with Tabitha Pierce as our chair. Sweeney and Cal got it into their heads that I should be on this council, and even though I told them I'd knock them out if I got picked, they still campaigned for me. I won, and I got stuck going to boring-ass meetings.

There were a lot of arguments through the summer like we had during Operation Exodus and during that first meeting in the library, but we worked it out. The council set up food rationing and duty and shower rotations. People mostly worked and ate the same shift as their families, but we had a couple complicated ex-spouse situations, so that wasn't always the case. The council spent hours figuring out rotations for kids so that they could have time with this parent or that parent when they worked other schedules.

The work schedules themselves were a whole other challenge. In the end, the council made a huge list of duties and asked everyone to apply for their top three choices. Then the thirteen of us spent days working out the assignments. Of course, it wasn't always possible to give everyone a job from their top three, and even people who were given one of their first choices bitched, but we set it up so that people who did good work for a month could apply for a duty change. The system even allowed people to cycle through a period of days off. At first, the idea floated around that we might build some sort of punishment cell, a solitary confinement box to penalize people who refused to work. After all, there was so much to do, and we needed everyone's help. But Mrs. Pierce crushed that idea at once. "We're not going to build trust and community, we won't have peace, if we start out with threats. We need to work together because we want to help one another and to honor the sacrifice of those who didn't make it here with us."

"Some gave all," I said, remembering something I'd read online once.

"And so all must give some," said Mrs. Pierce.

It took forever, but eventually we had a workable system going. We had enough people willing to work guard duty that our "soldiers" only had to work six hours on/six hours off guard shifts for four days at a time. So, I would work the zero one hundred to zero seven hundred and thirteen hundred to nineteen hundred shifts. Then I'd have four days of other work. After that, I pulled guard duty from zero seven to thirteen hundred and from nineteen hundred to zero one followed by four more days of work details and then four days off. People who didn't cover guard duty simply worked different jobs. Kids mostly went to school, which was taught by Mr. Morgan, Mrs. Van Buren, and Mrs. Stewart.

Mr. Cretis offered to teach, but we needed his shop skills for other stuff. I helped him take the big solar assist power units off the buses. We used one to provide power for the kitchen. They actually had a working refrigerator, freezer, and microwave in there. Mr. Cretis custom-built wood-fired water heaters for two latrines and the kitchen. The other solar unit powered the radios that Sergeant Crocker set up in the room right outside the library. We tried to use our comms, but we gave up after we figured out the deep Idaho mountains weren't really the best place for Internet. Crocker directed me and my friends in setting up a huge, powerful antenna rigged with wires in these giant pines next to the guest dorm building, which we were calling the Council Building. The radio setup let us finally get some news from the outside.

It was strange for all of us who had grown up streaming music, shows, and movies online to now gather around the radio like old times, but plenty of people pulled up metal folding chairs for the Sergeant Crocker radio show. Once in a while, we were lucky enough to tune in to music, but most of the time, all we got was news, most of it bad. World War III had begun, and most signs indicated it was likely to be far worse than the previous world wars. When we heard the reports that I was dead, Sweeney and Cal made a big thing of it, patting my back and making jokes like "You look pretty good for a dead guy" and "Hey, Wright, if you're dead and JoBell's single —" I cut them off with a quick punch to the arm. I'm not gonna lie. I was happy to hear the world thought I was dead. It was the best way to drop out of it.

JoBell and some of the others got all excited about this Cliffhanger pirate radio guy. I had to admit he had serious balls, traveling all around and sneaking his way on the radio like that. He was a nice change of pace from the regular propaganda that the other radio stations put out. He didn't care which government he pissed off, but just talked about what was really happening. Better yet, he was the only one on the air with any good news. Although the war grew worse and worse, the Pan American Peace Movement was also growing in cities everywhere. The Cliffhanger reminded us that there were still good people, that some folks still worked together to help one another. That kind of news, and the peace we'd found together at Alice Marshall, made good comfort for our aching bodies at the end of long work days.

The solar assist units weren't the only parts we took off the buses. We completely cannibalized bus one. We didn't have enough bunks, so I helped remove its seat cushions. Me and Mr. Cretis took a cutting torch to that sucker to salvage the metal so we could make more wood stoves. We converted its engine into a generator that could provide limited electricity to the whole school. I was kind of proud of that. Hell, we even used the tires to make a bunch of swings for the kids, and after we found golf balls and a set of clubs in the rec lodge, we used the tailpipe and some scrap metal to build a mini golf course. Someone had brought an old portable DVD player with some cartoons for the little kids, and with that, the swings, the mini golf, the canoes and other sports equipment, the books in the library, and the growing band, we didn't do so bad for entertainment.

I'm not gonna lie. The band was pretty good. They called themselves the Deadbeats after Crystal Bean's uncle, who played guitar and said he'd never had a real job. Mr. Morgan's wife played flute. Their daughter was good on the violin. And Chase Draper had built his own drum set out of old coffee cans and whatever other materials he could find. His drumsticks were whittled from sticks he'd found.

Jaclyn had it rough. She pulled guard duty with us a few times, but she seemed to be sinking into such a deep depression that we seriously thought of taking her gun. She stopped showering, and even when we brought her clean clothes, she wouldn't always change. She barely ate.

One night after Jaclyn had skipped chow again, I explained to the people in the kitchen that I would be taking an extra helping of vegetable deer soup for her. With a couple spoons, bowls, and a full thermos, I went to her room and found her slumped in a chair, staring at the wall.

I was no shrink. I had no idea what I should say. Finally, I went for the practical. I poured her soup into her bowl and set it down in front of her. "The council's been talking. If you don't eat, they're going to try force-feeding you." That got her to look at me, at least. I ate a spoonful. "It's actually pretty good." I didn't know what else to do, so I kept talking. "I got some jobs I need help with. You any good with tools?"

She didn't answer, but she did pick up her spoon and start eating. We ate the rest of our little meal in silence. The next day she showed up at the shop. She'd cleaned herself up and changed clothes. She didn't say anything, but she and I went to work.

I worked with Jaclyn a lot through the summer. Sometimes she'd join me in the shop, helping me with welding or with fixing something. For a while the two of us spent time improving the trails around the school. I think she liked jobs with me because I didn't try to make her talk much. We had a nice rhythm. She told me one time that she kept working to keep her mind off how she lost her family. I could understand that.

Winter was coming, so one of our biggest tasks was getting ready for the cold. That meant wood. We created an old-time pioneer lumber camp a slight distance away from the school. Alice Marshall had a chain saw, which ran out of gasoline fast. We'd have been set if the thing ran on diesel. We had a lot of that left. But without the chain saw, we had six axes and a bunch of handsaws. Guys worked out a rhythm, with two men trading chops to a tree trunk. It took a long time, but eventually they'd bring the tree down. Then the rest of the crew would go to work with handsaws, cutting the trees into more manageable chunks of firewood. Lumber duty ran every day from sunrise to sunset, because not only did we need a lot of wood for heating water and our cabins, but we wanted a fire break and dead space around the school to spot and shoot any invaders.

We sent hunting parties deep into the woods so they wouldn't shoot close to the school and give away our position to anyone who might be in the area. These were groups of ten, half of them out there to bring in game, the other half to take down any dangerous people they might encounter. They never spotted any humans, but they brought in three deer and a giant moose. Since we had power in the refrigerator and freezer, we were able to store most of the meat, but we also smoked a lot of it in case our homemade generator failed. With that and everything the fishing team was bringing in, our biggest challenge was finding enough vegetables. JoBell, Becca, and Sweeney often joined the gardening team, trying to grow potatoes, carrots, lettuce, and tomatoes. We worried that the growing season would be too short on the mountain, but the team worked constantly in their giant garden near the classrooms, and they swore we'd have plenty of vegetables come harvest time.

"Ain't these supposed to be our off days?" Cal walked into the shop one day in late August.

I looked up from the piece of metal from bus one that I was beating and grinding into the shape of a snow shovel. When it started to snow, we'd have to shovel trenches so people could move among the buildings, especially out to the latrines. Jaclyn was screwing the wooden handles we'd made from branches onto the shovel blades. "Winter is coming," she reminded him.

I laughed. "Thanks, Ned Stark."

Cal frowned. "Yeah, I saw that show too. That guy worked all the time. It didn't turn out so great for him." He shot a look at the door. Even after the whole summer, he could never quite relax around Jaclyn. "JoBell, Becca, and a bunch of the girls challenged us to mini golf."

"Dudes." Sweeney came rushing into the shop on his cane, bumping into a pile of shovel blades and knocking them to the floor. "Sorry." He started picking them up. "The girls just dropped the big one. They figured out the kitchen's making blackberry crisp for dessert next week. They just bet the crisp. If we don't beat them, we're out of luck for the dessert from all those million berries we helped pick."

"Let me finish this shovel," I said. "Then I'll be right with you."

"Come on, man," Sweeney said. "We have to win this one. Just think, double blackberry crisp!"

"I said I'd be right there." I spoke a little harsher than I'd meant to.

Cal looked at me for a moment. "Well, if you —"

"Why don't you go with him?" Jaclyn said. "I can do this."

"Cal," Sweeney said. "Go tell the girls to wait a little. We'll be out there in a minute to win their dessert from them."

"Right." Cal ran off.

Sweeney tapped the ground with his cane. "Listen, Wright," he said. "It's like the end of summer. So we need to take advantage of being outside while we can. The biggest enemy we've had to deal with up here is deer trying to get in our garden. You have to relax a little, buddy. What's the point of finally finding peace if you can't have a little fun?"

Jaclyn frowned. "After everything that's happened, it's hard to laugh it up playing mini golf, like blackberry crisp is the most important thing in the world."

Sweeney fingered the shiny, twisted skin on his cheek. "Everybody's been working all summer, but you two have hardly stopped. Danny, sometimes you take a canoe out on the lake by yourself, to do what? I don't know. I don't *want* to know."

"It's just good to be alone," I said. "Peaceful. Quiet. Like the war never happened. Like the world is just me and the sky."

"Well, we're a part of your world too, buddy. I think we've earned that after everything we've been through." Sweeney nodded at Jaclyn as he spoke. "People *need* some recreation once in a while. It's good for them. Healthy. If you don't think you can have a good time, at least try to have fun and fake it for your friends." Sweeney offered me a concerned smile and then hobbled back to the others.

It was hard for me to think about having fun when I remembered all the terrible things I'd done. But maybe Sweeney was right about Jaclyn. Her pain was no fault of her own. Maybe taking a break would help her out. "Jackie," I said. "He's right. I think we need a break. Let's go whack some golf balls." I put down my hammer and forced a smile.

Jaclyn shook her head. "Fine." She smiled a little. "Say goodbye to your crisp!"

"I know these scavenging missions are kind of a pain —" Becca started to say. It was a little over a week later, and we were moving through the woods.

"Kind of a pain?" TJ said from a few paces behind me. "I *hate* these missions. Pale Horse drops us off in the woods, miles from the school. We walk for days, and as soon as our packs lighten up after we eat some of our food, we find a cabin or a shed with some crap we need, and then the load on the way back is twice as heavy."

"And I got to hump the radio and extra ammo the whole way," Cal said.

Sergeant Kemp was leading our file through the forest. "If First Sergeant Herbokowitz was around to hear you all complaining so much, he'd drop us all and PT us until we went blind," he said.

"That's what I'm trying to say," Becca said. "These missions aren't easy, but I still kind of like them. It's a chance to get out here with the whole original crew, just us. No council. No Craig Rankin telling stupid stories about his old Buick with the underglow lights."

"And the cherry bomb glasspack!" JoBell groaned. "I know what you mean. So dumb."

"Are you kidding? Those things are awesome," I said. "I don't know that I'd want one on a little Buick Regal, but they're still cool." I stepped over a large rock on the trail. "Damn, I miss working on cars."

"Becca, how are you and your parents getting along?" TJ said after we'd walked in silence for a while.

"It's great to be able to be with them again." Becca held up her M4 and pressed the barrel against her forehead. "But I'm not sure how long I can go on living with them. I'm eighteen now, and it's September. In a normal world, I'd be moving out to go to college. Where am I going to move at Alice Marshall?"

"There's room in my loft of love," Sweeney said. We'd made a loft for his bus seat bed, with support poles from small pine trees and a loft floor from patched-together lumber and branches. He'd worked for weeks to gather every branch and small tree trunk he could find, walling off his loft all the way to the ceiling.

"Oh hell no!" Cal said. "My rack is right under there. I don't want you two messing around up above me."

"Hey, at least my love loft is closed in," Sweeney said. "Danny and the kitten are just right out in the open."

JoBell sighed. "The 'kitten' is going to rip your face off if you call her that one more time, Eric."

"We have never messed around when you guys were in the room," I said. JoBell tapped me on the back.

"Dude, are you kidding me?" Cal shouted. "Sometimes you two think we're asleep, but we're not asleep!"

"Oh my gosh," JoBell whispered.

"See?" said TJ. "That's why I'm glad I live next door. All dudes. It stinks and there's loud snoring, but I'm okay with it."

Kemp stopped up in front. "There's a war going on and any number of psychos could be out in these woods. Can you act like you're soldiers and not still in high school?"

We walked in silence for a moment before Sweeney spoke up. "Well, we never did make it to graduation."

We all laughed.

A couple hours later, we found a small house with some outbuildings at the end of a dirt lane. The place was quiet. Nothing moved. But we still followed procedure and set up an overwatch position while Kemp radioed to Pale Horse to let the team know we'd found something. After watching the house for about an hour and detecting no movement or sound, we hid our packs in the woods and ran up on the place, rifles at the ready. We went in the back door and cleared every room on the main floor, the upstairs, and the basement. Then we checked out the small horse barn and the two old sheds. Yeah, it might have seemed a little overcautious, but even if we sometimes joked around on the trail, we were way past being stupid on ops like this.

After the security checks, we all gathered in the dining room. "Do you think it's abandoned?" JoBell said.

"It looks like it's in pretty good shape," TJ said.

"We'll look everything over more carefully now," Kemp said. "Check for the usual signs." We all nodded. We didn't want to be like the Brotherhood, breaking into occupied houses and taking people's stuff. But the war had messed up everything, and a lot of people had died or fled Idaho and left a lot of useful things behind, so we'd done this a bunch of times. If there was still food here, especially fresh food, then someone probably lived here. If we found weapons, they were probably coming back, because who would leave without their guns? But if the food and guns were gone, or if there was evidence of people packing up to leave, then we took what we needed.

"Okay, let's shake it up," Kemp said. "Rule number three. Becca and Sweeney, post a guard out front. And, um, Danny and JoBell, cover the back. Me and Cal and TJ will search the house. I don't have to tell you the nights are getting cold, so keep a lookout for coats, hats, gloves, sweatshirts, and blankets and things."

I sighed and my shoulders slumped. Guard duty sucked. And lots of times the guys searching had first dibs on cool things they found. Cal shot me a look like, *Sucks to be you, loser!*

JoBell took me by the hand and we went out to the little back porch. It was only about six feet square, but it was covered with a little aluminum roof and surrounded by a short brick wall. "At least we'll have good cover," JoBell said.

"I hope we don't need it." I sat down on the cement cap of the wall and leaned against one of the posts that held up the roof.

"How many places have we searched?" she asked. "Twenty, at least. And only once did anything happen."

One time we had scared the shit out of a family who was hiding from us in the basement. We apologized and left their house right away. "Yeah, we were damned lucky that old man didn't shoot us."

"Or that we didn't shoot him." JoBell nodded. "But most of the time, this goes smoothly."

"First Sergeant Herbokowitz always warned us about being complacent."

JoBell held up her M1A a little. "I'm never complacent." She sat down on the wall on the other side of the porch so she could watch the opposite way.

"Oh, kick ass!" Cal yelled from inside. "Comic books! Spider-Man, Captain America. The . . . the New Warriors? Point is, comics!"

"Keep it down, Riccon!" Kemp yelled back.

"You know, I was talking to Becca the other day," JoBell said after a long time. "She and Eric are getting serious."

"Yeah, I noticed," I said. "Sweeney spends a lot of time volunteering to help with the" — I made air quotes with my fingers — " 'gardening.' "

JoBell laughed. "He actually does a lot of good work in the garden. But I mean, they're getting serious. They want to get married."

I sat up. "Really?"

JoBell frowned. "Why do you look so surprised?"

Was I showing a hint of the old weirdness between me and Becca? If so, I had to cover it up fast. "Just, Sweeney always swore he'd never get married. How did he put it? That getting married was like going to a buffet, but only eating the salad. Every day of your life."

JoBell shrugged. "He's changed. We all have. My point is, they don't want to upstage us. And you and I have been engaged for a while now."

I smiled at her. "I'm glad."

"I'm glad too, but I think it's time we do this." She smiled back at me, and then checked her sector again. "I don't know, maybe I was holding out hope for a fancier wedding. But I have that wedding dress we found a couple missions ago. Becca could help me adjust the length. Maybe we could ask Chaplain Carmichael to make it happen? Daddy won't be there, but if he stays deep in that bunker and we keep safe, we may both make it through the war to have family Thanksgivings and Christmases in the future."

"You sure you don't want to wait until after the war?" I asked. "Until we go home?"

"You don't want to marry me?" She asked it playfully, but with a tiny note of concern.

I got up, walked over to her, and pulled her into a hot kiss. When we finally parted, our lips stayed only inches apart.

"Naughty boy," she whispered.

"This isn't close to naughty," I said. "Wait until we get back to —"

"I meant, you're not covering your sector, naughty boy." She laughed and pushed me away, then got serious again. "We were waiting until we were out of the war, but I think we're out of it now. The Alice Marshall School is our home. All our friends are with us."

I thought about it. Most of my old dreams for our future together had burned to ashes, but at the school . . . The library would make a good room for the ceremony. Sweeney could be my best man. Cal would probably try to give a speech at the reception in the chow hall. Maybe I could shoot a couple turkeys for the meal. How lucky was I to have a girl like this? No matter how much bad stuff had happened, JoBell always kept me going.

"Okay." I said. "You're right. When we get back, you and Becca get that dress all fixed up, and then we'll get married." I opened the back door and called into the house. "Hey, you guys! Let me know if you find a tux in there."

"Shut up and cover us," Kemp called back.

I went back to my side of the porch and looked out at the edge of the property. "It will be great. We'll finally be . . ." I spotted a flash of white a few feet back in the woods. "What the hell is that?" I said. There was something down along the ground. I brought my rifle stock up to my cheek and scanned the area.

"What is it?" JoBell asked.

"Don't know. Cover me." I jumped over the short wall and started walking out toward the woods, my eyes and rifle still on whatever was out there.

"Danny!" JoBell hissed. "Rule number one!"

"It's not that far," I said. JoBell could pick off any trouble with that rifle of hers. And if this thing was a person or an animal, it would have done something by now. "It's probably nothing."

I walked out past the first trees. The thing wasn't moving, so I stopped aiming at it and swept the woods with my M4. That familiar jolt ran through me again — the boredom of standing guard replaced with faster breathing, a rapid heartbeat, and an intense awareness of everything around me.

I rounded one last tree to get a better look. That's when I saw the white bones of the rotting bodies.

TWENTY

I ran back to the house right as Cal came out the back door. "Guys, this is a Brotherhood safe house," he said.

"This far out?" JoBell asked. "This close to the school?"

"How do you know it's the Brotherhood?" I asked before I could report what I found.

"I'm so stupid. I should have checked the front door right away." He shook his head. "When we . . . When *they* find a safe house like this —"

"Or take one," JoBell said.

Cal nodded. "They tie something, a necktie or a piece of rope, around both the inside and outside doorknob of the front door. That's a signal to any of them who come back that it's safe to crash there. If the tie has been removed, they know there's trouble."

"Cal, what are you doing?" Kemp came out on the back porch. Everyone else was right behind him. "You're supposed to get on the radio."

"Before you do that —" I pointed my rifle at the woods. "I found two bodies. Animals and maggots have gotten to them pretty good, but their clothes were sort of holding them together. Big bullet holes in their skulls."

"Probably the people who owned the house." Kemp sighed. "Okay. We're moving out. Right now."

"We're not even taking the food?" TJ said. "There's a whole case of beef jerky in there."

Kemp closed the door to the house and started leading us back to where we'd left our packs. "We're taking nothing. We'll leave the ties around the doorknobs. If the Brotherhood is operating in the area, we don't want them to know anyone was here. We don't want any search parties looking for who robbed them."

"But we're miles from Alice Marshall," TJ said.

"Should we at least bury the bodies?" Becca asked. "They deserve more than to be dumped out back."

"I'm not taking the chance that the Brotherhood might show up," Kemp said.

"He's right," I said. "Let's get the hell out of here before shit goes wrong."

We hurried into our packs and Kemp took the handset for the ASIP III. "Pale Horse, this is scout. Over." We were encrypted, so we didn't have to worry about any Brotherhood on the net who might know what Pale Horse was. Kemp waited a whole minute. "Damn it. They better be paying attention. Let's move. Wright on point." I started leading us out the way we'd come. "No, Danny, guide left. We'll go up that valley over there. Different route just in case someone followed us or was on our trail. I'll get out the map later and figure out our whole path." He kept holding the radio handset to his ear. "Damn it!" He keyed the mike. "Pale Horse. Pale Horse, this is scout. Over." After a moment, Kemp sighed. "Finally." Then he keyed the mike again. "Pale Horse, this is scout. We've located a Brotherhood safe house. Nobody there. We're taking an alternate route back to your location. Be advised, we may have Brotherhood in the area. How copy? Over." A moment later. "Roger that. Stand by on this freq. Scout, out."

I climbed down a small rocky embankment and led us along what might have been a dry creek bed. Kemp ran up the line to me, pointing to a big rock formation that rose up out of the ground. A large pine grew right next to it. "We'll halt there," he said.

After we reached the pine, we pulled in a tight security perimeter as Kemp went over his paper map of the area. He showed us the basic route. "I want to put as much space between us and this place as quickly as we can. We're going to move fast. Noise discipline at all times. Be sharp. Questions?"

"What if we run into Brotherhood guys?" Sweeney asked.

"What's our rules of engagement?" I added.

Kemp looked down for a moment like he was thinking it over. "We're going to stay out of sight. If they spot us, we'll run like hell, back toward Pale Horse. Maybe they'll ignore us."

"If they come after us?" TJ asked.

"Then we'll have to take them out," Becca said. "We can't let them follow us back to our people."

"Good thing we do these scavenging runs so far from the school," JoBell said.

Kemp was all business. "Anything else?" Nobody said anything. "Right. I'm not kidding. Absolute noise discipline. Be ready for anything."

I led us deeper into the woods at a pace just short of a run. We moved and moved, and when it got dark, we put in a radio call to Pale Horse, put on our night vision glasses, and kept pushing through the woods. I tried to stay focused on our mission, but after a few hours, I couldn't stop my mind from wandering. Wasn't this how it always went? As soon as things were going right — finding a house that had things we could use, JoBell talking about getting married — then it all fell apart.

When Kemp finally called a halt for the night, we were all fried, completely soaked in sweat, even though the night air was cool.

Everybody pulled out what blankets they had and did their best to sleep. I took the first guard shift, knowing sleep wasn't coming for me that night anyway. We were supposed to switch guards every hour, but I covered four shifts, until I actually didn't think I could stay awake anymore. Becca got up to relieve me. I slipped under a blanket close to JoBell and closed my eyes.

In what seemed like an instant, JoBell was poking me awake with a stick and the morning light had begun to fill the woods. Kemp popped a can of baked beans and we passed it around, each of us taking a couple mouthfuls using the spoons from our mess kits. Kemp contacted the team back at Pale Horse to make sure they'd had a quiet night. Then we moved on.

"There weren't any Brotherhood guys back at that house," Cal said a while later. "There are probably none clear out here. We can maybe afford to slow down a little."

But right then everybody in line in front of us threw up their fists with their arm bent at a right angle to signal a halt. We went to a knee, and TJ, who had been on point, rushed back to Kemp. "There's something up there."

"What is it?" Kemp said.

"I don't know." TJ looked scared. "I don't think it's on the map. You have to see this."

We all crawled up to a line of small boulders. About thirty yards ahead was a huge clearing, with a twelve-foot-high chain-link fence topped with a coil of concertina wire.

"The hell is this?" Cal asked.

Any kid who'd grown up in Idaho knew exactly what it was. "What the hell is a field of potatoes doing way out here?" I asked.

"All fenced in like this?" JoBell added.

"It's not on the map," Kemp said quietly. "Unless we are way off course. But I don't think we are." He pointed across the clearing. "We were supposed to move through that valley. There shouldn't be anything out here."

"We can just go around it, right?" Sweeney said. "We can still get through the valley."

"Yeah, but what the hell is this?" Cal asked again.

"Maybe we should cut through the fence and load up on potatoes," Becca said.

JoBell looked through her rifle's scope. "Buildings way down there. Something's moving." She slowly lowered her rifle. "I don't believe it."

"What?" I asked.

"This can't be happening," JoBell said.

"What is it?" said Sergeant Kemp.

Then we saw them coming over the top of the little hill. Four rows of about a dozen people each, moving slowly. Men walked beside the rows of people, some with rifles, some with whips. As they got closer, we saw the black armbands on the armed men. Metal chains jingled among the rows of people, forcing each person in line to take small steps.

"It's a Brotherhood slave camp," I said.

We watched in horror for a moment, until Cal started to stand up, beginning to draw his sword. Me and Becca pulled him back down.

"What're you gonna do, Cal?" I whispered. "Cut through the fence and charge those guys? See any problems with that plan?"

"They're human beings." Cal looked at me all frantic and wide-eyed. "They got 'em chained up like animals. We gotta —"

JoBell rubbed his shoulders. "Cal, honey. It's okay. Calm down. I know it's tough."

Cal crouched down behind a rock again. "I can't . . . I can't let these assholes get away with shit like this again. Not like last time. We have to do something."

"But we're pushing a bad position," I said.

"We don't have enough people or ammo to take this place down," Becca said.

Kemp looked out at the field again. "And we don't know enough about the place to plan an op. We stay down here, out of sight, until those — I guess you call them overseers? Until those Brotherhood guys are way back down at the far end of the field."

So we used the oldest of all Army skills. We waited. We watched modern-day slaves work the potato field. Most of them were black, Hispanic, or Asian, but there were white people too. All men or boys.

"What are they doing?" Sweeney whispered.

"I think they're pulling weeds," Becca answered.

"By hand? In a field that big?" Sweeney said.

JoBell held her rifle tight, keeping it aimed at the Brotherhood. "Right, because it would be okay if the slaves had tools and the field was smaller."

"I meant, they're going to break their backs bending over all day like that," said Sweeney.

"Oh no," JoBell said, watching the workers. "That's Kenny Palmer, the guy Becca said disappeared from Freedom Lake after he complained about the Brotherhood. Has he been here all this time?"

Kemp had put Cal and TJ on guard duty to make sure nobody sneaked up behind us. That was smart. I didn't think Cal could handle watching this. Whenever one of the workers stood up straight, or took too long to stretch with his hands on his aching back, an overseer would be on him with a whip in an instant.

Cal crouched-ran over and dropped down behind the rocks with us. "Sergeant Kemp, I been thinking —"

"Oh shit," Sweeney said.

"— that this here is a pretty big field. If we all picked a target and shot at the same time, we could bring all those Brotherhood bastards down at once before they had a chance to shoot back. The guys back at the base probably wouldn't even hear us. Then we use our bolt cutters to cut through the fence and get those guys out —"

"You're supposed to be covering our six," Kemp said.

"I know, but I wanted to tell you about my plan for —"

"You left TJ by himself," Kemp said. "No one goes alone. Always post a guard."

"I know!" Cal said, a little too loud. Everybody hushed him, and we watched the camp to make sure nobody heard us. "I know the damned rules. But we gotta do something about this. We can't just walk on by like we never saw nothing."

"Riccon," Kemp said. "We don't know if we have enough resources for an assault on this place. For sure, right now, this squad is not equipped for that mission. We need more information."

I'm not gonna lie. I'd done a lot of dumb things in my life. Right then, I had an idea for another one. "I'll get us some information."

I ran up ahead of the line of rocks, ducking under low-hanging pine branches to stay out of sight. I hooked around the back of a boulder, running toward the field, and then dove into a low crawl the last ten yards to hide behind a big tree trunk about ten feet from the fence. I'd noticed one of the chain gangs working its way close to the fence, while the Brotherhood scumbag overseeing them had gone over to one of his pals to bum a smoke, so I figured it was worth the risk.

Everybody behind the rocks whispered my name real loud. I sat with my back to the tree and pushed down with my hand like, *Quiet down.* Cradling my rifle over my chest, I risked a look around the side of the trunk. The Brotherhood guys were far away, smoking and joking, as our drill sergeants used to say.

"Hey," I said quietly, then, "Hey," a little louder. That time a couple of the workers heard me. A black man started to stand up and look in my direction, but another guy pulled him back down so they could keep working.

"Who's there?" said the closest man. He was white, wearing what looked like a tattered military flight suit.

"We're friends. We'd like to get you out of there. My name's Dan."

Some of the people on the chain gang were whispering, elbowing one another, I think to keep everybody working. JoBell crawled up next to me with her rifle at the ready.

"Hey, babe." I smiled.

"Don't 'Hey, babe' me. I'm just making sure you live through this so I can kick your ass later for being so damned stupid."

"That's my girl," I said.

"My name's Doug," said the flight suit guy.

I turned again to lean around the tree. "Doug, we want to get all of you out of there, but we need to know what's up. How many guards? How many prisoners? What kind of weapons, commo, transportation they got?"

"Hard to say," Doug said. "You can see they keep us locked down pretty tight. But I've talked to other prisoners when I can. My best estimate is that they have about fifty Brotherhood guards up here. Maybe a half dozen more work in the office trailer. Big radio field antenna, looks military grade. They have one semi-truck. They pack the trailer as full as they can with the people they capture. Some die on the trip here. I think they have one more pickup, but they hardly use it. There's not much gas."

JoBell said, "They're only using men?"

"There are about thirty men here working the fields," Doug said. "They keep the women locked in these big sheds. We don't know how many there are." He swallowed. "We hear their screams sometimes. We never see them unless we get put on detail to carry a woman's body to the pit. Sometimes women are driven away. We think they're selling them."

"Damn," JoBell whispered.

Doug went on, "Everyone in the Brotherhood has a rifle or shotgun. Some also have sidearms. Heaviest weapons I've seen here are at the main gate — a couple of M240 machine guns. I don't know what they have for guns in the guard tower."

The man next to Doug turned toward us again. "Can you help us? How many of you are there? Please. You gotta help us. They got my wife. They got my daughter. She's only thirteen."

"Hey!" one of the Brotherhood guys shouted. My instinct was to jump back behind the tree trunk, but I forced myself to be still. Movement attracted attention. "Get your lazy asses working!" I slowly eased myself back behind my tree, my whole body tense and shaking, ready for a fight if we were discovered. "Get. To. Work!" I heard the whip crack with each word. The man grunted a little. "Get up!" the overseer shouted.

"No, wait! He's fine," Doug called out. "He can work! You don't need to whip —"

The whip cracked and Doug cried out in pain.

"Mr. Air Force Hero, you really gotta learn when to shut the hell up and stay out of things. You interfere again, and I'll beat you so hard, the rest of the lazy pukes on your chain will have to drag your unconscious ass all the way back to the pit. Chuck you in there and let you bleed out with the rest of the bodies."

Me and JoBell stared at each other. Finally, we saw Kemp

motion for us to come back, like it was all clear. When we got back to our friends, Kemp chewed us out, but neither me or JoBell was listening.

"You said we needed information," JoBell finally said. "We got it. It's worse than we thought."

⌁—• *And so, my fellow citizens, as Montana, Wyoming, and Idaho come together as one free nation, dedicated to protecting the lives, liberty, and property of all our people, I, James P. Montaine, accept the nomination as interim president of the Northwest Alliance. To our country I dedicate my entire life. I swear to you before God that we will win this war for our freedom. Unto us a great burden has fallen, and our sacrifices have been costly indeed, but I promise you, my fellow citizens, that victory is within our grasp. Rise up! Rise up! Rise up! Defeat the enemy! Onward to victory for the Northwest Alliance!* •—⌁*

⌁—• *In the fifth Battle of Cheyenne, Northwest Alliance insurgents were able to gain temporary footholds in the area immediately north of the city and in nearby Laramie, but after two days of fierce fighting, the United States prevailed in keeping southern Wyoming free. While the official casualty report is still being compiled, the number of insurgent dead is estimated to be well over one thousand. You're listening to the Unity Radio Network. Hope for a united America.* •—⌁*

⌁—• *BBC now goes live to the House of Commons, where Prime Minister Carman is about to make an address."*

"Over eighty years ago, Mr. Speaker, another British prime minister had the duty of reporting difficult news to this chamber during a world war. I am no Winston Churchill, and I would that this duty fell on someone else, just as I wish this war fell on another people. But this is our hard lot, and never in our long, illustrious history have we the British people backed down.

"Nevertheless, the reports that many of you have seen through a variety of media are true. The German cities of Dresden, Leipzig, and Berlin are now occupied by Soviet military forces. The enemy deployed out of occupied Poland with remarkable speed and deadly precision. Their armored and infantry divisions, supported by an air force far superior to that which our intelligence community estimated, moved quickly first to Berlin, and then into many other cities in the eastern part of Germany. The Allied military faced particular danger from the Soviet Air Force, a large component of which had been expertly concealed from satellite surveillance. It would appear that these additional Soviet air assets had been kept in reserve as part of a coordinated effort toward a surprise attack. The enemy made no distinction between military and civilian targets, but unleashed near total devastation wherever they went.

"Doubtless the murderous Soviet leadership is celebrating what it believes to be a great triumph, what it believes to be a sign of its coming victory. But when Allied forces regrouped, we dealt decisive damage to the Soviet military, crushing any hope of their continuing advance. I spoke via video conference to German Chancellor Jutta Martell, who leads her government from a secure location. I do not think Chancellor Martell will mind me repeating her words, that the Soviets' mistake of believing they can divide Germany again will cost them their lives.

"The Soviets have misjudged our allies. And I would suggest to you, to the whole British people, and to the world, that the Soviets have greatly misjudged us and our history if they believe, for one moment, that the people of the United Kingdom will ever capitulate. Sir Winston Churchill's sentiment from so long ago rings no less true today. We shall fight in Germany and in Poland. We shall fight on the seas and oceans. We shall fight in the air. We shall fight on the beaches. We shall fight in the fields and in the streets. We. Shall. Never. Surrender! •⟶⋏

~~• Because the civil war has disrupted vaccination production and distribution, millions of parents no longer have the ability to protect their children against measles, mumps, and rubella, among other diseases. The result? An outbreak of measles affecting thousands of children. Worse, for the first time since polio was eradicated in the United States in 1979, the Pan American territory now faces the threat of an epidemic. Dr. Byron Hoffman of the Centers for Disease Control and Prevention in Atlanta read a prepared statement today."

"Our leader, General Jonathan Vogel, understands the importance of immunization and assures the Atlantican people that all Atlantican citizens will be fully vaccinated, by force if necessary. He is deeply saddened to hear of the children suffering from measles, and offers his condolences to the families of those who have died. General Vogel is also disappointed to hear of so many suffering paralysis from polio. While the Centers for Disease Control and Prevention has an ample supply of all vaccines needed to protect Atlantican citizens, those vaccines cannot be shared with any nation currently engaged in war against Atlantica. Full nation recognition as well as other military concessions must be made before the CDC can offer assistance in combating the growing health crisis in the United States and other Pan American countries. Atlantica is victory! •~~

~~• Soviet Television Online is proud to present this address from Soviet leader Vladimir Putin, translated into English for our supporters around the world."

"Peter the Great once said that our military is paramount to the Fatherland's defense, and this love and respect for our military is something that lives in the memory of every Soviet family. We will defend this truth from lies and from being forgotten.

"The courage, integrity, and professionalism of our great military is unparalleled, admired by our allies and feared by our enemies. It was the courage of our soldiers in battles for Moscow, Stalingrad, Kursk, Warsaw, Budapest, and finally Berlin that made it possible to defeat Nazism.

"Now the Germans have attacked Soviet forces again at our bases in Prague, Poznan, and even Warsaw. But our enemies should read their history books! They should know that those who serve beneath our battle banners will always look to the example of past Soviet victors and never flinch or retreat. No one should make the mistake of believing for one moment that it is possible to achieve military supremacy over the Soviet Union or to pressure us in any way or form. We will always offer the strongest response to any such reckless actions.

"Our response to the current aggression is much as it was decades ago. The Soviet Union will never surrender! We will never relinquish our right to defend ourselves, and if we are forced to seize the territory of our enemy aggressors to protect our families and loved ones, then that is what we will do! My comrades, in the coming struggle, in the great crusade before us, I wish you success! •⌐√

√—• *As the hottest summer on record winds down, experts estimate the number of deaths from heat-related causes in the thousands. But given that the northeast region of the Pan American territory has experienced harsh winters in recent years, many now fear the coming cold. Empire News's Erin Heddleson reports."*

"Coping with record snowfall and cold is nothing new to the hearty citizens of the Keystone Empire, but with gas and electricity supplies uncertain this winter, national and local authorities are rushing to prepare safe houses. These will be large barracks-style

buildings where those whose homes lack heat can come to get warm. Keystone Empire President Caroline Craig warns that besides United States military aggression, the coming winter is the greatest threat we face. •⌐√

√⌐• Adam Coleman has recently returned from a long reporting trip around Pan America. Adam, what can you tell us about the war? How long do you think this can go on?"

"That's a good question, Adrienne. I have been to each of the now fourteen countries in Pan America, and I wish I had good news. The last time I traveled this widely was covering the US presidential campaign, and on the campaign trail, you see a lot of the country, the best of so many great cities and towns. Now those communities are in ruins. I saw millions of homeless refugees, desperate for even the most meager scraps of food or basic supplies."

"But without food, how can the soldiers go on fighting?"

"Oh, the soldiers are well fed, Adrienne. But more and more, this isn't a fight among the different Pan American armies, but among rogue groups battling over dwindling resources. These are good, honest people, whole families that have been forced to band together and arm themselves for protection. Then they run into another group that has been forced to do the same. Throw some food or a little gasoline in the middle, and suddenly the members of the groups are killing one another. I saw this over and over, nearly everywhere I went. It was heartbreaking. •⌐√

√⌐• Brothers and sisters in Christ, I call upon you to repent! Repent of your sins! For the time is near. For the day of the Lord will come as a thief in the night, in which the heavens will pass away with a roar and the elements will be destroyed with intense heat, *and the earth and its works will be burned up. Second Peter, chapter three, verse ten.*

And I know, brothers and sisters, that in this war, you think you have known fire. You think you have seen suffering. But in Ezekiel chapter twenty-five, verse seventeen, God warns us: "And I will execute great vengeance upon them with furious rebukes, and they shall know that I am the Lord, when I shall lay my vengeance upon them." For now this evil and corrupt nation pays for its sins. Our people have worshipped false gods! We've forbidden prayer in our schools and in all our public places, and put in its place the mosque, the Buddhist temple. And some of you listening to me even now say, "Reverend, we have not gone to these temples of false gods." But you put your faith in your government! You worshipped at the altar of your technology! Your military and your own weapons have become your idols! And what have your false gods brought you? They've brought you death. They've brought you disease.

Repent! Throw yourself on your knees before the righteousness and the power of God. "For it is written," Romans chapter fourteen, verse eleven, "As I live, saith the Lord, every knee shall bow to Me, and every tongue shall confess to God." But time is running out. Now the signs are clear. The signs are clear! The vengeance of the Lord is upon us, and you must repent now, brothers and sisters, or face the hellfires for all eternity! •—⅄

CHAPTER
TWENTY-ONE

"Absolutely not!" Mr. Keelin leaned forward. "They aren't our concern. Our job is keeping our families safe, not running around trying to play superhero."

Us thirteen members of the council were in our seats around the long wooden table, arguing whether we should try to free the people we'd found in that Brotherhood camp. Mrs. Pierce sat at the head of the table with Dr. Nicole around the corner to her left. Then it was Mr. Shiratori, Pam Bean, Dwight Robinson, me, and Mr. Morgan. Mrs. Stewart sat across from Mr. Morgan. Alissa Macer was on her left. Then it was Samantha Monohan's dad Jim, Kristie Ericson, Mr. Keelin, and finally Mr. Grenke up by Mrs. Pierce.

The weirdest part of today's meeting was that Sergeant Kemp, JoBell, Sweeney, Cal, Becca, TJ, Jaclyn, and some others were standing at the end of the table opposite Mrs. Pierce. I should have been with them, not sitting at this table. But I knew they were all eager to attack the camp and try to save those people, and when I looked at them, I wondered how many of my friends we'd lose if we tried a mission like that. We'd come here to hide from the war. Why charge into the middle of another fight?

Kristie Ericson spoke up. "Even if we wanted to help those people" — she nodded at Toby Keelin — "and I'm not sure we do — I don't think we are *capable* of helping them. This isn't an Army base. We're not soldiers."

"Some of us are," said Sergeant Kemp.

"Isn't everybody a soldier now?" said Mr. Shiratori.

Dr. Nicole smiled. "This war has forced all of us to take on roles we didn't plan on."

"You stitched me up just fine." Mrs. Stewart laughed. "For a veterinarian."

"Yes, but how much more stitching am I going to have to do if we attack this Brotherhood base?" Dr. Nicole asked.

I was kind of surprised she'd said that. I would have thought she'd be up for the mission.

"These people are locked up as *slaves*," Alissa Macer said. "And it sounds like the men are the lucky ones. They just have to work the fields. How am I going to look Cassie in the face knowing that there's a Brotherhood camp where girls like her are being . . ." She looked at her mother, Mrs. Pierce. "Tell me that if I were locked up in a camp like that, you'd do whatever you could to save me. Please say you wouldn't leave me there to be . . ."

"They're being raped," said Mr. Morgan. "They're being used as sex slaves. Let's not confuse the discussion by an unwillingness to face all the facts."

"Let's also face the fact that most of the slaves are people of color," Mr. Shiratori said. "The Brotherhood may have locked up a handful of others who have caused problems for them, but for the most part, they are gathering up anyone who's not white, and enslaving them."

"But the team said they talked to a white man," Mr. Keelin said.

"There were some white guys." Cal spoke up. "Most were Hispanic, black —"

"Or Asian," Sweeney said.

"I don't think we need to go making this a race issue," Mr. Keelin said.

"You know, I am getting a little bit tired of white people

343

complaining about things not being 'race issues' when they are absolutely all about race," said Mr. Shiratori. "And I don't understand why it is so hard for you to grasp the idea that people of color here take it a little personally when we hear about people like us whose lives are being destroyed, simply because they're not white."

"I'm sorry," said Pam Bean. "But we came up here, brought our children up here, so we could escape the Brotherhood. We need to stay out of their way."

"The fact that people tried to stay out of the way of the Brotherhood is what led to my parents' deaths," said Jaclyn. Jackie didn't talk much anymore, but when she did, people listened.

"We're all horrified by what happened to your parents," said Dr. Nicole. "But this situation is different. Let's suppose we launch this mission, and it goes exactly as planned. Our people don't get killed or wounded. We don't use up a ton of the very limited and important ammunition that we'll need if we ever have to defend our community here. The Brotherhood doesn't follow you back here and kill or enslave us all. Let's say your mission is a complete success and you free those people. What will you do with them then? Hmm? You can't send them back to their homes, because their homes are probably all over Idaho and the whole damned northwest, and we almost died trying to make it here in the first place."

"And their hometowns are probably run by the Brotherhood," Mr. Shiratori said. "They'd be killed or recaptured immediately."

"We'd have to bring them here with us," Mrs. Macer said. "We'd have to find room for them."

"Room for at least thirty men?" Toby Keelin asked.

"Probably fewer, because some would be killed trying to escape," Dr. Nicole said. "And who knows how many women? And who knows what diseases those poor people have? Who knows what injuries?"

"We could get you some help taking care of them," Mrs. Stewart said.

"I've already learned so much from you," Becca said. "I could help."

Tears stood in Dr. Nicole's eyes. "I'm not a doctor. I'm a veterinarian. If I have the right drugs and supplies and equipment, I can help most animals the best that we know how to help them, and some of that knowledge works for humans too. But there are things about treating people that I do not know."

"Everybody here is grateful for all you've done," said Mrs. Pierce.

"You saved my life," JoBell added.

"That's not the point!" said Dr. Nicole. "I'm not sure you all understand how fragile our situation is. I have very little medicine. I'm low on surgical supplies and every other basic medical tool. You think that joke of a hospital in the Freedom Lake gym was bad? Think we were underequipped there? That place looks like an advanced medical facility compared to what we have here. What if the war goes on for years? What if it lasts a decade? We have to accept that this could be a permanent community. And I have no vaccines! Zero. None. Our children will not have the same immunity we have. If one of those people we rescue brings any kind of disease here — not just measles or whooping cough or one of those nineteenth-century nightmares, but anything, the flu — we could all be in serious trouble."

I finally spoke up. "Those are good points. And there are problems with the mission. It would have to be a full-on assault. Getting those people out of there would take time. We can't move all of those exhausted people out on foot. That means we'd have to take the whole place over, take out every Brotherhood turd in the entire camp." I saw Jaclyn had started crying. "I'm sorry, Jackie. We all came up here to get away from the war. We can't go back to it."

"And how would we feed them?" Mr. Keelin asked.

"Where would they sleep?" Mrs. Ericson said. "We're squeezed pretty tight into our cabins as it is."

"Then we build more cabins," JoBell said in a what-the-hell-type voice. Silence hung in the room. "Or we put them up in the chow hall or the rec lodge or the hallways of this building. Damn it! These are human beings we're talking about." She shook her head. "I was in the radio room last night and heard some scary stuff about Russia and the war. It's getting worse out there, all over the world. Dr. Nicole is right. We may be here for . . . well, forever." JoBell gestured toward the walls lined with books as she turned around. "Look at this place. This might be the last library. The kids we brought with us will grow up here, others will be born here, and these books, along with what we teach them, will be all they know about the old world we grew up in." She pointed at Mr. Shiratori. "There's our historian, writing down the minutes of these meetings, laying down the first pages of a new book. The story of us. What story do we want our children to read? That we knew there was a terrible evil, and we didn't even *try* to stop it?"

Mr. Grenke was about to speak, but JoBell held up her hand. "During the occupation, I was down in the dungeon, in the secret bunker under Danny's auto shop. Montaine had just made a radio address, telling people that southern Idaho was still holding out. He asked everybody to start fighting the United States."

"Right!" Mr. Keelin said. "You used to be against fighting, weren't you? I know you were at protests and —"

"I was against the war because it was a mistake. Look what it's cost us. Everything. First Sergeant Herbokowitz said then that the world is governed by the gun, that whoever has the biggest, most powerful guns, or whoever fights with no rules and nothing to hold them back, gets to choose the way things will be.

"But it's not always like that. It doesn't have to be that way. We can choose something — we *have* chosen something better! Right here! Where we share with one another and help each other and live in peace!"

Mr. Shiratori was smiling. "But you're not suggesting peace. You want us to attack this Brotherhood camp."

JoBell stepped forward to face the council. "The Brotherhood are the guys with the bigger guns, the ones who have no rules, no conscience. And the big-gun psycho can't always win. Damn it! Not this time. Sometimes good people have to take a stand, even if it requires our own guns. Sometimes in the face of pure evil, we have to say, 'Enough.' Sometimes the weak have to win one." She shrugged. "We just have to."

She paused. "These books are a record, a monument to a world that has failed, a way of life that doesn't exist anymore." JoBell pointed at Mr. Shiratori's notes. "Don't let the story of us be a record of failure."

She put her arm around Jaclyn, and the two of them walked out of the library. The room was silent for a long time. Mr. Shiratori seemed happy. Maybe he was proud of JoBell, his former student. Nobody else on the council would even look at one another.

Finally, Sergeant Kemp approached the end of the table. "I've talked it over with a bunch of people, and we think we can figure out a way past the difficulties Private Wright pointed out. We're willing to give the mission a try. It is my professional opinion that we can succeed if you want us to."

"Thank you, Sergeant Kemp. That will be all," said Mrs. Pierce.

Kemp nodded at me and then at Mrs. Pierce before my group of friends walked out, leaving only the council in the room.

"Right," said Mr. Keelin. "I call for the vote."

Mrs. Pierce nodded. "The question is, should we attack the Brotherhood slave camp to free the people trapped there? We'll go around the table." She pointed to Dr. Nicole on her left. "Dr. Nicole?"

"No," said Dr. Nicole. "I'm sorry, we just don't have enough —"

"Debate is closed," said Mrs. Pierce. "Votes only, please. Mr. Shiratori?"

"Yes," Coach said.

"No," said Mrs. Bean.

"Yes," said Dwight Robinson next to me.

I hated the idea of another op, another firefight. It had been great to live here in peace for the past few months. I was almost getting used to it. But JoBell was right. We had to do this. Otherwise it really would be just like letting Jaclyn's parents hang all over again.

"Danny?" Mrs. Pierce asked.

"Yes," I said. There were some *hmm* sounds. I guess people were surprised I'd changed my mind.

"No," said Mr. Morgan.

"Sarah?" Mrs. Pierce asked Mrs. Stewart.

"Yes," said Mrs. Stewart.

Alissa Macer smiled at her mother. "Absolutely yes."

The yes votes were ahead five to three, but we were coming up to Mr. Grenke's crowd.

"No," said Jim Monohan.

Mrs. Ericson shook her head. "Hell no."

"Nope," said Mr. Keelin.

The vote was six to five against the mission. All eyes were on Mr. Grenke to see if he would kill the mission or send a tie to Mrs. Pierce. I couldn't remember the last time Keelin, Ericson, and Grenke hadn't voted together. It was like they'd formed a political party on the drive up here.

"When our bus was pinned down under Brotherhood fire, Danny and his guys came back for us," Mr. Grenke said slowly. "I know if I was in that camp, I'd be praying for someone to come break us out. I vote yes."

It was a tie, then. Mrs. Pierce would decide.

She stood up. "We need to make plans to feed, clothe, house, and otherwise take care of a lot more people." There were a few groans around the table. Mr. Keelin slid his chair back and folded his arms, looking pissed. "Danny?" Mrs. Pierce let out a long breath. "Please go tell Sergeant Kemp to begin preparing for the assault."

CHAPTER
TWENTY-TWO

When I got back to our room, everybody was busy cleaning weapons and loading rounds into magazines. I paused outside the open door. My friends and I were heading into another firefight. Voting for the mission had seemed like the right idea at the time. Of course we shouldn't allow human beings to be treated like cattle or worse. Through the whole war, I'd been wondering if it was right to continually value me and my friends more than the Feds or others we'd fought. But now, facing a situation where we were going to risk our lives to help strangers, tipping the scales the other way, I wasn't sure it was the right thing to do.

Or maybe this mission wasn't a change for us at all. We'd be going into that camp, having decided that the lives of the Brotherhood guys running it were less valuable than our own, less than the lives of the people locked up there, and so we'd kill them. I squeezed my rifle. But the Brotherhood had already decided their lives counted more than those of the people they'd captured. With that in mind, maybe this battle would be the clearest case of right and wrong in the whole war. I prayed it would be our last fight. I rubbed my hands over my eyes, my head almost aching just thinking about it all.

"I know I've been . . . kind of out of control . . . sometimes. One time Danny even told me I shouldn't fight with this sword anymore. But I . . ." I looked inside the room, where Cal ran an oiled whetstone along the blade of his cavalry saber. "I can't wait to get back at these bastards, you know? One final battle with this sword."

"The mission is to kill 'em all?" Jaclyn smiled bigger than she had in months. "Yeah, I'm in."

I swung the door open all the way and came into the room. "I stop to take a dump on the way back from council and everybody knows how the vote went?"

JoBell didn't look up from cleaning her rifle. "It's a small village. Word travels fast. Anyway, I knew the mission would be approved."

"It almost wasn't," I said.

She looked up and smiled at me. "I knew you'd convince them." But her smile told me she knew it was her speech that had swayed the vote.

"Kemp and Crocker are drawing up the plan," Sweeney said. "Kemp said he wanted to go in heavy, with a lot of guys. He'll be asking for volunteers."

Attacking those Brotherhood bastards with a large force sounded like a good idea. Going in big would help us overwhelm the enemy and make sure we came out on top. But it also meant running the mission with a lot of people who didn't have much experience. I worried about Jaclyn. The only action she'd seen was pulling guard duty on Pale Horse while my team ran scavenging missions. Who else on this op would have barely fired a weapon? I was still right about what I'd said about the tactical situation. The Brotherhood had the advantage.

"You know, Jackie," I said. "We already have pretty good coverage on this one."

Jaclyn slammed a magazine into one of her handguns. Another into the other. She set them down on the table with loud thunks. "Those bastards murdered my parents. I'm going to kill them back." She fixed me with hard eyes that dared me to argue.

It was so quiet that I jumped when someone knocked on the door.

Brad Robinson poked his head in. "Danny, Sergeant Kemp and Sergeant Crocker are in the radio room. They sent me to get you."

"What do they want?" Becca asked.

"Help planning the op," Brad said.

I gave the doorjamb a light punch. "Remember last year, when we were just kids?" I asked the room.

Sweeney touched his mangled skin where he had been burned. Becca rubbed his back.

"Last year was like ten years ago," JoBell said quietly.

I went with Brad to the radio room in the Council Building. "I'm volunteering for the attack," he said when we were outside. "I can shoot, and I've been working out all summer, push ups and curls with logs and stuff. I'm strong. You know, if we gotta carry some of those people out."

"I hope it won't come to that," I said.

"Crystal's mom is pissed about the whole thing," Brad said. "She already told me I couldn't go. But it's like you were saying when we first moved to the school. We gotta stick together like in football, you know? A team. I got your back."

He fist-bumped me, but all I could think was that this mission wasn't going to be like a damned football game.

I joined Kemp and Crocker in the command center they'd set up around Crocker's radios. "Sergeants." I nodded at each of them, standing at something like parade rest out of force of habit, even though we'd ditched that kind of formality by now. Still, demonstrating proper respect to rank made it easier to criticize what I'd heard of the plan. "I heard you were asking for volunteers."

"Geez. At ease, Wright," said Sergeant Crocker. "This isn't basic training."

Sergeant Kemp leaned back in his folding chair. "Yeah, we're taking volunteers. You signing up?"

"Right. Would you let me stay out of it if I asked?"

Kemp frowned. "I'd be disappointed, but I wouldn't force you to go."

"I'm going," I said. "But what about the others? It's not like you're picking trained soldiers from back in our unit. People with zero combat experience like Jaclyn Martinez are volunteering."

"How many battles were you in before this war started?" Crocker asked.

"You know what I mean," I said.

"I hear you, Wright," said Kemp. "But you make it sound like we're going up against US Special Forces. It won't be easy, and we'll take every precaution, but we have to remember we're taking out a bunch of barely trained, ignorant, overconfident, racist thugs. And if we charge in there with Pale Horse and then keep up the momentum, we'll have surprise and overwhelming firepower on our side."

"Kill them all before they have time to react," I said.

"Exactly," Kemp said. "Beat them with brutality."

We got down to planning the fight.

One thing I'd learned about the Army is that the nights before shipping out to training or for missions were always sleepless nights. The soldier lays there, loving his soft, warm bed, but unable to sleep, a little more fear coming with each hour that slips away. The best I could do on the night before our op was settle into that sort of half-sleep-half-waking-type rest.

JoBell had been resting her head on my chest, but she slid up a little bit to reach the pillow. "Have you slept much?" she whispered in my ear.

"A little," I whispered back.

Her arm was warm across my chest, and she squeezed me closer. "Liar."

We lay there in silence for a long time. There was something I wanted to talk to her about that I hadn't found the guts to bring up yet. "JoBell, will you sit this one out?"

"Mmm." She took in a breath. She'd fallen asleep. "What?"

"Will you sit out this mission?" I whispered. "Stay here and keep watch over things?"

"You're going to need me." She breathed the words in my ear, and a hot tingle went down my spine. "The plan calls for snipers, and I'm the best shot you got."

I ran my hand down her soft blond hair, down her back, until I squeezed her ass and pulled her on top of me. "You are the best shot, which is why you should stay here in case someone attacks the school."

"There won't be any attacks." She moaned a little when I squeezed her again.

I gave her a quick kiss. "We were going to get out of the war."

"One last mission," she said.

"You could stay here and get ready for our wedding. When I get back, we'll get married. That day."

She propped herself up on her elbow, smiled in the faint moonlight, and pressed a finger to my lips. I kissed her finger, and she trailed it down my chin, down my chest. Down. Down. Then she kissed me, hot and hard, before we melted into each other. And we were so, so, so good. Together.

It took a long time to get into position for the op. I drove Pale Horse. Kemp worked the radio in the passenger seat. Cal ran the turret. TJ manned the right side .50 and Becca had the left. Sweeney covered our tail with the M240. JoBell and Jackie sat right behind the hatch between the cab and the ambulance pod. Brad and Dwight Robinson rode in back with Tim Macer. Our call sign was assault one.

Assault two followed us. Norm had volunteered to drive our remaining bus. I was surprised when Mr. Grenke signed up too. He'd be backup for Norm, and he'd work the door, helping people who were escaping the camp to get on board. Dr. Nicole would be on the bus to take care of any wounded. Mr. Morgan, Lee Brooks, and Tim Macer's dad would provide fire support out the bus windows. I worried about assault two. It didn't have the armor or firepower that protected Pale Horse.

The scariest part of the plan was assault three. Sergeant Crocker was leading a team on foot in the open, with Chaplain Carmichael, Chase Draper, Skylar Grenke, Aimee Hartling and her first stepdad, Darren, and about five other people. Mr. Shiratori had signed up too, quoting something about evil succeeding when good men chose to do nothing.

The plan was simple. Pale Horse would ram through the gate and start blasting every Brotherhood bastard we saw. We'd hit just before dawn, so hopefully most of them would still be groggy with sleep. We'd take out the radio antenna to stop them from calling for help. We'd made contact with Doug, the former pilot. He was supposed to tell the rest of the prisoners in the camp to hit the dirt when the bullets started flying, and to make their way toward the potato field when they could.

Eventually Kemp would take over driving, and me and everyone else not manning a gun in Pale Horse would dismount to help the prisoners get over to the bus. Assault three would be protecting us the whole time, and they would have holes cut in the fence for the prisoners to escape if things went wrong.

My stomach felt cold and tight, and the back of my throat burned as I sat behind the steering wheel in Pale Horse. Kemp had spent a lot of time with the paper maps of the area that we'd used to find the Alice Marshall School. He'd guided everyone to their positions. We were parked in our release area. The camp was up the dirt road ahead of us.

"All assault elements. All assault elements. This is assault one. Assault one is go. I need a sit rep. Over," Kemp radioed.

"Assault one, this is assault two. We are go. Over."

"Assault one, assault three. We're go. Over."

"All assault elements, all assault elements, this is . . . shepherd." It was Chaplain Carmichael. He shouldn't have been on the channel, but Sergeant Kemp didn't seem to mind. *"As the old hymn goes, 'Onward, Christian soldiers.' May God be with us in what we are about to do. Amen."*

Kemp pressed the radio handset to his forehead. "Amen," he whispered. Then he keyed the mike. "All assault elements. All assault elements. This is assault one." He paused but kept the mike keyed and looked over at me. I nodded. "Execute the mission. Assault one. Out."

"Let's kick some ass!" Cal called out from the turret.

"Hit it," Kemp said.

I put her in drive and stomped on the gas, speeding up the dirt road faster and faster. The camp gates were a couple hundred yards ahead. The plan was to break through at full speed, firing on the way. Soon I could see the tall fence, the big chain-link gate with barbed wire on top, that damned flag of my bloody fist fluttering in the breeze. "Okay, assholes," I said quietly. "I will give you a war." Seventy yards out.

"Are you going to do it?" Kemp asked.

"Do what?" I said.

"The thing."

356

"Oh, right," I said. "And I looked!" I called out.

"And behold a pale horse!" Sweeney, Becca, Cal, and TJ yelled back.

Fifty yards. The gate guards had come out of their little shack. They were readying rifles.

"And his name that sat on him was Death!" JoBell shouted.

Twenty-five yards.

"And hell followed with him!" Cal screamed.

"Give it to 'em, Cal!" Kemp yelled.

The .50-cal on our roof opened up. The gate guards' bodies popped into pulpy meat and blood. We crashed through the gate, ripping it off its poles. I checked the side mirror and saw two more guys come out of the guard shack. Sweeney gunned them down, splitting one guy's skull and sending more rounds slicing through the other's crotch and chest. By the time we made it up the road toward the buildings, our bus had hooked off to the right, running behind some trees toward the potato field.

About a dozen men that we'd caught off guard had come out of an RV and a larger trailer house, all in different stages of dress. They were firing back, most with rifles, but a few with shotguns and at least two with SAWs. We took fire from a tall guard tower on the far side of the cluster of buildings. Hot bullets thumped our armor like hard, short cracks of thunder.

"I got the tower!" Cal yelled.

"Get up here in the middle of these buildings!" Kemp shouted.

"They'll surround us!" I answered.

"Get up there so we can use our side guns better!" Kemp said. "TJ, here you go! Mow 'em down!"

"Eat it, you racist bastards!" TJ fired a series of five-second bursts.

"Jo, I'm gonna need more ammo!" Cal yelled.

"On it!"

As I circled around in the middle of the ring of buildings, we took more bullets. I worried about Cal getting hit. Becca, TJ, Sweeney, and Cal were burning through rounds.

A pickup rolled out from between a big aluminum shed and the trailer that must have been their barracks. One man fired a rifle from the passenger seat, but four guys standing in the bed of the truck were loading a .50-cal they had fixed to a custom mount. Once they started shooting, we'd be in trouble. I swung Pale Horse hard to the right to hit their front fender with our heavier front corner.

"Jo, you got the gun," Cal yelled.

"Idiot! Don't!" JoBell screamed.

"What's he doing?" Kemp called back.

But we were too late. In the mirror, I saw Cal leap from the roof of our truck to the back of the enemy pickup. His sword speared one man in the throat, slashing out sideways and down to take off another's hands. He kicked back to push a third man out of the truck before he brought the sword around to thrash open the guts of the fourth. The driver and the shooter in the passenger seat of the pickup were so distracted that the pickup rolled away from us.

"Damn it!" JoBell shouted. "I can't get a clear shot! Cal, get out of there!"

Cal sheathed his sword and jumped to the ground, rolling like a commando. A second later, JoBell shredded the whole cab into a pink mist. The truck crashed into the corner of the big shed.

"Get us around the back of that building," Kemp said to me. He turned his head to yell back to the others, "Get ready to dismount! I want that radio antenna taken out!"

The shed gave us a little cover from the guard tower, and our back door swung open. Me and Kemp jumped out. I ran with my M4 and joined Jackie, Tim Macer, and the two Robinsons.

"We'll never get to the antenna until we take out that tower!" I said. "Cover me. I'm going up there."

But when we rounded the corner, we saw the tower was already taking heavy machine gun fire. Cal had jumped on the pickup's .50-cal. "Jackie, Macer, cover Cal. Robinsons, shoot the shit out of the cables on that antenna," I said to my group. "I'll get those bastards up there." I ran like hell for the tower, slinging my rifle as I jumped to the ladder and scrambled up.

"Go, buddy, go!" Cal shouted. My rifle slapped against my back as I flew up the ladder, focusing on every rung so I didn't slip. "'Bout outta rounds!" Cal yelled.

Near the top, some dumb bastard peeked over the side. Three rounds from Cal tore away his head, arms, and upper body. Blood rained down on me. Cal let off the machine gun. I pulled the remains of the body out of the tower and dropped it to the ground. I brought my rifle to the ready, held tight to the ladder rungs with my legs, and emptied fifteen rounds into the little room up there. When I climbed in, the guards' bodies were huddled at the back of the shack. I grabbed their M240 machine gun and draped myself with belts of ammo.

Cal had cross-loaded the pickup's .50-cal ammo to Pale Horse. I think he'd cooked off the enemy gun's barrel. Pale Horse made another run through the main camp, tearing up everything.

From up here, I could see the whole compound. Four black men used their chains to choke a group of Brotherhood, then they used the captured guns to shoot their chains and break free. After that, they tore through whatever Brotherhood guys they saw.

Another group of Brotherhood thugs were shooting at our other two teams from behind some junked-out cars near the field. Prisoners in ragged clothes were rushing to the bus as fast as they could while still chained together. It looked like a couple of our people were down. A few prisoners on one chain gang took rounds, falling, so the rest had to drag them.

I aimed at the Brotherhood guys in the field and fired. Missed. "Jo!" I screamed down to Pale Horse. She never missed. She could hit those Brotherhood bastards from here. I yelled down to the others, "Get out to the field! The prisoners need help. JoBell, get up here! I need you!"

Cal jumped up on Pale Horse's hood, was on the roof in two steps, and hopped down into the turret to replace JoBell, who came out the back and sprinted for the tower. A fat, bearded man in that damned armband rushed out from behind some trees and fired twice.

Blood erupted from my JoBell's chest. Her thigh tore open. Her scream echoed over the roar of the whole fight as she fell.

JoBell.

I dropped the machine gun, slung my rifle, and climbed-fell-slid down the ladder. My legs stung when I landed. I slid to the ground next to JoBell. "You're good. You're okay." My shirt was off and wrapped around her, but I couldn't get it tight enough to stop the blood. "Jo. Jo. Jo. You're okay. JoBell?" I kissed her. I had to stop the bleeding in her leg. "Somebody help me!"

JoBell stared at me wide-eyed. Blood rose in the corner of her mouth. A smile came to her face. "I would . . . have made you . . . such a good wife."

Screams and bullets echoed around me. A wave of smoke passed as something burned somewhere. I should have screamed. Cried. I should have tried to save her. But I knew she was gone. My JoBell. My life. Was gone.

I yanked the snap on my nine mil's holster and pulled the gun out. I worked the slide, clicked off the safety, and put the barrel into my mouth, aiming up through my brain.

The gun flew out of my mouth and my face hit the ground. A heavy weight crushed me. Was I dead?

Then I was pulled up by my arms, being shaken around, my head flopping loose. "What are you doing?" Cal screamed, his spit in my face. A vein bulged on his forehead and tears ran down his cheeks. "You trying to kill yourself, you son of a bitch!? You try to kill yourself!?"

There's nothing left for me. No words would escape. Tim and Jackie were by our side. Tim heaved JoBell onto his shoulder, blood rolling down his body, dark red staining his T-shirt.

Cal slapped me. "You wanna die!? Then we go out fighting! Let's kill these bastards!" He hauled me to my feet.

"Cal . . ." A tiny breath made it out of me. "I can't . . ."

"I'm with you all the way!" Cal said. "I'll die with you if that's what you want. But let's die fighting. Let's go!"

He pulled me, and I ran with him. I think Jackie and Tim ran beside us. Some Brotherhood guys were up ahead, shooting at us from behind some pallets and fifty-gallon fuel drums.

"Kill 'em, Wright!" Cal's voice echoed in my skull. "We'll kill 'em all!"

I screamed, aimed my nine mil, and fired again and again. Then I was flying over a pallet, my boot landing on some guy's throat. I shot three more of them. Cal slashed with his sword, opening one man, then another. Two men came out of a steel door in front of a big shed. I sprinted to them, shooting, shooting, shooting. I was in the shed. Full of cages, some beds with stained mattresses. Crying women huddled in the cold dark.

Cal was behind me. Some guys up on a catwalk fired. My leg burned. Cal shot back with his rifle, dropped a guy from the catwalk. He pulled the rifle slung on my back and put it in my hands. I ran all over the place, shooting anyone with a gun. One shot. One kill. Move.

The bastards could shoot me. I didn't care. I didn't want to live. At the door to one cage, I shot off the lock, threw the door open. "Come on!" Cal did the same at another cage. Women poured out of the cages. I heard Cal shouting directions to the buses. Six Brotherhood soldiers ran into the big room from the far door. I screamed and fired and sprinted at them. Firing. Firing. Firing. Three of them dropped. I was out of rounds. One woman prisoner slammed into one of her former captors. Her teeth sank into his throat, and she jerked her head to the side, ripping flesh and spraying blood. I understood her furious shriek as red blood ran down the brown skin of her chin. I hit the button to drop a mag while I pulled another from my pocket. My left shoulder screamed with fire inside. I emptied half my new mag into the last two Brothers in the room. The door was open and we ran.

"They're pinned down!" Cal caught up to me.

Up ahead, a dozen of the enemy had good cover in a ring of junked cars. Our people couldn't get to them. I could. These were the bastards I'd needed JoBell's help to shoot. They were here. She was not.

They saw me when I screamed at them. Some of them fired at me, but I shot round after round after round, sliding into their circle over the hood of an old Pontiac Grand Am. Cal was behind me, cutting them. One raised his hands to surrender. I felt the squelch as I shoved the barrel of my rifle into his eyeball. I pulled the trigger and the back of his skull blasted into a red spray. I turned, shot another.

Someone pushed me up against the side of a minivan — one of the Brotherhood with his hands on my rifle. An Asian girl yelled as she swung a fist-sized rock into my attacker's head. He fell to his knees. She crashed the rock into his skull again and again, taking him down. One of the Brotherhood called out from the ground as he held his gut, which Cal had slashed open. I felt the crack of his spine as I stomped on his throat.

Then Becca was beside me, tears in her eyes. She put her arms around me, saying something, but I pushed away from her, my fingers smearing blood on her cheeks. Sweeney tried to take hold of me too. TJ and Kemp grabbed Cal, but he broke free and ran up to me.

"Come on, Cal!" I shouted. "We gotta kill 'em! We'll kill 'em all! Come on! We gotta move. We gotta keep going! Let's go!" The ground wobbled, and I stumbled.

Cal's eyes were wide and wild. Then they blurred. He grabbed my head. "There ain't no more. We got 'em all." He was crying. "End of the line."

⌐—• is why the Brotherhood of the White Eagle exists! For you! Think about your lives under United States domination. How many of you felt fulfilled? How many of you felt as if your work were truly meaningful? How many of you felt that anything you did would be remembered when you were gone? What did life under United States tyranny bring you? Endless dissatisfaction in your useless quest to get more of their dollars. The indignity of debt and dehumanizing work for too little pay or recognition.

The old world is gone! And it falls to this generation to build a new and better one. The members of the Brotherhood of the White Eagle have risked their lives again and again in pursuit of the shared glorious future of all of Idaho. We did this not for our own reward, but for you!

It is not enough to live off the scraps from the United States' table. We will not be their dogs. We will rise up. We have dedicated every spare inch of our land to growing food, to pasture for cattle. We must all work together to make our fields thrive, to feed each other, to feed ourselves! The work will be hard. The Battle of Spokane has been won, but the wolf is still at the door! The United States will return, and the war is difficult, but always keep reminding yourself that someone has it worse than you.

All of us have done so much through this challenging struggle, but more is expected of some. It is not enough to simply believe in our great new destiny. So far I have limited membership in the Brotherhood to a select group of men. I have done so to spare you as much as possible from the dangers that always loom over such a monumental struggle. But we must act now before it is too late. Beginning today, we are asking all interested men to join in our fight to protect our home. We are opening membership in our forces to all young men over the age of fourteen.

The Brotherhood calls upon all of you to fight! If you were alone, what would you be in this world if your wages and your debt were the only things you considered to be your community? You owe this to everyone! I expect every decent Idahoan to join our cause, because the generation of today, right now, is the bearer of Idaho's destiny! •—ᴧ

ᴧ—• *The Israeli military has faced the toughest fighting in its modern history, losing control of almost all of its northern territory, from the Golan Heights to the northern edge of the West Bank. Soviet and Chinese leaders promise full nuclear retaliation if Israel uses nuclear weapons in its present conflict.* •—ᴧ

ᴧ—• *There are now an estimated four million refugees living in filthy camps across Pan America. These camps don't have enough food, clean water, waste disposal, or security. In many camps you have starving people suffering from cholera, typhoid, and dysentery, while a growing number of criminal elements are luring desperate women and girls into sexual slavery.* •—ᴧ

ᴧ—• *Joining us today in the WGN studios is Dr. Dennis Pierson, an expert in epidemics and immunization, who will talk to us about outbreaks of diseases that have long been under control in most of North America. Doctor, why have these diseases returned, and is making a deal with Atlantica our only solution?"*

"The reason for these new outbreaks is quite simple — and no, General Vogel isn't our only hope. He's nobody's hope. Look, the Centers for Disease Control and Prevention in Atlanta isn't the only producer or supplier of vaccines and medicine. There are other places around the Pan American territory that have stockpiles or

can produce pharmaceuticals. The problem is the United States built up its transportation and distribution systems organically, over the course of over two hundred years, and that system has now collapsed. The materials used to manufacture drugs and the facilities in which they were manufactured are now spread out across fourteen different countries, many of which are at war with one another. To make matters worse, the useful medications that remain — the antibiotics, the pain medications, even the immunization doses — mostly go to the military. If they do reach civilian hands, they are understandably hoarded by doctors who want to save them for the patients who need them the most. That just creates an enormous segment of the population that is largely unprotected.

"The situation is a little better here in Liberum than in some of the other new countries. We're witnessing major problems with disease in the Southern Alliance of America, Appalachia, and even in parts of what remains of the United States. But treating and preventing diseases is an area where, I think, if we don't have more cooperation among the nations soon, we're going to see devastating health consequences, possibly pandemics. Bacteria and viruses don't care about politics, borders drawn on some map, or the war. More needs to be done to bolster our medical community before it's too late. •—⌄—

KINLEY VEGA ★ ★ ★ ★ ☆

The sadest thing. My neighbors just killed, cooked, and ate their golden retriever. I don't think they told their kids what the meal was made of. Is that what it's come to in Santa Fe?

★ ☆ ☆ ☆ ☆ This Post's Star Average 1.07   [Star Rate] [Comment]   36 minutes ago

---

NATALYA JOHNSTON ★ ★ ★ ☆ ☆

Oh, I don't care how hungry I get, I could never eat Poofer.

★ ★ ★ ☆ ☆ This Comment's Star Average 3.26   [Star Rate]   3 minutes ago

TATUM LOWE ★ ★ ★ ☆ ☆

Ur dogs name is Poofer? He deserves to die.

★ ★ ☆ ☆ ☆ This Comment's Star Average 2.13   [Star Rate]   2 minutes ago

KINLEY VEGA ★ ★ ★ ★ ☆

Tatum Tots, your such a hardass! LOL!

★ ★ ★ ★ ☆ This Comment's Star Average 4.22   [Star Rate]   1 minute ago

CALEB WOOD ★ ★ ★ ★ ☆

Glad to see some people can still joke about this. You might think about the situation a little different if your kids were starving. Losing a family pet is tough, but when you see that empty look in your kid's eyes. Hear their bellies rumble. See their skinny arms and legs and their ribs. You'd do anything to help them. Anything.

★ ★ ☆ ☆ ☆ This Comment's Star Average 2.13   [Star Rate]   30 seconds ago

⋏• *Groups of farmers are forced to take up arms and stand guard over their fields or herds as desperate people attempt to steal whatever they can to eat. In Dakota and other new countries, there is very little legal framework in place to prosecute crimes or enforce anti-theft measures, making the law of the gun increasingly the deciding factor in who gets to eat.* •⋏

Cold on my arm. JoBell looked down from above me, her hair hung down around her face. But her hair had changed color. Dark brown. And some gray. "JoBell?" Fire burned in my shoulder. I screamed out, "JoBell!"

Lights moved past me. Crying people. A weird shape blurred around next to me. I could kind of see she had arms. "Jovell." Mouth wouldn't work.

"It's Nicole." A woman's voice echoed. "You've been shot. Sleep."

"Dunwanna wake up."

"Can we get him something for the pain?"

"The morphine he's been given already represents a good-sized portion of our entire supply. He's stabilizing from the blood transfusion. He's going to have to tough out the pain from here."

" . . . be pissed if he misses it."

"We can put off the funeral, but we can't wait to bury her. The body . . . it's not good. We have to bury her today."

". . . have been me."

"You don't mean that."

"She was so much better than me. She was honest, and good, and a better friend to me than I ever was to her," said Becca.

A sharp ache began to throb in my thigh and shoulder. When I opened my eyes, I stared at log rafters above me. A few oil lanterns hanging up there cast a faint light and weird shadows down on wherever we were. I dragged my tongue over the sandpaper roof of my mouth. "Wa —" I tried to speak. "Water?"

"He's awake," Becca said.

My shoulder burned like hell as I turned my head to see her. She was propped up on pillows on a cot, wearing a puffy bandage around the right side of her chest and shoulder.

Sweeney stepped up beside me. I must have been on a table. "How you feeling, buddy?"

I closed my eyes and let out a breath. "I hurt like hell."

"Join the club." Becca pointed to her chest. "I never had much up here, and now I'm gonna have a nasty scar for the rest of my life." She looked down. "But maybe now isn't the time for jokes."

"Cal wanted us to get him when Danny woke up." Sweeney started for the door.

"No, you stay," Tim Macer said. "I'll get him."

I looked over at Macer. His cheek, neck, and shoulder were bandaged. A few spots of blood showed through. That blood. And the sad look on his face. A memory flashed through my head. I was running. Shooting. And Tim carried her on his back. Her legs dangling limp behind him as he carried her. That was a dream. A jacked-up, terrible dream. I always had bad dreams.

It was so quiet in the room. Why was it so quiet? Mr. Morgan had propped himself up on his elbows from where he'd been laying on his back on a cot. His right leg ended in a bandaged stump just below the knee. How had this happened? It was probably a dream. Maybe I was still dreaming.

"S-Sweeney?" I couldn't hold back the first shakes of a sob. "Whe-where's . . . Where's JoBell?" The guy blurred in my tears. When I wiped them away, I could see tears in his eyes too. "How'd I get here? Where's . . ." Sweeney grabbed my good shoulder and leaned down over me. He was crying. My body tensed. I couldn't breathe. He didn't have to say anything. I knew. "Oh God. Eric. Oh please. I'm not . . ." I gasped in air. "I'm not supposed to . . . be . . . alive."

Careful of my bad shoulder, Sweeney hugged me. His sobs shook my chest. "No!" I screamed until I had no air. "No. No. No. Damn it, no. JoBell. Please, Jesus, no. Take me instead." I could hear Becca sobbing from where she lay. "What the hell . . . w-was the poi-oint?" I gasped for air again. "What did we do all this for!?"

Cal came in. "Brother, I'm so sorry."

"Hey!" A sharp voice cut in. Dr. Nicole pushed Cal and Sweeney away from me. "What did I tell you? Stay back."

"He just woke up," Cal said.

"Did you even wash your hands?" Dr. Nicole asked. "No. You want him to get an infection? You want to lose him too?"

"You should have left me there to die," I shouted at Cal. "There's nothing left for me. Everything's gone. E-everyone's dead!"

"We're here, Danny." Becca spoke through sobs. "You got us."

"With you all the way." Cal was weeping too.

But I didn't want Cal. I didn't want Eric Sweeney or Becca. I wanted my JoBell back. But she was gone. I'd gotten her killed. *JoBell . . . I need you.* I'd called to her, and she'd come running, and she was shot and died.

"It should have been me," I said. My leg and shoulder throbbed. Maybe it could still be me. I reached over to my left shoulder, grabbed my bandage, and yanked hard.

"Damn it!" Dr. Nicole was by my side in a second. I pulled the bandage harder. Heard it rip. My fingers clawed over stitches. If I could get 'em out, I'd bleed. "I worked all night getting you fixed up,"

Dr. Nicole said. "You're not gonna — Sweeney, help me!" The two of them pulled my hands away.

"No!" I shouted. "Leave me alone. Let me go! I don't wanna . . ."

"Danny, please," Becca cried.

Sweeney and Cal had hold of my arms. Dr. Nicole put me in some kind of headlock. Something cold and wet dabbed my neck. Then I felt a pinch. After a while, she let me go. My head slipped sideways. Floating. Falling off. My mind spun inside it.

Daylight filled the room. I tried to sit up, but my arms and legs were tied down. My head sloshed around when I moved, though, so I stayed down.

I thought I could see a girl sitting next to me. For just a moment, with my blurred vision and the sunlight shining on her hair from behind her, I thought it was JoBell, like maybe she was still alive. Or maybe I'd died, and she was greeting me in Heaven. Then I remembered all the things I'd done and realized this couldn't be Heaven. "Jackie?"

"Yeah. It's me. I'm here for you. We're all here for you, Danny." She spoke quietly. Like a river. Like when we spent the whole day on the river and we found that little beach. I remembered the sunlight sparkling on the water, in a million little flashes of light, and JoBell's perfect body as she whipped her wet hair back and smiled at me.

"Too much drugs," I mumbled.

When I woke up, it was still daylight, but the light wasn't shining in on me the way it had been before. Posters with equations and formulas told me I was in the math cabin. My arms and legs were still tied down. My shoulder and leg burned, feeling like they were stabbed from the inside. My headache throbbed. I tugged with my arm, tried to raise my leg. Nothing. Some kind of Boy Scout had tied me down good.

Cal spoke from my left. "You tried to tear out your stitches."

"She's really dead," I said. Tears stung my eyes.

"Danny, I . . ." Cal's voice trailed off. I don't know what he was going to say. It didn't matter. There were no words to make it right. No kind of comfort to push back the pain, to stop the movie clip of her death from endlessly playing on loop in my head.

"Who else?" I asked.

"What?"

"Did we lose anyone else?" I asked.

"Maybe we should talk about this when you're feeling better," Cal said.

"She's dead, Cal! I'm never gonna feel better. Did we lose anyone else? How did I get here? What the hell is going on?"

"Everybody else in Pale Horse made it." He looked down.

"What happened to Tim Macer?" I asked.

Another voice came from my right. "One of those bastards cut me pretty bad. But I'm okay."

I turned my head the other way to see Macer sitting in a chair, holding a ragged old magazine. The kid looked a lot different than that day before the Battle of Boise when I gave him a ride in the Beast. "You got her out of there," I said. "Thanks. I was . . . kind of out of my mind."

Tim made a little bow. I think it hurt him to nod. "I know it won't fix anything, but I grabbed her rifle too."

"In assault three, Clay Ratcliff took a head shot. Chase Draper —"

"Oh no," I said.

"Chase went out like some kind of action hero. There was this woman, a prisoner, you know? She was hurt, trying to get away, couldn't run. Chase ran out there, picked her up in a fireman's carry, and ran like hell back for the bus. They say he took four bullets, but he got her to safety. He didn't make it long after that." Cal stood up and started pacing. "Mr. Morgan lost the lower part of his right leg."

"Damn. That sucks," I said. "Anyone else?"

"Mr. Grenke was shot three times in the back while he was getting Mr. Morgan to safety." Cal paused for a moment. "Skylar Grenke was way out in the open, trying to help a prisoner or just returning fire. I don't know."

"Damn. Skylar too." The Grenkes would be out of their minds with grief.

"No," Cal said sadly.

"What?"

"Crocker pushed him out of the way. He was hit twice. They say he just screamed and ran at the enemy, shooting five or six of them before they finally took him down."

"Sergeant Crocker," I whispered. If Major Leonard had somehow survived his injuries from the US drone attack in Washington, and if Specialist Sparrow was alive somewhere, that would mean only four of us were still alive out of my whole National Guard company. "Crocker was always such a dork. A sci-fi nerd screwup at drill."

"War changes people," said Tim Macer.

I nodded. "Sergeant Crocker was one of the best." My nose itched and I tried to scratch it, forgetting I was tied down. The ropes bit into my wrists. "How many prisoners did we get out of there?"

They told me that our team had completed the mission. We'd taken out every Brotherhood guy at the camp. We'd even stolen some useful stuff like ammo, food, fuel, their radio equipment, and some generators.

They told me the stories of some of the people who were now living with us too. A man who'd been on a chain gang for over six months had been reunited with his wife, who'd been locked in that warehouse. The woman who'd bit through that scumbag's throat had managed to protect her daughter the whole time they were prisoners. A couple white guys who'd been yanked from their apartment in the middle of the night after they'd complained about how the Brotherhood distributed supplies unequally couldn't stop thanking us for their freedom. I guess the woman who had pulled that Brotherhood guy off me to smash his head in with a rock had come to check on me a bunch of times. The former prisoners said that a lot of other people had fought so hard against even coming to the slave camp that the Brotherhood had killed them in the streets. Everybody had made sure to remember them and the prisoners who had died fighting to help set the others free.

"Twenty-six of the thirty of us men made it." The prisoner I'd spoken to, Doug, stepped into view. A couple old bruises stained his face, and his arm was wrapped in a sling. "Eighteen out of twenty-one women and girls."

"A nineteen-year-old girl hung herself last night," Cal said. "I think they done some, you know, some real nasty things to them."

"Girls?" I said.

"The youngest they had in those pens was ten years old," Doug said. "She hasn't said a word yet, but they finally convinced her to eat a little. Another girl was twelve. She's not much better."

It was quiet for a moment. "You're really PFC Daniel Wright?" Doug said, looking at me closely.

Oh shit. Not another "rise up" maniac. But he'd been wearing a flight suit. He could be a US pilot. He might want to kill me. Maybe he would. "Yeah," I answered.

"I want to thank all of you for getting us out of there. I know it cost you a lot. I'm grateful. We all are — everyone you rescued. That's why I'm going to be honest with you." He took a deep breath. "I'm Second Lieutenant Douglas Griffith."

I looked at him for a moment. "Bullshit," I said. But I saw his resemblance to the photos I'd seen on the news.

Griffith laughed. "No, it's true."

Cal stood up straight. "You with Idaho, er, the Northwest Alliance, or are you with —"

"Cal, he's President Griffith's son," I said.

"Bullshit!" Cal said, bringing his rifle around from where he had it slung over his shoulder. "They reported you dead."

"Well, shot down," I said.

"I was shot down, but I ejected. I destroyed my transponder signal, figuring Idaho had the same technology and could find me the same as the US. I had a knife, my sidearm, and my flight suit, and I was way the hell out in the middle of the Idaho wilderness." He smiled. "You people have a lot of wilderness."

"How'd you wind up in that camp?" Cal was almost pointing his AR15 at the lieutenant.

"Cal, put the gun down," I said. "I'm pretty sure he surrenders."

"Well, all of us pilots get SERE training. That's survival, evasion, resistance, and escape. Standard procedure for being shot down and alone, deep in enemy territory, is to stay alive and evade — avoid contact with the enemy. But once when I was hiding, I saw these guys on the road hauling a whole group of terrified people in chains. I guess I was like you. I couldn't stand by and let that happen. So I ran out to try to rescue them. I got three of them before one of the guys knocked me out with a baseball bat. I woke up on a chain gang, and I've been there ever since. They had me for about four months." He looked down. "It was pure hell. Thank you so much for getting us out of there."

I turned away from him to hide my tears. In my head, it made sense. We lost five people and had four wounded, and we saved almost fifty lives. But in my heart, if I could go back in time, I swear I would have scrubbed the whole mission. Voted no. Forced JoBell to sit it out, at least.

"You know she believed in what we were trying to do," Cal said. "She made that big speech. She couldn't stand the idea of a camp like that going on."

I knew he was right, but that didn't take away the pain that was hurting me far worse than the bullet holes in my shoulder and thigh.

I heard there was a big debate on the council and around the Alice Marshall School about what to do with Lieutenant Griffith. I was glad to stay out of it. I wanted out of everything. Eventually, after making Griffith swear to never reveal the location of the school to anyone, and after he volunteered for a work detail, they let him stay.

After about four days, they decided they trusted me enough to leave me untied, and I joined the others in the bitter cold Alice Marshall School cemetery for the one funeral they'd saved for me. Seventeen crude headstones made out of chunks of basalt marked the place now. Nine were for the bodies of our people. Seven marked the prisoners who had died in their fight to be free. One memorialized the girl we'd rescued from the camp, who had hung herself. Nobody had known the girl's name, so the gravestone was marked FREE WOMAN. Now a bunch of us were gathered around the cold stone that was all we had left of JoBell.

The wind tore through the sad little meadow, bringing with it the first stinging snowflakes of the coming winter. Becca, Sweeney, Cal, and TJ moved in closer to me on my homemade crutches so we could protect one another from some of it. Chaplain Carmichael quoted scripture about Heaven and sacrifice, that part that talked about the greatest love being when someone lays down their life for someone else. I wondered about that. Thousands were laying down their lives all around the world every day, but it didn't seem like there was any great love involved. I thought about Specialist Sparrow and how she didn't believe in God. Once, Luchen had asked her why she didn't believe. She'd asked him how he could.

I knew God was real, because I knew how much I was being punished for all the wrong I'd done.

Finally, Chaplain Carmichael stopped speaking. Before we came out here, he'd asked me if I wanted to say a few words, and I'd shaken my head sadly. I had nothing left to say.

We stood in silence for a long time, but right as we started to head back to our rooms, Mr. Shiratori stepped into the middle of the circle. "JoBell was one of the most brilliant and courageous students I ever had the good fortune of working with. Rarely have I encountered anyone with as much passion, and as much *compassion*, as she had. In fifteen years of teaching, she was the only one I ever worried might beat me in a classroom debate." People laughed a little through their tears at that one. Mr. Shiratori wiped his eyes. "Actually, she did sort of beat me in a debate. She changed my mind, and the vote I would have made, when she gave her historic speech in front of our council, convincing us to authorize the mission for which she gave her life.

"I say it was historic, because she said it was up to all of us to make sure ours was a *good* story, to make sure our history book chronicled the *best* of us for our children and those who come after. I know none of us, nor the forty-four people she helped liberate, will ever forget her. She was taken from us far too early, yet we will always remember the love and respect we all share for JoBell Marie Linder."

Afterward, we walked back toward our building, Sweeney, Becca, Cal, TJ, and me. JoBell was gone. The thought of it pulled the hope and air from my lungs, the strength from my legs. I couldn't hold my tears back, and I couldn't hold myself up. Cal and Becca put their arms around my back and waist, and together, all of us, except for the one I needed most, went back to the tiny room we called home.

The snow on the day of JoBell's funeral was a dusting. The snow that fell near the end of October was not. The snow that hit us a couple days after that was worse. They hadn't given me back my gun by then, but I could at least walk, and though Dr. Nicole said I would probably have a limited range of motion in my left shoulder for the rest of my life, I could shovel snow. The sting of the cold and the burning in my shoulder and thigh hurt like hell, but I liked the hurt. Sometimes when I hurt enough, or when I worked hard enough, I could almost forget.

So I worked my ass off all winter. The snow got deeper than I thought was possible. Our farthest-out guard bunkers were completely buried in snow, over and over again. Digging out to them became a real problem, and we worried our guards might get stuck out there for a long time and freeze or starve to death. Finally we figured that if we could hardly get to our guard positions, anyone else would have an even harder time getting up to us, and we brought the outer perimeter guards in for the winter.

I didn't interact much with the people we'd rescued, but for the most part, they were a big help. Yeah, they made the food supply stretch a little thinner, but most of them were so happy to be out of that terrible place that they were eager to join our community and help share the workload. More people allowed us to get more wood chopped, more snow shoveled, more cooking and cleaning done, all faster.

Not all of them stayed. Just before the snow came, three men and two women asked us to take them as far as we dared take anyone, to the outskirts of the city of McCall. The rest of them figured their old homes were all run by the Brotherhood or otherwise destroyed by war, and few of them wanted to take their chances out on the road. Since we blindfolded the ones who wanted to leave for most of the trip away from the school, there was little chance they could give away our location to anyone who wished us harm.

I didn't go to all the council meetings anymore, and when I did, I rarely joined in the discussion. But I did get into it at one meeting, mad as hell. Pam Bean was leading an effort to keep the prisoners we'd rescued off by themselves in a couple of the classrooms. Mr. Shiratori and some others argued that people should move around, so that the newcomers could live spread out with everyone else.

When I heard about what Pam wanted to do, I shouted her down. "Pam Bean! JoBell did not die —" I stopped, chest heaving, and then pointed at the chair where Mr. Grenke used to sit. "Ryan Grenke did not die so that we could keep all the brown people in segregated housing!"

"We don't even know who these people are," she fired back. "Some of them don't even speak English."

"You know Kenny Palmer from Freedom Lake! You going to say he isn't one of us just because he was captured and had a far rougher time than us? You don't *know* the rest of them because they've been kept apart," I yelled. "One of the guys we got out of there, Chris Stone, used to be a broadcast engineer. He probably knows more about radios than Sergeant Crocker did, and he's been working on them constantly. But he's not good enough to live with the rest of us?" I shook my head. "It doesn't even make tactical sense keeping them separate! You've been getting people all scared that they might do something bad to us. If they were dangerous — and they're not, but using your twisted logic — if they were dangerous, that's all the more reason to have them living with the rest of us, so that we can keep an eye on them, and so that they become a lot more *us* and a lot less *them*." I slapped my hands on the table and looked straight across at Mrs. Pierce. "When you vote on this, I vote to move the newcomers in with us. Any of you who vote to put them off by themselves are sick. Almost as bad as the Brotherhood, who had them locked up in cages." I walked out of the room as straight as I could with my bum leg.

The newcomers began moving in with the rest of us the next day.

We'd done our best to prepare for the winter, rationing food all summer, smoking rabbit, duck, deer, and moose meat, chopping and stacking what seemed like millions of pieces of wood. We rationed food even more carefully through the winter. We had a slightly larger meal for Thanksgiving, with wild turkeys our hunters had brought in, and the kitchen people saved a few treats for Christmas, like chocolate and stuff. But other than that we ate simply, and not a lot. The biggest priority was making the canned and preserved fruit stretch to make sure everyone had enough vitamin C. By late February, supplies were running low, and people were starting to worry.

Always, I kept working to try to keep my mind off JoBell, and always I failed. I shoveled snow, carried wood to where it was needed, volunteered in the kitchen washing dishes, and pulled a hell of a lot of guard duty, sitting in the dark in the council building, looking out the window with night vision glasses. I figured I hated the nightmares that came with sleep, and I'd be up anyway, so I might as well let others sleep. Of course, nobody went on duty alone. Sweeney,

Becca, Cal, or TJ joined me sometimes, but Jaclyn stayed up with me the most. It's like she knew I was trying my best to put all that hurt away so that I could function. So she just talked about football or some crazy stuff that had happened at some old party. Anything but the terrible thought that always ached inside.

By the middle of March, the days were getting longer and a little warmer. Some of that snow had finally begun to melt.

"Come on, Wright, you gotta see this thing before it's gone," Cal said. He was wearing about six layers of clothes — jeans, sweat-pants, a snowmobile suit that fit a little too tight, gloves, and a big, dumb, poofy hat. He'd dumped a pile of extra winter gear on the floor next to my rack, all over the pieces of a kerosene heater I had taken apart for repair.

"I told you. I'm busy," I said. "I ain't got time to go build snow forts with you."

His shoulders fell a little. "Sweeney and Becca are already out there waiting for us. I told 'em I'd bring you."

"Well, if those two are out there, I don't want to interrupt them."

"It ain't like that," Cal said.

Jaclyn knocked, and the door swung open. She leaned against the door frame, all suited up for the snow too. "Wright, you seriously need to see this. It's three stories high." She shrugged. "Well, two and a half."

"Right! The roof on the top room fell in this morning, but the rest of it is holding up." Cal pushed the pile of clothes with his foot. "That's why you have to come see it before it's gone. I ain't asking you to come play, just to see it. 'Cause the kids who built this thing, they're like snow fort engineers." He looked up like he was thinking real hard. "Snowineers? Fortineers."

Jaclyn smiled. "Maybe snowengiforts."

"Exactly." Cal couldn't tell Jackie was making fun of him. "Or like snow . . . like fortisnow. Snowfoneers . . . wait —"

"I will go out there and see this thing if you two will shut up," I said.

"Yes!" Cal started to head out. "You won't regret this."

I suited up. I didn't know where Cal had found all this gear, but it didn't all quite fit. I figured I wouldn't need more than I wore shoveling. I'd only be out there for a little bit.

Jaclyn and I walked down the hall toward the stairs. "Why won't Old Man Winter die already?" she asked.

"I know, everybody else does," I said.

She stiffened and stopped. We were on the landing, halfway down the stairs, and with no electricity, the stairway was kind of dark. "Can I ask you a favor?"

"Can it wait until I finish fixing that stupid kerosene heater?"

"No, actually. It can't." Jaclyn sounded serious.

"What's up?

"Look, there's no way for me to say this without sounding like a giant bitch, so I'm just going to say it. Just hear me out." She sighed. "It's been six months."

I stopped on the landing, thinking about turning around and going back to my room. I'd been getting through the day, the last week or two really, pretty much okay. I didn't need her bringing up what I knew she was going to bring up. "Oh, six months? Is that the time limit? I'm not allowed to be sad anymore because it's been six months?"

"No, of course not. That's not what I meant."

I was so pissed, so frustrated, that I wanted to hit something. "We were engaged to be married. We'd been dating for almost five years. I've known JoBell since I was like five years old."

"I knew my parents since I was born!" Jaclyn glared at me, fists at her side. She wasn't backing down. "Other people have had losses too."

"So?"

"So, believe me, I get it, you wanted to go numb at first. You threw yourself into work to distract yourself. But your friends want to be there for you. This whole town, or whatever it's called, wants to help you. But you keep pushing everybody away."

I leaned until my back hit the wall, and then I slid down to take a seat on the carpeted wood stairs. "You don't understand," I said.

"I don't understand? Are you kidding me?" She spun away from me and started down the steps.

"There's nothing left for me in this world!" I called after her.

She stopped and faced me. "Then maybe you find something to start living for. Instead of spending all your time thinking about all that's been taken from you, maybe think about what you have left to give."

It took a while, but eventually I got up and went out to the snow fort. Cal was right. This place was impressive. I'd heard it started out as a pile made from the snow everyone had shoveled again and again around the latrine cabin and the dining lodge. Some kids had started digging tunnels into the pile, and some of the tunnels were higher than others, so they began to hollow out different floors of the hill.

"This is genius," I said when I walked onto the bottom floor, almost standing straight up. The kids had found half of an old pipe, about four feet long, but split open down the side like a little trough. They filled it with water, let it freeze, and then popped out ice poles, which were thick enough to act as a frame for the fort.

"Wright!" Cal called from above. "Get up here!"

Sweeney slid down a snow chute into the bottom room. "Dude, if we would have had this much snow as kids, we would have *lived* in the snow."

"Don't say that, Eric." Becca came down the packed snow steps. "We almost did live in the snow."

"So it's held up with ice beams?" I said. "I'm not sure we would have figured all this out."

Becca smiled. I hadn't seen that much excitement in her eyes in a long time. "They linked some of their beams end to end, and then covered them in slush to freeze them together."

I walked up the snow steps to the second floor. Jaclyn and TJ were talking there. I gave her a nod and a smile. I wasn't sure exactly what she'd meant back there on the stairwell, and I wasn't sure I could measure up to her expectations even if I did figure it out. But I could give it a try. It had been a long, terrible winter.

"Pretty cool, huh, Wright?" TJ said.

"Is that a snow joke?" I said. TJ's smile fell. "I'm just messing with you."

"Hey, you pussies!" Cal yelled from the floor above us.

"Cal, do you really think that top level is gonna hold up your fat ass?" TJ answered.

"Hell yeah it will! Because . . ." He drew out the last word. "Because I'm king of this damned mountain, and none of y'all can unthrone me!"

"Cal, the only throne you'll ever sit on is the toilet," I said. I'm not gonna lie. It felt good to joke.

"Bring it, bitch!" Cal said.

"I thought you said I was only supposed to come out and look at the place," I said.

"Well, if you want to see the top floor here, you'll have to take me down."

I looked at TJ and Jaclyn, who smiled and nodded. "Let's beat that smug bastard."

Becca and Sweeney hurried up to join us. "Not without us," Becca said.

"You two were down there for a long time." Jaclyn gave Becca a little shove.

Becca looked at me nervously for a moment, but then went on, "Yeah, well, we were trying to keep warm."

"You guy-ys!" Cal called out in a singsong voice. "I'm getting bored up here."

"Becca and Jackie, take the stairs," Sweeney said. "We'll go up the slide. But give us a head start. It's hard to climb up that thing."

Sweeney led us out to a snow slide that sloped down pretty sharp as it curved around the outside of the tower. Still, the snow was a little wet, so we could dig into its outside edges with our fingers and make our way up.

"I hope you like that slide, boys," Cal said above us. " 'Cause I'm gonna knock your asses back down it."

"Charge!" Becca shouted before we'd reached the top. We could see her and Jaclyn grab Cal and shove him hard down the slide. He laughed as he knocked into us, sending us guys down the snow chute as well. We all collapsed on the ground at the bottom of the slide. "Sorry, Jackie," Becca said from above us. Jaclyn came tumbling down the slide too. "Nothing personal," Becca called, holding her hands up in the air. "New game! *Queen* of the mountain."

"That was a short reign, Cal," Sweeney said.

Jaclyn laughed. "You'll pay for your treachery, false queen Becca!"

"False queen?" Becca said. "I'm right here. Where are *you*, my servants?"

"Are we gonna stand for this, you guys?" TJ was on his feet. He laughed as he ran back into the bottom room. "I'll take the place myself!"

Cal was right behind him. "You'll never make it up before me."

Sweeney leaned closer and put his hand on my good shoulder. "Stupid and childish." He tipped his head toward the snow fort. "But fun, right?"

"It's not that fun," I said sadly.

"What?" said Sweeney.

"You okay, Danny?" Becca called down.

Shooting my foot behind Sweeney, I pushed him back to trip him. Then I threw Jaclyn to the snow in the same way and ran for the snow fort. "*That* was fun!"

TWENTY-FOUR

We battled for control of that stupid snow fort until it got dark. If we'd had moonlight, we would have kept going. It was the first outright fun I'd had since JoBell died, the first laughter, the first time — the guilt flooded in as soon as the thought hit me — the first time I'd been able to do something without her on my mind. Is this what Jaclyn had been saying about living for others? Forgetting the woman who was almost my wife?

Those kinds of thoughts cut through my mind during chow. Afterward, me and my friends went to the library, where all guards coming on shift were supposed to report before going to their positions. The fireplace was kept burning, and coffee was on all night. It had become the place where my group all hung out. Usually I only stopped in right before I went on duty. I hadn't been in the mood for fun and joking around.

Now it was just my group, plus Tim Macer, Brad Robinson, and Samantha Monohan, sitting in a semicircle in front of the fireplace. I sat on one end of the couch with Jaclyn next to me and Sweeney and Becca on the other side of her. Cal and TJ each had one of the two big, comfortable chairs. Sam sat on Cal's lap. The rest had pulled up business chairs from the council table, where Lieutenant Griffith sat reading a book.

"Dude, it's seriously great to have you with us again," Sweeney said to me. "It's good to see you have some fun. And since we're actually off the guard duty rotation tonight, I have a surprise for you." He got up and pulled some books from one of the shelves.

"You know I'm not a big reader," I said.

Sweeney flashed a grin that, except for the burn scar on his cheek and neck, was just like his old I'm-up-to-something-type smile. He reached back behind some books and pulled out a flat, wide bottle of brown liquid. He held it up like a trophy. "I found this on one of our scavenging missions. I know we're supposed to share everything, but I was saving it for a special occasion." From the way his eyes fell, I figured the occasion he was talking about was me and JoBell's wedding. "But since . . . Well, since you're back with us now, I think that calls for a celebration."

"Hell yeah!" Tim Macer said.

"Who says you're getting any?" Cal said. "You're just a sophomore."

Tim's mouth dropped open a little. It was one of those expressions where you could tell someone was hurt, but he was trying to act like everything was cool.

Sweeney burst out laughing. Cal joined him. "Macer, I was just giving you shit. You better have some of this."

Samantha laughed and kissed Cal's cheek. "You guys are so mean to him."

"Gee, Eric." Becca spoke in an exaggerated acting voice. "If only you had little cups so we could all have some together."

Sweeney leaned his head against the bookshelves like he was sad. "I know. I'm a failure." He looked up. "Unless . . . Wait a minute. What is this?" He reached back between some books and pulled out a plastic sleeve of little wax paper Dixie cups. "Would you believe these were back there the whole time?"

Jaclyn laughed. "No, I wouldn't believe it. Now would you pass the cups and pour us some of that already?"

Sweeney bowed. "Yes, my lady."

"Hey, I was the last queen of the mountain," Becca said.

Sweeney passed out the cups and then filled them. "Yeah, we're all going to get at least three big shots out of this bottle."

Lieutenant Griffith pulled a chair up to our circle. "Do you mind if I have some? Maybe pour one for Chris Stone, around the corner in Crocker's room?"

"Make that two and a half shots." Sweeney poured some for Griffith and Stone.

"I don't know if you officer types can handle it, sir," I said.

Everybody whooped at that. The lieutenant smiled. The whole thing felt so normal. And underneath it all, I couldn't shake the feeling that normal was wrong.

When Griffith came back with a smiling Chris Stone, Sweeney tapped his cane on the floor to shut everyone up. He raised his cup, and we all did the same. He looked us all over and nodded. "To the best of friends."

"Hell with that." Cal held his cup high. "To family."

"To surviving," Griffith added.

"Amen," said Stone.

We all knocked back our drinks, and then came the usual *wow! whoo! strong stuff!* and gasping after a round of shots.

"Hey, none of you are underage, right?" Lieutenant Griffith smiled and pointed at us with his cup. " 'Cause I could tell my mom on you."

"I swear, sir," said Becca, holding up her hands in surrender. "This is the one and only time I've broken the law."

We laughed again, and this time Sweeney passed the bottle

around for people to pour their own. "Don't be hogs, everybody. About an inch should do it."

Brad Robinson laughed. "So fill it about as high as your dick is long." Sweeney flipped him off. Stone filled his cup again and nodded to all of us before he went back to his radios.

"I can't believe we're drinking with the son of the president of the United States," Jaclyn said when the bottle got to Griffith.

The lieutenant filled his glass and raised it at Jaclyn. "I can't believe I'm alive and free to drink this because I was rescued by the US's number-one most wanted rebel insurgents."

I took another shot, and then opened my mouth to blow out the heat. "We ain't insurgents. We gave up on the war. Now there's just . . ." What? What was left after JoBell was gone?

"Staying alive," Samantha said.

We went on like that, sitting in front of the fireplace, drinking and joking, for a few hours. Kemp came in after a while, the flickering light from the flames making weird shadows dance on his black eye patch.

"Sergeant Kemp!" Cal held up the bottle of bourbon, sloshing around what little was left in the bottom. "Polish 'er off fer us, wouldja?"

Kemp raised his eyebrows, took the bottle, and downed the rest, closing his eyes and taking a sharp breath in through the nose to savor the burn. "Thanks. Hey, you guys might want to hear this. All that work Stone's been doing to our radio and antenna system seems like it paid off. He's got something on speaker in Crocker's room."

We made our way to our feet, if a little shakily. Cal reached over to Macer, who was nearly passed out. "Shtop. Wait minute." He grabbed Tim's cup. "Masher's cup. Shtill some liquor in it." He held it up. "To Sergeant Crocker. Helluva man."

He drank the bourbon that was left in the cup, and we went to the next room, the radio room we'd named in honor of Sergeant Anthony Crocker.

Stone smiled as we came in. "You all ever hear about this guy called the Cliffhanger?"

"We've listened to him sometimes," I said. I thought about how JoBell had loved that show. Always JoBell.

"That dude supposedly's been all over Pan America —" TJ started.

"He *did* go all over. There's nowhere he wouldn't go," said Stone.

"Broadcasting about peace and stuff, like out of the back of a van or something," Sweeney said. "Everybody else is locked in a war, and all he's worried about is radio."

"Pretty gutsy," Becca said.

Stone nodded. "Not only radio, but he also got his message out by Internet, TV transmitters, podcast, and even paper flyers he'd leave around town. He must be transmitting from a real commercial radio station tonight, must have the transmitter power as high as she'll go, because it is coming in crystal."

"In almost every city in the Pan American territory, you'll find message boards, scraps of paper tacked to walls, bits of hope carrying messages to loved ones. The Cliffhanger always tries to get these messages on the air. And you know, I can read the writing on the wall. I've found more than a few notes thanking the Cliffhanger for helping to reunite lovers, families, friends.

"Anne Chambers has left a message, dated today, in Caldwell, Idaho, for her family. 'I've gone to Twin Falls looking for you. I have a motorcycle and a shotgun. If you make it back here, stay here. I'll be back in two weeks.'

"Ca-aldwell is just outside of Boise," I said quietly, my head spinning in booze. "Place'sh taken pounding. Fed soldiers come in from Oregon. They fought it out there couple times."

Two days ago in Boise, Evangeline Jennings posted a photograph on the wall of a bombed-out coffee shop near what's left of the Idaho capitol building. She asks, 'Has anyone seen my baby girl? Charlotte Jennings, four years old, went missing last night. Police can't help. She also goes by the name "Charlie." I will check back here every day at noon. If you know where she is, please help. I'll pay anything. Do anything. I need my daughter back.'

"You know, listeners, I see more and more of these missing persons notes everywhere I go. Too often, it's a young child, a teenage girl. A fractured nation hangs on the edge of a chasm, and in those dark depths is a nightmare reality in which women and girls are sold for the use of their bodies, in which others are sold into the bondage of slavery.

"No, I'm not reading some old book from before our first Civil War. I'm talking about what we've come to now, in our time. A lot of the Pan American territory is ruled, not by one of the fourteen governments who claim legitimacy through votes or force, but by fear, as people live in terror of ruthless criminal gangs and brutal warlords. One such dangerous militia rules in northern Idaho and eastern Washington. The Brotherhood of the White Eagle proclaims itself to be the protector of all people, a force for freedom, but the Cliffhanger has seen the truth! The Brotherhood seizes what they want for themselves by force, playing the part of the merciful protector when they allow their allies and supporters a few scraps from their feast. The Brotherhood is, in fact, a dangerous white supremacist organization, the leadership of which is far more organized and cunning than the dregs of our former society who populated the Ku Klux Klan or the Aryan Nations. What is more, the government of the Northwest Alliance works openly with the Brotherhood, relying on them for security in the region, so busy in their war against the United States that they are unable — or unwilling — to put a stop to *the atrocities committed by the Brotherhood. What atrocities? Murder! Extortion! Arson! Theft! Rape! Slavery!*

"You may not believe me, but truly, the Cliffhanger came back to Idaho after hearing a tip on the location of one of my closest friends. He's a technical whiz who helped keep the voice of truth coming to you over the airwaves night after night. And he was cap-tured, chained up, and made a slave by the Brotherhood of the White Eagle, until his camp was liberated back in September."

We all looked at Stone, who backed up in the rolling office chair a little and shrugged.

"You know the Cliffhanger?" Becca asked. "You worked with him?"

"It's not easy rigging all those transmitters and the generators to power them," Stone said.

"And I have more news for you, my friends. The Brotherhood of the White Eagle and the Northwest Alliance have been generating sympathy, drawing people to their twisted banner, with the sad story of how the United States killed PFC Daniel Wright and his friends, how Wright died fighting for the Brotherhood. It is a lie! Daniel Wright was alive as recently as last September when he fought to liberate the slave camp that held my friend. He fought against the Brotherhood! He helped rescue almost fifty people!"

"Oh shit," Sweeney said, grabbing my shoulder to steady himself.

"I wish he wouldn't have said that," Kemp said. "It was better, safer, when nobody knew you were alive. We left no Brotherhood survivors, so until now, they couldn't have known you were involved in wrecking their camp."

"The Cliffhanger doesn't hold back the truth," Stone said. "But this also shows that at least some of the people from the camp who went on the road survived long enough to spread the word about how they got out. They might have told people about this school."

"We don't know that," Jaclyn said.

"Shtill." I shook my head against the booze. I needed to dry out. "I better tell da council. We gotta be ready in case da Brotherhood comes for us now. For me."

"The Brotherhood and other groups have been hunting for me, offering rewards for my capture or for even a snippet of information about who I am. Well, tonight I will tell them, tell everyone, the exact truth of the identity of the Cliffhanger.

"The Cliffhanger is a mother in Kentucky who goes without food for days so that her children can eat. The Cliffhanger is the tornado victim in Nebraska who has lost his home, when there are no insurance companies to help him rebuild, no materials on the market with which to rebuild, and no disaster relief agency to assist him in his time of need. The Cliffhanger is the exhausted soldier, the people on the run from bullets or bombings, the grandmother crying in the street because she has outlived her children and her children's children. The Cliffhanger is the family huddled in the dark basement where they thank God they've made it through another day, the laborer with no work, the child with no food, refugees with no home! The Cliffhanger is an entire generation of people holding on to the edge of hope and humanity with their last . . . sliver . . . of strength.

"This war isn't about freedom, democracy, or security. It's no longer even about a handful of opportunists who will do anything to take what they want from this world. It's about death, suffering, indignity, and the collapse of our civilization. The Cliffhanger is everywhere, and calls upon people everywhere with one question. Where does it end? If we continue to trade an eye for an eye, a life for a life, we will grind our society into dust. We will drive our species toward extinction. Have hope, my friends. True justice is not a futile quest to balance a scale. It isn't a scale at all. It is a book, the pages of which are not yet written. We must make the right choice for the

next chapter in our shared story. What will you do to throw away the scale, and make sure the story of us continues with hope?"

The Cliffhanger went on longer like that, but I sort of stopped listening. That last bit stuck with me, and it took the party spirit out of me so that I didn't hang around down there much longer but went up to my room. I lay awake in my empty bed until long after Sweeney and Cal had hit the rack. The Cliffhanger's words wouldn't leave me alone.

That night I walked out into the bite of the cold night air, my boots crunching on the hard-packed snow of the empty path. A light breeze whispered through the needles of the trees overhead, like the whispers of the ghosts of everyone who'd died in the war. If the people who'd died at the Battle of Boise could make their voices heard right now, what would they say? If Lieutenant McFee were here, what orders would he give? If the wind carried the wishes of Staff Sergeants Kirklin and Donshel, Sergeant Ribbon, PFC Nelson, and Specialist Stein, what would they tell me? If Herbokowitz, Bagley, and Luchen could speak again, what would they offer? I closed my eyes. What would my mother say?

I slid down a frozen rocky slope into the sad little valley where our people had buried our dead. Moonlight glinted on the snow that covered the gravestones. It was older snow, and heavy. I brushed off one of the markers to reveal her name.

JoBell Marie Linder.

If I could hear my JoBell's sweet voice one more time . . .

She'd probably remind me about rule one. "I'm not alone," I said quietly. "I feel like too many people are here with me tonight."

The wind died down and the cold night fell absolutely still.

"That show you like. The Cliffhanger? It was on tonight," I said. "He said kind of what you said once, about books, about how we should do things to make future books about us say the right things."

My eyes stung, and not only from the cold. "I thought you would have liked that.

"He said something else, though. He said we gotta stop thinking about justice, payback, and how much is owed, like it's all on a scale. You know? Like the US killed some of ours, so we have to kill some of theirs back? But I think . . . it goes back farther than that. Democrats like President Rodriguez would pass a law, and maybe it was a good one, but that didn't matter because Republicans like Montaine would have to oppose it, or the scale would tip too far in the Democrats' favor. Democrats would do the same. Republicans and Democrats. All they did was push the scale for the sake of pushing. Then that summer in Boise."

As I said the words, I could hear the screams from that night, and from a lot of bad nights that followed.

"It. Was. An. Accident. And that should have been the end of it. But it had tipped the scale, and others wanted to push it back. So they sent men to arrest us. So the pressure of the scale made Montaine block out all the Feds. Rodriguez himself said he didn't want to launch the blockade in response, but that he *had* to. It's all because one side or the other can't stand for the balance to be off, no matter if what tipped it was good or bad. But it's like each time they tip the balance, they push it farther and farther, until finally the only way to move it back is with guns."

I shivered in the cold and wished for the millionth time that JoBell's arms might be wrapped around me. "A long time ago, Sweeney asked me how we deal with having killed people in this war. Becca wondered the same thing. Cal was all tore up after what happened to Jackie's folks. He blamed himself. I . . . I told him it wasn't his fault. And I believed that." I tapped the side of my head. "In here." I tapped my chest. "And in here. I believed that because it's true, and because I knew the weight of the guilt for those deaths would crush his soul.

"We had kind of a party tonight, JoBell. You would have loved it. Everybody together, safe, and joking around. Even Lieutenant Griffith and this guy Chris Stone that we freed from the camp joined in a little." A tear rolled down my cheek. "But when we listened to the Cliffhanger talking about war, I felt guilty, you know? Because what right did I have to be safe, to have fun, when so many others are suffering so much in this war? But I was glad that my friends could have a good time."

I shook my head. "Sorry. I know I'm not too good of a speaker. Maybe I'm still drunk. I can forgive Cal and I believe it when I tell him it's not his fault. But I blame myself for everything else that's gone wrong. And I'm happy that my friends are safe and having fun, but I feel bad for doing the same thing. And then when the Cliffhanger talked about what we want to put into the next chapter of the book about us, just like you had, I could almost imagine you with us, and I wondered what you'd say. And I think . . . JoBell, I know you'd tell me it's okay if I have fun. You'd tell me this . . . oh God . . . that it isn't all my fault."

I dropped down to my knees in the snow before JoBell's grave. "I can't keep weighing the war and suffering against my life. I gotta get off the scale. And to do that —" My whole body twisted in sobs. "I gotta let you go, Jo. I can't keep figuring the crime versus the cost and all the things I maybe coulda done so that you'd still be here. *You* argued for the mission. *You* wouldn't listen when I said you should stay back. Who's to blame? How much do they owe?" I shouted up to the trees, "I don't even know anymore!"

I wiped away snot and tears. "But trying to figure it all out is killing me worse than any bullet. I gotta get off the scale. We all do."

I turned around and sat down with my back leaning against JoBell's headstone. "I told Jackie there's nothing left for me in this world, and she said maybe I should see what I can offer to others instead. And that's what I gotta do. Not because I owe it for the wrong I done, but because I care about my friends, and the people here."

I was silent for a long time. The cold bit harder and harder through my clothes. "I'll always love you, JoBell, and I'll never forget you. But I gotta let you go. I gotta get off the scale and let it all go. In my heart, I don't know how I'm going to do that, but in my head, I know I have to."

I stood up and brushed the snow from my jeans, looking down on JoBell's grave. "I think this is the kind of thing you'd tell me if you were here. But I'll never truly know, and it's up to me." I leaned down and rested my hand on her stone, warmed a little where my back had pressed over her name. "I love you. Goodbye, JoBell."

TWENTY-FIVE

After explaining to the council that the Cliffhanger had revealed that it was us who took out that Brotherhood camp, it didn't take long to convince them that we all might be in more danger. They had some questions: *The Brotherhood haven't found us in almost a year. Why would they be any more likely to find us now?* Or: *Maybe we can find somewhere else to hide?* But most people accepted that the Brotherhood was expanding its territory, and now that they knew we were somewhere around north central Idaho, and we'd beaten them twice, they'd be more likely to step up their search for us. We had nowhere else to go. The Alice Marshall School was our last stand.

Even before the last of the snow had melted, we launched into an unending stretch of the hardest work I'd ever done. It made winter seem like a vacation. Sergeant Kemp directed the construction of our new defenses, with help from Mr. Cretis and Mrs. Pierce. Mr. Cretis was a whiz with our tools, and Mrs. Pierce had studied some of the kinds of traps that had wounded her patients way back in Vietnam. She had plenty of suggestions for setups that would work just as well against the Brotherhood.

We worried about the Brotherhood or some other dangerous group driving up the road to the school, so Mr. Cretis spent over a week designing and planning a system to launch a rockslide. He figured out a sort of giant basket-type thing that a bunch of us filled with big rocks, almost boulders. If our guard pulled a rope to release a certain pole, the basket would dump the rocks, letting them roll down the steep hillside to completely block the road.

Our other new defenses were built in two ringed perimeters. The first defense was mostly an early alert system. We built scout and sniper platforms high in the trees. We'd be able to see people coming from far away, and take them out from up high, where they might not be looking. Above all, our tree guards could spot the enemy and let everybody at Alice Marshall know of the danger early enough for the rest of us to get into place for the fight.

Those scouts and snipers could then fall back to our main protection, a series of ten fighting positions in a circle around the school. Each position was reinforced with huge logs and camouflaged. When the bunkers were finished, they were hard to spot and would be even harder to beat.

Mrs. Pierce had us dig a bunch of shallow pits in front of the circle of bunkers. These pits weren't deep enough for the enemy to use as decent cover, and they were made deadly with sharpened sticks or even sharp pieces of metal from what was left of our scrapped bus. Each pit trap was covered with a mesh of thin, easily breakable sticks that were then covered in pine needles to blend in with the rest of the forest. If the enemy stepped on the sticks, he'd fall right through and be stabbed by the sharp spikes or metal bits. Our fighters would practice navigating the pits and learning the safe paths back toward the Alice Marshall School.

One day in the middle of April, me, Cal, Sweeney, TJ, and Jaclyn were way up on the north edge of the school's land, digging traps beyond fighting position six.

"Damn it." TJ threw his shovel handle to the ground. His shovel's blade was still in the dirt. "That's the third handle I've busted this week. Worthless things."

I tried not to take his words personally. I'd built a lot of these shovels from bus steel and pine limbs. They were the best we could do, but they were kind of junk. "You gotta —"

"Scoop smaller and faster! Yeah, I know the drill. I've been digging for a month," TJ said. He wiped the sweat from his brow, went to our open water bucket, and drank from the ladle.

"Cheer up. We'll only be digging till the ground freezes again," Jaclyn said.

Sweeney tossed another blade full of dirt and then leaned against his shovel like a cane, rubbing his bad leg. "You think this pit's deep enough to spike?"

I couldn't blame him for being tired. We'd been out here digging since five a.m, and it had been like that for a month. Every muscle in my body ached, but we had to do the job right. "I think we have to go a little deeper. The farther they fall, the deeper the spikes will stab them."

Sweeney sighed. "Even if we are attacked, the mathematical odds of anyone stepping in this trap are about a million to one. They'd have to send hundreds of guys up over the mountain to come down at us from this side anyway. And then, once the first guy hit a trap, they'd be more careful."

"That's what makes it great," said Cal. "They'll have to slow way down to be careful, and that will make it easy for shooters at bunker six to pick them off. If they do send enough guys to overtake the bunker, they'll be shot down by our people back by the school."

Jaclyn shoveled more. "At least the fighting positions are done. I'm glad we're not working on that project today. This is easy work compared to carrying the logs into place for the bunkers."

"Speaking of easy work." Sweeney smiled and pointed. We turned to see Becca and Sergeant Kemp heading our way. Radios had to be saved for our scout teams or for emergencies, so messages had to be run the old-fashioned way. Becca had lucked out with that job for the day. I didn't know what Sergeant Kemp was up to.

"Great," said TJ. "Maybe she can go pick me up another shovel."

Cal made a big show of being in pain, standing up from digging and groaning as he pressed his hand to his back. "Oh hey, Becca. Tough day running messages? Your back must be hurting. Maybe some of this cushy work shoveling would help. Your feet got lots of blisters from all that walking?" Becca smiled and flipped Cal off. Cal grinned. "How you doing, Sergeant Pirate?"

"Just missing a hook," Sergeant Kemp said. "So I can shove it up your ass." Everybody laughed.

"How's Angeline?" Jaclyn asked with a big grin on her face.

Kemp shrugged, trying to hold back his own smile. "She's . . . fine, I guess."

"Especially after your long, romantic walk by the lake yesterday," Jaclyn said.

"She works hard, raising little Josie and babysitting other kids," said Kemp. "She needed a break."

"Well, that's *very* considerate of you," Cal said. "So is she a good . . . you know . . . *walker*?"

"What are you, a seventh grader?" TJ said to Cal.

Cal laughed and nodded like he was so smooth. "He knows what I'm talking about."

Sergeant Kemp stared at Cal with a confused look.

I'd served with Kemp for a long time. I could tell something was bothering him beyond the teasing. "What's wrong?" I asked.

"Our long-range scouts ran into a Brotherhood patrol, a dozen well-armed men on horseback about four days' hike from here."

I started toward the tree against which we'd leaned our guns. "How many of our people made it back?"

"They're all fine," Kemp said quickly. "It was Lee Brooks's team. It was all by the book. Radio check-in at all the right times. They went out in total camo with the ghillie suits we made and everything, staying hidden while the enemy rode by about twenty yards away."

"They were heading south, away from us," Becca said.

"Still, four days' hike is pretty close," TJ said.

"Really close on horseback," Becca said.

"So what?" Cal said. "Let them come. We'll kick their asses."

I met Kemp's eyes. Our defenses were a little better than they were before, but there were still problems. We had three .50-cal machine guns, but we were down to about 350 rounds. The guns would eat through those real quick. The M240B had only about 500 rounds. If the Brotherhood came for us in force and took out even one of our fighting positions, they'd be inside our perimeter no problem. Then there'd be chaos, and a lot of bodies on the ground.

Cal held up his shovel and pointed it out at the woods like a rifle. "The bunker walls are like four- or five-feet thick. We got these traps. Anyone who attacks this place don't stand a chance."

"That's what the French said about the Maginot Line in World War II," said Sergeant Kemp.

"Yeah, but that's the French," Cal said.

Kemp shifted his gaze out to the woods. "If the Brotherhood is being smart about their search, covering ground with any kind of system, there are good odds they'll find us. The bunkers and these traps will help, but . . ."

"So what are you saying, Sergeant?" Sweeney asked. "That we should be ready for war?"

"We are ready!" Cal said.

"Maybe we can go someplace else?" TJ said. "Higher up the mountain, maybe? Someplace safer?"

If TJ hadn't turned out to be such a solid guy, if I didn't owe him my life so many times over, I would have answered him with a real smart-ass comment. "There's nowhere else to go," I said.

Jaclyn jabbed her shovel in the dirt. "I wish the Idaho Army would *do* something about the Brotherhood! It's crap that we're stuck in a war against the United States, *and* the guys who are supposed to be helping us fight the United States."

"Montaine would probably send the Idaho Army to take the Brotherhood out if he didn't have the US military threatening him all the time," Kemp said. "But for the foreseeable future, we're stuck in the middle of a war, and it looks like our safe place is getting less and less safe all the time."

That night me and Sweeney sat on tree stumps inside the position one bunker. Logs above, in front, and on both sides of us. We had nothing to do for the next six hours except stare out the windows to make sure it all stayed as boring as it was now.

"No offense, dude, but this is crap. I've been pulling guard with Becca for months. Why the reassignment?"

"Are you being serious right now?" I asked. "I think it has something to do with Sergeant Kemp catching you and Becca . . . doing whatever you two were doing while you were supposed to be covering your sector."

"We had it covered," Sweeney said. "It's just that things with Becca have been really great. I honestly believe that she's the one. My *real* one. And, well, it's tough to find anywhere to be alone."

"Yeah," I said. I really wasn't in the mood to talk about Sweeney's love life. He held out a cigarette. "Where the hell did you get that?" I snatched the smoke and lighter he offered.

"Darren Hartling's been holding out on us. Secret stash. Won a whole pack off him with my full house over his straight."

I grunted, stood, and went to the window, looking out at the forest as shadows slowly thickened to dark.

"You okay?" Sweeney asked. "You've been kind of quiet all night."

I blew out smoke, coughing. I hadn't had a cigarette in ages. "Just, poker . . ." How could I explain this to him?

"You never complained about my gambling before."

"It's not that. Before we busted up that slave camp, we were safe up here. Nobody knew where we were. Nobody was hunting us."

"As far as you know," Sweeney said.

"Well, now I *know* we're in greater danger of being attacked."

Sweeney lit up his own cigarette. "So, we're doing the best we can."

"No," I said. "No, we're not. We ain't gonna win the fight if the Brotherhood does find us."

"What more can we do?"

"I'm going to go to Montaine and get help." I'd been thinking about it all afternoon.

"What?"

"If he won't put a stop to the Brotherhood, maybe I could bring back help to protect the school. At least I could get more ammo to give everybody here a fighting chance."

"He's in Boise!" Sweeney said. "If he's still alive. And how you gonna get there?"

"I'll take Pale Horse."

"What, are you going to sneak out again on some secret superhero cowboy mission? Take all the best weapons away to leave this place really unprotected?"

I took a drag on my cigarette. "No, I'll let the council know what I'm doing. And I'll leave the machine guns here."

"Dude, this is crazy," Sweeney said. "I know you feel responsible for the people we lost at the Brotherhood camp or on the way here. You're probably still blaming yourself for the whole war, but —"

"It's not that," I said. "It's just a tactical necessity. If the Brotherhood are coming, I have to make sure I do all I can to help keep people here safe." I hesitated a moment, wondering if I should tell him the real crazy part of my plan. "And, who knows, but maybe I can convince Montaine to call for a cease-fire." Sweeney's jaw dropped, and I could see he was about to argue with me, so I went on. "Montaine's said over and over that all he wants is for the US to give up, for the Northwest Alliance to be left alone."

"The US isn't about to give up," Sweeney said.

"President Griffith might have a change of heart —"

"If she's even really still in charge."

"— if she finds out her son is still alive," I said. "If Lieutenant Griffith calls for a cease-fire too."

He paused, thinking about it. "It'll never work. The war's too big, man."

"Maybe, but I'm doing this. I don't have any choice. At the very least, I got to get us more food and bullets. Hopefully, I can get Montaine to do something about the Brotherhood."

Sweeney was quiet, thinking again. The ash on the end of his cigarette was really long. "How do I keep letting you talk me into these stupid —"

"I wasn't asking you to come with me."

He stood up. "Oh, come on. I ought to knock you on your ass. What part of 'with you all the way' don't you understand? But I . . . Are you sure about this?"

"This is as sure as I've felt about anything in a long time," I said. "I have to try."

⌁—• Those of us inside the United States are fortunate. Even though more US citizens are being called upon to fight, most of us still enjoy many of the freedoms we had before the war. The United States invites those of you listening in rebel states to return to America. If you and your family can reach United States territory, you will be welcomed home with open arms. You're listening to the Unity Radio Network. Hope for a united America. •—⌁

⌁—• Welcome back to the Civil War Situation Room here on the Atlantica News Network. I'm Al Hudson. We're joined today by a senior official from the Atlantica War Department, Colonel Bradley Yates. Colonel, as you know, one of the many things our leader, General Vogel, has done extremely well is to keep a digital communications grid operating in our country. This allows us to hear from patriots all over our nation, and tonight we've been in touch with people in Spartanburg, Greenville, and other northern cities, who are concerned about the fighting going on so close to their homes. Colonel, what should those patriots understand?"

"Thank you, Al. That's a great question, but before I answer it, I just want to say that I've spoken directly with General Vogel himself, and he has expressed a great deal of appreciation for everything you and your fellow journalists at ANN are doing. It's great to see that patriotism for the great nation of Atlantica can march side by side with the kind of excellent fair, free, and independent journalism you people are delivering every day. To answer your question. I will not lie to you. It's a difficult battle. We're fighting a war along old state lines that were arbitrarily drawn up hundreds of years ago. When you're out there on the border, you can't see that line. There is no line. That's a meaningless, archaic marker. We can all see the wisdom in the Vogel Doctrine, which

dictates we will seize territory anywhere if it promotes the peace and safety of Atlantica. So Charlotte, Fayetteville, Wilmington — the whole state of North Carolina! Those are all areas that will soon either be under Atlantican control or be destroyed. The fight is difficult now, and clearly we should be on guard against our many enemies, but what is also clear is that General Jonathan Vogel is leading this nation to an amazingly bright future. •—∿

∿—• The conclusion we've been able to draw so far is that the greatest losses are in border cities. Appalachia continues to hold Cincinnati and the southern territory of what used to be Ohio, but Liberum's continued attempts to take back that territory have left much of that city in ruins.

Here's an image from our NBC drone cam — we apologize for the poor quality. There you see the broken arch in what is left of Saint Louis. Fighting there between US and Liberum forces has intensified in the last few days as US Marines are securing their position on the east bank of the Mississippi •—∿

∿—• German armored and mobile air defense artillery suffered another setback today as Soviet cruise missiles pounded German positions around the Polish city of Poznan. To the southeast in Prague, the British and French clashed with Soviet infantry units, a setback after Turkish forces were compelled to answer attacks on their homeland from Iraq and Iran.

While the United States has been too preoccupied with the North American war to assist its allies against the Free Federation of Nations, today several United States submarines contributed to the sinking of the Soviet flagship missile cruiser Admiral Kuznetsov. The ship is believed to have been destroyed with most of its over seventeen hundred crew members aboard. •—∿

‑√‑• Keep it tuned to WGN Chicago, Liberum's superstation. With fourteen different countries across the Pan American area, each of them doing their best to appear invincible, getting accurate casualty figures is exceedingly difficult. However, many people now believe that not counting the nuclear attacks on New York and Washington, DC, Pan American casualties have likely topped two and a half million. This staggering death toll has risen thanks to continued brutal fighting, starvation, a terribly hot summer and desperately cold winter, and now, a new horrible killer — the improvised explosive drone. These bombs can be rigged on old, inexpensive, commercially available drones, allowing opposing armies or violent militias to easily inflict massive casualties from a distance. Several trucks out of Oklahoma crossed the border into Missouri within drone range of the city of Joplin. In a little over an hour, an estimated two hundred drones, each carrying at least a full pound of a high-explosive compound wrapped in metal shrapnel, flew into the city and attacked United States positions. Remote drone pilots were able to maneuver the tiny aircraft wherever people tried to take shelter. Over a thousand were killed. •‑√‑

‑√‑• That red light means this is on, yeah? We're not professional broadcasters. All right. Please, everyone watching the Atlantica News Network. General Jonathan Vogel is dead. We have killed him ourselves. Several of his top officers are dead as well. We represent a large group of Atlantican citizen-soldiers who refuse to suffer under Vogel's brutal police-state tactics and who want an end to the war. At this time, all Atlantican forces are withdrawing to the original boundaries of South Carolina, Georgia, and Florida. Citizens of Atlantica should stand by for further announcements regarding reforms. For now, please join us in celebrating the end of the tyrannical military dictatorship led by General Vogel. •‑√‑

⌐• Greetings, fellow patriots! Welcome back to the Buzz Ellison Show. *It's another great day of freedom here in the Northwest Alliance. Those of you who were listening before that last update from the War Department heard my conversation with a very interesting caller. She was a Northwest Alliance citizen who was asking if the war — our struggle for freedom, dignity, and conservatism — was worth the enormous cost. She was even thinking about joining that ridiculous Pan American Peace Movement. She was calling on a comm that was just about out of charge, and she had it plugged in, but then her city suffered a power outage and we lost the call. I assure you, I did not hang up on her. The Buzzmaster does not shy away from the tough issues.*

Over the many, many years I've been broadcasting my genius, I've become quite skilled at reading people. Some people have a rare gift for listening and understanding, and I happen to be one of those people. And I sensed some worry in that last caller. I think she's worried that we are getting closer to losing this war.

Fellow patriots, let me assure you: It's the other way around. The United States is losing this war! They're fighting on how many fronts now? Yes, US forces have retaken most of the state of Washington, but they had to destroy it to do it! They had to bomb the hell out of Washington to get it back! And even then, they couldn't retake Spokane and Fairchild Air Force Base there. The US lost so many soldiers, so much ammunition and valuable equipment and . . . and aircraft, folks, in their failed attempt to destroy or dominate Spokane. They are on the losing side of this war. Our job is to hold our ground and inflict as many casualties on the United States as we can. And if we keep our faith, if we maintain the strong foundation of our conservative principles, then victory is right around the corner. •⌐

⎯⎯• I am Vice President General Charles Jacobsen, making this address on multiple television, radio, and Internet channels and frequencies at the behest of the United States Congress and President Laura Griffith. Leadership and people living in rebel states, listen carefully. Every possible effort has been made to limit the number of civilian casualties in the process of ending your rebellions. The United States has been generous in welcoming, with open arms, refugees from your impoverished and suffering states. But our patience is nearing an end. You will stand down your forces and surrender, or the United States will have no mercy on your people. We will, if necessary, completely destroy your cities, using any and all methods available to us, including nuclear weapons. You have one week to comply. Surrender now, or you will die. •⎯⎯

CHAPTER
TWENTY-SIX

I'm not gonna lie. It was not easy to convince the council to authorize the mission to Boise. A lot of people pointed out the terrible cost of freeing the slave camp. But I responded that this wasn't an assault operation, and Sergeant Kemp helped me out, reminding them of our troubling tactical situation. "Even if Danny just brings back a few cans of ammo," he said, "it would make a huge difference." In the end, the vote was tied and went to Mrs. Pierce. She stared at me in silence for a long time, and somehow I got the idea that we had an understanding, veteran to veteran.

"I wish you success," she said quietly, "for the sake of us all."

The next three days were full of frantic but quiet planning. It didn't take long until my whole group — Sweeney, Cal, Becca, TJ, and Jaclyn — had volunteered for the mission. Then, after we explained to Lieutenant Griffith our hope for how he might help us convince the Northwest Alliance and the United States to agree to a cease-fire, he volunteered to come with us.

Chris Stone approached me one night when I was checking over Pale Horse's engine. She hadn't run in a while, and I wanted to make sure she was ready. Cal was busy loading some extra five-gallon fuel cans onto the vehicle. Sweeney and Becca were stowing away some rations for the trip. I could tell something was on Stone's mind, but I waited for him to speak.

"Listen, Wright," he said. "I want to thank you again, thank all of you, for coming to get us out of that Brotherhood camp. I owe you big."

"No." I smiled at him. "You really don't."

"It's just, you know, the Brotherhood snatched me off the street. Then I was in that camp. Then I've been here. What I really want to do is go back to working with the Cliffhanger."

"What?" Sweeney teased. "You don't like us?"

Stone grinned. "It's not that. You all are great. But besides this mission to Boise, there's no realistic way for me to get out of here. It's like I have no choice. I'm safe, but not exactly free."

"Same goes for everyone here," Becca said.

"Everybody who was working with the Cliffhanger knows a certain radio code he uses." Stone looked down for a moment. "When the Cliffhanger was broadcasting in the area, I risked sending a coded signal, asking him to stay around. He was heading out to Seattle, but sent a message saying he'd be back in about a month. I've been able to confirm he's back in Boise, and I'd like to rejoin him."

I pretended to think about it for a moment. "Well, the food will be lousy and Cal snores when he sleeps," I said.

"I do not!" Cal yelled.

"But sure," I said. "We can take you as far as Boise."

We told everyone that we'd be rolling out after breakfast Sunday morning. Our real plan was to leave a lot earlier, to avoid a big crowd gathering to say goodbye. Sergeant Kemp was the only one who saw through our lie. He joined us in the parking lot just before dawn. "You sure you don't want me to come along?"

"We *want* you to come along," I said. "But you're *needed* here to run the defense of this place."

"Plus," said Sweeney, "this trip will be dangerous, and we wouldn't want you to lose your other eye."

"Thanks." Kemp laughed a little. "You know this is crazy, right?"

"More than anything else we've done?" I asked. "You know I'm right. This is our best — our *only* — chance to get some help before the Brotherhood finds us. I know me and the president didn't get along so good last time we talked, but Montaine's always protected me. Maybe he'll do it again."

Kemp shrugged. "Good luck, then. I'll pass your apologies to the council for leaving earlier than planned."

Becca hugged him. "Goodbye, Tom. Take care of yourself."

"You too, Wells," he said.

I looked him in the eye as I shook his hand. "Sit this one out," I said. "Good luck holding down the fort. And good luck with Angeline."

Everybody started mounting up in Pale Horse. Kemp wasn't an officer, but he was one of the best soldiers I'd ever served with, one of the few from the 476th Combat Engineer Company who had survived, and protocol could go to hell.

I snapped to attention and saluted him. He smiled and saluted right back.

I think I'd been missing out on a lot by being the driver on so many missions. Up in the gun turret, with the sun shining on me, the fresh air in my face, and beautiful mountain and river views all around, I felt like a cowboy. I stood with my ass against the back of the turret hatch and my top half in the open air, leaning back like I was riding a horse.

We took a different road southwest out of Hindman, almost like a trail that wound its way along the banks of different little rapids-filled creeks and rivers. I could hardly figure out why this road was here in the first place. There were only a few houses and trailers along the fifty-some miles of dirt. A couple people at these properties watched us drive by, showing us they were armed. I made sure they saw my rifle in turn, and we passed on in peace.

We drove along slow and careful. In a couple places, the road was too jacked up to go very fast, so it took us the better part of a day to get near Highway 55 and the town of Cascade. We stopped before we reached the town and parked back off the road in the dark shadows under some trees. We set up the litters in the back of Pale Horse as well as a guard rotation for the night. TJ stood in the turret and Lieutenant Griffith sat on the roof to cover the first guard shift, while Cal and Stone slept in the seats up front in case we had to roll out in a hurry. The rest of us hit the rack. I was in the top litter on the driver's side. Jaclyn had the lower rack below mine. Becca was across from me, and Sweeney had the litter under hers. The quiet night settled around us.

"This will sound stupid," I said after a few minutes. "But here we are, out on the road again. Anything could happen. Any psychos could be out in the woods."

"Thanks for bringing that up, Danny," Jaclyn said. "Real nice."

We all got a chuckle out of that.

"I'm not gonna lie," I said. "I feel safer out here with you all than just about anywhere else."

"Oh, that's so sweet," Cal said from the front seat.

"Go to hell, Cal," I answered.

More laughter. But Becca reached across the gap between our racks and squeezed my hand. It wasn't weird or anything. It meant she understood what I was trying to say. It meant she felt the same.

The next day, our plan for getting through Cascade was to move fast and shoot any trouble before it turned into more trouble. As we drove south through town, an old pickup suddenly rolled across the road in front of us, and about six gunmen came out from some falling-down houses. Cal had to swerve off the road, and my shot went wide from the bumping around. Then we had a crazy run through town, trying to find an intact route to get back up on the highway. Four guys in an ancient Ford Focus with the roof cut off chased us for a while, but I dropped one of them, and then Jaclyn fired round after round from the rear gun port, taking out their windshield and radiator. Steam and smoke poured from the Ford's engine, and we left them behind.

By late afternoon, we'd reached the outskirts of Boise. We passed areas that used to be nicer housing developments. A lot of the houses looked blown out. Some of them had plywood over the windows. A fire had swept through at some point a while back. Many of the trees were burned down to scorched bones.

"Damn," said Lieutenant Griffith. "This is terrible."

"Yeah, you can thank your mom for that," Cal said.

"Chill, dude," Sweeney said. "There's enough war going on. We don't need any more here in Pale Horse."

"So what do we do?" Stone asked. "I assume the Idaho Army isn't going to just let us drive into their secret base."

"They might, if you turned me over as a prisoner," Griffith said.

"Not going to happen, Doug," said Becca.

"If Montaine doesn't seem like he's going to play ball, I won't even tell him you're with us," I said. "We didn't bust our asses getting you out of that camp just so you could be an Idaho Army prisoner." I looked ahead. "Hey, Cal," I said, "check out this burned-out old Gas & Sip." Only three of the four walls of the gas station and the charred sign out front remained. "Can we pull over and take cover there for a minute? I want to try something."

Cal drove right into the center of the old building, crunching over the ashes of Ding Dongs and beef jerky. If anything useful had survived the fire, it had long since been taken. My friends got out, stretched their legs, and set up a security perimeter around Pale

Horse. I stayed in the turret and took out my comm, which I had charged on our solar generator before we left the school. It had a lot better signal here in Boise. Some tech must still be running.

"Hank, you stupid piece of shit, let's see if you can still do anything. Get me a video call with President Montaine."

"Well, golly! My stars! I do declare it's been a month of Sundays since we last talked, partner! I'll put that rootin'-tootin' call through faster . . . than a drunken jackrabbit in the moonshine still. Meantime, here's a little taste of my new song, 'Troubled Times' by Hank McGrew —"

"No, Hank, don't play a —"

> *What's this war even for?*
> *Too many folks are dyin'*
> *And them kids don't play no more . . .*

A full-bird colonel came on-screen. *"Who is this? How did you get access to this number?"* He stopped when he recognized me. *"PFC Wright? So the rumors are true. You are still alive."*

"Yes, sir. I'm trying to reach President Montaine. I know you're all busy with the war and everything, but I was hoping to —"

"Nathan Crow told us you were dead, that US forces had attacked your town and kidnapped and murdered over a hundred people."

"Crow's a liar," I said. "I have dozens of witnesses to his crimes. Those hundred people? We escaped Freedom Lake to get away from the Brotherhood and have been hiding out together ever since."

"What is your location? Are you safe?"

"Yes, sir. We're fine." I didn't want to tell him where we were in case this went wrong somehow.

The colonel shook his head. *"The president will be thrilled to know you're alive. He could use some good news. Please stand by."*

Sweeney whacked a hanging piece of waterlogged drywall with his cane like he was golfing. "I swear, Wright. You're a magic man. You should just call all the presidents and get them to stop fighting."

"Maybe you should have them make you the president — no! The king!" Cal said. "King Daniel Wright the Third." He marched around with stiff arms and legs, exaggerated movements, like an antique toy soldier.

"Would you two stop screwing around?" Becca said. "Pay attention before someone sneaks in here and jumps us."

"*PFC Wright.*" President Montaine spoke in a kind of "aw shucks" tone. "*If this wasn't a vid call, I wouldn't believe it. You really are alive.*"

"Yes, sir. It's good to see you again, sir." But it really wasn't. The president, who had always looked sharp and commanded respect in every situation, now looked shabby and worn out. His hair was longer and shaggier than it usually was. I wasn't sure if he'd showered recently. He definitely hadn't shaved. He wore no jacket or tie, just a stained button-down shirt. There looked to be a lot more lines on his face, a lot more gray in his hair.

"*Your friends make it too?*" he asked.

I gripped the comm so hard that it shook. "Not all of them, sir."

"*I'm sorry for your losses. We've suffered too. General McNabb was killed while rescuing some of our civilian experts from a burning section of Idaho CentCom. He pulled almost a dozen of them out, and went in for more before that section collapsed.*" Montaine's stare went blank. "*He died in the finest tradition of the service.*" Then he seemed to snap back to the moment. "*He did save your fiancée's father. I'm sure he'd love to speak to her. Yes! He'll be thrilled to know Nathan Crow's report was in error.*"

I bit my lip. "Crow's report was a lie, sir. But . . . JoBell is dead. The Brotherhood killed her."

"*Damn. I'm so sorry. We've lost so many people. My wife . . .*" Montaine ran his hand over his face. "*So many losses.*"

"That's why I'm calling today, sir. This war needs to stop. It has to end. I'm asking you to reach out to the other leaders and call for a cease-fire."

Montaine waved my suggestion away. "*Griffith might've gone for that. But we don't think she's running the show anymore. It's all General Jacobsen now.*"

I couldn't tell if Montaine disagreed with me or if he just wasn't listening. He didn't seem like himself. If I didn't know better, I'd almost think I was talking to a digi-assistant version of Montaine. I thought about telling him that Griffith's son was alive and might listen to him if he asked for a cease-fire, but I hedged. "We could try. Sir, we have to at least try. We owe that to all those we've lost. We could just, you know, put out the word to everybody else, see if they're ready to stop fighting too."

Montaine shook his head and his whole body, like a cold shiver had gone through him. "*Stop fighting? When we're this close to victory? Never! I told those bastards we would never surrender! We're going to win this war!*" He pointed at me. "*This is some kind of trick, isn't it? Maybe you weren't killed but captured by the US. Brainwashed somehow! Or maybe you defected! Suddenly Daniel Wright appears, saying I should surrender to the United States?*"

Lieutenant Griffith stepped up, trying to get himself into the vid call, but I pushed him away. "No, sir. I'm fine. I'm not talking about surrender. Just a cease-fire —"

"The other part," Stone whispered to remind me.

"Or if I could at least get some ammunition and supplies, maybe an infantry squad or platoon, to help me protect —"

"*It won't work! You tell those Fed sons of bitches that the*

Northwest Alliance will win! It is the United States who will surrender to me! I'm President James P. Montaine! And I do not surrender!"

The call ended. We all stared in silence at the comm.

"Well, buddy, you tried," said Cal. "It was worth a shot."

I slammed my fist on the top of Pale Horse. "Damn it. Why won't he listen?"

"He seemed kind of . . ." Jaclyn started.

"Unbalanced," finished Sweeney.

"The war's gotten to him," said Stone. "Broken him."

"It must be hard being a leader in all of this." Griffith kicked a chunk of charred rubble. "All that pressure."

I held my hands up in the air. "Would everybody just stop fighting?" I shouted to the sky. My words echoed through the quiet neighborhood.

"Damn, dude," Sweeney said.

"Yeah, can you be a little louder?" Cal asked. "I don't think everybody heard you."

I set my comm down on the hood. "Cal."

Cal continued, "Just, you never know what psychos could be around."

"Cal, you're a genius!" I said.

"They hear us and find us and next thing — wait." Cal frowned. "What?"

"Everybody mount up." I pinned a location on my comm's map and handed it to Stone. "We're not finished yet."

As we drove into the heart of Boise, we could hardly believe the damage. In American History class, we'd seen photos and videos from Germany at the end of World War II. In some cities like Berlin and Dresden, there was nothing left but rubble. Boise wasn't in much better shape. It took forever getting around, because so many streets were closed by bomb craters or collapsed buildings. Still, some structures were mostly intact. And there were food distribution centers and places where people looked like they were trading stuff they had for stuff they needed.

We stopped at one checkpoint, hoping Montaine hadn't realized we were in Boise and put out an alert for our capture. Ahead of us was a woman in a dirty Idaho uniform, holding a shotgun, and an older man in torn jeans and a T-shirt aiming a bow and arrow at us.

"Halt," the woman said without much enthusiasm.

Up in the turret, I laid my rifle on the roof of Pale Horse and held my hands up. "It's okay," I said. "I'm —"

"Private Wright!" The man smiled. "It's you, isn't it?"

The woman frowned. "They said you were dead."

"You've been misinformed," I said. "But I need to get through. We're on an important mission."

The woman wasn't quite convinced. "Do you have a pass?"

"Are you kidding?" The man gently pushed the barrel of the woman's gun down. "This is Danny Wright! Let him through."

"That's pretty relaxed security," Sweeney said when we were allowed past the checkpoint.

"What do you expect when they're guarding a bombed-out wasteland?" said Stone. He handed my comm back to me. "He'll meet us at the station."

"I just hope they haven't moved," I said to myself.

We reached the corner where we were supposed to meet the Cliffhanger and stopped Pale Horse. After a few seconds, a black man in his thirties calmly stepped out from between two abandoned cars. He wore jeans and a black T-shirt that showed off respectable biceps. As he approached the side of Pale Horse, he took off his sunglasses and looked up at me in the gun turret. "So, you're Danny Wright."

"The Cliffhanger?"

Stone hurried out the back of our truck. "Joe Woodson!" He shook the man's hand and patted him on the back.

Woodson laughed. "So good to see you, man!" I got down out of the turret. Everyone else set up a loose security perimeter around us. Woodson turned his attention back to me. "Yes, I am the voice of the Cliffhanger. Thanks for setting my buddy free. I never thought I'd see him again."

"I'm hoping you can return the favor," I said.

Stone frowned. "I don't get it."

"There's a reason I asked you to meet us down the street from Buzz Ellison's radio station," I said.

Woodson laughed. "Want to do a show with the Cliffhanger, huh?"

"To call for a cease-fire, yeah."

"Seriously, Danny? You really think this guy's going to make a difference?" Cal nodded at Woodson. "No offense, Mr. Cliffhanger, but you've been doing the radio thing a long time and nothing's changed."

"Not true!" Woodson smiled. "The peace movement is growing. Who do you think set up the underground communication network that helped the rebels stop General Vogel in Atlantica?"

"Plus we have President Griffith's son on our team," Sweeney said.

If Woodson was surprised to see Lieutenant Griffith, he didn't show it. Instead he shook the man's hand. "Hoping your mom will go along with a cease-fire?"

Becca put her arm around me. "And we have Danny Wright."

"It's worth a try," said Woodson. "If I didn't believe in the importance of demanding peace, I wouldn't have been risking my life so much to get my message out on the air. The Pan American Peace Movement has been gaining strength. If we do this, maybe it will help push it over the edge, and we can make some real progress." He laughed. "And I can't pass up the chance to broadcast from that five-hundred-thousand-watt powerhouse transmitter."

We pulled up outside the building that housed the *Buzz Ellison Show*. I tried not to think about how the last time I was here, JoBell was with me. When I climbed down out of the vehicle and started up the sidewalk, SAWs were pointed at me from behind sandbag barriers, and three soldiers rushed out to block my way.

"This is a restricted area," said the youngest sergeant I'd ever seen.

"You have to let me through," I said. "Buzz Ellison is expecting me on the air today."

"I would have been notified, and you would have had a security escort." The sergeant gave a little push to my chest to back me up.

For a second, I wanted to punch the guy out, but I smiled instead. "Right. Sorry."

Back inside Pale Horse, Sweeney turned away from his gun port for a moment. "Now what?"

"Is there another way in?" the Cliffhanger asked.

"Cal, let's see if we can go around the block. Maybe we can get into the alley behind this place."

"Okay, man." Because of all the debris and so many road closures, Cal had to drive around three blocks to get us to the alley behind the building. But they'd blocked that too. Near the building that housed the studio, two young soldiers, male and female, stood with rifles behind another sandbag wall.

"What do we do about these guys?" Sweeney asked.

I'd ducked down into the vehicle and moved up to the hatch behind the cab. "Couple of kids. They look younger than us. Let's try the direct approach. Girls, come with me. Sweeney, Cal, when the guards aren't paying attention, spring the trap. Everybody else wait here. We just need to tie them up."

Cal pulled up to the barricade. I slung my rifle on my back and climbed out of the turret. An M4 and a SAW were instantly aimed at me. "Hey, guys!" I kept my hands up.

The male PFC with the M4 smiled and elbowed the specialist with the machine gun. "It's Daniel Wright!"

"I heard you were dead," the female specialist said. "They made us all watch a video about you and everything."

"Yeah, I get that a lot," I said. "You gonna shoot me with that SAW, Specialist?" I noticed she had only about a dozen rounds on the ammo belt in the weapon. That would be more than enough to finish me, but I wondered how hard up Idaho was for ammo.

"Hey, how y'all doing?" Becca turned on the charm as she got out of the turret, then helped Jaclyn out. I jumped down to the hood and was making my way off the front of the vehicle when I saw the specialist tense up.

"This area is restricted," she said. "Nobody is supposed to be back here."

"What's your name?" I asked her.

"Specialist Harper." She'd aimed the SAW at me again.

I ignored the gun and laughed a little. "What's your first name? Your real name?"

"Courtney," she said.

"I'm Danny," I said. "This is Becca, and that's Jaclyn." I climbed down to the ground.

"You can't be here." But she lowered her gun, at least. "Okay? I'm going to get in trouble if they catch me letting people be back here."

"That's true," said the zit-faced PFC. "We have orders."

Jaclyn touched his forearm. "This is an awesome M4. Are you a good shot?"

"Mason," the specialist warned. PFC Mason backed away from Jaclyn.

"Right," I said. "You don't want people too close to your weapon." I noticed one unopened MRE on the ground, leaned against the sandbags. Were they supposed to share it? What kind of rations were they on? "I'm supposed to pass on good news. A load of steaks is coming in from Montana. Should be here by tonight. President Montaine is going to make sure all the troops get a big meal."

"Seriously?" Specialist Harper said.

"Seriously, don't move," Cal said.

I moved quick and grabbed Harper's SAW. When I yanked it away from her, she threw her hands in the air. Jaclyn grabbed PFC Mason's rifle. Cal and Sweeney had stepped out of Pale Horse with weapons drawn. We had them.

"Please," said Specialist Harper. She was shaking, tears in her eyes. "Please don't shoot. I didn't even want to be in the Army. They made us."

"I just signed up for the food," said the PFC.

I handed Becca the SAW. "Cover the alley," I said to her. I turned back to Specialist Harper. "Courtney. We're not here to hurt you. Did you ever see the video of me that went all over the Internet?" I held my left fist up at an angle over my head. "The one they made the day my mom was killed?"

"Yeah," she said.

"We all watched another video on the first day of basic training. You were in Idaho Army uniform, giving a speech," said PFC Mason.

"Right," I said. "Well, we're here to go on the radio and ask soldiers everywhere to stop fighting. We're trying to end the war." I squeezed my rifle. "It's cost everyone too much. So we can either tie you up out here, or you can come with us."

Cal was about to argue, but I held up my hand. I knew what he was going to say, but he was wrong. These two weren't dangerous. I don't think there had ever been any fight in them in the first place.

Moments later, they nodded. "We'll come with you," Harper said.

"Great," I said. "Cal, cover our six. Becca, bring that machine gun up here in front. You keep an eye on these two. Sweeney, Lieutenant Griffith, protect Stone and the Cliffhanger. Remember," I said as we took off running and entered the building, "we're trying to *stop* the fighting. This is not a shoot-first-type situation."

We sprinted down the hall to the stairs, and in moments, we reached the door to the studio offices. Locked.

"What now?" Cal said. He was breathing heavy and moving fast, in battle mode again.

"Get back." I aimed JoBell's badass rifle at the door. These were heavier rounds than the 5.56 from my old M4. I should be able to shoot it open. I pulled the trigger, squeezing off four rounds and tearing the hell out of the door all around the lock. Then we were in, and soldiers were shouting from somewhere down the hall toward the front of the building. I sprinted through the front business office. A man rose from his seat at his desk, and I aimed my rifle at him. "Sit your ass down and stay there!"

Paul the producer came around the corner holding up some kind of a metal microphone pole as a weapon. Cal dropped him with one punch.

Behind the glass I saw Buzz Ellison talking frantically into the microphone. Beads of sweat rolled down his forehead and temples. I tried the door to his broadcast room. Locked. I shot it open and we all rushed in.

"Fellow patriots, I cannot stress enough the danger of this situation. Gunmen are breaking into my studio. They're being led by —" He finally seemed to recognize me. "But that's impossible . . ."

The soldiers from out front ran into the control room outside Buzz's broadcast studio. My friends held up their guns. Sweeney and Griffith were keeping the unarmed guards from the alley covered, while Becca, TJ, Jaclyn, and Cal aimed at the two guards from the front. Stone and the Cliffhanger were already at work on all the broadcasting and computer equipment in the control room, total professionals, wasting no time making sure our message would go out on as many channels as they could get.

We were locked in a standoff with the other Idaho soldiers, gun to gun, just like that horrible afternoon back in Spokane when I'd killed a man for the first time. Sure, we had more guns. We'd win if everyone started shooting. But I was unwilling to lose any of my friends. This situation was like the whole war. Victory had become meaningless. The cost was too high.

"This time it's going to go better," I whispered.

"What do you people want!?" Buzz shouted, red-faced. "If you think I'm going to make statements for you or —"

"Buzz, the Cliffhanger needs your microphone and your broadcast system." Woodson laughed as he sat down behind the microphone in the other booth.

I pulled Buzz out of his seat and looked him in the eye. "We've come to stop the war."

✓—• *Fires burning across the Dakota prairies are the largest and most devastating in Dakotan history. The problem is compounded by United States snipers and drones, which have been shooting at firefighters attempting to contain the blaze. This fire has already consumed several small towns and cost the lives of hundreds. The Dakota Leadership Assembly has promised a brutal retaliation for United States interference in the humanitarian firefighting effort.* •—✓

✓—• *The United States is doing its best to broadcast this important address throughout North America, and in particular to all rebel states. I am Vice President General Charles Jacobsen, speaking on behalf of President Laura Griffith. The end of the war is at hand. The leadership of all thirteen so-called independent countries must understand that you have exactly sixty minutes to unconditionally surrender to the United States. If you do not, all of your capital cities will suffer total nuclear annihilation. After that, you will be given an additional half hour before —"*

"THIS IS A UNITED STATES EMERGENCY BROADCAST. PLEASE STAND BY. THIS IS A UNITED •—✓

✓—• *of the food shortage made worse, now that war has broken out around the world and emergency relief supplies are no longer being brought into the Pan American area. Some experts believe that if something isn't done soon, as many as 15 percent of children born this year will die or suffer serious health problems from malnutrition before the age of five.* •—✓

✓—• STATES EMERGENCY BROADCAST. PLEASE STAND —"

"*I am United States President Laura Griffith, and I freely admit to shooting General Charles Jacobsen just now. My loyalist forces have arrested the United States officials who were helping the late vice president circumvent my constitutional authority. Let the courts judge me for the general's death. Let history judge me when I, as commander in chief, order the immediate and complete stand-down of all US nuclear forces. All pending nuclear attacks will be aborted immediately, and I will never authorize nuclear attacks here at home or anywhere in the world.* •⌁

⌁• *You're listening to the Cliffhanger, broadcasting with five hundred thousand watts from the Northwest Alliance superstation here in Boise, Idaho, and streaming video via the Internet. I'm afraid we've had to ask Mr. Ellison to stop spewing his warmonger hate so that we could bring you a message of peace and hope. Today, I'm reunited with my friend Chris Stone. Chris will be recording this program for both my video and audio podcasts, because this is a show you don't want to miss! This is history in the making. My friends, for many months the Cliffhanger has dared to shine a light on the darkness of deception, and right now, the propaganda lies of the Brotherhood of the White Eagle are about to be shattered against the solid rock of truth. My friends, here's Private First Class Daniel Wright."*

"This is Danny Wright. Yes . . . um . . . that Daniel Wright. I'm still alive, and still in Idaho. For over a year now, I have found myself trapped. I've been, um, in the middle of the controversy that started at a protest here in Boise, and expanded into a civil war and World War III. Although I know nothing I can do or say can ever make up for the pain I've caused, I want to say, first of all, that I'm sorry. I'm sorry for the people I've killed, for the lives I've helped destroy by inspiring people to fight.

"A good teacher of mine once warned me about slogans in war. People talk about freedom. They say they have to beat tyranny. On

the day my mother was killed, before this war really flared up, I was mad at the United States about her death, and I shouted, 'We will give you a war.' Those words were turned into a slogan. They were put on flags and T-shirts. People said them before they were killed. They were shouted as soldiers rushed to their deaths."

"And what would you say to people now, Danny?"

"I'd say I want to give you all a new slogan. 'No more. End the war.' We have almost as many people dying now from starvation and exposure to the elements as from bullets. Some say that we're free. But free to do what? Die? Scrounge around looking for a tiny bit of food?

"'No more. End the war.' I like that. From my travels around Pan America, I truly believe people are ready for this message."

"I'm just a soldier. And I'm putting this call out to all the other soldiers around all the countries of Pan America and even the world. If you too are tired of fighting. If you've had to watch too many good people die. If you miss the old world we had, the food and the freedom from fear, then join me. Join me in saying, 'End the war.'

"Our leaders may continue to order us to fight, but it's time to stop obeying those orders from our chain of command. This time, let the order come from the bottom and work its way up to the top. Let's tell them: 'That's it! We're done. War's over.' We can demand peace. It's not up to them. It's up to us. Two Idaho soldiers, who were assigned to guard this radio station to prevent anyone from breaking in, have had machine guns pointed at me this whole time. But now they've chosen peace and lowered their weapons. All of us can choose to put down our guns."

"Thank you, Danny. And now the Cliffhanger has a special message for United States President Laura Griffith, from her son, Second Lieutenant Douglas Griffith."

"Madame President? Mom? We believe we're getting a comm video out over the Internet, but in case it isn't working and you're only listening, it's really me, Doug. I had a rough time of it for a while, but Danny Wright and his friends saved my life. In case you think this is some kind of trick, that this isn't me, do you remember that time I was maybe six, and you'd made that big birthday cake for me, but when you came inside, I'd dug into the whole thing with my hands and had cake and blue frosting all over the living room couch? Or maybe you remember when I was ten and you took me to that peace rally. You talked about how terrible war is, how we have to work hard to avoid it. It's time to end this war, Mom. We saw your broadcast. We know you're in control again. Please. Call a cease-fire. Here's Wright again."

"I'm asking all the leadership and all the soldiers everywhere to end the war. End the war. I . . . had a girl. I loved her very much. We grew up together, been dating for years. Me and JoBell were going to get married. I spent most of my money from basic training on a ring, and we'd found a white dress in an abandoned house. She died in a battle to free Lieutenant Griffith and a lot of other innocent people from a slave camp run by a militia group, the Brotherhood of the White Eagle. But before this war killed her, she reminded me that it's our job to decide what will one day go in the history books. When the next generation asks us what we did in the war, let's make sure we can look them in the eye and tell them that we did our best to end it. ●—⋏

THREE WEEKS LATER

"I hate this stupid shirt." I pulled at my buttoned-up collar and the dumb tie. Sweat rolled down the middle of my back. "It's too hot for this anyway."

Jaclyn pushed my hand away. "Would you leave it alone? This is an important day. You don't want to look like a slob."

"Yeah, you convinced everyone to stop killing each other long enough to have this meeting," Cal said. "But mostly people just heard you on the radio. Be a shame if they saw how nasty you look and started the war again."

I was with Sweeney, Becca, Cal, TJ, and Jaclyn in the hallway behind the Idaho legislative chamber, which was lit only by a few dim emergency lanterns. In a few minutes, I would have to go into the chamber itself and stand at the central podium in the round room with its white columns and balconies. After a lot of arguing, it had been decided that nobody would occupy that high central desk in the room during the meeting. It would be used only for speeches, and everyone else would sit on an equal level on the floor.

The colonel I'd seen on my comm the other day approached. Colonel Kidd was a good man. He'd found a way to have some ammunition and a lot more food flown up to Alice Marshall via helicopter. Sergeant Kemp and everybody else there were still doing just fine. Colonel Kidd had even promised to order the Idaho military to do something about the Brotherhood, as long as the cease-fire held. "Private Wright?" He shook my hand. "I'm sorry it's taken so long for me to get here. As you can imagine, things have been very hectic at Idaho CentCom."

"Where's Montaine?" Sweeney asked.

The colonel looked down. "President Montaine is . . . not well. He couldn't handle his troops refusing to obey his orders and giving up the fight. He's resting comfortably in a secure location. I've been appointed to negotiate in his place." He nodded at me. "It's almost time."

Sweeney and Becca moved aside as two people stepped out of the shadows, approaching me.

"President Griffith," I said. Her son was right behind her, back in Air Force dress blues and promoted to captain. I didn't know the rules here. Should I shake her hand? Should I salute?

"Daniel Wright," Laura Griffith said. She kept her hands tight at her sides. "We meet in person at last."

"Hey, Danny." The captain shook my hand. "It's good to see you again."

President Griffith looked so much older than she had before the war. Her suit-dress-type thing was frayed a little at one shoulder. Her eyes looked tired, and tears welled in them. "I wish now that I'd pardoned you a long time ago. Maybe then —"

"I wish I had surrendered myself to the FBI right at the beginning," I said.

She nodded. "Thank you for bringing my son back to me."

"I didn't do much."

She reached out her hand. "Nevertheless, I am grateful."

We shook hands, and then she moved past me into the chamber.

"Private Wright?" the colonel said again.

I was about to address the leadership of the thirteen countries who had come here to negotiate with the leaders of the United States. The goal wasn't to remake the old USA, but to work out a lasting peace. Maybe later there could be trade negotiations and defense pacts. But for now, it was all about recognizing the borders of all fourteen countries and ending the war.

I turned to follow Colonel Kidd into the legislative chamber. Sweeney stepped up to me on his cane and patted my shoulder. Becca squeezed my hand. TJ offered a fist bump. Cal gave me a little salute. I took one more look at my friends, these people I'd gone through hell with, who'd saved my life. My family. I stopped in front of Jaclyn and nodded. She'd wanted me to tell her when I started the long process of letting go of a war's worth of guilt. "Jackie, the time has come. I'm ready."

She smiled. She knew what I meant.

I entered the hot chamber on shaky legs, climbing the steps to the podium. Like the hall, the room was dimly lit. Every chair was full, and camera operators stood in the back. Joe Woodson, the Cliffhanger, was back there with a camera and microphone. He nodded to me.

I looked down for a moment, thinking of all the good people we'd lost to get to this point. Then I tapped my comm to open the file for the speech that Becca and Sweeney had helped me write. I held my head up and met the crowd's gaze to begin my talk.

"I am Private First Class Daniel Christopher Wright, and I fired the shot that ended the United States of America.

"At least, it set off a chain of events that led to the end of the United States as we knew it. What's left of the United States has gathered itself at its new capital in Colorado, the most powerful single military in Pan America. And a couple weeks ago, we saw the danger posed by a madman who had too much control over that military, as we were moments away from nuclear annihilation. But courageous citizens of the United States, led by President Laura Griffith, were able to stop the nuclear attack. In the same way, brave citizens of Atlantica ended the rule of the Atlantican dictator, General Jonathan Vogel. And all over the Pan American territory, people began to realize that even if victory were still possible, it was no longer worth the cost."

I looked out over the room. The air-conditioning didn't work, and sweat pooled on everyone's brows and ran down their cheeks. My words seemed to be swallowed by the dark heat. I found my place in my script and read on.

"I looked up the list of the dead yesterday. With the cease-fire in effect, we finally have time to begin to add up some of that cost. It is estimated that about thirteen-point-seven million people died as a result of the nuclear attacks on New York and Washington, DC. Some estimates project deaths related to any combat, whether official fighting among the fourteen countries or in smaller, gang or militia warfare, at over two million. Those who have died from disease, starvation, or exposure? Perhaps another half a million. Over sixteen million dead. And the true number is likely much higher."

I wiped the sweat from my upper lip and read on. "But . . . I think the problem is that after a while, that's what it becomes. Numbers. A horrible, massive number. I never saw sixteen million anything. I don't even know what one million looks like. But I know the look on the face of this redheaded girl, dead on the ground at the Battle of Boise. I see her every night in my nightmares. I also dream of my mother, and I still hear her screaming like she did as she bled out from US bullets. I remember the pool of blood around Staff Sergeant Kirklin, the first man I ever killed, and I wonder every day if there was any way out of that situation without having to shoot him." I sighed. "I will never wash away the guilt from the dozens, maybe hundreds of soldiers and militiamen that I've killed in combat. I can never apologize enough to their families.

"I remember Lieutenant McFee, who killed himself because he couldn't handle the grief and guilt after the Battle of Boise. I remember Staff Sergeant Shane Donshel, First Sergeant Scott Herbokowitz,

Sergeant Adam Ribbon, and PFC Henry Nelson. I think of Specialist Will Danning, who slowly died of an infected wound he received the night the US invaded Idaho. I miss PFC Nick Luchen, who sacrificed himself to save me and Specialist Shawna Sparrow from torture at the hands of United States Army Major Federico Alsovar. I remember how hard Major Alsovar fought until the very end. There was Captain Peterson, who helped me and Shawna Sparrow escape those torture cells. The Brotherhood of the White Eagle hung him. I remember my friend Jaclyn Martinez's parents, who were also lynched by the Brotherhood of the White Eagle — how Jackie screamed and tried to save their lives even though it was too late."

My hands shook as I gripped my comm, and I fought to keep from crying. "I think of the Brotherhood slave camp and the men there, chained together and forced to work. The women and girls there who were used for far worse. I remember how hard they fought to break out of that place. And every second of every day, I miss JoBell Marie Linder. We were going to be married, but instead she died along with others in the fight to free the people from that camp. She was my . . . She was everything.

"Each of us who has survived this long carries our own personal list of the dead. It is for those people, for the people on *your* list, that these talks must succeed. It is for the people left in our lives who we can't live without that you all agreed to meet here to bring about peace.

"I'm not asking for your pity, or your forgiveness. If all the nations in Pan America insist that I be arrested and punished, I won't run. I won't put up a fight.

"I am Private First Class Daniel Christopher Wright. I have had too much of war. It's time to end the fighting. We must enter earnestly into the long process of healing and forgiveness, both for ourselves and for others. It's up to all of us to work for peace."

✓—• The cease-fire seems to be holding, for the most part. We have reports of some clashes among various militia groups, but these appear to be small and isolated. It's too early to tell how long this relative peace will last, but medical professionals and other relief organizations no doubt welcome this break in the fighting, an opportunity to better assist many who have suffered for so long through the war. •—✓

THEO APONTE ★ ★ ★ ☆ ☆

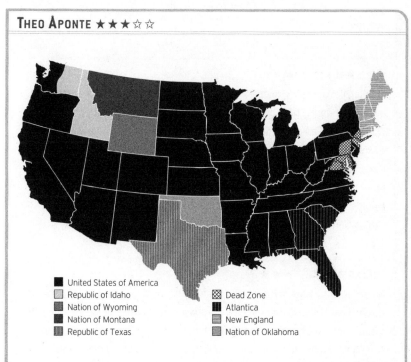

■ United States of America
▨ Dead Zone
▨ Republic of Idaho
▥ Nation of Wyoming
▥ Atlantica
▥ Nation of Montana
▨ New England
▥ Republic of Texas
▥ Nation of Oklahoma

The Pan American Peace Treaty is signed! Just like that, the war is over and there are officially 14 countries where there used to be just the USA. Now we need to start working together to make sure we don't have another war like this! If you live in Appalachia, join the Cooperative Party, a growing group of Cascadian citizens working to improve cooperation with the other Pan American countries, including the United States.

★ ★ ★ ☆ ☆ This Post's Star Average 3.14   [Star Rate] [Comment]   26 minutes ago

439

PHUNG MEEKER ★ ★ ★ ★ ☆

Work with the United States? Are you $@($ing kidding me! We've finally won our independence, and now you want to give it up!?!? People of Appalachia, the Independence Party is growing! Our dependence on the US federal government is what got us into this mess. If you believe it is time to create a strong society that can stand on it's own irregardless of what is happening elsewhere, join the Independence Party! We want to get as many IP candidates elected to the new Appalachian Congress as we can, so the time to act is now! We'll see how long until my old buddy Theo deletes my comment.

★ ★ ★ ☆ ☆ This Comment's Star Average 3.25   [Star Rate]   21 minutes ago

THEO APONTE ★ ★ ★ ☆ ☆

Meeker, I'm not going to delete your comment. I'm not saying we shouldn't be independent. The Independence Party keeps distorting our position. We Cooperatives only want to deal productively with other Pan American countries. The United States has already suggested it wants to shut down most of its nuclear power plants. I think they're spooked after the Indian Point disaster. They've suggested they may want to buy our coal. That would be a good source of revenue. The Cooperatives are the way of the future. Sometimes you Indies sound like you want to go back to war.

★ ★ ★ ☆ ☆ This Comment's Star Average 3.80   [Star Rate]   19 minutes ago

PHUNG MEEKER ★ ★ ★ ★ ☆

How long until Appalachia is dependent upon that revenue, until the US can threaten to cut back on their coal purchases, leaving us all the sudden with a bankrupt government! That's how they're going to control us, man! Why can't you Cooperatives see that? Well, it doesn't matter because the Independence Party is taking over. We lost too many good people in the war to let your party give it all up!

★ ★ ★ ☆ ☆ This Comment's Star Average 3.15   [Star Rate]   17 minutes ago

⌁—• *WGN. Liberum's Very Own. While isolated sniper activity and ongoing militia violence hampered early efforts to protect communities from the dangerous flooding of the Illinois River, more and* more citizens have joined sandbagging crews to protect homes and reinforce dikes. People who helped supply food to the work crews have now expanded their cooperative endeavor to feed others in need. This effort has become a much-needed symbol of hope in these challenging times. •—⌇—

⌇—• Peace has allowed the restoration of electricity to some areas of northern Cascadia that have been without power for several months. Graham Keefer, the Cascadian secretary for restoration and regrowth, made a statement today in •—⌇—

⌇—• We are live via satellite link with Captain Clarence Benedict, the commander of Rogue Fleet, in his first interview since Carrier Strike Groups 9 and 11 left the United States Navy. Shortly thereafter, Rogue Fleet was recognized as a full nation-state by Japan and Korea, and it has since been active in World War III, helping those two countries in their fight against China. Captain, thank you for joining us. I'll get right to the question on the minds of many people in the former United States. The civil war is over, and the Pan American countries have, for the most part, been able to stay out of World War III. Why hasn't Rogue Fleet come home?"

"That's an excellent question. There has been a lot of discussion in Rogue Fleet's parliament about returning, but simply put, we cannot decide to which nation we should return. We do not entirely trust the new peace, with thirteen countries spread out on the fringes of a very well armed United States. Moreover, the sailors, Marines, and civilian personnel of our fleet have been through a lot together. Pan America's war is over, but World War III has not ended, and the Allies have finally begun to make some difficult gains in Europe and Israel. The Koreans and Japanese are still holding off the Chinese invasion. Rogue Fleet has been able to make a *difference for the better in the war. So for the foreseeable future, we will sail on.* •—⌁

⌁—• Today Jake Rickingson became the fourth member of the Brotherhood of the White Eagle to be convicted in a Northwest Alliance court on charges including theft, extortion, murder, human trafficking, and crimes against humanity. Despite the testimony of hundreds of people who were liberated from Brotherhood-operated slave camps by the Northwest Alliance Army, Rickingson denied the camps even existed. He justified his other criminal activities by arguing that he was merely following orders from former Idaho President James P. Montaine and the Brotherhood chain of command. While Montaine himself remains in treatment and is not mentally fit to serve as a competent witness, a number of senior Idaho officers have denied prior knowledge of the Brotherhood's crimes.

The search for other senior Brotherhood leadership continues. In particular, a manhunt is under way deep in the Idaho and Montana wilderness for Brotherhood leader Nathan Crow. Colonel Kidd of the Northwest Alliance Army spoke at a press conference yesterday, promising that "the forces of justice will never relent until Crow and his vile militia are made to pay for their crimes." •—⌁

⌁—• We at ESPN have reorganized MegaSports in our commitment to provide unparalleled coverage of red-hot sports action across all the Pan American countries. So welcome to the inaugural broadcast of Pan American SPORTS! I'm John Soto."

"And I'm Lindsay Nang. It will likely be at least several months before the leagues are able to reestablish teams and schedules, but Major League Baseball commissioner Joseph Jackson and NFL commissioner Ronald Goodman gave rousing speeches in Colorado

Springs yesterday, extolling the power of athletics to bring people together for peace.

"And one bright point rising from the devastation of the civil war? Preliminary talks are under way for the Peace Games, a sort of American Olympics that would celebrate the best athletes among us and serve as a sign of our cooperation and community. Pan American SPORTS! *will bring you more on that exciting story, as it develops.* •⌁

⌁• *has been out of the public eye since the May fourth Pan American Peace Treaty was signed last year, but I was able to catch up with Daniel Wright at the secret, remote community he and his friends and neighbors established during the war. All appearances suggest that the settlement is self-sufficient, with its own livestock, crops, and solar and wind electric generators. An excerpt from our recorded interview:"*

"Most of the people who lived here in the war have stayed. We've all worked real hard improving the place to make it more livable. We've even converted one of our big rooms into a chapel. Worship services have become a big deal here. There's a lot of soul-searching. Um, I've started reading a little. I don't know. I'm just happy to be alive, to be with my friends and these people I care about."

"You're so far out here on your own, I don't know how much news you get from elsewhere, but how do you react to US President Laura Griffith's recent announcement that she is retiring from politics and will not run for reelection next year?"

"You know, I try to stay out of politics. But I'd say good for her. There was a time I thought I was real mad at President Griffith. But toward the end of the war, I became friends with her son, and the more I think about it, the more I figure she was like a lot of us, kind of trapped by the war. I mean, she was appointed to the vice presidency, and then when President Rodriguez was assassinated, she got dumped into the middle of an impossible situation. I wouldn't have wanted to be in her position. I'm glad she's getting out."

"But even getting out of the war and the public spotlight doesn't mean Danny's challenges are over. Like millions of others in every Pan American country, and indeed around the planet as World War III continues, Wright suffers from ongoing post-traumatic stress disorder.

"You say you're trying to let go of the war, that you're trying to move on. Can you describe that process, Danny?"

"I think you know it's not easy. I have a lot of nightmares. Sometimes I feel angry or anxious for no reason. If someone startles me or if there's a loud noise, I get . . . tense up, you know? Like I'm back in the fight.

"And I miss the people I've lost. It's been over a year now since my JoBell was killed . . . Whew . . . Sorry. There is not one single day that passes when I don't think about the war in some way. And I feel like my life is always going to be divided, that there will be the me from before and during the war, and there will be the me after the war, after it was all over. I've lost a lot. We all have. I'm going to do all I can to care for my friends and the people in my community, to live my postwar life the best I can. •⌁

⌁—• *The process of reestablishing the Internet across so many new and war-ravaged countries is slow. But a video of Ron Porter went viral last week, appearing to show the handsome young actor cheating on his baby mama, pop singer Molly Curtis, with his former lover and* Nightfall *co-star, Kat Simpson. Fans everywhere have been using the hashtag #stayforpeace, begging Ron to stay with Molly for the sake of their daughter, Peace.* •—⌁

⌁—• *Although the course of our future is not easy, although we all face and will continue to face many challenges, I hope the courageous people across Pan America who helped their neighbors and demanded peace will continue to reach out a helping hand. No victory has been won in our civil war. Nothing has been achieved but fear, famine, indignity, sickness, and death. The scars of our great tragedy run deep, and we will never be the same. We can't put our trust in political parties, governments, or militaries anymore. Life should not be about ideologies, but individuals. Trust your neighbor. Work to help your community. And do what you can to foster the same cooperation in other communities. I ask you all to join with the Cliffhanger as we actively commit ourselves to peace.* •—⌁

⌁—• *Thousands of people attended a rally in Boulder yesterday afternoon in support of presidential candidate David Trapp, chanting his name and interrupting his speech with nearly frantic applause when he spoke of, quote, 'returning the United States to its rightful place of control of Pan America.' Trapp, the former mayor of Denver, favors negotiating with the other Pan American countries from a position of military and economic strength.*

Reconciliation Party candidate Ben Swanson attempted to give a speech in response at a slightly smaller event in Boulder, but encountered an unexpected obstacle. "The struggle for control and dominance is what led to the death of millions in our tragic civil war. Respect and understanding are essential if peace is to contin —" A group of Trapp supporters then seized the stage and took away

Swanson's microphone, shutting him out with their own speeches about Trapp Party positions. Boulder police were on guard against violence, but the rally dissipated peacefully when Swanson left the stage.

In a press release, Swanson criticized the heated argument between the two new major parties as the same kind of divisive bickering that contributed to the civil war. David Trapp was quick to dismiss such allegations as paranoid and naive, saying, "It's different this time. We've all learned too much." •—⌁—

ACKNOWLEDGMENTS

The Divided We Fall trilogy is the result of several years of work and of the support of many good people. I wish I could individually thank everyone who contributed to the effort behind these books, but the list would be longer than all three novels combined. Special thanks:

To Sergeant First Class Matthew Peterson for his advice about the modern military and for his speculation about near-future military updates.

To Staff Sergeant Ryan Jackson for the excellent explosives training he helped provide me in the Army National Guard and for his advice about the advanced explosive techniques featured in the trilogy.

To Dr. Bryce Hoffman and Dr. Dennis Straubinger, for all their medical advice about everything from the way Major Alsovar might keep Danny Wright alive through interrogation, to the way Danny and Sparrow could conduct basement surgery on Will Danning, to the basics of burn treatment for Eric Sweeney. I appreciate their patience with all my horrific hypotheticals. Any medical errors are entirely my own.

To Dr. Nicole Knaack, for her careful explanations of the various medical tools and supplies found in the average small-town veterinary clinic and their practical application on human patients when used by people in a war-type situation who lack Dr. Nicole's level of expertise. Again, any mistakes are all mine.

To Erin Saldin, author of the wonderful novel *The Girls of No Return*, for allowing the use of the Alice Marshall School that is featured in that book. Thanks for giving Daniel Wright and his people a place to hide, Erin.

To Chris Stengel, the wizard designer who made all my interior image requests come true.

To Paul Gagne, who did so much to make the Divided We Fall audiobooks so fun and unique.

To Emily Heddleson for lending her singing talents to the Idaho national anthem in the *Burning Nation* audiobook.

To Charisse Meloto for getting the word out on my books.

To all the incredibly talented and dedicated people in the Scholastic family in general and in the Arthur A. Levine Books imprint in particular. I'm very grateful for your creativity and support.

To Clete Smith, Carol Brendler, and Cori McCarthy for feedback on early versions of *Divided We Fall*.

To all my brothers and sisters in the Vermont College of Fine Arts community, with special gratitude to the members of my graduating class, the Cliffhangers.

To my wonderfully kind and supportive agent, Ammi-Joan Paquette, for giving this writer his first "Yes," and for sticking with me through my first six books. Six! Thanks, Joan.

To Colonel Kidlit, my premium friend and brilliant editor, Cheryl Klein. It's been so much fun working with you. Thank you for your patience, wisdom, and understanding.

To my beloved new daughter, Verity. Thank you *so much* for sleeping and letting me write. Thank you for the joy you bring to my life with your cute little smiles. I'll pay you back someday.

And, as always, all the gratitude and love in the universe goes to my wife and best friend, Amanda, who continues to light up my world with possibility. Amanda, you are my life.

ABOUT THE AUTHOR

TRENT REEDY served as a combat engineer in the Iowa Army National Guard from 1999 to 2005, including a year's tour of duty in Afghanistan. That experience led directly to his first novel, *Words in the Dust*, which won the Christopher Award and was selected for Al Roker's Book Club for Kids on the *Today* show. His other novels include *If You're Reading This*, *Stealing Air*, and the first two books in this trilogy, *Divided We Fall* and *Burning Nation*. Trent lives near Spokane, Washington, with his family. Please visit his website at www.trentreedy.com.

This book was edited by Cheryl Klein
and designed by Christopher Stengel.
The text was set in Sabon, with
display type set in Conduit and
Grotesque. This book was printed
and bound by R. R. Donnelley
in Crawfordsville, Indiana. The
production was supervised by
Elizabeth Krych. The manufacturing
was supervised by Angelique Browne.